About

Liz Tyner lives with [...] acreage she imagines [...] children's book *Where* [...] lifestyle is a blend of o[...] sometimes comparable to the way people lived long ago. Liz is a member of various writing groups and has been writing since childhood. For more about her visit liztyner.com.

Janice Preston grew up in Wembley, North London, with a love of reading, writing stories and animals. In the past she has worked as a farmer, a police call-handler and a university administrator. She now lives in the West Midlands with her husband and two cats and has a part-time job with a weight management counsellor (vainly trying to control her own weight despite her love of chocolate!).

... lives with her husband on an Oklahoma
... is similar to the ones in the
... the *Wild Things Are*. Her
... old and new, and is sometimes

GOVERNESSES
UNDER THE
Mistletoe

LIZ TYNER

JANICE PRESTON

MILLS & BOON

First Published in Great Britain 2018
By Mills & Boon, an imprint of HarperCollins *Publishers*
1 London Bridge Street, London, SE1 9GF

GOVERNESSES UNDER THE MISTLETOE © 2018 Harlequin Books S.A.

The Runaway Governess © Harlequin Books S.A. 2016
The Governess's Secret Baby © Harlequin Books S.A. 2016

ISBN: 978-0-263-26852-2

Special thanks and acknowledgement are given to Liz Tyner and Janice Preston for their contribution to The Governess Tales series.

9-1118

MIX
Paper from
responsible sources
FSC™ C007454

FSC
www.fsc.org

This book is produced from independently certified FSC™ paper to ensure responsible forest management.

For more information visit: www.harpercollins.co.uk/green

Printed and bound in Spain
by CPI, Barcelona

THE RUNAWAY GOVERNESS

LIZ TYNER

Dedicated with gratitude to Laura McCallen who
helped me find the story I wanted to tell.

Chapter One

Isabel watched from the window as the older couple's driver stepped on to his carriage perch and called to the horses. She'd not believed her luck when she'd spotted the man and woman waiting for their carriage to be readied. It had taken her all of a minute to find out their destination and pour out her sad tale.

She didn't want to think of what might happen when the other coach arrived in Sussex without her. But the family could find another governess. This was her one chance. Her chance to soar.

Isabel turned to the man whose eyelids almost concealed his vision and the woman who matched him in age, but her eyes danced with life. Isabel clasped her hands at her chest and promised herself she would never again lie, except in extreme circumstances such as this. Taking a deep breath, she let the words rise from deep within herself. 'You have *saved* my life.'

A barmaid, hair frazzled from the August heat, stood

behind the couple. She looked up long enough to roll her eyes heavenward.

'Miss…' the wife patted Isabel's glove '…we just could not bear that your evil uncle was selling you into marriage to a man old enough to be your father—and your betrothed a murderer as well.'

'Thank you so much.' She sighed. 'If my parents were alive today…' they were, but they'd understand and forgive her once they discovered how famous she'd be '…they would fall upon their knees in gratitude for your saving my life.'

The barmaid snorted and Isabel sighed with emphasis, knowing she mustn't let the couple notice the scepticism.

'You're sure if you go to London with us, your family will give you a home?' the wife questioned.

'Oh. Yes.' The word lengthened to twice its usual length. 'Aunt Anna, my mother's sister, who has no idea of the tragedy that has befallen me as my great-uncle would not allow me paper or ink, would give me refuge in a heartbeat. I have always been her favourite niece, of course. It is just that my uncle told her I was…tragically killed in a fall from a horse, trampled by hooves and had to be immediately buried because the sight was too exceptionally hideous for anyone to see as I would not have wanted to be remembered as such.'

The woman's eyes could not have been more kind. 'Tragic.'

'Yes. Frightfully so.'

The man arched one brow, enough that Isabel could

see the scepticism. 'We will certainly deliver you to your aunt in London,' he said. 'To her doorstep.'

'I will be in your gratitude for ever.' Oh, good heavens. That might not end well as she had no aunt in London. 'It is near Charles Street—Drury Lane.' She almost shivered, just saying the words *Drury Lane*. Not that she was going to be an actress. Oh, no. Not something so disreputable as that. Her voice would be her fortune. Her very best friends, Joanna, Rachel and Grace, had told her time and time again at Madame Dubois's School for Young Ladies that she could sing better than anyone else they'd ever heard. Even the headmistress, Madame Dubois, had commented that Isabel's singing voice was bearable. Since Madame Dubois had called Grace Bertram 'passable,' whom Isabel thought favoured a painting of a heavenly angel—then to have a bearable voice was the highest praise from Madame Dubois.

She'd been so lucky Mr Thomas Wren had heard of her when he attended one of the school presentations. Now he was her patron—albeit a secret patron. She would be the lead of his new musicale. She would sing her heart out. Even though her voice was not perfection itself, something about the way she sang stirred people. When she was performing, others would listen and eyes would water. Nothing made her happier than when someone gave her that rapt attention and they were brought to tears. She *loved* making people cry in such a way.

She gathered her satchel and linked her arm around the older woman's. 'My Aunt Anna will be so grateful.'

'We must meet her and make sure she will not return

you to that dreadful man.' The woman's voice oozed concern.

Isabel leaned forward and batted her lashes. 'Of course. You simply must meet my aunt.' Easily said, albeit completely impossible.

The couple's meal was left behind, crumbs still clinging to the man's waistcoat, and they spirited her to their carriage.

When she stepped into the vehicle, she slumped a bit, keeping the man's frame between her and the windows of the coaching inn. It would not do for anyone from the other carriage to note her leaving before the end of the brief stop. She grasped her satchel and settled into the seat, ever so pleased to be leaving the governess part of her life behind. True, she had enjoyed the friendships of the school. But as she became closer and closer to graduation, she'd felt trapped. Mr Thomas Wren's notice of her was indeed fortunate. Apparently another student's father had informed him of Isabel's voice. Mr Wren had known the rules of the school and had known to be secretive in their correspondence. He'd offered her the lead in a new production he'd planned.

She could barely concentrate on the task at hand for thinking of the good fortune of her life. This change of carriage would even make a grand tale. She could imagine recounting the tale of how she stowed away, risking all to travel with a couple she could but hope was reputable, and who transported her at great personal risk to help her achieve her life's dream.

Isabel spoke as quickly as the wheels turned on the carriage, not wanting to give the couple a chance to think too much of the events of the day. She recounted honest tales of her youth at the governess school, leaving out the parts about the visits to her parents—and keeping as close to the facts as possible. She had already used her share of untruths for the year and it would not be good to blunder at this point.

When the carriage neared Drury Lane, Isabel kept one eye to the road, knowing she must make a quick decision.

A woman wearing a tattered shawl and with one strand of grey hanging from her knot of hair walked near an opening between two structures. Isabel saw the chance she had to take.

'My aunt,' she gasped, pointing. 'It's my aunt.' She turned to the man across. 'Stop the carriage.'

He raised his hand to the vehicle top, thumping.

She bolted up and tumbled out the door before the conveyance fully stopped, scurrying to the woman. 'Aunt. Aunt,' she called out. The woman must have had a niece somewhere because she paused, turning to look at Isabel.

Isabel scurried, then darted sideways behind a looming structure, running with all her might, turning right, then left. When she knew she was not being chased, she stopped, leaning against the side of a building. She gulped, and when her breathing righted she reflected.

She would become the best songstress in all London. She knew it. Mr Thomas Wren knew it. The future was hers. Now she just had to find it. She was lost beyond hope in the biggest city of the world.

Isabel tried to scrape the street refuse from her shoe without it being noticed what she was doing. She didn't know how she was going to get the muck off her dress. A stranger who wore a drooping cravat was eyeing her bosom quite openly. Only the fact that she was certain she could outrun him, even in her soiled slippers, kept her from screaming.

He tipped his hat to her and ambled into a doorway across the street.

Her dress, the only one with the entire bodice made from silk, would have to be altered now. The rip in the skirt—*thank you, dog who didn't appreciate my trespassing in his gardens*—was not something she could mend. She didn't think it could be fixed. The skirt would have to be ripped from the bodice and replaced. That would not be simple.

How? How had she got herself into this? Oh, well, she decided, she would buy all new clothing when Mr Thomas Wren gave her the funds he'd promised.

Yet, she didn't quite know where to begin in her search for him and she'd have to find him before nightfall. She would certainly ask someone as soon as she left this disreputable part of London. The dead fish head at her feet didn't give her the encouragement she needed.

But then she looked up. Straight into a ray of sunshine illuminating a placard hanging from a building. A bird on it. She didn't have to search. Providence had put out its golden torch and led her right to the very place she was searching for. This sign—well, the sign was a sign of her future. This was Mr Thomas Wren's establishment. The man with the ill-mannered eyes had gone inside but still, one did sometimes have to sing for unpleasant people and one could only hope they gleaned some lesson from the song. She had quite the repertoire of songs with lessons hidden in the words and knew when to use them.

She opened the satchel, pulled out the plume, and examined it. She straightened the unfortunate new crimp in it as best she could and put the splash of blue into the little slot she'd added to her bonnet. She picked up her satchel, realising she had got a bit of the street muck on it—and began again her new life.

Begin her new life, she repeated to herself, unmoving. She looked at the paint peeling from the exterior and watched as another man came from the doorway, waistcoat buttoned at an angle. Gripping the satchel with both hands, she locked her eyes on the wayward man.

Her stomach began a song of its own and very off-key. She couldn't turn back. She had no funds to hire a carriage. She knew no one in London but Mr Wren. And he had been so complimentary and kind to everyone at Madame Dubois's School for Young Ladies. Not just her. She could manage. She would have to. His compliments had not been idle, surely.

She held her head the way she planned to look over the audience when she first walked on stage and put one foot in front of the other, ignoring everything but the entrance in front of her.

As she walked through the doorway, head high, the first thing Isabel noticed was the stage. A woman was singing. Isabel concealed her shudder and hoped her

ears would forgive her. She supposed she would be replacing the woman. The songstress's bosom was obviously well padded because it would be hard for nature
to be so overzealous, but perhaps it had been to make
up for the error of her voice.

A man with silver hair and a gold-tipped cane sat
gaping at the stage. The woman put her arms tighter
to the side of her body and bent forward to emphasise
her words.

Isabel turned her head. She could not believe it. She
would have to have a word with Mr Wren about this,
although—

Then her eyes skipped from person to person to person. It would take more than a word. Men sat around a
table playing Five Card Loo, but it seemed only pence
were on the table.

The men at the game could not decide whether to
watch the stage or their hand. Two women obviously
championed their favourites, alternately cheering and
gasping at the cards. Then the game ended. Whoops
erupted. A man stood, bowed to the table, and waited.
The other players reached into their purses, took out
coins and handed them to the women. The winner
put his arm around the women's waists and led them
through a curtained hallway.

She let out a breath and all her dreams fluttered away
with it.

William strode under the faded placard and stepped
into Wren House, giving himself a moment to let his
eyes adjust from the bright August sun to the dim light

of a world only illuminated because men needed to see the cards in their hand. He'd have to go to a stable to get the scent of Wren's out of his nostrils.

If his father knew this was where Cousin Sylvester spent every Wednesday night, things might have been different. But now Sylvester had Marvel and Ivory, the two best horses in England and the only ones whose eyes flickered regard when William neared them. The beasts would always stick out their necks for a treat when William appeared. 'Spoiled,' the stable master muttered each time.

William always replied, 'And worth it.'

William surveyed the table, and spotted his cousin immediately. Sylvester mumbled a greeting and two others looked over, recognising William and giving him a grunt of their own before they returned to the cards. William jerked his head sideways, motioning for Sylvester to join him. The answer, a quick shake of Sylvester's head, and a brief upturn of the lips, didn't surprise William. He took a seat near the corner where he could watch the room. He didn't want anyone at his back. A woman on stage finished singing, thankfully.

He ordered an ale and when the barmaid brought the drink, her brows lifted in question and she looked to the curtain at the back. He shook his head, smiling to soften the refusal. His fingers clasped the mug, but as he lifted it, he paused. Sticky residue lay under his touch. Jam? He gazed into the liquid, half-expecting to see something floating, but nothing looked alive in it. Then he sat the mug back on the table.

A perfect ending to a perfect day, but Marvel and Ivory were worth it.

And having a roof over one's head did have some merit.

William's father had visited early in the morning and had pontificated well into the day. The Viscount had picked a fine time to regain an interest in life and an excellent plan to disinherit his only son. The Viscount knew the entailment laws as well as anyone. He had to leave his property to William. But he could, however, lease his nephew the estate for the next fifty years. Upon the Viscount's death, William would receive the proceeds of the lease. A bargain to Sylvester at one pound per year.

If his father had mentioned that once, he'd mentioned it one hundred times. And he'd had no smell of brandy on his breath.

The inheritance could be dealt with later. Marvel and Ivory were already gone from the stables.

Sylvester smirked at the cards, but William knew the smugness was directed his way. No hand could be that good.

William glanced around and, even though his eyes didn't stop until they returned to his mug, he noted the woman sitting on a bench at the other side of the room. She sat close to the wall, her body slanted away from the group of men. The shadowed interior hid more of her than it revealed. He was certain she had a face, but she'd pulled the bonnet off-centre and it perched askew so he couldn't see her features unless she turned his way. If not for the plume, he wouldn't have noticed her.

In one movement to relax his frame, he twisted his chair just a bit in her direction so he could stare forward, but see her from the corner of his eye.

The barmaid sauntered by him. He waved a coin her way and asked for another drink, discarding any thought of asking for a clean mug. He didn't imagine she would take kindly to that, particularly when he saw the crust at her fingernails.

He thought the lady at the bench was above the others in the room, particularly by the way her back didn't leave the wall behind her and her hands gripped the satchel as if it might protect her. He wondered why she stayed.

The barmaid plunked another mug in front of him and brushed against his side before leaving.

Nothing floated in the liquid. Nothing stuck to his hand. He would take that as an omen that the ale was— he took a drink and smothered a cough. The mug's contents could have been watered down more. He hoped his tongue hadn't blistered. The owner apparently didn't mind if his customers wobbled a bit and knew drink could loosen the ties of a purse.

The door opened and light dappled across the bonnet the miss on the bench wore. She turned towards the light. For an instant he could see wisps of her hair. Copper.

He took a small sip. The ale tasted better than it had before.

Copper. Just under the ghastly plume. His favourite colour of hair—now. He didn't think he'd ever seen a woman with just that shade of hair. A shame the bonnet covered it.

Someone from Sylvester's table belched and the woman with the falling plume stiffened even more and twisted away from them.

William noted the dress. Not quite the dash of colour his sisters insisted on. It reminded him of something he might see on a miss at a country fair, yet not a walking dress. Not a soirée dress either. He could see underskirts peeking from a tear in the skirt. All his muscles stilled. A woman would not be going about with such a rip in her skirts. Particularly not one sitting so straight and gloves locked on her satchel.

He stood, mug still in hand, planning to offer her his assistance. At his movement, her eyes darted to him. She took in a breath and the back of her head bumped against the wall.

He gave her a grim-lipped smile. The woman didn't want him to approach her, obviously. Perhaps she was at Wren's hoping to find her husband. In that case, William certainly didn't want to draw notice her way. He sat the mug at the table and moved to stand at Sylvester's side.

Putting a hand on the woollen shoulder of Sylvester's coat, William leaned forward. 'I must talk with you.'

'Anything you have to say,' Sylvester's voice boomed, 'you can say in front of my friends.'

'I'm sure I can,' William answered. 'But I thought we might step out to speak of family matters.' Sylvester had to have noticed if the Viscount was sotted when he gave the horses away.

'These men are like family,' Sylvester answered.

'Only better, because they do not gift me with horses not worth feeding.' He spoke to the man on his left. 'Did I tell you my uncle gave me two horses? Broken-down old things. I could hardly refuse them and hurt the man's feelings, particularly if his mind is clear as a cloudless day.'

Sylvester wouldn't have said the Viscount's mind was clear if it wasn't true. 'I will take them off your hands.'

'Oh, I could not do that to you.' Sylvester let out a breath. 'I'll just keep them for now, though I don't see feeding them like they're used to. A bit on the plump side. A few less rations will be good for them. Or maybe I should just put them down.'

William tightened his grip on Sylvester's coat. 'You will feed them properly and you will care for them.'

Sylvester laughed. 'Just having a jest with you, dear Cousin. I know those beasts are your favourites. Your father does as well. Can't think what he's up to.' He brushed a hand over his chin, tugging at it. 'Or maybe I can.' Sylvester spoke to the other players. 'If Cousin William doesn't get it on his mind to marry and have an heir, sadly, the title will pass to my son, should I have one, and I intend to have a full brood. I can't think if I were in his boots that would be difficult. I'd be wed-ded, bedded and enjoying the bondage of matrimony, although that is not how I put it to Uncle. I told him I'm deeply in love and near to proposing. And I am.' He smirked again. 'Deeply in love with William's inheri-tance and near to proposing to…' Looking around the table, he asked, 'Any of you have an unmarried sister who wants a husband?'

'Not that we'd let wed you,' one of the men answered. The rest laughed.

'I will have Marvel and Ivory back.' William released his cousin's shoulder.

'Well, I'm going to wager the horses if I run out of funds. Of course, with the way my luck is going tonight, I'll own everyone's livestock before I leave.'

'I'll buy them from whomever you lose them to.' William leaned forward and briefly met eyes with the others at the table. 'If any of you men win those horses from Sylvester, I'll buy them from you at double what you'd get at Tattersalls.'

The others grinned, chuckling.

'That's why Uncle is concerned about you, William.' Sylvester pulled out a card, waved it for others to see the back of and then dropped it on to the table with a flourish. 'You're planning to buy a pair of old horses not worth a pence when you might be able to win them with a single game of chance. Yet, you gambled away a carriage once. You've even lost your own boots and then threw in the stockings. It's all a game to you, but you don't care if you win or lose.' He raked in the coins. 'I play to win.'

'I enjoy the sport,' William said. He'd had enough of the night.

Turning to leave, he made it as far as the door before looking back at that feathery trimming. His youngest sister had once pulled such an adornment from his middle sister's bonnet and the roof had barely stayed on the house in the aftermath.

He retraced his steps to the sticky mug. He sat, staring straight ahead. The joy of being called a wastrel by one's father meant William could sit all night watching a plume on a bonnet. He tried to imagine the bird that lost the feather, but he could only see a caricature of a bird prancing, preening, and sprouting a blast of unnatural feathers from its head, while wobbling under the weight.

He needed to stop with the ale.

The singer returned to the stage and opened her mouth. He would not call it singing, exactly, but if one didn't care much about quality of voice, then it could pass the time. He swatted at a fly that landed on the edge of the mug. Just because he didn't want the drink didn't mean he intended to share.

The woman with the tear in her dress adjusted the bag in her lap. The singer hit a high note, or had her foot mashed by a carriage. He squeezed his eyes shut, wishing he could do the same for his ears. As the note ended, he opened his eyes while pulling the cleaner mug to his lips. His hand stopped when he caught Miss Plume watching him.

She looked away and his hand moved again. He finished the drink, not tasting it. He would wait until her husband arrived to take her home. If the husband walked in with some woman hanging on him, William would make sure to give the man a reminder of propriety. A man didn't embarrass his wife so. To let her wait alone in a place like Wren's was unforgiveable.

William looked directly at her, not able to see through the glove on her left hand, or into her mind to see what memories resided there.

He eased back in the chair. He wasn't leaving until she did.

Isabel knew the man who wanted his horses was aware of her. But he was hoping to get his stock returned and he wanted them fed properly. The other men even seemed more decent after he'd spoken with them. When she'd noted him walking to the door, leaving, fear tremored in her midsection and she'd had an urge to follow, not wanting to remain without his presence. But he'd paused and returned to his chair. He must want to be certain he received those horses.

She peered around her bonnet brim, searching for Wren.

Mr Wren should be about. Earlier she'd asked that barmaid and the woman had glared and mumbled that he'd be in when he walked in. Wren had told Isabel he would meet her. He'd said he spent each day working, except when he attended Sunday Services. She no longer believed that, unless he attended with her aunt.

The one, William they'd called him—his face had pinched when the singer got stuck on that dreadful note. Apparently he could hear quite well. And when he'd opened his eyes and caught her examining his expression, he'd looked startled.

He was rather ordinary except for those legs that didn't want to fit under the table, but yet, he made her feel safer.

Then the barmaid approached and brought him another mug. He'd not requested it, but he took it. The woman brushed a lock of his hair over his ear, which hadn't needed touching, but Isabel couldn't blame the woman. That hair did make a person curious about what it felt like.

The woman whispered something to him. He laughed, changing everything in his face, and creating the same thump in Isabel's heart that she felt when the music was perfect. His smile could carry its own tune.

He saw Isabel watching. He gave a flicker of a smile and shrugged his shoulders.

She ducked her head, pleased not to feel so alone.

The barmaid was a tart, but Isabel couldn't blame her for noticing him. He was the only man in the place who didn't make her feel like bathing.

The door opened and she saw the familiar checked waistcoat of Mr Thomas Wren, his eyebrows as light as the gold buttons on his coat. She wasn't as impressed with the fastenings as she'd been before.

He made his way to her bench, his grin almost suffocating her. She scooted away, gently wedging the soiled side of her satchel in his direction as she put it between them. Half her bottom was already off the bench, but she could not let Mr Thomas Wren's breath closer. Apparently he'd had something to do with the fish she'd seen in the street.

She forced a positive lilt to her voice. 'Mr Wren, I do believe you forgot to tell me something in your letters.'

'No.' His eyes widened. 'I can't think I did.' He put

an arm at the back of the bench. He could not possibly have eight hairy fingers on one hand, but that's what it felt like when his knuckles brushed at the top of her glove. 'You really do sing quite well, Miss Morton, and I am happy to have you on my stage.'

'You mentioned a suitable chaperon.'

'Why, yes, I believe I did. And if you look around, you'll notice there are plenty of women here to…'

She lowered her chin, but raised her brows at him. He didn't appear chagrined at all. Instead, he grinned while his eyes devoured her.

The air in the room boiled into her and she could hardly force the words past the sweltering heat. 'I fear that on the way here,' she spoke, 'I realised that I cannot forgo my duties as a governess. I will not be able to accept the position.'

She didn't know how she'd manage or what she'd do. She had hardly enough coins in her satchel to buy bread. She could only hope for another married couple to notice her and this time she would tell the truth. Some of it. She hoped she had not totally used her portion of lies for the year.

'Oh, my.' Wren's words mocked themselves. 'I seem to recall in your correspondence a distinct aversion to those duties and a sincere wish to follow your true talent. And you are quite talented, Miss…Morton.'

'I can't. I wouldn't be—'

He leaned forward, his voice covering her with fumes of the summer heat. 'I am saddened. But I admit, I considered the possibility you would not wish to continue in our bargain.' He stood, his tongue clucking as if he'd caught her doing something terribly wrong. He whisked one hand to the bottom of the satchel and the other over hers on the grip. Involuntarily, she jerked her hands from his touch.

Brows lifted, he turned, striding away. 'Come with me to my office and I will see what we must do now.'

'We can discuss it here.' She stood, running a hand down the side of her skirt, hoping to pull that rend together just a little more.

He paused, turning back. 'Will you be needing funds to return to your home?' His voice faded so low that she read the words on his lips more than heard them.

He hadn't given her money for the trip to London, saying he'd once done so and the woman he'd hired never arrived.

She couldn't answer.

'Then come with me,' he continued. 'We can discuss it in my office. The funds are in my safe.' He looked to the window. 'The hour is getting late. I hate to think of you alone on the streets, in darkness and finding your way. It's not safe at night for a woman out and about. Just last month, one of the women, Molly, went out. They found her the next morning, bruises on her neck. Blood on her hands. Buried her in a pauper's grave.'

Before she answered, he was at the curtain, her satchel clasped in his hand.

She stood, glancing around, hoping no one would see her follow. She would be ruined. If she wasn't already. But it was better to be ruined than buried in some lost grave. She didn't quite think Mr Wren would be rushing to see that a proper burial would take place.

She watched his retreating coat. She would never again complain about being a governess.

He had the only funds she had—hidden in the bag. An unmarked grave would not quite fulfil her dreams. She followed, planning to grab the satchel as soon as he released it and run.

Stepping through the curtain and into a cramped office, relief brightened her spirit. A copy of a Mrs Radcliffe novel lay on his desk. Surely a man who liked to read had some refinement.

'Please sit.' He indicated a chair, one rung missing from the back. She did, noting he sat the satchel down at his right side, his body between her and the bag. He still stood. He turned.

'I don't believe you realise what position you put me in.' He shook his head while picking up the novel. 'We can't have that.'

'I just—' She moved to rise, the fish smell wafting over her.

He crashed the novel to the wall. Before she could believe what her eyes told her had just happened, his hand clamped on her shoulder. The surprise and force thrust her on to the wooden chair seat.

'I—'

'You *wish* to hear me out.' She could feel all of the fingers again. This time they pressed. Pinched. His hand slid, not releasing, until his thumbnail rested in the soft skin at the base of her jaw. He took a step, moving his body forward, still beside her, her head held back by his thumb. Her backbone firm against the chair, him above forcing her neck back. He untied her bonnet strings and pushed it to the floor.

Her mouth dried. She could breathe—just. Her hands clasped his wrist, pushing. But she could not move him.

'Sweet, you have to understand, I looked for a long time to find just the right woman. Just the right blend of woman. Taller than most so she stood out. A haunting voice that could also trill in happiness. A look of freshness. Eyes that made a man think he could see her wanting him. Lips that he could imagine on his body.'

'No,' she gasped.

'Do not interrupt.' He put his other hand over her mouth and leaned closer. She shuddered. All of his bulk loomed over her, his cheeks ruddy. 'You understand that even the other women would increase their coin by satisfying your cast-offs. You would even be a boon to them.' He paused. 'Feel free to nod.'

He took his hand from her throat, but not her mouth. One of his legs pressed against hers.

'Nod.' His eyes glistened with an intensity that covered her like the coil of a serpent's skin against hers.

She didn't move. Her lower face was in his vice-like grasp. She could feel the pressure of his thumb. The tightness. But no pain. Nothing hurt. Nothing. Except she could not breathe.

His clothes rustled and he moved so that she could see nothing but his face.

'You understand, I have to have you. I have no choice. No choice. I've spent too much time finding you and waiting on you.' He reached to his waistcoat and a thin sliver of steel flashed in front of her. The blade pressed at her neck. 'Nod, Sweet.'

She did—the barest amount.

'You understand there are rules one must observe to work here. You will learn them in time.' The knife moved, tracing the circle of her neck. 'Nod, Sweet.' He moved her head up and down with his hand. 'Get used to that.'

She remembered how easy it had been to convince the couple of a lie. She nodded, moving her hand from his wrist. He trailed the blade in the same way of an artist's pen making swirls on a page. He slipped the tip to her shoulder. 'You don't have to worry about me hurting your face, permanently. But a man might be aroused by a gentle scar trailing away under clothing.' The blade caught her sleeve, but rested at skin, pressing. Testing. Drooling, he stared at the blade. 'He might wonder where a scar led. Where it ended.'

The blade pressed harder, and the sleeve pulled, fabric falling away—no barrier to the steel. Pressure flared at her arm.

Spit pooled at the edge of his lips. 'Scars, in their way, can be beauty marks.'

William glanced across at his cousin. Sylvester scratched his earlobe, stared at the cards, and grumbled.

Something had thumped in the back, but none of the others' attentions wavered from the cards.

Miss Plume was beyond the curtain with Wren. William tapped the side of his mug and pushed his chair back, standing. With the woman on the way to finding whatever she looked for, he had no wish to continue enjoying the smell of worn boots.

He stared at the curtain, unable to move, imagining the look on the woman's face as she'd left the room. Wren had swooped up the bag and darted to the back. Miss Plume had hesitated before moving.

He shrugged, noting the worn threads where so many had touched the curtain before him, but striding towards it.

He walked through and saw several doors. This would not be the time to open the wrong one.

Ignoring his misgivings, he pressed a hand to the first door and pushed it.

Wren stood over a woman, a blade at the woman's arm. Instantly, it moved to her throat. In seconds Wren could slice and nothing would be able to erase the moment, ever.

William's breath left his body. His mind took a moment to adjust to the sight his eyes tried to make sense of. The woman was one movement from death. Wren's face had the look of a rabid animal, all thoughts absorbed by the sickness. No way to understand reason.

William could not move forward to rescue the woman because Wren could act on impulse. The knife pressed against the slender neck. Wren could kill in the moments it would take William to close the distance. A jolt against Wren's arm would press the blade into skin. She would be dead and nothing could ever change those seconds.

Chapter Two

Wren increased the pressure of the blade. Isabel's pulse thumped against the tip.

'My pardon,' the man at the door spoke. 'I didn't realise this was a private conversation.' Nothing flickered on his face. He didn't even seem to see her.

'Get the hell out,' Wren rasped.

Isabel swallowed. Could the man not understand there was a blade at her neck?

'I certainly will,' the man at the door spoke. He leaned back a bit, turning his head.

His hand tightened on the door and he was going to leave, letting Wren do as he wished. She could tell. The stranger had not once looked at her eyes.

'But, I was thinking of making an investment.' Soft words from the man at the door. His body stilled before turning in her direction.

Finally, he noticed Isabel. His brows lifted and he wet his lips. He appraised her in the same way a butcher might decide which chicken was to be the first to the block. A nausea filled her.

'I would like to invest, Wren.' He chuckled. 'And all it would take would be a bit of pleasure to convince me.'

'I need no investors.' The knife didn't lessen. 'I own everything under this roof. Everything.'

'True enough,' the man spoke. His eyes were again on Wren. 'I hear nothing but good about this establishment. Nothing. And an investor like myself feels a bit left out.' His gaze locked on Wren's face. 'I have a good bit of coin. A good bit, and I certainly can find better ways to spend it than on gaming.'

The pressure at Isabel's throat lessened.

'A man cannot have too much coin,' Wren said. 'But he can have too many women about.' At those words, the knife jabbed forward, tapping Isabel's neck like a pointed fingernail with a razor at the end.

The stranger's eyes widened and he caught his breath, speaking as he exhaled. 'Don't damage the goods, Wren.' His voice strengthened. 'Wouldn't want to hurt an investment.'

Wren took the knife from Isabel's neck, looking at it as if he'd forgotten he had it in his hand.

In that moment, the man threw his body in front of Isabel, knocking her backwards with a crash.

For less than a second she could only see the ceiling. She pushed herself up, scrambling to her feet. Wren's back was on the desk and the stranger's right fist plunged into Wren's face.

Wren rolled, falling from the desk, kicking the man's ribs when he moved forward. But the stranger only turned with the blow. He continued forward, driving on to Wren, using his body as a battering ram. His left hand gripped Wren's neck and he rose, just enough for leverage, keeping Wren pinned to the floor.

The stranger's fist rose and hammered Wren's face, pummelling a groan from him.

She could not bear it. 'No,' she shouted, the words more a scream than a command. 'Stop. No. I beg you, please stop.' The words could have carried to the top of the Tower.

She shuddered, her voice now pleaded. 'Please stop.'

The stranger looked at her. His eyes held no recognition of the moment, but his fist stilled on the upswing. Nothing from inside him acknowledged her words, but he stopped pummelling. Again his arm moved up, ready for a downswing.

'No…' The word pulled her last thread of strength.

William stopped, pulling the world around him back into focus. The woman's body trembled in a circular motion. Another second and she would topple. Dazed eyes locked on him, but he didn't think she truly saw anything.

William lunged upwards and scooped the knife from the floor so Wren couldn't grab it. He had to get the woman away from the place. Neither she nor his family would be helped by tales of these events.

In one stride, William had a hand at her shoulder. 'Miss?' He tightened his clasp.

She blinked, but didn't speak and her glance fell to his hand.

'Miss?' he repeated. 'Where do you live?'

He released her shoulder and took her chin in his gasp, pulling her gaze to his. His heart slammed against his ribs with a stronger punch than any Wren had managed.

Seizing her around the waist, he lifted her to the door. Stopping outside, he let her feet flutter to the floor. She kept moving downwards and he pulled her up, tight against him. Her colourless face wasn't far from his own, yet she offered no resistance.

He had a knife in one hand and a woman in the other. The door still open, he led her to the taproom, trying to keep her on the side opposite the patrons.

Everyone in Wren's looked towards the curtain when he strode through. They'd heard the commotion apparently, but hadn't moved. Sylvester's cards fluttered to the table.

A customer entered at the door. Light filtered on to the woman's hair, showing the unusual colour to all in the room. The stranger stared at William, unmoving. Uncertainty stilled him as if he couldn't decide whether to enter or run for safety.

Sylvester's voice jarred the moments, reminding William of the others. 'Cousin—you must introduce us to your friend.'

'Yes, I must.' William tramped forward. 'Just not today.'

He glared at the man at the door, gesturing him aside—and then Will realised he gestured with the knife. He dropped the weapon and the man jumped backwards, pulling the door with him. William stopped the swing with his boot. The man darted away.

Sprinting the woman into the fading sunlight, William moved towards his carriage. He shouted to the driver, 'Just go. Keep us moving.' The driver stared, then his posture straightened and his chin snapped up in agreement.

Once inside the vehicle, William reached across her to lower the shade on her side. She gasped and the sound slashed into him. She pressed against her side of the carriage.

With the same control he'd used when he spoke to Wren, he turned to her.

He opened his mouth to ask her where she lived, but closed it again. He could not deliver such a bedraggled miss anywhere. She'd been so prim on the bench. And her dress had been ripped even then.

'You must stop shaking.' He spoke in the tone that could soothe two sisters trying to strangle each other over an apricot tart.

One at a time, he reached for her hands, holding tight to one when she tried to pull away, but freeing the other. He couldn't have her darting from the door of a moving carriage.

He stared at the slice on his own knuckles and then remembered her arm. If it had meant losing the horses to put himself in Wren's while she was there, then he would thank Sylvester—at least silently.

He reached into his pocket and took out a handkerchief. Even in the darkening light, he saw the moisture, but the wound on her arm only trickled blood.

He pressed and waited, making sure it wasn't serious. 'Just relax,' he spoke in the apricot-tart tone, 'you'll be all better in a minute.' If it would have been his sister, he would have started singing a nursery song, because it always worked, even if they complained about the nonsense.

'You're hurt,' she said.

Relief flooded him. She was aware of something other than the fright.

'I'm fine.' He daubed at the dried blood on her shoulder. 'My horses give me worse bruises and we call it fun.'

She looked at the handkerchief and then her shoulder. 'Oh,' she squeaked, not in pain, but surprise.

'Yes.' He pressed the cloth at her injury again, not really needing to. 'But it will mend quickly. I'm sure you've had worse.'

She reached up to relieve him of the cloth and for a moment their fingers tangled, then their eyes met, and she breathed in and pulled away.

He hated to move, but he did. He would ask her the location to deliver her and he would see that she arrived safely. Even if it was some distance away, he could direct the coachman easily enough. But his question changed before he spoke.

'Why were you in Wren's?' he asked.

She gazed at him. 'I was seeking work there.'

He'd been so wrong. His voice strengthened and the first words he thought flew from his mouth. *'In a brothel?'*

Life returned to her eyes. 'You insult me.' She

straightened. 'Do I look like someone who would—?' Her eyes opened wide. She cried out, using both hands to pull the dress over her bare shoulder, then adjusting her grasp, pulling the rip in her skirts closed. 'Do I look like a...*fallen woman*?'

'Not... No. No. Not at all.' She looked well past fallen, but he had learned as a youth that a pre-emptive reassurance was easier than stopping tears.

'I must go back,' she said. 'You must take me back to that terrible, forsaken place.' Her eyes widened. Pleading. 'I need your help.'

'No. You are not going back.'

'You don't understand. I left my satchel. All I have in the world. A dress. My funds.' She held the handkerchief at her shoulder while reaching to clasp his wrist. Her eyes searched his face and then she sighed, and relaxed.

Letting her hold him, he extended an arm around her shoulders, barely touching, but close enough that he could free her hand of the fabric and hold it in place for her.

'Is it a great sum of money?' he asked. She certainly shouldn't have been in Wren's if she had funds.

Her voice barely reached him and her head tilted so he couldn't see her expression. 'It's not truly all I have in the world,' she said. 'It is not truly all I have. It is just the rest of my things are on the way to Sussex.'

'How much did you leave in Wren's?' he pressed.

'My songs. A dress. A fan which had paste jewels on one edge. Hair ribbons. Enough to buy a bowl of soup.' She made a fist. 'I cannot believe I left the fan. The fan was a gift from three dear friends, but I'm sure they would understand if I sold it to buy food.'

She tensed, moving to stare at him. 'I am not a tart. I am not a fallen woman. A Jezebel. Or whatever else. I am a…' Her chin rose. 'A singer.' She lowered her face. 'Or I was to be. That evil debacle of a man was to pay me to sing.'

'You *sing*?'

She looked directly at William. 'Yes. Songs. To sing songs. Wren hired me. He'd promised me wages.' She snorted, then caught herself. 'I do have a good voice and the wages were not such a large amount to make me suspicious.' She straightened her fingers, saw blood on the gloves and shuddered. 'I have always been told my voice is a gift.' Her words faded away.

Her hand rested in her lap and her head bowed. 'My songs are in that satchel. With a picture my friend Grace drew of us singing and laughing with Joanna and Rachel.'

'So you are a Songbird.' He reached and tugged at the fingertip of her glove. She didn't need to be staring at blood.

'Not any longer,' she said, pulling away to remove the gloves herself and fold them.

'Nonsense. Don't let one person stand in your way.'

'It's not one person.' Shadowed eyes stared at him. 'It's everyone. Everyone says I should be a governess. Everyone. And this proves it.'

'This proves nothing of the sort.' His words were firm, but Isabel discarded them with a wave of her folded gloves.

'I will never sing again,' she said. 'Madame said it would be the ruin of me and she didn't know I listened so I suppose she was right. I just couldn't believe it— until now. She was *always* right.'

She met the view of the brown eyes. 'Even when we didn't let Madame Dubois know she was right—she was right. I should have learned from my friend Grace how things go awry.'

'And what has happened with this friend, Grace?'

'She explained to me how...' She fluttered her hand at her head before pulling the bodice of her dress for more covering and leaning against the inside of the carriage which smelled a bit like a blacksmith's shop. 'People make mistakes. And I see now that perhaps I should have been happier about my chance to be a governess. Not everyone is so fortunate to have the parents such as I do who are willing to send a daughter away for education.' She winced. 'But I wanted to sing. I truly did. For audiences.'

She remembered the joy flooding her when music sounded. 'I had to know. Wren and I exchanged many letters and I believed him reputable. I had to know if he had a true job for me. I might have suspected that it would be all for naught, but all my life I would have wondered. Perhaps it is worth the risk of death to know.'

'No. It was not.'

His words brooked no argument. She examined him through the fading light. He sat, unselfconscious of her perusal, and it didn't seem that she was being impolite or forward, but just learning what he looked like and trying to learn his thoughts.

But she had to think of her future now.

'I will send a post telling how I was waylaid,' she said. 'I will leave out certain parts and I will hope that Madame Dubois accepts it, and will again reference me to a family. I will be a...' She shut her eyes and forced out the words. 'A governess.'

'The children will be fortunate to have you.'

'I must hope I am allowed to regain my position.'

'A governess could sing to her charges.'

'Of course.'

'Sing for me,' he said.

'No.'

'Please.'

She tried, but only three words came out before her mouth dried. Her voice wavered, cracking, and no longer sounded her own.

'I never want to sing again,' she said. 'I sang because *la vie est trop courte pour boire du mauvais vin.* I wanted a chance to drink the *good* wine.'

'The results can be the same. But do not give up something you love—something so sweet as song.'

'My voice has always brought me notice,' she said. 'Always, and so many times Madame told me that pride goes before a fall and that it doesn't cushion the ground a bit.'

'Songbirds don't have to remain on the ground.'

'My wings have been clipped,' she said.

'I will find you a safe place to have the good wine tonight and tomorrow you may send the post to your friend. You will have many chances to make the children happy in your care.'

'If you would just deliver me to a place where I might find suitable lodging.'

'I know of only one place that would have what you need. My sister's home. She's married and too proper for good health. Tomorrow, my sister can quickly send a messenger to your destination and make up some folderol about how you aided her, causing you to become separated from your carriage. She'll even put together a new garment for you. This will only be a small detour in your travels.'

She let out a breath. 'Thank you.' The words hurt her throat. Wren must have pressed against it more than she'd noticed. She trailed her fingers over her neck, searching for a cut but finding none.

He leaned forward, sliding the wood aside which covered the small trap window. 'Sophia's.' he called out. But before he closed the window, he added, 'Slowly,' before glancing at Isabel and smiling.

That one word wrapped around her, suffusing her with wellbeing.

He relaxed to put an arm at the back of the seat, not touching her skin, but enveloping her all the same. 'So, Miss Songbird, let us introduce ourselves on the way. Just listening to your speaking voice is quite the treat.'

Chapter Three

⤜❧◈❧⤛

The carriage creaked to a stop and instantly Isabel saw William's eyes shutter, then he straightened, slipping his arm from behind her.

'If you will wait for a moment,' William said, hand on the door. 'I'd like to send my sister's butler on an errand so you can go into the house without being seen. It's better if it's assumed you arrived with Sophia.'

He lowered his voice. 'And you can trust the coachman to keep his silence, I assure you.' Jumping out, he exited into the dark night. She pushed her hand against the warm leather of the seat, loneliness creeping about her. She wished he hadn't left her—now the memory of the knife resurfaced.

She was alive and, except for a detour, her life was going to continue on just as planned. Now she could embrace being a governess. She'd seen the truth of what a singer's life was really like. Her mother had warned her countless times that people assumed all singers were really paid to do other things. That hadn't mattered then, but now it did.

She shuddered and opened the carriage shade. Enough light filtered from the moon so she could see a mansion. A mansion. William hadn't told her his sister was wealthy. Immediately, she dropped the shade and worked with the pins in her hair, ignoring the sting the movement caused to her arm.

She was arranging pins when the door opened and William looked inside. His lips quirked up. 'Songbird, do not do yourself up too pretty. My sister is used to looking at me.'

Her hands stopped. 'I'm a sight.'

'You—' he reached in, took her hands and pulled her with him, as he backed from the carriage '—are a sight like a swan in the moonlight. And all swans do not have their feathers always perfect. Sometimes the birds flutter about and feathers fly everywhere, but not for one moment do they stop being swans.'

'You're quite flattering.'

'You deserve it,' he said, leaning low so he could speak quietly as they walked up the steps. 'But with three sisters, I've had lots of practice, not that they don't deserve it as well. But my sisters gave me a list once.'

'A list?'

'Yes. A list of compliments. They had sat around one evening and decided what wonderful phrases they should like to hear from me instead of my asking if they had memorised their lessons, or practised pianoforte or were kind to each other. Every time I corrected them in any way, I was to repeat one of their compliments and add one of my own.'

'I should have liked to have had a brother like you.'

Opening the door, he ushered her inside. 'Sophia said she married in spite of having a brother and Rosalind claims she and Harriet are unwed because if I am among the best of men, then she fears for her sanity should she end up with someone only twice as good as I am.'

Gazing at him, she tried to think of suitable words to thank him for what he'd done. But her voice fled. She brushed a hand to her neck, wishing she could find something to say that explained what she felt.

'Oh…' Gently, he took her hand from her throat and his forehead almost touched hers. 'Please don't look so stricken.'

'I owe you—' she breathed out '—so much.' She clutched his lapel to remain upright.

With the lightest touch at the small of her back, he kept her steady, his whisper caressing her. 'I would have done the same for anyone.'

She tightened her clasp on his lapel. 'That only makes you…even better.'

He shook his head, darting a glance upwards, before returning his gaze to hers. 'I'm only two whiskers away from being a drunken, gambling, rakish, penniless, thankless, conceited heir to a viscount. Please don't let anything else get out about me and ruin my carefully earned reputation.'

'You were the only one who came to my rescue and I screamed. I'm sure I did.' She flattened her palm against the wool of his coat. 'I'm so fortunate you were there.'

'I just wish…things had been more like you wanted,' he said and his eyes fell to her arm.

'I couldn't have…' She tugged at the gown's shoulder, aware that only a bare inch held the garment. 'It was almost worth it to know there are men like you in the world.'

He grunted a denial and he watched her hand struggle with the fabric. 'Do not think about that, Isabel.' His words softened into a whisper. 'It is beyond your repair.' He took a smallest lamp from the side table and held it aloft so she could manage the stairs.

When they reached the sitting room, he led her to an armed chair upholstered in burgundy. He lit another lamp and put it on a table at her side.

'I'll get Sophia,' he said, leaving.

She'd expected him to ring for a maid, but he'd acted much like someone of her own means would. Her mother's maid-of-all-work wouldn't have been roused this late in the evening because it would have taken more time than the simple task of fetching someone.

Isabel glanced around the room and found it little different from her parents' home. The lamps were more plentiful and the painting above the fireplace had quite a large frame, but other than that, the chamber could have been in a country squire's house.

William returned, and shook his head. 'She has to put her hair up.'

Immediately Isabel took in a breath.

'Do not concern yourself,' he said, his face reassuring. 'It's Sophie. My sister. The one with—'

'With…?'

A woman walked in, hardly looking old enough not to have her own governess. Her hair frazzled around its pins. The dressing gown had the same capped sleeves of a day dress, but the drape and sheen of a something one could wear at a soirée.

'With the most beautiful smile in the world,' William continued.

William introduced them, talking as smoothly as if they were at a morning call and the day was dawning with the promise of sunbeams and wildflowers.

When Sophia saw Isabel, her mouth opened and she said nothing at first. Then she said, 'Your arm… I must get a cloth to clean your arm.'

Isabel stood. 'It's dried now. And only stings a little. Your brother saved me.'

'Oh, him.' She shrugged the words away. 'I slipped and fell into a stream head first and he tugged me home by my ear because he said I scared him so.' She thrust her hand sideways, giving a punch to William's arm. 'I still haven't forgiven him for making one ear crooked.'

William examined her ears. 'Yes. Hideous. Makes me shudder.'

Sophia waved his words away and stepped towards Isabel. 'So let us get you all mended.'

'Soph—' William interrupted. 'There is one other thing. I would not want to send a rider in the darkness, but you must pen a quick post in the morning for delivery to her employer. Just make up something about her rescuing you and a companion from a horrible attack of wasps or something and how she could not leave you abandoned… You know, the same story you told Aunt

Emilia.' He winked. 'It is a shame to let such a tale fade away when it could be used twice.'

Sophia shook her head. 'I don't think Aunt Emilia believed me.'

William snorted. 'I know she didn't. She told me I must get you married off immediately, so I looked about and tossed a suitable fellow your way.'

Sophia raised her chin, smiled and added drama to her voice. 'And all it took was *one* dance and he was *smitten.*'

'See, Miss Morton…' William tucked his hands behind his back '…she is good at folderol.' He turned to leave, then stopped and looked at his sister. 'You might let Aunt Emilia know of the tale. Just in case.'

'I shall. But she'll not be awake early in the morning. She's attending a dinner at the Brownings' tonight and she'll not be the first one to leave as she has put on her marriage-mart gloves again. She thinks our sisters should not rusticate away in the country.'

'She may be right.'

'Oh, please.' Sophia's voice turned whimsical. 'Once it's known that Ros and Harriet are interested in courting, Aunt Emilia will be sorting out the proposals and you will be complaining because the suitors are not worthy. Aunt Emilia is planning to get an early start on the Season. Even the people who have been in the country for the summer are returning to be at the dinner. Apparently it is quite the event because they all wish to discuss Nash's plans for our town. We can't let Bonaparte outshine us.'

'I'm surprised I found you at home.'

'Only because I do not wish to get into a heated discussion about architecture or Napoleon and prefer to spend the evening with my *smitten* husband.'

'Now you will be hearing about Nash's plans from Aunt Emilia, or her battle plans for capturing beaus for our sisters.' He raised his chin and smiled at Isabel. 'Our aunt does like to go about. Even though she has a home in the country near my father, she prefers her residence here. She considers good society vital.'

'Which means she has to ignore tales of my dear brother,' Sophia inserted.

He inclined his head to his sister and Isabel. 'And now your dear brother must take his leave as I trust two such enterprising women will have this night well in hand.' His glance lingered on Isabel's face, then her injured arm.

'Miss Morton, it might be best if you stayed at my sister's an extra day or so, unless you have a dress with long sleeves with you. That cut on your arm might raise questions.'

'Yes,' Sophia inserted. 'I'll be able to get you a gown with longer sleeves, but wearing too much covering in this heat might cause more notice. You even have a slight bruise...' She tapped a spot near her cheek. 'But after all, the wasps were chasing me at a rapid pace before you flung your bonnet like a sword and frightened them away.'

William's smile turned to Isabel alone. 'Do not let her get too carried away or she will have you saving scores of infants and battalions of soldiers, and it will get difficult to remember the details.' He leaned so close to Isabel that she could feel the flutter of his lashes, but the motion was in her chest. Almost whispering, he said, 'But don't even tell her one tiny little untruth and expect her not to remember every last detail.'

'I heard that,' Sophia said, voice loud. Then she resumed her regular tone. 'It's true.'

William murmured assent and spoke to Isabel. 'I regret we met under such unpleasant circumstances and I hope you forget all about this night soon.'

The doorway framed him, then he left. His footsteps faded into distance and the room became just a room and she could feel the bruise on her face without touching it.

William trod down the stairs, forcing himself not to turn around. He rang for the butler and waited, tapping the pull against the wall.

Finishing the last two buttons of his coat, the butler arrived and asked, 'Yes?'

'I realised my sister has a friend visiting, so I'll not be staying.'

'Yes.' He pulled his coat tight.

'Watch over them.'

'I always do.' The knowledge of the first time William had visited Sophia in the middle of the night with his own key and nearly got his head bashed in by the servant reflected from the man's eyes.

'I know.' William stayed a second longer, acknowledged the memory with a grim-lipped smile and walked out into the night.

The bolt in the door clicked.

William looked at his carriage, the three-quarter moon and the houses with mostly dark windows.

He heard the woman's voice again and turned to the open window well above him. Murmurings and a *'Goodness!'* from Sophia, and then more murmurings and a shocked exclamation. Sophia should know better than to let in the night air, but he stood until one of the carriage horses whinnied and then he turned to go home.

He sat in the carriage, crossed his arms and leaned back into the leathered cushions. A hint of her rose fragrance remained in the vehicle. The knowledge of how close he'd been to leaving Wren's earlier in the night gnawed at him. He needed to push all recollections of the past hours away and think of nothing but the fact the woman was safe, alive and cared for.

The vision of her face when the knife had been at her throat stayed in his mind. He'd been so close to walking out the door and the Songbird's life would have been altered for ever. If not for the waggling feather, he would have.

He ran a hand over his knuckles and swollen fingers, inspecting them. When they healed, he might visit Wren again.

Then he brushed a smear of dried blood away. But before the singer left London, he would make his way to his sister's house and ask Isabel to sing something for him. He smiled. He imagined them standing side by side at his sister's pianoforte and music filtering through the room.

* * *

The thought remained in his head until he walked inside his parlour. The view from the window was not fascinating, but he never seemed to tire of it. He stood at the middle of the three windows looking down and could hardly see outlines in the darkness below. Another row of town houses, just like his. Another row of windows, just like his. He didn't care to see the interiors of them or what lay beyond the panes. He feared he might see a rug, just like his. But he knew he wouldn't see furnishings like his. The room had almost none except for the two tables, the stiff-backed chair and a pretence of a desk with serviceable lamps. The servants' quarters were better fitted than this room, he hoped. The starkness suited him. Kept him from getting too close to the memories of the past where the picture of home could be painted by the fripperies spread about and the little flower shapes sewn into table coverings.

None of that appeared in his domain and his bed was the only softness in the entire house. A large beast of a bed that had once been his grandfather's and had been no easy chore for the workman to reassemble.

But he didn't want to go to bed because he kept reliving the quiet moments with the woman in the carriage, trying to think of the exact tilt of her nose. The colour of her hair was easier to recall and in all the upheaval he wasn't quite sure what had happened to the plume.

He shook his head. He was standing at the window, thinking of a bit of fluff just as a schoolboy would do. His head must have been hit harder than he realised. But the moment he'd stepped into the room at Wren's and seen the knife and her eyes widened in fear had left more than a few scrapes on his hand. The knowledge of how fast a person's life could turn to dust shook him. Now his insides shivered.

His eyes flittered to the decanter on the side table. Half-empty. The servants were not allowed to refill it until it became completely empty. If his father had walked into a room in the family home and not found it full, someone would have heard about it. If not everyone.

His father. William wished the man still looked at the world through hazed eyes.

William resisted the urge to walk forward and put a boot through the bottom glass. That would change the window, but as soon as a servant became aware, the window would be fixed.

One by one he could smash out each pane, yet the world would go on as it always did before. He could not change the way the world rotated and even if he broke the glass, other people would rush to bring the order back.

And his father, after years of a waking sleep, had truly awoken and decided he needed order back and he wanted the world on his path, a path he'd ignored the presence of for years. His father didn't remember the broken panes swept into the dustbin. He didn't remember the shattered glass.

Now, the Viscount just cared that his son be married and provide an heir. He had instructed William much like he might tell him to go to a sideboard and pick a confectionery.

The man planned to force marriage on to his son by any means possible—taking the rents William lived on would accomplish a lot. Removing the funds wouldn't hurt William alone, though, and William knew it. Twelve servants lived in the town house. Thirteen if he counted the little child he pretended not to know about—a boy who had some claim on the cook the housekeeper had hired the year before. He'd only found out about the lad because one of the servants had hidden a badly written note near William's pillow. Apparently life always didn't run smoothly among the staff either.

William took the decanter and filled his glass almost to overflow—just to see how close he could get to the edge without a spill. He placed the decanter on the table and slowly brought the liquid to his lips, not spilling a drop. He drank the liquid in one gulp, enjoying the burn.

The glass still in his hand, he stretched and strode to the windows. The servants needed their employment.

William would somehow get the horses back, then he would attend a soirée and dance with all the unwed ladies. Give his father some hope. Fruitless hope, but it wouldn't do to torment the man.

Everyone would be happy. William would find a way to have the horses returned to the stables. His father would believe a search for a bride had commenced. Sylvester would know his son would inherit the Viscount's title. Everyone satisfied if not happy. End of plan.

William slept well into the next morning and lingered through his morning wash. His dreams had been of birds fluttering about with feathered bonnets.

When dinnertime came, he would be at Sophia's house. He pulled a book from the table where it had sat for a year, planning to read enough of it so he could say he'd finished, then he would return it in time to sit for a meal with his sister, and her guest, and hopefully an evening around the pianoforte. It was only natural that he might want to visit and make sure their plans were progressing well and offer assistance.

With the mostly finished book tucked under his arm and his chin feeling raw from the second shave of the day, he strode to the front door when a carriage pulled to the front of the house.

Sophia didn't have a town coach. It could only be his father.

William put down the book and walked to the staircase before the butler could answer. The front door shook with a violent knock.

William opened the door. His father brushed by him, bodies connecting as a shove, and William stepped back.

His father raised his eyes to his son's face, slammed his beaver hat and gold-tipped cane into William's hand and said, 'Get used to that.' He continued up the stairs. 'I will see that if you are not hanged, then you will be transported. It is apparently your wish.'

Transported? Hanged? His father was daft. Completely. The years of liquid grief had turned his mind into pudding.

The Viscount rushed ahead, more at a run than William had ever seen him. William followed, knowing he didn't want his father's conversation carried to the servants' quarters. His father stopped inside the parlour, whirling around. 'You thankless piece of conceited tripe. You've gambled your name away and mine, too. Generations of our heritage. Destroyed. For ever. By you. I thought you cared more for your sisters than this.'

William put the hat over the globe of a cold lamp and propped the cane against the wall. 'What are you talking about?'

'My sister—' his father jabbed his own chest '—my sister, Emilia, came to me in tears. You are less than a son.' He splayed his hands, fingers arched. He pulled in air through his teeth. 'You called my bluff, only it was not bluff. I merely threatened to circumvent the inheritance laws. But I had no need. You were quite willing to take care of that yourself.'

'I've done nothing wrong.' His voice grated on each word. 'I only wished for the horses.'

The Viscount whipped his head away from William and stared to the windows. 'I cannot even bear the sight of you.' His words raced. 'I didn't think you would perhaps jump to marry someone suitable, but I didn't expect you to destroy our entire heritage.'

'I've done no such thing.'

His father waved his hands in the air. 'You wanted to make sure no woman would consent to wed you. You abducted a woman in daylight, in front of as many witnesses as you could find.'

'Abducted? Are you foxed?' His voice rose. The man had lost his senses.

'Do not try to turn this back at me.' He rushed by

William and to the windows. He stretched his arms at each side of the window, as if holding himself erect. His head dropped.

'Your Aunt Emilia has even begged to say that you were with her to save you. But I have forbidden it. Besides, too many have seen you.'

'The woman was attacked.'

'Attacked? Of course she was attacked. It's said you near dragged a reddish-haired woman screaming from a brothel.'

'No.' William's throat clenched. 'No.'

'Why am I not surprised? I have heard. Always I have heard. I have heard of the night you were foxed and fought the Duke of Wakefield's brother. I have heard of your gambling. But I never thought you to be so low as what transpired last night.'

The Viscount put closed fists over his eyes. 'My son,' he gasped out the words. He pulled his fists away, eyes reddened. 'I caused this. I caused it.' His voice cracked, then gained momentum. 'But I can correct it. You will vacate the premises by the end of a fortnight. I suppose sleep in your new carriage. I do not wish to see you again.' His lips trembled. His voice had the same fury as when he had told William to take the ring from Will's mother's finger on the last night of her life.

The jewellry had slipped easily from her finger and he'd felt as if he had stolen her last breath.

Pushing the memories aside, William turned so he would not see his father's face. The same vice clenched him that had surrounded him so many times before, only this time, he had to use all his might to push it away so he could speak. 'What happened?'

'Tonight,' the older man said, 'I have lost my only son. I could not sup with someone such as you.' He stepped around William, pulling his hat from the shade and grasping the cane.

William turned. 'Father. What is going on?'

The Viscount took his hat, and clenched the cane. 'I must blame myself, William. But it does not change a thing. I shouldn't have mourned your mother so long. I should have opened my eyes before it was too late. But it is now too late.'

He stepped forward, but lowered the walking stick. 'Oh, you showed me. You really did. But I will not ignore such behaviour. No longer. This was beyond the pale. Even for you.'

William squinted at his father. 'The woman is safe at Sophia's house. I took her from Wren's, but she wished for me to.'

'Sophia?' His father started. 'What does she know of this?' His fists clenched. 'I could pay the hangman myself for you attacking an innocent woman.' He stepped back. 'Your sisters. Think of your sisters.' He dipped his head. The room was silent. 'This will reach their ears. They'll be humiliated.'

Attacking an innocent? His father believed William attacked Isabel? The vice gripped again.

'The whole town will hear of it.' His father's voice ended on a high shriek. 'Apparently the talk of your— behaviour became the centre of the dinner. Your aunt was mortified. The whispers have already started and will become shouts. She came to me in tears. She found Sylvester and he agreed that you dragged a woman from Wren's. He said he was so shocked he didn't think to chase you and rescue her until after you had spirited her away in your carriage.'

'I didn't do anything wrong.'

'All the men saw you leave carrying a woman of quality from Wren's. A copper-haired woman with a bruised cheek. The men at cards heard her scream. Saw her in tatters. Blood on her sleeve. You forcing her out the door and into the carriage. Leaving a knife behind. It is thought her body was tossed into the Thames.

'Oh…' William stepped back, reaching a hand to the wall, steadying himself. 'No. No. It is not that. I didn't—'

This… This would destroy his sisters.

'You will never step foot in my house again. You will distance yourself from your sisters for their sake. I hope you care enough for them for that.' His father's eyes twitched.

Events of the night before careened through William's head. He'd done nothing wrong, except perhaps in letting Wren escape a magistrate, but he'd not wanted any notice of the night.

Now his name would be destroyed. The tales of his past weren't enough to grieve his sisters, but with this added, everything would be embellished. The tarnish would never be cleansed.

William took in a breath. 'Father.' He laughed, but could barely manage the sound. 'That is so absurd.' He waved a hand. 'She was to meet me, but was early and confused at her direction. When she was alighting the carriage, a dog, obviously trained by a cutpurse, ran out and startled the horses. The culprit knocked her about, but Isabel fought back before running into the back door of Wren's. The criminal chased her and caught her there.' He hoped no one had truly noticed her in the shadows before. But he doubted they had. At first, the bonnet had hidden her face and covered her hair. She'd remained in shadows, her presence overridden by the woman on the stage. Then, when he'd moved her outside, her clothing dishevelled—everyone had noticed them and the light reflected on her hair when the door opened.

He took a breath, gathering his thoughts. 'The driver had to keep the horses steady while fighting off the dog and didn't realise Miss—' If he'd heard her surname, he'd forgotten it '—my Isabel had exited the carriage and been attacked.'

His father stared. 'And why would a woman of quality be wishing to meet you there?'

'We had corresponded. We were to go to Gretna Green. I plan to wed her, but could not start out with her in such a state. That is why I bought the new carriage. To elope. She is waiting at Sophia's to recover and then we will marry.'

The heat of the day had collected in the room and the Viscount rubbed sweat away from his forehead with the back of his hand.

'She is alive? A reddish-haired woman?'

'Very much alive. She is a good woman. I wish to marry her. We are betrothed.'

His father examined William's face. 'Without so much of the piffle spread in—did you attack her?'

'No. I could never do that.' He used his eyes to convince his father. 'She didn't realise where she was.'

'You believe her?'

He nodded. 'She is a country squire's daughter. She had no notion.'

'From the country, you say?' He shut his eyes. 'And you have been corresponding with her and she agreed to meet you—'

'Father. We have corresponded many times while she trained to be a governess. We were not certain, with the differences in our station, that people would accept our union. So I thought it best, to avoid dissension, to present Isabel as my wife.'

'You can produce her for view?'

'Of course.'

The Viscount slammed his cane against the door frame. 'I will remember this story well enough. I cannot have my only son accused of defiling a woman. I cannot.'

'I didn't. When she didn't meet me as planned, I found her crouching behind Wren's and without thinking I took her through the place, hoping I might see the cutpurse and have him contained.'

'I could not believe what the others are saying, but I have heard the tales of your courting the women of the *demi-monde*. You are known in every gambling hell and tavern in London. And yet, you say you were with an innocent miss. If she weds you I will know you tell enough of the truth. If she doesn't, I forbid your name spoken to me and I'll not have it said in my presence that I have a son.'

He stopped mid-turn to the door and then returned his gaze to William. 'Should I trust you enough to spend the day at the club laughing at the tale Sylvester is telling because he thinks to get me to switch funds his way and a jest got out of hand?'

'Yes.' The word had the strength of a church bell.

He turned his back to his son. 'I will explain this fluff to your Aunt Emilia and she will begin combating the tales. But you must produce this sweetheart of yours and she must be at your side. And she'd better have red in her hair.'

Every rail on the bannister sounded to have received a thwack from the cane as the Viscount left the house.

William went to the window. His mouth was dry. He put a hand on the wooden shutter running the length of the door. No, the houses across the way were not like his. He swung his leg back, planning to kick out the window, but returned his boot to the carpet. He could not. If he did, they would think him the one cracked and no one would believe him innocent.

He would marry. Isabel must understand. His future depended on her saying yes.

Chapter Four

The clean dress looked more mending thread than cloth, but it did wonders for Isabel's spirit. She held the skirt away from her body and curtsied to her image in the mirror. She dreaded sitting down to dinner with Sophia and her husband because she'd never eaten in such a fine house and she hoped she didn't embarrass herself.

A maid knocked, then entered when Isabel answered. 'Miss, you are requested to the mistress's sitting room.' The woman darted away before Isabel moved.

Truly, she didn't want to step outside the bedchamber. But she must. She must put on a brave face and accept her fate as a governess. Quickly, she practised the brave face in the mirror and then she laughed at herself. To be safe was all that mattered.

She would regain that governess position without losing her reputation. Her parents had sacrificed so that she might attend Madame Dubois's School for Young Ladies and have the best education they could provide.

She could not reward them by failing to be able to care for herself.

When she walked into the sitting room, Sophia wasn't present. A lone figure sat on the sofa. William, legs stretched, his gaze on some distant thought. Her spirit leapt. Isabel rushed forward to thank him again. William rose from the sofa, legs straightening in a controlled slowness.

She lost her thoughts. She'd not seen a man such as him. Ever. He could have trampled any man in one of her novels. This lone man had saved her against a man with a knife. His inside was as magnificent as his outside.

A true rescuer in gentleman's clothing. The cravat, perfect. The waistcoat under his dark coat gold with matching buttons.

'I do not know how I will ever thank you,' she said.

His lips thinned, then turned up. His kept his gaze on her. His eyes had no true happiness in them, but his mouth seemed determined to laugh.

'Marriage?' he asked.

She leaned forward. 'I didn't hear you.'

He clasped his hands behind him. 'Will you be so kind as to wed me? Vows. For ever. All that nonsense.'

She needed two tries before she could speak. For ever? Nonsense? 'You did save my life,' she said. 'Perhaps I could stitch you up a rather nice nightcap. My father quite likes the one I did for him.'

'We have quite a kettle boiling around us,' he said, leaning his shoulders forward and tipping his head close to hers. He smelled better than any perfume she'd ever scented. Perhaps like lilacs, but not flowery. More like something to deflect the scent of shaving and masculinity and things that might tempt a woman.

Yet the words he spoke had no sweet fragrance in them.

For ever? Nonsense? She had dreamt of true love. Of all that 'for ever' and 'nonsense'. And even asked that if there were angels up above, one might send a nice vicar or soldier her way. He didn't need all his teeth, or hair or even the usual number of fingers or toes, and this man seemed to have all that, whereas a man missing a few parts might be more willing to share all his love to find a wife. She wanted someone who gazed upon her as a shining star. Someone who could shower her with love…and perhaps *not* be found in a brothel. Although she could not complain he had been at Wren's the night before, but still that didn't induce her to wed him.

She put a firm, competent look on her face. 'I am quite good at making stockings which keep the feet warm on a cold night,' she said.

He shut his eyes briefly and pulled back, lips up-turned, as if they knew no other direction. 'You would not ever know I was about. I doubt I would be home enough you'd notice. You would be a governess of sorts still, but it could be for your own children. One would hope for children to be a part of the endeavour.'

Oh, that was what this was about. The man needed some sons and perhaps he'd only been at Wren's and not noticed the many fine places where a decent woman could be found.

'Children?' She looked past his shoulder to the wall.

'You're not unpleasant to look at,' she said. 'I could recommend several young women who are now at Madame Dubois's School for Young Ladies who would be quite good wives.' She appraised him and fought to keep speaking. William had helped her most efficiently and she should do the same in return. 'What colour hair do you prefer?'

He appraised her, eyes lingering at her head. 'A copper colour. Like sunlight has softened it.'

'Um…' She looked at him. 'I admit, my hair is a good shade. I have heard that all my life. And I can understand you might think to have children with this colour of hair, but it is indeed a bit rare and one cannot count on such a thing.'

'Probably a bit much to expect the sky-blue eyes to go with it.'

Her stomach curled, making it hard to maintain her composure.

'Yes, I'm a bit of an aberration.'

'A lovely aberration.' He paused. He looked at her without flirtation. 'And your voice. I like your speaking voice. It doesn't grate on my ears.'

'Oh, my…' She put her hand to her bodice and ducked her head in the way she did when someone praised her singing. 'You are quite efficient with the compliments. I hope that is one of your own and not from the list.'

He nodded and his lips turned up at one side before speaking. 'You would be surprised how many times a woman's voice has grated on my ears. I have three sisters, remember. So when I called you Songbird, it was not idle. But it would be best for us to wed.'

She put her palm out, touching his coat just above his elbow, giving a brief pat, trying to ease the rejection. *Oh, candlesticks, no one would ever believe she had refused a viscount's son.* 'You do not have to concern yourself with my honour. Your sister has agreed to help me get to Sussex. If that does not work out, I can return to my parents'.' She could not go home in disgrace though. She would have to find a post.

'I am not concerned only about your honour.' His eyes sparkled and his lips, still firm, returned to their rueful smile.

'I know a quite lovely girl of near marriage age,' she said. 'I could see that you have an introduction. Blonde hair. Eyes the same colour as mine.'

'Do they sparkle quite as well as yours do?'

'I'm sure when she looks at you they will quite outshine...' She paused. Cecilia was so sweet and kind and rather younger. An older rake would not do at all. 'She may not quite suit you, though. I think perhaps all my friends remaining at the governess school might be young for you and the ones who graduated with me are quite busy. Perhaps, um...' she stumbled '...a nice widow. A woman with some—knowledge. More your age.'

'I'm twenty-four. Not quite ancient.'

'Oh,' she muttered, 'I thought you older. At least thirty. Closer to thirty-five.' Particularly if he seemed desperate to find a wife.

One brow rose.

'I suspect you have rather included many adventures in those years. I do seem to remember asking if it was your first time at that horrible place and I think you answered that you were long past first times at anything.'

'Except marriage. It would be my first time at marriage.'

'I fear you do not understand the concept.'

'I disagree.' He took a step away. 'I have seen it quite close. Love and all that…conflagration of mindless emotion.' He stopped. 'Isabel. I am quite slogging in the wrong direction. I hate to tell you what has transpired, but I feel I must…'

'The talk is out about my misfortune.' She met his eyes. They confirmed her words. She continued, 'You are asking for my hand in marriage to save my honour.'

He was valiant. No knight could surpass him.

His eyes shut. 'Not entirely.' He stepped forward.

Again, when he stood so close, something about him distracted her thoughts and took them as directly as one might take the bridle of a horse and turn its face in a desired direction.

'I would hope that I would be so noble as to marry to save you, but I am not sure.' He took her fingertips. She could not move.

Now he spoke softly, conveying the importance of his words with his gaze.

'It is said that I ravished you in Wren's. I spirited you out by force. The dishevelment. The torn dress.'

'*You* didn't ravish me. You rescued me.'

'Yes. But to have that untrue story—no matter how it is said—your presence in such a place will cast aspersions on you. I would prefer us both to get out of this as best as possible. I would not wish to spend the rest of my life with the lingering question in the minds of others as to whether I truly attacked you or not.'

She balled her fists within his hands. 'I will tell them. I will tell them all.'

'You may,' he said. 'Other questions will arise that neither of us particularly care to be subjected to. You will be seen as a woman afraid to tell the truth about a wayward viscount's son for fear of repercussions. I do not have a…' He searched for a word. 'A sombre past.'

Her stomach bunched into a gulp and then bounced from one side of itself to the other. 'William, I fear you would not make a good husband.'

'I know I would not. That is one of the reasons I have not considered marriage in the past. I think it a suffocating, strangling gaol. It is not a leg shackle. It is a throat shackle. I have said it is likened to having leeches attached to bleed the body dry and leave it a desiccated shell. Much like the body left behind centuries after death.'

She pulled her hands away. 'You have worked long on this proposal?'

'Twenty-four years.'

'Am I the first to hear it?'

'Yes. This is a first.'

'I dare not ask…'

'I don't think I should talk of my life if we are to be married. Last night I thought never to see you again so I didn't care overmuch. If we might be seeing each other at a marriage ceremony, then I don't care to discuss how I spend my nights.'

'The socks and night caps would probably not make a good gift for you.'

'No.' He gave the saddest smile she'd ever seen. 'All that I ask is that you stand at my side and answer a few words.'

'Those vows and nonsense?' She might end up the desiccated shell, but she was not quite doing as well on her own as she'd hoped. And she had no desire at all to be a governess. None.

'Yes.' He stood. 'I see a bit of concern on your face. But you do not have to worry I will be a brute like Wren. I will not…be unkind.'

She didn't speak.

'Ours would be the most perfect of marriages.'

She lifted her brows.

'Yes. If you have need of me once we are married, you will only have to give a note to my butler and he will see that it is delivered and I will read it immediately. We won't see a great deal of each other. I truly do not like to be home.'

'You did rather help me,' she said. When she looked into his eyes, it was as if they begged her to say no. Forces behind him pushed him her way, much like a pirate would shove a person into the deep. 'Do you not think you are making a terrible mistake?'

He shook his head. 'All my sisters' lives I have been there for them. Perhaps even when they had no one else. I have had one unselfish task, only one, and that has been to see that they are safe and have a home. When that is provided, they content themselves. I cannot bring disgrace upon them. A few tales about my revelry doesn't hurt—that is shrugged away. But that I might harm a woman would not be tolerated. A man who hurts weaker people for his pleasure is condemned. His family—particularly sisters of a marriageable age— would be tarnished.'

He moved to the window, looked out, shook his head and returned to her. His smile was directed inwards, but the question in his eyes was for her alone.

'Can you not think of another solution?' she asked.

'Not at this moment. If I could, I would give it.'

His words rested in her like a wooden ball rolling down a stair, clunking to the bottom.

'If you do not wish to wed,' he said, 'I understand. But, Sophia will be damaged if you do not. So will my other two sisters and my Aunt Emilia. My father will manage to consider Cousin Sylvester his heir. I will be tossed from my home. At least half of the servants will be without employment.'

'You do not play on someone's sympathies…do you?' She brushed her fingertips over the sleeve of his coat. They had only met the night before, but they were not strangers. Nor friends. Nor enemies. But they had shared a moment of decisions together that few ever faced and her life would plunge one direction or the other based on her response.

'And there is the fact that I found you a place to stay last night. Although I understand if you have no wish to marry,' he said. 'I certainly can understand that. Perhaps better than anyone.'

That he could understand her wish not to marry *per-*

haps better than anyone' was not a resounding push in his favour.

'I must give this some thought,' she said. 'But you should give it a great deal more consideration as well. Marriage is about love and holding the other person in the highest esteem. At least it is for me.'

'As a governess you would not be allowed to have a marriage.'

'I can eventually leave a governess post. Or I might fall in love with a tutor, or stable master, or linen draper—on my half-day off. And if that person loves me back, just a little, it is more than you're offering.'

'I'm wealthy.'

She paused. One shouldn't marry for money. But one shouldn't overlook funds either. 'How wealthy?'

'My children will have a governess. A tutor. And if you wed me—' He shrugged. 'Your children will have a governess. A tutor.'

'My son would be a viscount,' she mused.

He frowned. 'Bite your tongue. There is never any rush for that.'

'He would. Just not until he was very old.'

'So we will wed.'

'My daughters would be able to have the finest things.'

He nodded. 'I can also ensure that you have reputable avenues for your talent. I would consider it a way of thanking you for taking on the misfortune of marriage.'

'I don't— Marriage is not such a thing.' She turned away. 'As your wife I wouldn't wish to sing. That's over for me and I can accept that easily.'

'You would be giving your chance at love away, but it would enable more choices for the children you might have. A sacrifice, for sure.'

The clouds inside her head cleared. A mother did such things, or should.

'You may wed me,' she said. She could pretend. Perhaps if she didn't pay attention to the marriage words they would not quite count as much and she could pretend to be a governess with the children away on holiday. That could be pleasant. And she would not mind to have a little family for herself. And if the boys favoured him, oh, she would preen, and it would not be a problem for the daughters to inherit her hair colour or his.

'I don't see that either of us have many other choices. You are all the things a woman would want in a husband,' she said, giving a smile that didn't reach her heart. 'And all the things she would not.'

Isabel sat at the writing desk which had been moved into the room. She didn't feel like opening the ink bottle. She'd never written a letter while wearing a borrowed chemise, but the garment would do her well to sleep in and by the time she woke, her own laundered dress would be dry. She didn't have to worry about choosing matching slippers, as she should be pleased her slippers were mostly free of the muck.

She would be quite the lovely bride in the patched-together dress. Her marriage would take place some time the next day as William was getting the special licence and telling all his friends how delighted he was to be married.

She could marry, or, she could go home in disgrace.

She chose to take the stopper from the ink bottle. The letter would be easiest. She would write her parents of how wonderful everything was as she had met the man of her dreams... She shut her eyes and tapped her closed fist at her forehead. Oh, this news had to be delivered in a letter. They would never believe it if she said it to their faces.

Or they might.

She remembered her father picking daffodils for her mother each spring. Roses in the summer. Walking hand in hand in the crisp autumn air and calling her the best gift of his life—one he could hold each day of the year.

Her parents loved her. She knew it. But when they looked at each other an affection shone in their faces, along with something else. It was much like a clock-maker might want to see how the mechanisms worked to turn the hands of a timepiece. Isabel had imagined how it would feel when her own husband cherished her so.

When she had realised that she was being trained to be a governess and a governess didn't have a husband, she'd felt tossed into a rubbish heap. She could never be loved in the same manner her parents loved each other. She'd put all of her spirit into her song the next time she sang—the very first time she had noticed tears in a listener's eyes. Her dreams had soared. Singers could marry. They could have their own family.

She imagined the devotion she wished for. She began

to write. The man she wrote of in the letter was so deeply devoted that he could not bear to be away from his beloved one moment more. He had cherished her from afar...

She tapped the nib against the inside of the bottle, planning just how it would have been.

Her parents had missed one of the events where the school had let her sing, so that was where she had met William. And he had been instantly smitten. Tears had flooded from his eyes—no, scratch that. He had shed one lone, intense tear as he had thanked her for the overwhelming performance and called her a songbird. She smiled when she penned the word *songbird.* He *had* called her Miss Songbird.

She dipped the pen again. He'd begged, yes, begged that they might correspond. She had refused, most assuredly, but he had managed to get his letters to her, and after great personal dilemma, she read them. Slowly her heart had melted—*but, no*, she'd insisted, she could not neglect her dream to become a governess. Over time, however, his devotion had overtaken her and she had agreed to wed.

William stared at the darkened ceiling in his bedchamber. The ceremony would be in a few hours.

He'd not slept at all. He'd kept remembering the deep love his parents had had for each other and then his mother had died. The world had gone silent that night after her last breath. Then he'd had to remove her cherished ring from her finger. None of them had been the same after that night. His father began to substitute liquid for air.

Love had destroyed his father. Took him from them in the guise of drink. But William didn't blame his father for that weakness.

William had heard the noises the second night after his mother's death and crept to his mother's room. His father had been huddled on the floor, arms around himself, rocking. He'd been crying out his wife's name over and over.

William had pulled the door shut and walked the hallway. Silence had followed, and permeated deep into the walls around him. In the days afterwards, he'd watched the family move about and it had felt as if he watched a play. He could see the actors and hear them. But he wasn't even standing near the stage.

He rolled in the bed, kicking the last of the covers to the floor.

Marriage. Children. Such a risk.

But he didn't love Isabel, so marriage could not destroy their lives. He would not allow her to love him either. He imagined himself standing beside Isabel as the vicar asked—

He had forgotten a vicar. No one might be standing there to marry them.

He'd been so concerned with getting the special licence, the town coach, and telling as many people as he could think of to expect the happy event, he'd forgotten someone to make the words official.

Within moments, his boots were on and his shirt stuffed into his trousers. He tied his cravat as he rushed

down the stairs and he had no idea of how to progress
but he was certain the butler would know of someone
who could perform a marriage.

The butler chuckled as he gave William direction to
a vicar's home.

William had had a bit of difficulty finding the house
in the darkness, but he banged on the door. He heard
a voice grumble out, and then he waited, rubbing his
chin, feeling the stubble.

The vicar, a wisp of a man, finally appeared, his hair
falling in snowy frazzles around his face and a scrap of
a belt around his nightshirt covering. Without speaking, he waved William inside.

'I have a special licence.' William shot out the words.
'I need to be married quickly.

'Is the babe arriving now?' the vicar asked, tugging
the belt tight.

'No,' William said, taking a step back. 'There's no
child.'

'Well, then, what's the rush?' He squinted.

'I'm marrying today and I didn't remember I needed
someone to speak the words.'

'Are you going to battle?' the man questioned. 'Leaving soon?'

'No.' William shook his head. 'I just need to be married.'

'Ah.' Again the man tugged on the tie at his waist and
then stepped back, peering through squinted lids. 'You
might come back after breakfast and I'll decide then.'

The speck of a man was saying no? 'It's your job.'

'A young man pounding on my door in the middle of

the night when there is not a babe arriving before morning makes me concerned that he might not be considering the options.'

William tightened his stance. 'I cannot go into the details. Just tell me who might be able to say a few quick words to take care of this for me.'

'I suppose *you should* prepare us a pot of tea and tell me about it.'

'Tea?' William gasped out. 'I do not know how to make tea.'

The man grunted. 'And you expect to be able to handle a marriage?'

'The servants will handle the tea.'

'Would you like my advice?' the vicar asked.

'No. But if I stand here much longer I suppose I will be hearing it.'

'Yes. And I know how to make tea, so I do have more knowledge than you on some things and I am not rushing about in the wee hours. So perhaps you should come in.' He walked away as he talked. 'You owe me that for waking me. And if your reason for pounding on my door has merit, then I can take care of the marriage for you.'

William ducked his head, stepping into the scent of tallow candles and well-settled dust. A floorboard creaked under his foot.

'Come into the kitchen with me and I'll light a candle,' the vicar said. 'Don't bother bolting the door. I always open it anyway, no matter what kind of person is pounding.' He chuckled in William's direction.

After the kettle started, he whisked a glass and wine

bottle from a shelf. After placing the glass in front of William, he poured without asking and then concerned himself with his own drink.

'So,' the older man asked after he finished preparations and settled to sip his tea, 'what is all the rush about?'

'A young woman and I need to be married. We do not wish for any tales about us to be spread.'

'A compromising position?'

'You could say that.'

'Perhaps you're overreacting. Tales can fade.'

William snorted. 'Not this one.' He leaned forward. 'I know what I am to do. We are to be married and we won't cause interruption in each other's lives.'

'I have never heard of a marriage which does not cause some interruption in life.'

'I have the funds to see that it happens,' William said. He stopped. 'I am very adept at dealing with such things. I can live separately if needed.'

'Marriage. The specialness in part is that it cannot be walked away from. That is what makes it different than, say, not marriage. Love is fickle, though.'

'We are not in love.'

The vicar sputtered into his tea and set down his cup.

William continued. 'We are in agreement. She and I have discussed it. I told her what nonsense love is.'

'Ah.' The vicar nodded. 'You shouldn't have told the truth on that. Not even to me. But if she agreed with that, then I suppose she will have no one to blame but herself.' He chuckled, and mumbled, 'Do not expect that reprieve, however.'

'Isabel is not like that.'

'You've known her long?'

'Long enough.'

'A lifetime can be not long enough to know what a woman is like before you marry her—from what I've seen.'

'The woman *I am* going to marry is…' He paused. 'She's almost alone in the world, or that's how she feels. I don't want her to be alone. I may not be able to give her everything, but I can give her a home, safety and a haven. She'll have servants. Children, perhaps.'

In a flash of memory, he could see his parents laughing at the table and then his father throwing crockery about after her death, acting in the same manner as Rosalind when she'd been cross. Only he could not send his father to his room and tell him that the governess would not be reading him a bedtime story.

His father had never even raised his voice before his wife died. Never acted anything but sensible and selfless. Then he'd become senseless—and selfish.

William's eyes flickered to the small man who stared into him. 'I need to marry her—for my own purpose, but it is not an entirely bad thing for her. Without me, she will likely remain unmarried and not have children of her own.'

'Why do you think she won't find someone else? Is she unappealing?'

'I wouldn't say she is unappealing. In fact, she is too appealing—to be safe—alone in the world. It isn't beauty, though I am not saying she isn't.' William smiled, staring at the empty glass. 'She has this cop-

per-coloured hair.' He held out his hand, thumb touching forefinger, making the movement as if holding a
strand. 'The light shone on it and she had her bonnet
off, and the other men saw it and they saw her eyes,
and ten years from now, she could walk into a room
and they will remember her.'

'There are other ways to protect a woman besides
marriage.'

William let out a deep breath. 'Not this one.' He put
the glass on the table and leaned back, stretching his
legs. 'Not this one. She's been at a school in the country or she would have had suitors lining up. Even at
the school, someone found her who wished to take advantage.'

The minister stood. 'You think to love her later.'

'No.' William breathed out the word. 'I don't. That
could never happen.'

'If she is so appealing—' He moved, standing by a
shelf with a basin on it, keeping his back to William.
'Another man should easily fall in love with her.'

'That's true. But I've seen what love does—I'm not
in favour of it.'

'My wife might agree with you,' he said. 'But you
might fall in love if the two of you are married.'

'No. I do not have it in me.' William considered the
words.

'How does she feel about you,' the vicar asked, 'this
daft woman who has agreed to wed you?'

'She doesn't know me.'

The man turned around, wiping his hands on a cloth
from beside the basin. 'I would say she doesn't.' He

peered at William's face and reached under the shelf
and pulled out another bottle from the dark recesses.
He popped the cork and put the bottle on the table between them. 'Drink up and tell why I should perform
this ceremony.'

Chapter Five

Isabel examined her patched dress and stained shoes. She'd once wondered what she'd choose to be married in. It wasn't this.

Her invisible groom's father, Viscount Langford, sat in Sophia's overstuffed chair as if it were his throne. He patted a chair arm and stared, emotionless.

'It'll just be a few minutes more,' Sophia said, perching at the end of the sofa and resting one hand on the brocade between them. The other hand held a fan that flitted more than any butterfly wings. 'And William will be here. He's not really late yet.'

Isabel raised her head in acknowledgement.

'If he doesn't appear, I will find him and drag him here myself.' Langford stood, walked behind the sofa and patted his daughter's shoulder.

'This almost reminds me of the day—' Sophia stopped fanning, glanced at her hand, then spoke to Isabel. 'One day, in the past, my sisters and I waited for Father and William to return. It was in August, too, and a much warmer day than this.'

'Do not speak of your mother today,' the Viscount commanded. 'If she were here, William would have married long before now.'

Isabel stood, turned to the Viscount, gave a small bow of her head, and put a smile on her face. 'William—' she fluttered her hand over her heart and paused '—was waiting for me. His whole lifetime. So it will not concern me to wait a few moments for him.'

Thoughts flickered in his eyes. 'Welcome to the family. I do beg your pardon if anything I have said this morning offended you and I beg forgiveness for the errors I have made in bringing up my son, which I feel are about to be visited on your head.'

She gave the assured blink she used for the audience before she sang. 'Then when my husband does not do quite as I expect, I will keep my words kind to him and my ire will be directed in your direction.'

He turned halfway from her. His voice was soft. 'Do as you must.' Then he turned back to her. 'Isabel, I will be prepared for your visits.'

Laughter sounded as a door on the lower floor opened. A scattershot of noises sounded.

Sophia and the Viscount looked around as if a gunshot had landed nearby and no one knew which direction it came from.

Sophia's words were a whisper and she looked to the ceiling. 'Thank you.'

The Viscount turned to the wall and sighed, then said, 'What did I do?'

Isabel could not think which face to use and she settled on the one she used at the governess school after she sang and everyone praised her.

William appeared at the doorway, with two men behind him, one with a book under his arm. William hadn't shaved. Isabel couldn't concentrate on the greetings around her, but examined William. He only looked her way a half-second or less. Blazing determination flashed in his eyes. The same stare he'd had when he'd pounced on Wren.

Then the cleric made some jest about reading the right portion of the prayer book. William glared and the other man's eyes darted downwards, but his smile beamed. She wondered if the Book of Common Prayer had a section for words said at funerals because that would be the only jest she could think of to use.

The wedding would not fool anyone present that it was a love match. She in her patched clothes and him appearing as if he'd just rolled from a bed.

She glanced to the door. A quick dart and she could be down the stairs. She opened her mouth, thinking to conjure up another aunt. She could rush away to retrieve her aunt to attend the wedding, but then she shook the thoughts away. William had saved her and he wished to protect his sisters.

The cleric spoke to William, patting him on the back. William swayed and she could have sworn the older man gripped the back of his coat to hold him steady.

Now she knew why men often had a friend at the side when they spoke their vows.

'Let us begin.' The cleric moved, directing the other man to stand by William.

'Miss,' the cleric said, taking the Book of Common Prayer from under his arm and looking to the vacant spot beside William.

She bit her lip and looked at the empty place at William's side. She would be standing there a long time.

She moved into place, but not quite. Another person could have stood between them. Stepping sideways, he put his hand around her waist. For a moment his fingers rested at her side. Then a tug and she had no choice but to follow his clasp. She squeaked and her feet caught up with her body.

They were close. Very close. And he was strong. Her hip tingled where it brushed against his side. The tingles spread around her body. This could work.

The minister opened his mouth to speak, then closed it. Then opened it again, looking at William and not at the book. Then he shook his head.

'We shall proceed.' William spoke. It wasn't a question. He dropped his hand away from Isabel, and cleared his voice.

Internally, Isabel stumbled, but nothing changed in front of her face so she didn't think she'd really moved. She leaned closer to him, her bare arm against the sleeve of his coat, and she took in an easing breath.

The Book of Common Prayer opened and the world outside the windows stopped. Isabel became a wife and she couldn't hear the words but his arm rested against hers, comforting.

In the last dress and pair of shoes she would have

ever chosen, she wed William, and even though he looked as if he'd fallen from a horse and smelled of an alehouse, he'd charged a man with a knife to save her and he'd married a stranger to protect his sisters. She stole a glance at him. Behind the ragged façade, she was certain some part of him wished for the marriage. He'd pulled her to his side and she'd felt it.

William listened to each word, committing them to memory. Blast. He had not expected them to sound in his head as if blared from a trumpet. Nor had he expected them to sound so real and sincere.

Words. They were just words. But they weren't like any he'd ever heard before. He was listening to a decree of the rest of his life. Vows of spiritual portent, spoken from a prayer book, with family around, to bond. Marriage had not been invented by a sane man. The vicar was right after all. The process was necessary for the sake of the children and the record-keeping of whom they belonged to. One didn't want to pass a title too far from the lineage.

She stood beside him, chin high, eyes forward, pale and…kissable lips.

He'd never kissed her, though it wouldn't be a problem. He'd held her in the carriage. If not for her misfortune, he would have kept the coachman driving circles in the town all night. He never seen a woman so *just right* as her. Tall enough for him. Short enough for him. Curved and straight enough. Just right.

All things considered, Isabel was a fortunate choice. His thoughts raced among the other ladies of his acquaintance. What if he had rescued one of them? She would be standing beside him now.

He imagined someone else at his side and felt a shudder. He had certainly missed cannon fire on that regard. At least fortune had chosen Miss—Isabel. He had forgotten her name again, but it would not be a concern now. She was Isabel Balfour now—which didn't quite seem to fit her. Yet speaking the vows with someone other than her would have been—unfathomable. In relief, he huffed a sigh—just at the moment the vicar pronounced them man and wife together.

His sister hissed.

The vicar tutted and William shut his eyes. That was something that could not be explained away.

Then the vicar prayed over them. And prayed. And prayed. The ceremony ended and the air dripped with the heat of the day.

William glanced at Isabel. No songbird's feathers had ever drooped more. A stab into his midsection. Guilt. Remorse. Anger at the ironic situation. All flashed into him.

She looked at him and when her eyes met his, the wilt disappeared. In his whole life no woman's eyes had ever pinched in such a way when she gazed at his face.

Pleasantries sounded and everyone disappeared from the room, except William, his wife and his father.

The Viscount's eyes rested on Isabel. 'I wish you both all the best. And I am pleased to have you as a daughter.' He took her left hand and pulled it to his gaze, looking at her wedding band. His eyes darted to William's long enough to spear him and back to her simple gold band, then to her face. 'Isabel, if I can ever be of any assistance to you in any way, please do not hesitate to contact me. I will accept your criticism freely and direct it in the proper direction.'

He looked at his son. 'Let me know when the heir is on the way.'

William blinked once in acknowledgement that he'd heard and his father left the room.

'Well, we are married,' his Songbird chirped, but her profile had quite a strong jaw. William offered his arm. She took it without looking in his direction and then a sigh exploded from her lips. If candles had been lit nearby, that blast would have easily extinguished them.

This would require something expensive or rare. It always worked for his sisters.

'Perhaps we could take a ride in my carriage and I might select a gift for you,' he said.

'Oh... Thank you so very much, but I do not need a thing. Your sister has sent for my trunk—she is so thoughtful. She also instructed a burly footman to Wren's as I mentioned that my satchel is there.' She paused. 'She is quite thoughtful.' Her face ever so innocent, she sighed.

'I didn't mean it the way it sounded,' he said. 'I was merely thinking how fortunate I was to have you by my side instead of someone else.'

'I am sure that is how everyone took it. Husband.' She stepped to the stairs and he followed. 'For ever... nonsense...' She sighed again, much in the same way a cat's hiss might turn into a growl.

Chapter Six

He'd taken Isabel around London after the marriage even though she'd refused to shop. He'd made sure she could later and let her know where he had accounts.

At his town house, he'd shown his bride to her room. She'd immediately spotted the trunk and while the door hadn't slammed in his face, or even shut, it had been nudged his direction, but his boot had stopped it. He'd left her when she'd hugged a dress to her face and the sniffles had started. It wasn't even a pretty dress. He'd had a good look at it when he'd said her name and she'd flung the clothing past him.

So, he'd moved to his room, took off his boots, stripped to his shirt and trousers and lay on the bed, giving her some time to orient herself before he returned.

Isabel was more in agreement with his plan for marriage than anyone else he could have chosen. She'd not even wanted to shop with him. And the little nudge of the door hadn't been an accident. She would be the perfect wife once she stopped sniffling and throwing things at him. He didn't blame her.

He would make it up to her. He would.

He promised he would get her a beautiful piece of jewellery soon. If there was one thing he had learned, the bigger the mistake; the bigger the gift. And sometimes it was best to wait before delivery so that it didn't get thrown back.

He shook his head. He was a rake. What kind of rake was reluctant to visit his own wife's bed on their wedding night? It was just that she'd felt so fragile in the carriage. And then the tears. She'd hugged some garment and cried. He didn't wish to cause her more pain and so soon after the attack. She had to be bruised as she'd fallen to the floor. His own ribs still hurt.

The turns of the past few days passed through his mind and he realised he hadn't slept the night before, and his eyelids weighted him down until a sound woke him.

Tap. Tap. Tap. He looked to the door. No servant would be…on this night.

Tap!

He opened the door, and a rigid, wan face glared. 'It is my wedding night and I would prefer to get some sleep and I cannot because I feel like you are going to slip into my room any second.' She paused. Her hair had been taken from the knot and cascaded about her shoulders. 'Where have you been?'

Just enough light illuminated her to give her the gentleness of a lost waif.

'I fell asleep.'

'Well, that is a good plan.' She whirled away.

He took a step, following her. He reached to clasp her arm. 'Please.' Gently, he led her back to the chamber.

'My ribs,' he said and patted over them. 'I should have told you.' In truth, he'd had many worse bruises, but a woman shouldn't be alone on her wedding night. Neither should a man for that matter. 'And I didn't ask about the cut on your shoulder.'

'It's well enough.'

He led her beside the light and her hair showed glints of the copper. 'Isabel.' He touched the strands, letting them slide through his fingers, and he remembered a tale of a woman whose hair was so alive that she could let it down at her window and a prince could climb it to be at her side. He felt like the man trying to find the princess.

Burying his face against the silkiness, he slowly pulled her close, breathing in the soap-clean scent mixed with a reminder of spring flowers. *Just right.* She was not just right. She was perfection.

'I told the truth about the sigh,' he said. 'I thought of my misfortune, should someone else have been at my side at that moment.'

'Surely you—'

'I could not imagine how lucky I was to have you there instead of anyone else.'

Isabel put her palms out and a fortress of male was at her fingertips. Instead of fear to have a male so close, his strength flowed into her.

'Are you hurt badly?' she whispered.

He rested his face against her hair. 'It does not hurt at all, but…you're certainly making it feel much better.' His thin shirt was no barrier to the chest beneath. Warmth raced from her fingertips into her heart and she splayed her hands to feel more. She had not realised. He had not looked so formidable only inches away, nor so gentle.

Kisses sprinkled her whole body with sparks of warmth.

He stepped aside, pulled off his shirt and leaned into the light. Purpled skin, half the size of a boot.

She reached out, swirling her hand along just above the skin, not touching. 'I am so sorry.'

'I'm not.'

He clasped his hand over her wrist and moved her hand to the centre of his torso, just above his waistband. He pulled her hand close. Her fingers spread naturally, fitting against the taut skin. He trailed her fingers upwards, moving them over the ribs, the orbs, the lines and swirls of his chest.

Silken. Taut. Flexible and firm.

She'd never heard a song written about such an experience, never understood why people acted in manners not suitable to their station. In one brush of her hand against William's chest she understood things no one could have explained if they'd spoken for a million years.

Like a creature burrowing against another for shelter, William put his face closer to hers. 'Isabel… Is…I don't think we've kissed before. I wanted to—I wanted to lean towards you and kiss you during the wedding. I ached to do it.'

He loosed his clasp and took his hand away, but her fingers stayed above his heart. He touched his lips to her nose, petal-light, brown velvety eyes watching blue.

'Our first,' he whispered. 'But do not try to keep count, because if you can do so the night will be counted a miserable failure in my eyes.'

The world disappeared when he pulled her close and melded her into his arms. Her mind could not think past the feel of being held and she became light as thistle-down, and wafted along on the warmth, held aloft by the rushing breaths. The soft brush of lips against lips joined them in a world of nothing but their heartbeats.

She didn't know when the sash on her gown loosened and the garments fell away. But somehow, without her knowledge, William removed her clothing and his, and lifted her to the bed.

Their bodies twined close, skin heating skin, and for once, warmth on an August night soothed.

He paused, pushing himself up so that she looked into his eyes. The darkened room didn't allow her to see the exactness of his features, but she could visualise him easily. His lips were parted and he studied her face, then moved to the side enough that he could reach to her cheek. She didn't feel the touch, but his hand heated much like sunbeams travelling over the skin.

His fingertips dropped to her skin, moving to her jawline and down her neck to her shoulder. He trailed down her arm and took her hand, putting it against his cheek, moving to place a kiss against her palm. The bristles of his face mixed with the softness of his lips. She traced his jaw, taking in the transition to a world she'd not known existed. Tendrils of his hair brushed against her knuckles.

'Isabel,' he whispered, so softly she knew it was not a question, but a caress with words.

He moved forward to kiss her, but something inside her had changed so that the tilt forward seemed to take a thousand moments, but she savoured each one.

His lips, warm and moist, took her thoughts away so that she could only feel.

His hands brushed over her breasts, bringing the feel of a caress to her entire body. He outlined her hips, her stomach, and pulled her against him, his hardness between them.

Again the warmth of the night became a balm as the slickness of his heated body bonding to hers swathed them in a cocoon of togetherness.

When he entered her, the murmurings whispered into her ear made her feel more protected and loved than she'd ever imagined at any moment of her life.

In some knowledge she didn't know how she'd gained, William did all he could to protect and cherish her with his body.

William stood at the side of the bed, looking down. His head kept lowering as he fell asleep on his feet and then he'd raise it and jolt himself awake. She lay so still and looked more fragile than any glass figurine with her resting lips, the lashes resting over closed eyes and the skin pale in the moonlight.

He leaned over her and brushed a kiss at her hair, hoping she would wake. She didn't move. Then he brushed a knuckle against her cheek, and her eyelids flickered and she rolled over.

Stepping away he turned, controlling his breathing. She was well. She would remain well.

He should have met Isabel in her chamber. Even after she'd knocked on his door, he could have easily walked her back to her room and then left as she fell asleep.

He was not cad enough that he could ask her to leave his bed, and he didn't think she had plans to go. If she had, she would have left earlier.

He could not become attached. He could not experience anything deeper than he might feel for any other person. To care enough that you didn't want to hurt someone was how it should be. But he could not care enough that the person could damage him. If he had learned one thing in his life, that was it.

He didn't don his trousers or shirt, but slowly began gathering his clothing. Devil take it. His face itched. He touched it again. This would be the second day without shaving and he simply could not stand another moment of it.

But he couldn't ring for his valet and ask the man to simply ignore the woman in his bed—the wife in his bed.

This was what the vicar had meant about marriage, but William had been too absorbed to see. A wife did differ from a mistress. He'd not expected that since no love was involved.

The simple act of declaration of marriage in front of a few witnesses and it wasn't just nonsensical words. But he had suspected that all along.

His thoughts had tried to warn him when he'd not been able to think the night before. He'd babbled on to the vicar as if he'd swallowed a crate of ale, but he'd not had any spirits until the one before the wedding, hoping it would steady him. The portent of knowledge, and the sleeplessness, had taken him out at the knees and gutted what was left of his thoughts.

This oddness, at seeing Isabel asleep in his bed, helpless in her slumber, was a reminder of all the conflagration he'd experienced during the past days. Surely, soon this would dissipate. Distance would help.

With his clothing bundled in one hand and his boots in the other, he made it out the door and pulled it closed behind him. In the hallway, he dressed, resting his back against the wall as he tugged on his boots.

Marriage had reduced him to—secreting himself out of a married woman's bed in the night as if she might have a husband appear at any moment.

He would have to find another place to stay, at least temporarily until he had accepted the routine of someone living in his house. But he could not turn to his friends. He would be the laughingstock. *So, Will, wife toss you out on the wedding night? What didn't you know how to do?*

He would go to his sister's house. He wouldn't have to explain there. It wasn't as if he hadn't stayed there many times before when he'd been playing cards with her husband, or talking with her, and the night had flitted away. The servants always let him in as if he owned the property.

Someone knocked at the door and Isabel's eyes opened wide and she pulled the covers to her neck, feeling the strange slide of bed fabric against bare skin. She was in the middle of a monstrously large bed, she was naked and she was alone.

'Yes?' she asked, that being the only word she could think of. William. He didn't wish to startle her.

'Pardon.' A male voice, rising high at the end, as if his foot had been trampled. Not William. 'Later, sir.'

Oh, that was most likely William's valet to wake him.

She looked around the room. He was not about, nor were his boots, nor any sign of the clothing, except hers.

Well.

She jumped out of bed, dressed as best as she could and darted to her room. How did one approach the servants and ask where one's husband had wandered off to? She could not pen this in a note to the butler.

Back in her chamber, she sat on the mussed covers where she had tossed about the night before waiting to see if Mr Husband remembered he had got married. She reflected on what a small bed the room contained. Oh, it fitted her shape perfectly, but didn't quite measure up to his chamber.

Little embers grew inside her, fanned by every deep breath she inhaled.

She stood, arms crossed, and examined the bed. The room was not nearly as nice as she'd thought it the night before. Oh, it was beautiful and pleasant, all the things a woman could wish for if she had not awoken alone in a much larger tester bed.

No lovely posts raising high in the room to declare the owner worthy of the best.

She tamped her hand over the covers. Lumps under. She was certain.

This was what he had meant about marriage. The tenderness of the night before was like the empty— smaller bed. It had...a rather nice cover, but underneath it was just workable. Nothing alive in it.

Oh, what a fool she was for neglecting to believe the truth told to her.

She whirled around, saw her face in the mirror and picked up her brush and pointed at the reflection. 'He told you. He didn't wish to be married. Vows and nonsense. Vows and nonsense.' She combed her hair and reminded herself that it was not his fault. None of it. He had rescued her.

They had met in a brothel, lest she forget. He was not a saint. He was probably back at Wren's hoping to... win something.

She put her brush on the table.

It wasn't as if she cared for him overmuch. Her feelings for him only stemmed from the fact that he had saved her life. He could have turned and left her to Wren. None of the other men there had even noticed her—so she was indeed fortunate he had seen something other than his ale and the lightskirt trying to entice him.

This day would have started very differently if not

for William. Very. She didn't want to contemplate how. She would be in worse shape if she'd returned to her parents. Disgraced. And *only* disgraced might be an overly hopeful thought.

She looked around the room. He'd married her. Kept her from being a governess. She needed not be so harsh on him. Not that there was a thing wrong with being a governess. She just didn't wish to be one. Or at the moment, a wife.

She refused to sigh and hissed instead.

Her stomach plagued her. The same way it had hurt the morning after her parents had left her at Madame Dubois's School for Young Ladies. They had waved goodbye and said it would not be long before they would be back for her. And she'd really thought they would leave and realise how they could not continue on without their one and only child and return. Even the next morning she had expected them back at any moment and was reprimanded by Madame Dubois for running to the windows.

She had just known they would miss her so badly that they would return. Every day she had expected her mother to rush in, tears streaming down her face, arms outstretched, and pull Isabel close and say she could not bear another moment without her precious daughter.

Finally her parents had returned on the appointed day and the hug had been tight, the smile sincere, and then they had all got into the carriage and Isabel had talked and talked and talked and her mother had not once mentioned the absolute misery of having Isabel away from home. Not once.

Isabel had been the most wonderful daughter ever on holiday from the school, showing her parents all the things she had learned. She had assisted her mother without being asked and had even helped the maid-of-all-work, who had said Isabel was the best child she'd ever seen and that she had missed her terribly and it was so good to have her home again. The maid-of-all-work had hugged her three times when she'd first seen Isabel. Three.

And then when the holiday was over, her parents had taken her back to Madame Dubois's School for Young Ladies Who Were Tossed from Their Homes and left her again. Isabel had not spoken on the trip and she didn't think her parents had even noticed. Again they had waved goodbye and smiled at her.

Then Grace had rushed to Isabel and had hugged her and said she had missed her. Joanna and Rachel had mentioned how much they had missed all their dearest friends.

Still, Isabel had not felt as alone the first day of the school as she did on her first day of marriage. No noise of other students chattering and playing reached her ears. No instructions shouted about. Perhaps she would have liked being a governess more than she realised. Over time she would have sneaked into those children's hearts and they would have missed her *terribly* on her half-day off.

Chapter Seven

'William.' His sister's voice.

The door opened a peep. He raised his head from the pillow.

'William.'

'Stubble it, Soph. I'm trying to sleep.'

She was halfway into the room. 'You look hideous.'

'Thank you. Go away.' He kept his eyes shut. Feigning sleep never worked, but one could hope.

'The maid told me you were here,' Sophia called out rather more cheerily and loudly than necessary.

He tamped the pillow with his hand, still not looking at her. 'She was right.'

'I was married a whole week before I showed up on your doorstep and you sent me right back home again.'

He felt the depression of the mattress as she sat.

'So what did you do?' she asked.

He didn't answer.

Then she laughed. 'Oh, I remember. At the wedding. Oh, that was endearing.' She mocked a man's gruffness. 'I now pronounce you married.' Then her voice rose and she emitted a very feminine, six-syllable sigh.

He half-opened one eye. 'I meant nothing. I was pleased to be wed and thankful I had found Isabel. I sighed because it had taken me so long.'

'Didn't take her long to toss you out.'

'She didn't.'

The mattress shifted as she rose. 'I'm sure she didn't.'

'Send some hot water this way.'

'I think I shall visit Isabel.'

He opened his eyes and snapped out the words. 'I forbid it.'

'Mmm...' she said at the doorway. 'Remember what you said to me? That sometimes it was fine for me to pretend to be wrong even when I was right because sometimes men were just too thick-headed to see what a treasure was before them.'

'I would have said that the sky was made of gooseberries if it would have convinced you to go home.'

'The sky is made of gooseberries, but you may stay as long as you wish. I will send some water for you, though, because you have a forest growing on your face—' The last of her words were lost in the closing of the door.

This would not do. He merely suffered from the shock of the wedding and the fact that the country miss had not known the proper rules of marriage. A wife didn't visit her husband's bed. And he had simply not been thinking when she appeared or he could have handled it so diplomatically and swept her up into his arms and whisked her down the hallway into her room.

He realised he had to go home. He'd had some rest now and he could see things much more clearly. Once he got the ragged mess of a beard taken care of he would go home. He would explain the way of the *ton* to her. Bedchambers were sacred by morning light. He could no more stay in her bed and risk the ladies' maid walking in than she could stay in his bed and be awakened by the—

Oh.

Walking inside the doorway to his house, the familiar scent of lemon let William know his housekeeper had been working.

His steps lightened as he moved to his private chambers to drop off his coat and then he would find Isabel.

Inside the room, he stilled. He could see nothing different. Nothing. Yet, he felt he'd stepped into someone else's room and not his own. Perhaps it was some lingering perfume or just the knowledge that she'd been there that disconcerted him.

But he supposed it was normal. Even his sisters rarely visited his town house and he'd invited no other woman inside, ever. The servants were mostly hidden in their duties. Sylvester sometimes visited, but was never invited. One allowed for Sylvester.

The room was no different. He was no different. And the woman in his home had no ties on him other than the fact that they had married. An arrangement that would suit them both for their futures. The vows were just words. But very loud ones, he admitted. Ones still ringing deep within.

William had escaped the need for courtship. He was as pleased with his wife as if he had chosen her from a fashion-plate magazine. The house was certainly big enough for the two of them, though he wasn't certain how he would have felt if he'd walked into the bedchamber and she'd been inside.

Well, he smiled, shutting his eyes briefly. He wouldn't have minded in one regard. His shoulders relaxed.

He examined the room. The bed. The walls. Everything was the same. Except the folded paper on the nightstand. He moved to it, picking up a note.

He stared at the words decorated with swirls and loops. She'd asked for his presence in her bedchamber.

Well, if one were to lose one's privacy, then it could have a pleasant side.

A night of little sleep with all the events around him—well, two nights of little sleep had disconcerted him. He must not let his imagination take him down some path that only he saw.

If she asked him of his whereabouts in the night, he would tell her. He would reassure her that he would bring no disgrace on her.

He strode the hallway to her bedchamber just as a maid exited the door and his eyes flickered to the servant. She scurried away, but his hand went out, stopping the door before it closed.

Isabel hummed beyond the door, unaware of his presence. The sound flashed into him like a gunshot wrapped in velvet. He could not move. Her voice, even without words, controlled his heartbeats and whispered endearments.

His fingers tightened on the wood and he listened, his body swathed in the sense of song and Isabel.

Oh, he had not planned for this.

The humming stopped suddenly and he blinked, deserted.

He stepped inside. Isabel stood in front of the window. Light haloed her copper hair and emphasised the contours of her clothing.

One blink of the lashes over azure and his words fell to their knees. 'Good morning.' He could think of nothing else.

Her smile knotted around him and he had to shake himself internally to step back into his realm.

'I have a plan.' She moved as if a wind had lifted her an inch taller. 'A plan you will like so much.'

Yes. He stopped the word from falling from his lips. He needed to hear her voice. He waited.

'I will change my name.' She clasped her hands to her chest. 'You can tell everyone I am away visiting my family and then, after time has passed—' She shivered with excitement. Her eyes shone. 'You can tell everyone I am dead.' She tilted her head to the side. 'You cannot marry again, but…' she shrugged one shoulder '…you do not want a wife.' Then her face brightened. 'I will tell only my family and my dearest friends I am still alive.'

Dead. Dead? The word flamed inside him, dried his mouth, slapped him back into the world he'd left behind. He didn't know if he'd spoken or not. And her face, it didn't shudder in fear at the words passing through her fragile lips, nor did she gasp at the finality of what she said.

'Yes. I will change my name, alter my hair, use face powder, perhaps spectacles and I will find a reputable place away—far away.'

She might have said more. He could not comprehend. His legs tightened. He turned himself into a wall of stone. 'No.'

'Why is that not a grand plan?' Eyes clear and innocent fluttered at him.

He took everything he felt from his words and his body, and made himself an empty slate. 'I need an heir.'

She put a hand on her hip and pointed out the window. 'Tell your cousin to get married. It shouldn't all fall on your shoulders.'

'It doesn't work that way and you know it.'

'I was not born to be a governess. But I don't think I was born to be a wife either.' She indicated the inkstand. 'I was just writing to my friend Joanna and I didn't know what to tell her, so I told her almost nothing but that I was married and would write more later. That is when I realised how confused I was with the events raining about like a tempest. We don't know each other and yet we are married.'

'I know you well enough. You are a good wife— these past few hours. I see no reason for that to change.'

She cleared her throat, which if he was not mistaken was a feminine growl. The sound pulled him back into the light.

'It's not working out too well,' she said.

'I thought you might want to stay in London, if for no other reason than to sing again.'

She shuddered. 'I do have a good voice, but singing doesn't appeal any more. I cannot bear the thought of it.'

She stepped back into the light, rubbing under her chin. 'Some moments I can still feel the knife. Mr Wren had watched me from the audience and I had not suspected it anything but enjoyment of the song. And he had such other plans. I walked about with pride, singing, and I was no different than a hare playing in a field being watched by a hawk.'

William's mind raced ahead. His mouth dried. The thought of other men viewing Isabel tumbled around inside him. He would certainly make sure she had a strong servant with her when she ventured about and he'd tell the coachman personally to keep close to Isabel when she was outside the house. He didn't want any harm to come her way. Instantly, he added plans to tell the butler to hire a sturdy servant who could always be spared when Isabel went out.

She waved a hand. 'I will disguise myself if I leave London. You will not have to fear anything. And if by some chance I am recognised you can merely say some sort of truth. Perhaps that I disappeared and you lied to protect me. That you feared me mad.' She smiled. 'A dead, mad wife would surely cause you no censure, but sympathy. If I need to act like Lady Macbeth, I can. I am quite good with theatrics.' She shivered and let her hands wrangle over each other.

'You are quite good with the imagination.' He'd seen

the same smugness she wore on each of his sisters' faces—when they were not listening to a word of reason and had no intention of unlocking their ears.

'You're needed here,' he continued, his words almost a retreat because dealing with his sisters had taught him that was the best way of attack. 'While you were born to sing, I was born to be a viscount, to produce children and take care of the properties that I inherit. And I rather hoped you would help with some of the parts of that which I cannot possibly manage alone.'

Her hands stilled, but remained clasped. She looked at the floor. 'I am sorry that my leaving will prevent the heirs, but I do not know how I could leave children behind, so…perhaps I should go soon.'

'It doesn't work that way, either.'

She twirled and plopped down on the bed. 'I have your interests at heart, of course. I know you do not want to be married.' Her shoulders wobbled, but it wasn't in weakness, more of a stance he'd seen on a bull as it locked hooves into the ground, ready to charge ahead.

Life with Sophia, Rosalind and Harriet had prepared him for this. 'You are very correct.' His sisters would have pulled a face, but Isabel had not heard him make that same remark a score of times.

He gave her a chance to absorb how correct she was, then added, 'We do not have to think of ourselves as married. We are merely two friendly people under the same roof.' With his sisters, he would have retreated before they realised they'd been contradicted, but they were used to his instruction. Instead, he planted his feet firm. 'Friendly.'

Dismay flitted across her face, but then she looked up.

Her shoulders relaxed. 'But I could go for a while to the Americas. Do not rule out the value of having a wife who doesn't live in the same country.'

This would not be the time to agree. 'I want you with me.'

'But you left. In the night,' she said.

'I went to Sophia's.'

'You left.'

'Yes. I felt the need to.'

'I understand.' Her lips tightened after speaking. She looked at the healing mark on her arm. 'I suppose it is all right.'

'We hardly know each other.'

'Which can only be corrected one way.'

He moved to her and knelt on one knee. He clasped her fingers and waited until her eyes met his. 'I do not have it in me...to form a close attachment.'

'Not if you are leaving before morning.'

He squeezed her fingers, hoping to soften the deter-mined chin with his earnest words. 'I can't change the side of the world the sun rises on. I can't change much in this life. I had thought to love before, but I discov-ered it cannot be done.'

'Give me a chance. Just to know that you like me would be pleasant.'

'I do like you, Isabel. Of course, I do.' *Of course. Of course.*

'Then why does it matter that I stay?' she asked.

'I need an heir.' The next words almost hurt his mouth and he chose them carefully, realising them for the first time himself. 'And I would not mind some respectability in my life. While I don't intend to become a doddering old saint, I would like, should I have children, for them to have a pleasant childhood. I would like them to have a mother, and a woman trained such as yourself would be the best, absolute best, mother a child could have.'

She lowered her chin and gazed up. 'I was not the top student at the governess school.'

'I'm sure you'll make a good mother.'

She looked at the side table. 'If they were my own little ones, I think it might be wise if a true governess were hired—I did not pay as much attention to the lessons as perhaps I should. I planned to forget every study as soon as I walked from the door.' She clucked her tongue. 'Sometimes my plans are successful.'

'You'll be able to love the children and that's what's important.'

'Of course.' Her smile beamed. 'I did like it when a new student arrived and I loved them all. Miss Fanworth sometimes chose me to take them around the first few days, but she never chose me to help them with lessons.'

'I can help with the studies,' he said, leaning just close enough that he could get a whiff of roses. 'And you can bring sunshine into their lives.'

'I could.'

He rubbed the knuckles of her hand against his

cheek. 'And why don't you get a larger bed—one big enough for two to be comfortable?'

A quick dart of her head took her full expression from his view.

'And would you be spending the night in it?'

'It would not do for a lady's maid to walk in to help you wake and find me half-naked.'

'My parents were quite comfortable to sleep in the same room. It is not entirely unreasonable. A servant can wait until summoned.'

'But the town house is large enough for comfort. In the country, roosters crow to wake the house. Here, servants open the curtains.'

She took in a breath and her eyes didn't return to him. 'It is indeed unfortunate that no roosters are about.' Pulling her fingers from his, she tapped her chin. 'But, in that case, I want to keep my present sleeping place. In the night, I need to be able to feel both sides of the bed.'

'I understand.'

She took in a breath and moved her body aside and hopped to her feet. 'So do I. I will not trouble you. You will not even know I am here. I will send notes to the butler when I need something from you and he will relay it. You need not see me except for the briefest moments and a few events needed for respectability. I know that I owe you and I will repay you in heirs.'

At the door, she grasped the frame, but turned to him. 'Please do not get too attached to me as I do think the idea of moving and changing my name has much merit.'

In two steps he was at the door.

'Is—' He put his hand over the one she rested on the door frame, holding her steady. 'You must give me your word you will not act on that thought.'

'I would ne—'

'Isabel.' Innocent, innocent, innocent eyes stared at him. 'Your word.' He could not risk her rushing off to some destination only she thought wise.

A frown. A pause. 'I will not leave.' She met his eyes. 'I will make this my home. I will make this a home.'

Chapter Eight

Isabel listened to the clattering of the carriage wheels over stones and the sound vibrated into her ears and stayed. The maid sat beside her. The servant was a good two score older and would be the proper chaperon. Isabel didn't want to be alone. Choosing whom to call on was easy because the only person she knew was William's sister and the driver knew the direction there.

She had to get something in her head other than the repeat of marriage vows and a sigh. And the memory of William's eyes begging her forgiveness while his words ran through her like a pike.

The maid darted a look at Isabel.

'It is just…nothing…' She kept her next sigh internal. It was nothing. Her marriage. Nothing. She felt no different. Just odd. Everything around her except her clothing was different. Even her name.

The clatter of thoughts in her head didn't cease when the carriage stopped. She didn't want to leave the vehicle, but she put her hand on the door, and descended.

She had to speak to someone and William's sister was most likely to understand. Besides, Sophia already knew the details and Isabel would not have to guard her words.

Once inside Sophia's home, she was taken to the sitting room with light-coloured walls and matching brocade on the sofa. This was a far cry from Madame's school where all the furnishings could withstand constant use. In the centre of the room, a small table for a tea service had an oval rug under it and two chairs were aligned for easy conversation, with the sofa just on the other side in case two more people wished to join in.

This was the same room she'd visited before, and yet, she didn't recall any of it.

She waited, careful not to disturb anything. A clock pealed in the distance and a dog barked several times, then stopped.

Finally Sophia entered the room, steps slow. She took a breath. 'He is not here.'

They only knew one person in common. Thoughts buffeted Isabel. Sophia thought William had already left the marriage. 'I know.'

Sophia's lips turned up. Her face eased. 'He *was* here. Almost all night.' She added the last words quickly. 'He has a chamber of his own here. He often comes to the house early in the morning and sends his coach home. Then we have breakfast and he falls asleep, and slips out in the evening.'

Sophia indicated Isabel sit, but Sophia remained standing.

'Does he talk much?' Isabel asked, making herself comfortable.

'No. But we don't have a lot to say. It is almost like a pair of slippers who've been stored side by side. He goes his places and I go mine, but we spend time together while nothing else is happening.'

'Oh.' Isabel imagined herself as another pair of slippers. Now she understood the marriage William wanted. But she preferred to be the same shoe and match. The one that was part of a pair.

She dismissed her thoughts. The marriage was still fresh. It would take at least a few days for him to understand how wonderful it was to have a wife. A cold thought hit her. Just as it had taken her parents a few days to understand how much they missed her and return.

Sophia interrupted Isabel's memories. 'William says you have a voice like a songbird.'

'I am pleased with it.' Isabel smiled.

'Would you sing something for me? I would like to hear it.'

Isabel opened her mouth, then stopped. Never before had she felt the slightest hesitation for singing. If someone asked a question, she had to prevent herself from giving the answer in song.

Shaking her head, she touched her throat. 'I can't. Today I woke up with a soreness and it would hurt to sing.'

'Later, then?' Sophia asked.

'Of course.' Isabel smiled, but her thoughts didn't match her face. Her desire to sing had fled in the same way a clock that had ticked a whole lifetime suddenly stopped and would not work again. She could not bear the thought of being watched while singing. Just could not. And it had been her favourite part of the performance before.

'I look forward to meeting your sisters and your husband,' Isabel said, turning the conversation in a different direction.

Sitting in the chair adjacent to Isabel, Sophia shrugged. 'You'll know sooner or later—my husband and William do not get on overly well. They are friendly.'

'It is not uncommon for a man to not think someone good enough for his sister.'

'It's not that.' She waved away the words. 'My husband is a few years older and he treats me as if I were born on a cloud and my feet shouldn't touch the ground. He feels William does not take life seriously enough.' She grimaced. 'William does take life seriously. Too seriously, I think.'

That was not quite how Isabel saw him. She raised her brows in question.

'He is quite determined to wring all the excitement out of it he can,' Sophia said. 'He may be out at all hours but it is a seriousness in itself—to grasp the spice of life. I became aware of it about a year after our mother died. He does not talk of what he does much. Sometimes he checks with the man-of-affairs to see how the finances are going and watches over what our sisters are doing. He has been counting on Aunt Emilia to find them matches. Usually, he is ready to sleep when he is here as he has been awake the night.'

'I do not know where he is right now, but he's not at his town house sleeping the day away.' She smiled to take any censure out of her words. 'But you know how we met so it is not as if it is a love match. I don't think he quite wants that.'

Calling it a friendship was even an overestimation. She would have liked nothing better to have been discovering his life from him, but instead she sat with his sister.

'I once had hope...' Sophia ran her fingers along the wooden arm of the chair, letting her words fall away into the room. 'I am only a year younger than he and closest to him. I was twelve when our mother died and our father grieved so much that William had nothing to do but take things in hand. My brother was quite the stickler with us. As he watched over us and made certain our lamps were out at a decent hour, he then bribed the coachman to take him about. He was tall even then and his ready smile helped get him wherever he wished to go. He told me the older men had no trouble testing the young pup's mettle and challenging him to keep up with them.' She grimaced behind her smile. 'He did, I'm sure.'

Isabel remembered his form flashing across in front of her as he tackled Mr Wren. 'Did he ever have cause to fight with someone?'

'I would imagine he did after our mother died. He would say he fell from a horse, and yet, he'd taken Father's carriage. The stories he tells me are all suitable for a grandmother's ears. My husband has privately mentioned a few escapades of my brother and they weren't saintly. William laughs it away when I ask and will not give a direct answer.' She paused. 'He never angers with me, except when I would jest at him about one of my friends hoping for his notice or ask him when he might marry. That is the only time he would anger. He would stay away longer as well.'

Isabel straightened her shoulders. William married because of his love for his sisters. He protected them. He wouldn't have wed her if not for the disgrace that would have been visited upon him and his family otherwise. She mustn't forget that.

'I do not want to be too inquisitive.' She used the same downward chin movement and the tilt of her head that could capture an audience's awareness. 'But has he ever been in love before?' Her demeanour was relaxed, but her heart braced for the reply. If he had been in love once, then he could fall in love again.

The thought jarred her. She wanted him to love her. Very much. And it was not as if she loved him. She'd been serious when she mentioned wanting to leave. Leaving could be much happier than loving someone who gave the highest regard to a friendly marriage. A Mr Grebbins.

Sophia laughed, leaning forward. 'You do not have to be jealous. I can assure you. Not long ago I asked him the same question. If you could have seen his face, you would have known he told the truth. He told me to bite my tongue. I have never known of any woman he has mentioned by name, although my husband has heard that William attended Drury Lane with someone on his arm.'

'I am so relieved.' Her shoulders dropped, but her smile might not have fooled friends who had seen her perform. William had not been in love. He'd started his adulthood earlier than many, yet had not even mentioned a woman by name to his sister.

'Does the—?' Sophia started, but then shrugged away her words.

'What?' Isabel asked. 'Please tell me what you were going to say.'

'I was going to ask about the ring. If he has mentioned it, or if you have it and have chosen not to wear it. I have not seen it since the night our mother died. William surely has it still.'

Isabel forced her hands to remain still and her eyes not to glance at the plain band on her finger. 'I haven't seen it.'

On the table beside her, Sophia touched the base of the lamp, turning it, staring into the glass. 'Our mother always wore the ring. The night she died, I was at the door because I'd heard a flurry of movement and knew something had happened. Father insisted William take the jewellery. Told him he must marry some day and it would be his wife's. William shouted he could not take something she loved so much. Father insisted.'

Isabel glanced at the gold band on her finger. It was like her own mother's wedding ring and her mother's band was a reflection of love. Now, the gloss on Isabel's seemed a jester's laugh, as practised as the words of songs.

She remembered the expression on her parents' faces

when they saw the other person enter the room—enchantment.

Kind Mr Grebbins and his wife had visited her parents often and both had the kindest words. Mrs Grebbins reminded Isabel of a fluffy hen clucking, preening happily in the sun, but almost unaware her husband was in the room. Mr Grebbins smiled often, in the way of a grandfather not seeing much more than a blurred shape.

Isabel had overheard her mother and father discussing how lonely the couple was. Mr Grebbins's first wife had died in childbirth and his heart had died with her. He'd married again, but he'd never danced with the same dash as he had with his first wife, nor had he laughed so heartily. He made the best of it and didn't bemoan his lot in life as Mrs Grebbins was a good sort, he was a good sort and that is what good sorts did. They had spent thirty years of their lives together. Good-sort years.

Mr and Mrs Grebbins had always ambled back to their home—silent—their shadows remaining alone, never touching.

Love is priceless and cannot blossom for every couple, her mother had said, and then her parents had shared a lingering glance.

At William's town house, when Isabel had left, William had wished her well with all the courtesy of Mr Grebbins suggesting to his wife they might leave before darkness descended.

Chapter Nine

Matrimony didn't agree with him. In fact, the whole house seemed out of sorts since his marriage. A fortnight should have been enough time for them to adjust. If it had been a manor, he would have called it Bumbling Hall. Cook didn't seem able to adjust to the circumstance of his asking for breakfast.

'My apologies.' The servant bowed her head as she exited his breakfast room, after replacing the drink. 'I brought you the mistress's chocolate and she does not wish for hers to be spiced as you do.'

He nodded, taking a sip from the glass left behind. The chocolate still wasn't correct. He tasted it again, drinking half of it to see if he could discern exactly what error had been made. He paused, realising why it tasted bland. His cook had not made morning chocolate for him in years. The only time he drank it was at Sophia's and he'd got used to the way her cook prepared it. If he ended the night at his own home, he sipped a brandy as he prepared for bed.

He left, returning to his sitting room. The newspaper lay on the table, but he had no wish to read it. He preferred his news from the club, either by men who had participated or men who'd seen it. Almost always the stories varied, but he sorted out the truth from them.

He picked up the print anyway. Reading through it, he then slapped it back down. Old news. He should have taken to the clubs. He would not make such a mistake tonight. All his friends would be abed now so he had no reason to trot out.

Sylvester had congratulated William on finding a bride who didn't curtail the nights out and said he planned to do the same.

He looked closer at the arm of the chair and pulled a bit of feather from it, then flicked the fluff aside.

William wasn't even certain if Isabel knew he was home or not.

Isabel was not like his sisters, always managing to burst upon him with some question, or leave this or that frippery for the servants to put away.

Moving to the door, he opened it and returned to his chair.

She'd not spoken with him since she had suggested she could leave and change her name. Perhaps that had been too imaginative, but still, she'd offered.

William had left each night at dusk since their wedding night, until the last one. He'd been arriving home some time after midnight because she'd listened and he didn't return before she fell asleep.

She could not imagine that Husband would be expecting her to provide an heir without his help. She'd also kept the smaller bed and although it had started as a rebellion of sorts, she'd considered it carefully and kept the plan. She looked at the paper in her hand, blowing to dry the inkspot she'd mistakenly made. Well, her penmanship never would win any notice.

She would not be able to send this letter to Grace. She hoped that Grace might meet William some day and draw a picture of him. Grace could sketch up anyone's face so quickly.

After Isabel realised she was to be married, she'd written to Grace, Rachel, and Joanna. Isabel had spent the entire day writing to everyone she knew—making sure they all knew of her good fortune so they would not suspect she'd made a judgement in error. She'd only admitted to Grace that the marriage was not exactly a love match, but more of a union of two sensible people in exact understanding of each other. Isabel's teeth had ached after writing the letters, but she was certain it conveyed a certain sophistication and a smattering of newly gained maturity.

Isabel knew she was indeed more fortunate than Grace, with the uncertainty of finding a child, and how horrible it was that Grace had not been able to keep the little one in the first place.

'Isabel.' William's voice interrupted her thoughts. She started. She hadn't heard him enter her sitting room. Her throat tightened and she nearly knocked the paper from the table. She caught it in mid-air and looked his way. His white cravat looped in a single knot. His face was freshly shaven, which jolted her. The other men she'd met had never looked anything but whisker-peeled after a shave.

She couldn't stare, he'd think her a twit. If she spoke, well, then she'd have to find words somewhere within her and she couldn't think of any.

'You look lost.' He took a step inside. 'What *are* you thinking of?'

Grace. Grace could rescue her once again. She couldn't tell him of Grace's misfortune, but she could talk of her schoolmate. 'My friend Grace, and how she used to make up tales about how the owner, Madame Dubois, obtained the governess school. My favourite was that she was a highwayman in her youth and robbed a merchant of all his gold. But one of the girls said her father insisted that the land was once owned by a peer. Madame spoke so elegantly, and I knew she was from France, that I could believe her somehow close to the aristocracy.'

Isabel picked up the paper she wrote on. 'Madame didn't like my favourite songs and told me I was only to sing ones approved by Miss Fanworth. Miss Fanworth approved few I liked.'

Isabel thought back to the excitement of watching the girls laugh and gasp when she sang the most gruesome songs, or sniffle when she chose a mournful tune.

But she had no more wishes to perform. The night at Mr Wren's had cured that.

'Are you settling in to your satisfaction?' he asked, lowering down into the easy chair across from her. The undersized chair gave him the appearance of even longer limbs.

'I am.'

'I don't know if I'm doing so well,' he said, laughing quietly. 'I've been home more these past few days than I'm used to.'

Her brows rose. 'You're serious?' He'd hardly been home at all.

'Usually I'm at Sophia's house. The club. Lord Robert has gambling events which last all night to several days, and he prefers them away from his home, so he finds a place where we can stay comfortably during breaks in the play.'

'Do you not like the town house?'

'It has my bed, a roof, room for the servants. That's all that matters.'

'It's a little sparse.'

He looked around the room. 'I suppose. I don't like tripping over furniture or lots of little cloths decorating here and there in a room.'

'Would you mind if I added just a few things?'

'Whatever you want to do is fine with me. Just not too many things that look like undergarments tossed about.'

'Table scarves?'

'That's why I have the inside shutters on the windows. I didn't want the look of chemises or a grandfather's coat hanging out to dry.'

'You've succeeded. It looks like you've either just moved in or are about to move out.'

He laughed, stretching one leg. 'I suppose you could be right on both counts. Sometimes that's how it feels.'

She studied him to see if he told the truth.

'Don't be concerned,' he said. 'I'll be visiting my father soon and I'll make sure the town house is in my name completely so that it can be yours for the rest of your life. You'll always have a home of your own now.'

'But, I…' She'd wanted him to say a home of their own. It wasn't as if she wanted him to say he loved her, but they were living together, married, and she wanted him to feel as if he belonged with her. 'I want you to like the house.'

His eyes wandered around the room. 'I like the windows in the front and I don't see you changing them.' He brushed back the hair at his temple. 'If you dislike the house, I can set my man-of-affairs on the search for another.'

'Oh, no.' She raised both palms. 'I just want you to feel like it matters to you. Like a home should feel.' She paused. 'I would hope.'

He put his elbow on the arm of the chair and raised his hand to prop his chin on it. He settled into the relaxed pose and watched her. 'It already feels more like a home than at any other day since I've moved in. No one moved above stairs before you arrived. Now, servants rush by with a plate of food leaving an aroma of a cooked meal behind. Or I hear you moving, or see you in the hallway and your cheeks light up just the barest, and your eyes smile, and I feel I've been bestowed a piece of treasure no one else even knows exists.'

She saw glints of a similar treasure behind his eyes.

'Thank you.' Warmth infused her cheeks, but she wasn't embarrassed.

'A songbird. Who doesn't have to be caged. Who flits

around and brings cheer. In this instance, my father was right. Marriage is an honourable state.'

He stood, planning to bend down to kiss her, but if he did, she might think it a sign of more affection than he could give.

He walked by, hoping she would retire early, and moved to his bedchamber.

William opened his nightstand drawer. Isabel had taken him at his word about penning notes. He lifted the last note passed along by the butler, opened it and read again. Isabel mentioned at both the beginning and end that it wasn't necessary for him to attend Lady Howell's soirée. He returned the note to the others, then flipped through them. The one before had mentioned the dress she'd purchased while out with his sister and she'd suggested the garment as suitable for an evening event. She'd also mentioned her wish to show them as deeply in love to the *ton* so no one would ever, ever hint of any impropriety of the past. For his future sons and daughters. Sisters. And himself.

Nothing truly personal was in the notes, yet he'd kept each one. The words of each breezed into the mind as if dashed from a smiling pen. Yet when he read the pages one after the other, the breeziness seemed procured.

Sadness touched him. Probably leftover-marriage tightness. He'd privately asked one of his older friends about the feelings a man might have after the deed was done and the answer had been little more than a shoulder shrug, and a discourse on the sanctity of friendships away from home, good libations, and how a lizard had been on the wall in 1797, or was it ninety-eight? That had helped tremendously and convinced him to spend another quiet night at home.

Waistcoat unbuttoned, he opened the bedchamber door, stepping into the hallway as Isabel rushed from her own room, a blast of feathers on her head. Even her reticule was feathered. He hoped there were no winds.

He paused as she caught sight of him. 'I thought to tell you I don't wish to attend Lady Howell's dance.'

Her lips rose at the sides. 'I don't either.' But something beyond the sky-blue eyes dimmed.

He didn't want to attend that soirée, but blue was his favourite colour, particularly when it had the sparkle of gemstones. He even liked the darkening blue of the sky before a storm. But he didn't like the dreary blue of sadness. 'But perhaps we should go.'

Her eyes brightened, then faded. She clasped her reticule in both hands. 'I do not know. It will…I don't want people to think I have married you for your…'

'Good looks?' he asked, raising his brows.

She opened her mouth briefly. Her cheeks reddened. She walked forward and slapped his arm lightly with the bag, causing a wisp of feather to break free and float between them.

'Oh, be serious,' she said, leaving, 'no one will think that.'

Chapter Ten

William didn't know if Isabel was aware he'd entered the parlour. He'd stopped at the doorway, watching. She was dressed for the soirée early, waiting for him.

She gazed out the middle window of the three, framed by the opening. If butterflies could become women, then Isabel had once had wings. It wasn't that she flitted around, although she could. Her reddish hair had the splash of colour that caught the eye and perhaps the same texture of a wing. The pale ball gown had hardly any hue in it except for the two flowing ties that attached at the back of her sleeves and flowed behind her. The fluttery azure fabric trailed down the back of her gown.

How did one manage a butterfly?

'Shall we leave?' he asked. Her reticule and fan lay in the chair beside him. To see someone else's property so at home in the chamber surprised him.

She didn't move. 'I suppose it is time.' She drew in a breath. 'I should not be worried. In the past, I stood in front of people easily. It's just now, it seems more daunting. The only person there I will know is your sister and she has said that her husband will certainly ask me to dance. I've met him.' She looked at her accessories. 'I do wish I didn't feel so much that I will be noticed out of kindness or curiosity.'

He leaned against the frame. He couldn't suggest they stay home that night. She needed to be comfortable in society and, with her nature, she would be as soon as she had a chance.

William snorted. 'You will dance many times,' he said. Cousin Sylvester would be sure to ask her as well. 'If my cousin approaches you, he will push the conversation in the direction of Wren's. He is an inquisitive little snipe, but we are related and he does have my horses.'

She turned, the fluttery ribbons of her sleeves emphasising movement. 'I won't mind.' Then her eyes widened before closing tightly. 'But sadly…' An internal wind buffeted her. Then she gazed again at him. 'But how can I talk of such an event at a soirée? I was indeed too frightened to move. If not for your presence, I would have expired from fright.' She touched the tip of her glove to her eye and wiped an imagined tear.

He watched and she gazed back. Within moments, her eyes saddened so much he wanted to reach to her, but then her lips turned up. 'I have heard but never tested it, that men do not always know how to speak with a tearful woman and might change the subject quickly.'

'You're quite good. How does one know if the tears are real?'

'They're real,' she said, lifting her brows. 'Always.' Isabel stared at him with wide-eyed innocence, causing him an inward chuckle. Sometimes her naivety appeared skin-deep to him. He wondered, if under the fluff and nonsense, hidden even from herself, an old spirit fought to reconcile with the world.

He held out his arm. 'Shall we leave?'

Her silent laughter brightened the room. She twirled and then closed the distance between them, the scent of roses swirling in the air.

He lifted the reticule and fan, holding them in her direction. She took them.

'Do you need anything else before we go?' he asked.

'Might you fetch me a compliment?'

Lightly he rested his hand at her back, the contact warming him and bringing a flush to her cheeks. He closed out all other moments by leaning in, whispering so his breath touched her ear, 'Compliments could not even begin to do justice to what I see.'

Her fan tip moved up, sliding down the smooth skin of his cheek, and stopping just over his heart. 'I think you managed it quite well.' She examined him. 'And I suppose your words of flattery are always real?'

'Never doubt them.'

She gave a tiny joust with her fan before putting it to her side. 'I won't.'

She turned, preceding him, and his fingers stretched so that the ties from her gown slid through them like gossamer.

* * *

Isabel gauged everyone in the room had known each other since before she was born. She was certain even the younger women had inherited some knowledge of each other well before birth. One woman raised a glass to her lips and three glittering bracelets slid on her glove. Four musicians played and only about twenty people bustled about in the room.

William led her to a woman and introduced her.

'So at last we meet your love,' the lady responded.

William's smile beamed. But his expression froze for just that instant the word *love* lingered in the air.

Their eyes caught. 'Yes, we have not been *wed* long,' she said, looking adoringly at him. Now *wed* caused his warm brown eyes to have flecks that looked like spear tips. She didn't wish to end the evening impaled so she struck the offensive words from her vocabulary.

Apparently, he didn't like profane speech.

'Ah.' A voice at her elbow jarred her. No one had been standing there a second ago. 'I believe no introductions are necessary for me,' the voice said.

'They are.' William's smile never faltered, as he introduced his cousin to her.

From a direct view, Sylvester's delicate features and long-limbed stance would have made artists ask him to pose, but when his head turned and she saw his profile Isabel noticed that, when in shadows, he could have passed for a well-attired weasel, in a handsome sort of way.

'May I have the first of what I expect to be many,

many dances throughout the years?' Sylvester bowed as he spoke.

William answered as Sylvester finished the question, 'As long as you mind your manners.' The commanding inflection in his voice couldn't be mistaken.

'Correct,' Sylvester answered, holding his arm for her to grasp. 'I could never do anything else with my enchanting new cousin.'

Sylvester whisked her away for a dance and she dodged his conversation easily. One didn't attend a governess school without having lessons in how to handle impertinent questions.

When the dance ended, he led her to the refreshments, and she suspected it was because the other guests had abandoned the area to begin a reel.

'I am impressed,' he said. 'Both with my cousin's choice and your ability to dance, not just with your feet, but with words as well, manoeuvring the talk back to me each time I spoke of Will.'

'The two of you are quite close and I'm sure you know all there is to know of him and only wish to learn my thoughts on the matter. I assure you, I feel the deepest loyalty to William Balfour.'

He grinned in response. 'My loyalty to him comes and goes, and I know it is not possible yet for you to have found out all the cracks and crevices in our world.'

'I would like to never find them out. So you may keep your silence.'

'Ah, Cousin. You speak the impossible.' He handed her a lemon drink, which surprised her as she expected him to give her the punch. 'I was merely a pawn in the elders' plan to shake William into the game of producing an heir. William may have let it slip to Mother that he never, ever intended to go through the uncertainty of watching children mature and having the responsibility. He may have felt that Harriet's birth contributed to his mother's illness. Everyone else thought so.'

'Your mother would scheme so?'

'It is not scheming—it is her family concern. She feels she didn't assist William enough when his mother died and she is making it correct now.'

The pianoforte sounded and the violinists began. Sylvester stepped closer so he could hear her.

Isabel took in a breath. 'He was hardly more than a child when his mother died. He couldn't have been expected to handle it all on his own. And yet I understand he certainly did much of it.'

'I would say he did all of it. Including the care of his father. The Viscount was near bedfast after the death just because he could not go on. My own mother had her hands full with her family and could not help. William had three sisters. Grieving.'

'He grieved, too.'

'I doubt his sisters let him.' Assured words.

She indicated a glass of the drink for him, but he shook his head.

'William often confided to me he expected never to marry,' he said, 'and part of that was because he wished never to have the worries of children. When I heard you were trained as a governess, the marriage made sense. A woman experienced in care for little ones. William has said to me many times that he managed his sisters and he does not wish to become a parent again. After Harriet got lost in the woods, I heard his recriminations to himself. When Sophia noted how dashing the foxed soldier was and thought he might need a wife to write to, William rushed straight to Mother to get her help. He now has enlisted her assistance on getting the other two wed also. Said she had had good luck with Sophia's marriage.'

She could not follow his conversation well because her mind had fixed on the first part of it. 'I don't think that my training as a governess mattered.'

'I would not bet the stables on that. Not that I do not think any man would find you appealing for a wife.' His cheeks reddened. 'But William was sincere in his intention not to wed. But I can see—' His face brightened more and he reached for the glass nearest and gulped down some of the lemon drink. Made a face and looked at the glass and swallowed as if trying to get the last vestiges from his taste. 'A governess. A person to care for the children. You know what I mean.'

'Yes. But, he is close to his sisters.'

'In a distant way. He is nearer Sophia now that she has married and has a husband to care for her. If you'll note, even the horses, Marvel and Ivory, were at his father's home. William prefers a wide swathe around him.'

'Thank you for keeping your cousin's confidences.'

'I have,' he said, leaving and tossing a wink her way. 'With family.'

He moved to the outer doors where William now stood and both began talking.

She didn't doubt a word Sylvester said. William had put some distance between himself and everyone else. It could have started when his mother died, or when he realised she was sick. Or earlier. It didn't matter.

Isabel took the lemon drink, finished it and noted the punch with reluctance. She was not sure how it had been mixed. She had heard the drinks ladies mixed for themselves often had more strength than what might be found in the men's glasses.

Isabel reached for a drink. The punch had its use. She was stranded in a sea of jewellery and wanted something to float about on.

On her first day at what she'd then called Madame Dubois's School for Abandoned Young Ladies, her parents had done exactly the same. They had introduced her, smiled all around and then she'd been on her own.

Her mother had made her leave her doll at home, telling her that she was all grown up. She didn't know what had happened to that plaything, but it would be nice to have her now, except, she supposed, the punch was the more mature version.

The liquid slid into her stomach, marking progress with heat. No, she'd never had any drink mixed quite so liberally. Putting the rim of the glass to her lips, she took an even tinier sip than before. Oh, she could quite shake the jewellery if she wished to.

More dancing. The music was quite good. The dancers were quite accomplished. The world was quite perfect around her. Just like the first day of school. Society, even a children's one, didn't allow cowering in the corner. Sipping very, very slowly, she examined the room, ignoring the glittery baubles.

This event was to set the stage for the rest of her life. She smiled and replaced the glass, reminding herself that no one could see beyond a confident smile into quivering insides.

Something bumped her from behind and she turned, a turban brushing her face. White hair straggled from the head-covering and one eye had a milky frost and the other a clear chill.

'Pardon.' The woman spoke. 'I have no time for proper introductions. One of my many faults. Not that I have many.' She looked to her right. 'You're not dancing. You should, you know. Does wonders for the complexion. I swear by it.' She chuckled. 'I'm at least eighty and I don't look a day over seventy-eight.'

'I would agree.'

'And your name is?'

'Isabel Balfour. I am married to the Viscount's son. He is—'

'Wait.' The woman raised a hand, stopping the words. Her gloves swallowed her thin arms. 'You may call me Lady Howell. If you forget, just think of a dog and its bark and then its howl at the moon.' Her nose wrinkled. 'That's how I remember it.'

She looked at Isabel's stomach. 'And are you increasing?'

'No. No.' Isabel narrowed her eyes, whispering.

'Well, you better get your mind to it,' the older woman said, voice strident. 'That's your duty now. Heirs.' She put a gnarled finger out. 'I had six in the first six years of marriage. Not many can carry that feat off. The trick is that the first one was very early—very early.' She leaned in and grinned. 'The second—I wasted no time.' She counted on her fingers. 'Three and four, twins. Five, well, what can I say, I had too much wine in celebration of finding a wet nurse for the twins. By six I put my foot down and said, I'd done my duty. I told Lord Howell to keep his distance. He howled.' She patted Isabel's arm. 'My favourite thing to tell people is how Howell howled. He never recovered fully.'

'I do think it would be nice to have children.'

The woman's lips tightened and her lower jaw jutted forward as she appraised Isabel. 'I recommend you stop at three. By the fourth child, they tend to put a strain on your temper.' She turned away.

Isabel heard her mumble as she left. 'The little chit cannot carry on a conversation.'

Then Lady Howell walked up to another sea of jewellery. The music ended and words jumped out from within the room. 'William Balfour's wife doesn't know her place in society.' All the faces turned Isabel's way.

The musicians even stared at her. How could they know who the woman spoke of? But apparently they did. They'd probably played at many soirées for the same people. This world was no bigger than a teacup and she was being examined as a speck in the bottom of the cup.

William stepped to her elbow and took her hand to pull it to his lips, then tuck it at his arm. 'Yes, she does know her place, Lady Howell. It is at my side.' He shot a look at the musicians and the next song began softly, easing the silence. 'Now we must be leaving, Lady Howell. Duties await us.'

He stood by his bed, hand on the post. He hadn't known the right words to say in the carriage and he suspected there weren't any. At least not that he could think of.

Leaving her alone at the soirée had been a mistake, but he'd been trying to get those horses—which could have waited.

He wanted to make it up to her. Neither of them deserved what had happened. At least she didn't. Society was not always easy for women who didn't live in it from birth.

Isabel shouldn't be belittled, except perhaps for keeping that ridiculously small bed.

Ridiculously small.

Somehow it had become a battlement. A territorial stake of some sort that he didn't understand. Why, the whole house was hers to command. Everything but his personal effects. And the valet. And the butler. But he wasn't certain she quite understood about the butler.

He pulled the tail of his shirt from his trousers. His boots were already put away. Reaching for his dressing gown, he placed it over the back of a chair and moved to the hallway.

'Isabel...' he opened the door and stuck his head in, inhaling the scent of roses and soaps '...it's too early to sleep.'

'No it's not. Not for me. Go away.' She rolled, putting her back to him. 'I have a headache that starts at my feet and goes straight to my forehead. The slippers were too tight.'

He left the door open. Moving to a chair, he picked it up and placed it closer to the bed. He sat, clasped his fingers lightly and stretched his legs, one foot moving to her counterpane. His heel rested at a covered mound which hid her leg.

'I know you're here for your duty,' she said.

'If I must, I must.'

He moved his feet to the floor, scooted his chair closer and pulled the cover from her foot and took it in his hands. Warm and delicate. She slid her foot aside, but he caught it. Covering her foot with his grasp, he kneaded the bottom with both thumbs. Her foot tilted towards him.

He pressed against each muscle, easing away tension, rubbing over the skin, soothing it.

'That is better than a warm bath,' she said.

He reached out, caressing the other toes with the same care. 'Is your headache any better?'

'I had thought not to wear those slippers again, but I do like the colour and if you could do this afterwards, I might keep them. Would save you the cost of another pair.'

'But is your headache any better?'

'I am not sure.'

He continued, sweeping his hands to ankles, kneading and rubbing. 'I suppose it will take me a while to get there, but I shall.' He continued sweeping his hands just above her heels. 'But not in that bed.'

'So,' she said. 'You will not do your duty while I am in this bed.'

He nudged her foot. 'Duty. That word is hideous.' He stood. 'Move over.'

'I thought you said…'

'Duty has nothing to do with it. Share the mattress.'

'There is not room in this bed for two people. It only holds me.'

'I noticed. Give me some room.' One knee on the bed, he wedged himself in beside her, tossing the covers away and rolling her to face him. 'See, it holds two people, except for my feet.' He moved one leg up and draped it over her thigh and adjusted close. The same delicate scent he'd noticed when he'd walked into the room engulfed him. 'I'm sorry you didn't enjoy the soirée. I didn't either.'

'I thought Lady Howell's invitation sincere.'

'It was—for her. If it makes you feel better, she has called me a tosspot and I believe she called my father a lovestruck chit.'

'It doesn't. Now I feel sad for you and your father. Well, for your father.' She snuggled. 'Are you a tosspot?'

'Who knows?' He shrugged.

Chapter Eleven

Arms tightened around her, embracing her so completely she could feel nothing but maleness and heartbeats. A wall of strength caressing her with the lightest touch. She'd never felt so safe.

Her hand clasped his side, over the cloth of his shirt, and her fingertips brushed back and forth, the friction the cloth created under her hand bringing his skin alive to her touch. 'Do you think you are a tosspot?'

'You are intent on that question.'

'And you do not wish to answer.'

His chest moved with a slow intake of breath, giving her room to get closer and yet, when he breathed out, she remained burrowed against him. 'I drink more than many, but not as much as I did. Several years ago, I noticed my friends were sotted every night and I was there as often as not.'

The room was silent before he continued, his words pulling her inside his thoughts. 'I wondered if I could go a fortnight without drink. On the sixth day, I was at the club and the scent of spirits lingered in the air so much I could think of nothing else. I was surrounded by desire for it. I ached for it.'

He stopped speaking. She pressed at his side. 'Well?'

'Sylvester put a drink in front of me and I sat with it for hours. But I refused. I went to Sophia's and slept a few hours until morning and then drank chocolate while I waited for her to wake. I drank possibly three glasses in three hours of waiting for my sister who'd decided to sleep in. Luckily, her cook makes very good chocolate.'

'I didn't like it so well as what the cook makes here. Your sister's burns the mouth.'

'Ah, yes. It's very good.'

'Did you finish the fortnight?'

'Of course. I didn't doubt it. I refused to let my want for it overcome what I truly desired and my biggest want was to be in control of the liquid. I didn't have to drink. Since then I have not felt as if it matters so much whether I have drink or not. On occasion, I even have a child's drink called milk. I have also discovered that one of my servants can take a jug to a home just outside of town and find water that tastes wondrous and refreshes my thirst better than anything. It is the best thing I've ever tasted.' He laughed. 'I can be as particular about the water I drink as some men are about their brandy. Makes all the difference. Even the tea is better.'

His hand ran the length of her back stopping as it slid to her hip. His face moved closer and his kiss barely brushed her lips. Tremors raced in her body. 'The best thing I've tasted, except for one other thing.'

His kiss didn't have the hint of brandy, or anything

but the freshness of him. 'That is much better than any drink.'

She hugged him tight, the length of his body pressing hers. The bed could have been half the size and they both would have fit. She could feel nothing in the world but him and it was the best feeling she'd ever had.

He pulled back, leaving one whisper of his lips against hers before breaking contact, and leaving her dazed with the loss.

'Isabel. I may not have been entirely honest with you.' He sat up, moving from the bed and reaching back to scoop her up into his arms. 'I will do my duty.'

She gasped, but her arms slipped around his neck. He moved, widening his stance, maintaining his balance.

'I am not at all concerned about the duty to the title,' he said. 'I am concerned about my duty to you. I simply cannot leave you in such a small bed. I cannot.'

'I am happy with it.' She put her arm around his neck. 'I mean that.'

'Well, you must give my bed one more chance.' Their faces close, he took her out the door. 'But do not destroy my manly pride.'

When they reached his bedchamber, she noticed the light flowing through the doorway. 'You left the door open. You planned this.'

He took her inside and the scent of shaving soap lingered in the air. 'I said I was a tosspot, not a fool.' He stopped in mid-stride. 'I must tell you that tonight—' His face rested near her ear. 'I would have built scaffolding to your window to hold you in my arms.'

A burst of warmth hit her when his nose nuzzled

at her ear, his voice barely aloud. 'And it would have been worth it.'

He turned so she could see his bed. 'We need more than that little pillow of a mattress you sleep on.'

With a sweep of his arms, he tossed her on to the bed and then he followed, landing around her, his weight cushioned by his arms.

'How is your headache?' He ran his fingers over her cheek, leaving warm rivulets larger than the path of his touch.

'It is completely gone.' She put one hand up, feeling the tendrils where his hair brushed his collar.

'Now,' he said, enfolding her in his arms, 'let me tell you how sorry I am that you had a bad experience tonight.' He squeezed lightly. 'But it's over.'

He'd just hugged her.

'That did make me feel better.' She reached out, clasped the front of his shirt and tugged.

He chuckled and squeezed her again and again and again, each time almost taking her breath away. 'Even better now?' The laughter in his voice, along with the hug, accepted her.

'Don't squash me in two pieces.' She lay in the crook of his arm.

'I wouldn't want to squash you in one piece.' He put a hand at her stomach. Waves of something delicious reverberated within her. 'Although in that tiny bed you have… See how much nicer this is.'

'I don't see that I have that much more room in it.' She wriggled against him. 'I can't even reach out my arm.'

He rolled her so that they lay facing each other, side

by side. 'Oh, by all means, reach out your arms all you wish, as long as it is in this direction.'

She pretended to push at his chest. He didn't move. She pushed. He still didn't move. He studied her, squinting. 'That's not what I meant.'

Reversing the direction, she tugged at his side. He tumbled against her. 'Ah, yes,' he said, breathing the words into her ear. She moved her head so their lips could meet and he pressed against her. Hunger grew inside her. She could not get close enough.

He tugged his shirt aside, moving apart long enough to pull it over his head.

Without her moving, his mouth found hers and he grasped the ties of her chemise, his fingers smoothing them, reaching to the very last of the ribbons, straightening, bringing the skin beneath the fastening to life before he slipped the knot loose.

He touched the chemise, his hands smoothing over the skin underneath while the garment moved up with each caress.

His legs brushed hers. A rough texture against the softness of her skin. Pleasure tingled from each movement.

He lifted the garment over her head and, as he pulled it up, his skin replaced where the fabric had touched. He could not possibly be surrounding her as closely as the clothing, but he did. She couldn't feel any other sensation of the bed, or time or presence except him.

'Songbird,' he whispered in her ear, the words hitting her in the way of music, a music shared by their bodies.

He cupped the underside of her breast and his face

moved over it, the sensation of the roughened chin and smooth lips interspersing one with the other.

His hand at her thigh caused her to writhe towards him, but he held her back, using touch to bring her to a crescendo of sensations, overpowering her with gentleness.

Then he moved his body close, sliding above her, his eyes holding her, until he shifted, enveloping her with their joining.

His shoulders held his chest above her and she pulled, but William's strength kept his weight from crushing down and her body moved up to meet his.

Their breathing increased, until the pause, and her heart stilled.

Neither moved, savouring one last second of togetherness, before he rolled to clasp her close at his side.

William stared overhead, Isabel nestled in the crook of his arms and her fingers swirled over his chest. She felt more comfortable against him than his own heartbeats felt in his body.

'Are you asleep?' she asked.

'Yes. I have been for this past hour.'

She laughed. 'Then I had best leave before you wake because I don't think I will be able to survive much more.'

He hugged her close, giving him a completeness he'd never felt before.

'You feel so strong,' she said. 'As if you are twice my strength.' Her palm flattened and stilled.

'You jest,' he whispered and rolled, keeping her

in his arms to stop above her. 'I am three times your strength at least. Four on a good day.'

She pushed at his chest, but he swooped down to cover her face with kisses before he rolled to his back again.

This was not working as he'd hoped. In truth, he didn't feel stronger, but weaker. He could not force himself to roll from the bed.

'Is this not better than being a governess?' he asked.

'I don't know it is that much different,' she said. 'My charge is just much more difficult to command. Did you not learn when you were a child that you must obey the governess?'

'No. I am quite certain only my sisters had a governess. I had a tutor. My father would step into the room as I studied my lessons and make certain to check with the instructor to ask what I was being taught. He was always enquiring if I had learned my numbers that day. Sometimes my mother would insist the tutor work with my sisters. Father would bluster that they didn't need to learn, because they were to marry. She would tell him that their husbands might need help understanding the sums.'

'I think I would have liked your mother.'

A grunt of agreement. Both his mother and father had seen that his days were filled with learning and responsibility. At least until his mother became ill. When she failed, the world changed. When the Viscount lost his wife, he lost all care for the world.

'We'd just finished a portrait sitting when my mother became ill. The paint wasn't dry. Immediately after her death, my father commissioned a larger portrait just of her. It still hangs in the library.'

The portrait was impossible to miss. His father had sat in the room days on end staring at the likeness, twisting her handkerchief in his hand. William had hardly ever entered the room. Seeing his mother's face had been like having a blade in his stomach. It reminded him that she was no longer with them. Seeing his father sitting there, dazed, lost to them, willingly, had been worse than his mother's death.

'I don't like to talk of it,' he said. 'The past is gone. It was not that hard for me to put it behind me. I loved Mother dearly, but it just was not the terrible tragedy for me that it was for my sisters. Oh, they carried on so.' He bumped his head against hers. 'You would not believe the tears. Rosalind was six and giving in to grief too much and would not leave her room, just as Father would not leave the portrait. We had to do something. Sophia and I picked Rosalind up. I had her under the arms and Sophia her feet and we carried her down the stairway. It is a wonder we didn't kill ourselves. Sophia had tears rolling down her cheeks. Then we locked Rosalind out of the house and told her she could not return until she stopped crying.'

'Did it work?'

'She totally destroyed the window, but she was not crying when she found us and told us we could not lock her out of the house. She said she would burn the house down before she let us do that. I believed her. Rosalind is strong-willed. The fuss upset Harriet. I had to drag her from under the bed, then she was afraid the house would catch afire while she was asleep and the nursery maid would not wake and we would all die. So she would not sleep unless Sophia and I were with her and then Rosalind had to be there as well because…I cannot remember why. Oh, yes. Harriet was afraid that if we let Rosalind sleep anywhere else she would start the house afire. She convinced Rosalind to stay with her and things got better.'

For three months his sisters had all slept in one bed and he had put two chairs together and tried to sleep. He'd hardly been able to get any rest. Then he'd started leaving the house after his sisters slept. He'd felt guilt for leaving that first night, but his father had remained staring at the portrait and William had not been able to stand another moment of the grief. The men at the tavern had welcomed him and they'd all known his mother had died. They'd drunk to life and laughter and pretty lasses.

Isabel's arms tightened at his waist. 'You were so young to deal with that.'

He snorted. 'I was not. I was a man at thirteen. When I was fourteen I discovered that my mother's cousin had diverted nearly four hundred pounds of my father's funds. Then, when I was away at university, at first Sophia would help me keep an eye on Father's affairs.'

Things had changed while he was at university. Rosalind and Harriet became more interested in the funds, particularly after he let them keep a portion of all increases to themselves. That had been a profitable decision. Rosalind had signed their father's name on to a letter hiring a quite good land steward.

'Rosalind became quite good at forgery and understanding accounts. Harriet reads all she can find about crops and livestock, and shares the information with the tenants. Harriet knows the number of eggs any breed of chicken should lay in the first year and how much the amount of eggs will decline in the second. She has also informed me that if a chicken starts laying eggs with thin shells, a solution is to crush eggshells and put them about for the chickens to peck. Father barely knows how the eggs get on the table.'

William turned to Isabel. He brushed a kiss on her nose, gave her a squeeze to pull her close and then rolled from the bed.

The most fortunate thing of the night had happened when he talked of the past. 'I cannot sleep this early.' He dropped another kiss on her forehead, softening his words. 'Goodnight, Songbird.'

Those last words were safe. They sounded pleasant, but meant nothing. He would go to the club and possibly visit Sophia later. One didn't want to start a habit which might be hard to break.

Isabel sat in front of the window, letting the evening light shine on the paper so she wouldn't have to have a lamp.

William had arrived home around midday. She'd heard his footsteps and then the door of his room closed, and nothing else.

Having him home pleased her, but she wished it didn't. It would be best if she celebrated his leaving.

Sylvester's words returned to her. William had taken

care of his sisters when he should have had someone caring for him. The memories of grief and responsibility had blended, causing him not to wish for children.

A maid opened and closed a door, bringing Isabel her tea.

'French apricot biscuits,' the maid said. Isabel nodded.

The maid opened the door to exit, holding the empty tray, then stepped sideways to give William room to enter.

Looking at the paper, she ignored his presence and gave a puff, pretending to dry ink.

'You should put on a performance for my sisters. I would like to see it as well.'

'I wasn't married when I wished to sing. I was younger.' Something had changed after the night at Wren's. The way the men had watched the singer. Before, she'd not minded the eyes on her. Loved the attention. After watching the singer warble and the men leering, now she could only think of the faded shading and the filth in the corner and the scurrying of insects. Just the thought tightened her stomach in the most unpleasant way.

Her eyes locked on his boots.

He knelt, holding her desk with one hand to keep himself easily balanced, but his face was now lower and she couldn't escape his examination.

'Sing a quick song. Just for me. Nothing particular. A lullaby.'

She shook her head and brushed across the papers with her fingertips.

'I can hear you hum when I am in the hallway.'

'I don't hum.'

He stared at her.

'I tried to sing for your sister Sophia and I could not. Never before had that happened. Not ever close to that. But the words were frozen inside me.'

The night she'd been attacked, she'd feared Wren might destroy her voice with the knife. He hadn't, but the blade had reached into her spirit and taken away her wish to sing.

'Isabel. You can't lock that voice away. It is a part of you. You must let others hear it as well.'

'No. Just the thought of singing in front of people now…' She touched her stomach, trying to brush away the coldness.

Chapter Twelve

He was a fool.

He let himself out the door and walked to the mews, escaping his house. Before, he'd wanted to go to the taverns and clubs, but now he felt forced away. Because he knew what would happen if he stayed in. He'd not be able to turn away from her as easily as he'd turned from the drink.

He wasn't deserting Isabel, but he could not bear the thoughts buffeting himself another second. He had one foot in the memories of the past and another dangling in Isabel's direction to be pulled even deeper into the strangling world of emotions.

He had a chamber that had a suitable bed and he could have used it. He just didn't want to be mired in thoughts and when Isabel was near he acted on impulse, and then his mind followed. The actions he liked; the thoughts he could do without.

He ran his fingers through his hair and ignored the darkness around him, reminding himself of the saying that it was darkest before the day dawned. But it was also dark in the light when grief took the day and choked it lifeless. If not for the nights of drinking and revelry, he could not have survived the past.

Three grieving sisters trying to find their footing and a father who could not move didn't spread joy and sunshine all about.

Some things were best forgotten. Thinking of the past only put one back into it. Life wasn't to be lived in memories, but in experiences. Forward at full rush, letting the wind of revelry breeze the thoughts away suited him best.

He owed Isabel nothing, other than material things and, of course, not to bring her public disgrace. He had saved her and in return had had little choice except marriage.

All in all, he felt rather fortunate when he truly considered the options of a wife other than Isabel. In fact, the one good thing of this was that Isabel would have been his choice had he wished to marry, but he hadn't.

He planned out the next few days of his life. He would work to get the horses back and he would spend an enjoyable time doing so. A few nights with his friends at the clubs should clear his mind.

'Are you going to stare at the cards all night?' Sylvester asked.

With a small shake of his head, William pulled a card from his hand and put it on the table. He'd lost again. He didn't care.

Lord Robert, younger brother of the Duke of Wake-field, made a rude jest. Sylvester laughed. The Duke didn't. William hadn't thought the comment insulting Sylvester humorous either.

The ale tasted off. He kept hearing Isabel's voice, and the tune she hummed. He stood. 'I'm finished.'

Sylvester looked his way, smiling. 'Leaving early?'

'I just want to go. My luck with cards is dismal to-night. Next time should be better.' He'd spent the last few nights running around the clubs with Sylvester and staying up all night.

When he returned home to sleep in the day, Isabel had been moving about in the house. He was certain she'd known he was trying to rest and had strolled about slamming doors. One could not accidentally create that much noise in the hallway outside his bedchamber door.

'I imagine you do,' Sylvester said. 'Ready to beg her forgiveness. You've not fooled me. I know she's got her chemise knotted around your private parts. You're going to be wearing a bonnet if you give in.' He leaned towards William.

'I told you we didn't have a disagreement,' he said. 'We are getting along quite well. She has no complaints of anything I say or do.'

'Unlike the rest of us,' Sylvester said. 'But go along home. You'd best enjoy the fruits of marriage if you have to wear the fripperies. If a woman such as she asked me to wear a bonnet, I would ask which colour was her favourite.' He paused. 'Which colour do you choose, Will?'

William clamped a hand on his cousin's shoulder. 'You should be so fortunate as to wed someone like Isabel.'

'I married a dainty little doll,' Lord Robert said, 'and the next thing I knew she had feet bigger than mine and had filled the house with crying babies, plus all her cousins and her mother, grandmother and grandfather.' He mused, almost whispering, 'I married one woman and ended up with a village under my roof.'

The Duke of Wakefield didn't raise his eyes. 'You just didn't find the right woman.'

'Because she does not exist,' Lord Robert grumbled, thrusting a finger under his eyepatch and rubbing at the eye he'd lost long ago. 'Even my mistress is more trouble than she's worth. I had to tell her I am with my wife tonight just so I can get some respite from her.'

The Duke of Wakefield stood, his chair clattering back, tossing his cards face-up on the table. 'I can see why you men prefer each other's company instead of a wife's.' His voice choked on the last word. 'A woman might expect something out of a conversation.' His eyes misted and he turned on his heel and stomped from the room.

'Blast,' Lord Robert said. 'He's acted like he's wearing a coat of brambles since his wife passed away.'

William stared after the Duke. Wakefield's loss had been months before. Months. In the early part of the year.

Lord Robert adjusted the patch, stared at the disarray on the table and then sorted the funds from the cards.

'That was a winning hand he forfeited. You can tell that my brother has never met my mistress. She doesn't expect anything out of a conversation.'

'Neither do my horses,' Sylvester said, glancing at William. 'I'm planning to dash off to see them. Autumn is a good time to visit the country. Marvel and Ivory should be ridden and not just by stable hands. If you want to see how they're faring, and take in the countryside, you might trot down to the estate with me, Will.'

'I'll think about it,' William strode to the hallway, leaving—going home. He had no desire to go to the country, but he kept remembering the pain in Wakefield's voice. The Duchess had been rather insipid, in William's opinion. Love had altered the Duke's mind.

The night air had cooled, giving a liveliness to the darkness. His mood lightened as the sharper air hit his face. He had no wish to be anywhere else. In a few moments he would be home and he would not have to see Isabel, but surely it would cause no harm to speak with her.

He frowned. He was rushing home like some besotted fool. A few more times of such and he would be strangled by those corset ties.

When he stepped into his house, his butler met him with a note, then whisked away.

Isabel had written to tell him that she was spending the night at Sophia's and would return later on the morrow than she expected. Of course, Sophia had invited him, too. He crumpled the paper and let it fall to the floor. Just as well.

He bent and swept the paper into his hand, smoothed and folded it. He'd have enough for a bonfire by Christmastime.

Walking up the stairs, he stopped at his room only long enough to add the notes to the rest, then he moved down the hallway. At her chamber, he opened her door and peered inside, just to make sure she hadn't returned. He knew full well the butler would have told him if Isabel was at home, but perhaps she'd returned and the servant hadn't seen her.

He inhaled, enjoying the soft scent. Roses again. Taking off his coat, he tossed it over a chair and added his waistcoat. Sitting on the dismal bed, he flattened his hand and pushed into the mattress. It should have been replaced years ago, but he'd had no reason to do so in the past.

Removing his boots, he let them fall to the side. Stretching, he lay down. His feet dangled at the end of the bed.

He had to find a way to cleanse her from his thoughts. He remembered staring at the glass of amber liquid. The feeling of power when he no longer wanted the taste in his mouth and could stand and walk away.

In her room, the presence of Isabel engulfed him. He breathed in deeply, noting only the barest hint of roses in the air. He imagined the taste of her, the lightness of his knuckles brushing against her skin and the way her eyes reflected the blue of the sky.

He imagined her twirling, taking in the world like a flower taking in the morning rain and savouring the drops on petals and the flourishing moments of being alive and at the height of a bloom.

He ached for her.

He rolled from the bed, grabbed his clothing and strode from the room, shutting the door with a slam which was much too muted for his own comfort.

He could hear Isabel at the stairway. She had not jested when she'd written that she would be home later than expected.

The paper tightened in his grasp. Footsteps tapped. Tap. Tap. Pause. Tap. Tap. Tap. He could imagine her stopping. One could almost read her thoughts by her movement. She would come in and beg his pardon for being about while he was at home. He was certain of it. Isabel was a generous-spirited person.

He lowered the paper and peered over it.

She stopped long enough to glance in, wave a parcel in his direction and then strolled by the door. A maid followed her, bowing under the weight of her load. He folded the paper, rolled it and popped it against his knee.

He would get someone to summon her. Or send her a note. They must talk. Not a single one of the parcels could have been a larger bed. Perhaps he should just move the little puff of furniture out of the room himself.

The soft voice jolted his reverie. 'Are you ill?' she asked. He'd not heard her step into the room. He looked up. She closed half the distance between them and peered at him with wide eyes.

He forgot. He forgot what he was so angry at her for. 'I am fine,' he answered. 'I didn't sleep well.'

'It is rather early for you to be awake.'

Her eyes blinked with the innocence of a babe and weakened something inside him so that he felt as if he were the one taking his first steps. Wobbling.

He unfurled the paper and looked at it again. 'I hope you had a good visit with Sophia.' The words reminded him. She had not alerted him beforehand of her plans. What if…what if she'd instructed the coachman to take her to her parents' home, or what if she'd decided to go to somewhere and sing something and someone had been about with evil plans? 'You must be careful when you are out.'

'Oh…' she raised her brows '…I took a maid. The burly one. And your coachman…'

'It is a dangerous world. As you well know.'

'Yes. Your sister has told me about the many times you have gathered bruises in the night hours.' She brightened. 'I admit. You dived at Wren as if you had done it before and I cannot complain.' She glanced at him. 'Have you had call to use your fists before?'

'Not in Wren's. Now let us change the subject.'

'Certainly. I don't wish to talk about Wren.' She raised her brows. 'Have you had many fights?'

'No. How is Sophia?'

'She is fine. How many fights?'

'I didn't keep records. And did you enjoy your visit?'

'Very much. She told of a time she thought your nose had been broken and you said you stumbled into a chair.'

'It was inconveniently in the hands of a man who also bumped his nose against it before the night was over.

And has that oaf of a husband of Sophia's whittled any more wooden hearts for her?'

'He whittles hearts for her?' Eyes gauged William's face.

'Yes. He's daft.' Inside William smiled. Subject changed. 'I'm surprised she didn't show them to you. Pulled them out every time I saw her for months afterwards.' Couldn't change that subject easily either. *You should marry,* Sophia had mentioned. Once. Each minute.

'We talked of everything from corsets to Christmas.' She beamed. 'I never thought to have a sister. And now I have three. Sophia plans a gathering with your other two sisters so I can meet them soon. I am looking forward to it.'

'Some post arrived for you.' He pointed to the letter on the table.

She opened it and read, and kept her eyes on the page. It could not take that long to peruse.

'What is it?' he asked, moving to her.

'From my mother. I did want her to think this a love match, at least for a time.' She handed it to him. 'She is not much for writing letters.'

He read, resisting the urge to shred the pages. 'She does not truly see you. I should write her and tell her the error in her words. But I am sure she does not realise what she said.'

Isabel's hand touched her plain wedding band. 'I didn't want her to know the truth any more than you wanted them to think you attacked me.'

He folded the missive, eyes on it. 'Did you need to

keep this?' Before she answered, he ripped it across, across again and then once more. 'If you save something that brings you unhappiness, it is like saving a stone for an enemy to throw at you again and again.'

Her azure eyes stared at him.

'It does not bring me unhappiness. It is just my mother's way of speaking. She does not always hear what she says.' Isabel watched him as if he'd lost his mind.

He held the torn paper to her. 'Burn it.'

'William.' She examined him. 'She didn't say anything dreadful.'

Returning to his chair, he picked up the newsprint. 'I just didn't like the way—Isabel, I am out of sorts today. I lost at cards the other night.'

'A large sum?' she asked.

He shook his head. 'No. I simply do not like to lose.'

'No one does, William. That is what makes winning so grand.'

'I do not need the grandness.' He had been reading the same publication for days now and the words had kept fading into the blue of Isabel's eyes. Perhaps once he went away he'd be able to think of something besides the azure.

'Thank you for the kindness you've shown.' She closed her fist over the papers. 'I'll toss this into the fireplace.'

She walked over, leaned his way and put a kiss on his forehead. Of all the places to kiss... He was not five years old. Then she turned to leave and something inside him plummeted.

The realisation of his dismay at her turning away

caused another bolt of something in his chest. His feet were on the ground, but his life didn't feel connected to him any more.

'I need to go to my father's home.' He did. He didn't feel he belonged in his house any more. He'd not spent a lot of time in it before, which had not mattered at the time. But now it did. In truth, William could hardly bear to spend so much time gambling now and counted the hours until he could return to the town house, only it didn't feel the same as it did.

And he longed for the scent of roses.

He just needed to get past this one hurdle of newness. Before the marriage, he had not wanted to be at home. But now he felt displaced from it by Isabel.

To go to the country could be reviving. The town house kept them too much in proximity. An outing could divert him. He needed a change from the blue eyes and wistfulness in them. It was not fair for her to have him underfoot so much. A woman learning a new home in a new town didn't need to be stumbling over a man as well.

He wasn't happy at the taverns, listening to the boasts and jests of the other men as they talked of their conquests, while he thought of Isabel.

'A change could do well for both of us.' He didn't look at her when he spoke. He could not bear to see innocent hope reflected from her gaze, or dismay, or relief at his departure. 'My cousin Sylvester is leaving to go to the country and invited me. If I go, I'll be able to purchase the horses back. You'll find your footing in the house without tripping over me. Sophia will be near if you need anything. And I'll have a messenger at hand for you to deliver notes as often as you wish.'

Notes, Isabel thought. Her arm would expire with the number of notes she could pen to him if that was what he wished to see instead of her.

'How long will you be gone?'

'I have not thought about it. With Sylvester, you never know what will happen. And Harriet has written that my father has been in the attic moving things here and there. It seems as if he has decided to look at every scrap of the past my mother touched. Rosalind worries that he has suggested some endeavours to my man-of-affairs that she doubts will be productive. Father has been so removed from the world he does not realise what we've done in the past decade.'

'He doesn't listen to your sisters?'

'As of last time we spoke, he didn't listen much to anyone. But it is good for him to be taking more notice of things. It's just that it is not needed now and he should find other ways to amuse himself than in prodding around in the affairs of the estate. We have managed well for years without his interference and we don't need him to muddle things now.'

'Perhaps he wants the feeling of being needed.'

William didn't move. 'It is a little late for that.' He took the newsprint from the floor and glanced at it again. 'But I will give him a listen. All the care of him shouldn't fall on Rosalind and Harriet.'

'Are you sure it is care of him that he needs? Perhaps he needs you to care *for* him.'

He turned and mused, 'I should take Harriet this paper as it has mention of events that could be planned for the Season. Perhaps she'll decide to stay with Sophia and attend the soirées. She refused last year.'

'William. Are you listening at all?'

Brown eyes landed on her, but flicked away. 'He is our father. Of course we care for him. Did we not manage his affairs—although I know it benefited us as well? We kept the roof over his head, the windows clear for the sun he could not see to shine in on him and took care of all around him. Soph, Ros and Harriet cajoled him to move about. I threatened.' He opened the paper, turning the pages, searching.

'So now he understands what you wished for and can do it.' Isabel stepped closer, almost against the newsprint.

William kept searching the words. '*Now* he wants to meddle in our work, but he must simply be shown that it is not needed. I will do as I did with my sisters who could be cajoled with a promise of fripperies. He will be soothed by the thought that two of his children have wed—two more could and soon he could have grand-children—something he claimed a necessity.' He folded the paper to the section he wanted. 'Yes, this should do for Harriet.'

'William, do you not think it unpleasant when your father wished you to wed?'

'I am merely dangling the possibility. I will not fuss if she doesn't wish to marry. Rosalind can stay unwed, too, for all I care. But they have stayed in the country to watch Father and I don't wish him to ruin their lives because they believe he needs them. I have fought against his neglect in the past and I will not let it happen because they have compassion for a man who had none for them.'

He tossed the paper into the chair. 'You were not there when he turned his back on his daughters. I really do not see any problem with him understanding our wishes. After all, now there is the possibility of an heir to mention and bring him to the realisation that we are no longer infants and can care for ourselves without help.'

He stepped to the window, glanced out and then said, 'I can understand his feeling that I was old enough to be left on my own when Mother died, but I cannot believe he ignored my sisters so. Mother would have wept.'

'Yes, some females do not like to be ignored.' She didn't linger, but moved to the door. 'You do not have to tell me goodbye,' she said. 'It will be little different anyway.'

Chapter Thirteen

She had received two notes from William. One mentioned the need for him to help his father longer as the man was trying to comprehend records William now realised the Viscount had never ever noticed. Not even when his wife was alive. William wished Isabel all the best and appreciated the notes.

She didn't quite think the last bit of the statement was written with the utmost sincerity.

The note she had received a fortnight before expressed that he would return soon, perhaps within days, and mentioned his happiness that she had met Rosalind and Harriet, and he wished Isabel all the best and so forth. It was surely a coincidence he'd written the second time after his sisters had returned to the country. They'd been quite curious that she'd not travelled with him, nor received a post from him, and they were certain he'd been getting hers. She'd mentioned a need to stay home to take care of her...aunt...who lived nearby. When the women remarked on their wish to meet the aunt, sadly, the aunt could not as she was quite reclusive. She always feared strangers would steal her gold.

When she'd said those words, Isabel feared she'd gone too far, so she'd added the mention of her aunt having no gold.

Isabel sighed. Soon, she expected she'd be writing letters to the imaginary aunt, thanking her for all the times she'd been helpful.

She'd like to write to her mother, but once her mother had asked Isabel to save the letters until she had five to combine as the cost to receive posts was dear.

If not for music she didn't think she would have ever managed happily at the school. Grace had heard her singing to a rag doll Isabel had traded her best hair ribbons for and asked to hear it again. She'd managed to feel at home at Madame Dubois's school after she began to sing with the others. And now she had made the town house her home.

If she were not to be loved wholly, then so be it. She could be married and yet happy. Some day. She hoped.

A spinster. She thought of Madame Dubois. A spinster. Not one to smile easily, if at all.

Isabel wrote a letter to William, telling him she was getting on quite well and wishing him all the best. She looked at the words and tossed the letter into the fire. She would not write him again.

Then she examined her room, picked up a fresh sheet of paper and her pen. Now she was wed and—she tapped the pen at her cheek—she assumed she had quite a lot of funds at her disposal. Definitely more than she had ever had before. When William's man-of-affairs arrived the fortnight before asking if there had been a mistake on the purchase, and she'd reassured him, he'd not returned.

No one had said a word about the new gowns and she quite liked the camel colour of the new pelisse she had. Trim had been added with wool dyed a lighter colour and frazzled to give a furry appearance around the hem, and adorned the shoulders like epaulettes. The sleeves purposefully gathered just above the elbow and flowed to the base of her thumb. The coat covered her from chin to heel in warmth.

She'd wanted to wear it earlier, but the weather hadn't cooled enough yet, even though Christmas wasn't far away.

She would be spending the holiday with Sophia as Isabel's mother had told her the trip would not be practical. Isabel's father's gout was flaring.

She had no idea if William might even appear on Christmas Day. And if she and the servants were to spend most of the days alone, then as mistress of the house she would begin the season as she wished it. She wished to have holly all about. Taper candles. Evergreen to the ceiling. She'd already given the housekeeper instructions to add some greenery about, telling her to replace it if it became dried before Christmas. Just no mistletoe as it caused her…aunt to cry. Because Uncle Horace, who had died, always pulled his wife into his arms and rained kisses about the tip of her nose—Isabel stopped to add that she had her aunt's exact nose and features—but Uncle Horace loved Aunt so much that he could not see mistletoe without clasping Aunt to his breast.

The housekeeper and Isabel had both given a sniffle when Isabel could not go on. She'd pulled herself together, until she noted something in the housekeeper's eyes.

Isabel realised she'd gone too far, spoken too much, of a couple who didn't exist. And the housekeeper was not thinking of Aunt and Uncle. She was thinking of a couple much nearer.

'That will be all.' Isabel held her chin high and left the room.

William gently pulled the ribbons of his horse and waited as Ivory took her time to stop. He looked up into the windows of his home. According to his butler's post it was painted in the same calming cream colour as he'd left it. She'd even had inside shutters repainted that closed over the parlour windows.

William had left behind the butler's messages, along with the man-of-affairs' letters, but he'd kept Isabel's in the portmanteau and he wondered if any ink remained in the house.

From the outside it looked exactly as he'd left it.

He'd had to return. With each post, he'd felt he lost a bit of grasp on his world. The paint. The two chairs sent to be re-upholstered.

The days with his father had been a trial. The man had forbidden the funds necessary to update the tenants' properties, thinking it far too much of an expense. They'd had to go back over the ledgers, take him to various properties, show him past repairs and it had been a trial for them all.

His father boasted to everyone they met of William's marriage. Twice he'd asked his son if a little one might be on the way and expressing worry that his son was away from his new bride.

But in the moments he was alone, with no more fanfare than a bird's wing, Isabel's face would flutter into his mind and he'd tried to push it away. But he'd kept noticing every time he saw something blue and he'd compare it to the colour of her eyes. Conversations outdoors were hard, because he'd kept glancing overhead.

The time spent with his father and then at Sylvester's country house had dragged and dragged, but Sylvester's mother had taken ill just as William was about to return to London. William could not leave while knowing Aunt Emilia might pass at any moment. Aunt Emilia had finally begun to speak and could take food, and a few days later all could tell she was on the mend.

And his father had even mentioned the coming holiday season, encouraging Harriet and Rosalind to begin the decorations early—a vast change from the past when he'd not been aware of a single sprig of holly.

William walked into the house, noting the scent of paint. He sent someone to care for Ivory, then paused. The house felt like home. Someone's home. Isabel's.

He stepped into the sitting room, but became immobile except for his eyes. The windows were still in place or he wouldn't have recognised the room. He perused each item. Sprigs of greenery dotted the room. He noted the new painting above the mantel—a land-

scape of a country glen. *That* along with the pianoforte
had been noted by the man-of-affairs in a rather rushed
post, mentioning their prices. The cost of the two items
totalled almost as much as he'd paid for the town house
and he'd grumbled over the expense of the house.

He didn't recognise his world any more. Just as when
his mother had passed away.

He moved to the doorway of Isabel's sitting room.
Paper rested on each flat surface. Isabel, lost in concentration, sat at a desk, her pen in her hand. The only thing
that looked like home to him. Stepping close, he had
to say her name. He wanted to hear the words. 'Isabel.'

She jumped and sheets fluttered about his head. He
caught one. 'You interrupted my letter writing.' She
tossed her pen on to the blotter and blinked several
times at him, her lips remaining in a firm line. 'You
did not knock.'

'No. I thought you might wish to know the horses
have been given to me.'

'What horses?' She stood.

'Ivory and Marvel.'

She picked up the paper strewn at her feet, then
reached to pull the one from his hand and added it to
the others in her grasp. She straightened them. 'I was
very concerned about the horses. Wondered about them
daily.' She turned her head to the side. 'Every day I
wondered how dear Ivory and Marvel were faring.' She
gazed at the papers. 'Of course, I didn't expect you to
write and tell me how they were.' She held up two fingers in a pinch just wide enough he could see one bit

of icy blue. 'Just that much time would have been all it would have taken.'

'I wrote. And I wrote to my sister once and I sent a message to the butler once. I have been kept informed.'

She sighed—and he could hear melody in it and it lasted long enough for a sentence in a song.

Papers flew up over her head again. 'I have shopping to do.' She made a brushing-away movement with her hand. He didn't leave.

She left the room momentarily and returned to the doorway, wearing a brown pelisse and carrying a bonnet with a small plume. The plume fluttered as she talked. 'And Sophia is expecting me afterwards.'

She turned, pulling the door closed, but reversed direction and poked her head back around it, one hand holding the wood firm. 'She has been so concerned about Marvel and Ivory. We have talked of little else.'

He clasped the door, immobilising it. He could not take his own gaze away. 'I think this is our first disagreement.'

'Oh, no.' She lowered her chin and fixed him with a gaze. 'It is just the first you are aware of.'

'My Aunt Emilia became ill.'

'I know. Sophia informed me. Thank you for letting her know when her Aunt Emilia was on the mend. She passed the news of the illness and the recovery along to me as you requested. Also the concern you had for me. Thank you.'

He flicked away the words with a blink. 'It was a serious time, Isabel. Rosalind and Harriet needed me to speak some sense into my father so he did not send us all into poverty. My sisters had tried and despaired, and Father wrested the control back, as he well could. It seems my marriage has made him take note of a world of things he's ignored for years. Now he wishes to make up for lost time. He has years to catch up on. And he would not listen to Rosalind. I had to convince him the girls know what they are doing and he can learn from them.'

She studied his face. 'Did it hurt your writing hand?'

'I didn't think you'd find it odd that I didn't correspond.' His eyes roamed around the room, taking time so she could note the appraisal. 'You have managed to find ways to keep yourself busy.'

He pulled the door wide so she could go before him and she returned to the room.

'You noticed.' Her smile brought the outdoors sunshine closer. 'I hope you like the changes.'

'Of course.' He examined the room. He could not tell her he wished the changes gone. He sat on the sofa and put his arm along the back. 'Do you have any more renovations planned?'

'Not at the moment.' She raised her brows and walked into the room, also spending more time examining the furnishings than warranted. 'But I have a cat. He's not a handsome cat, but he's very lovable once he becomes acquainted and if he's not startled.'

'I am sure it is a quite suitable cat.' The new arrival William's butler had mentioned during the entire contents of one post and said that he had personally overseen the hair-removal process from the rugs, daily, but he had not perfected a method to remove scratches on furniture or boots.

'Rambler.' Her voice rose with authority. 'He was meowing most pitifully at the gate and someone had thrown something at him. I had to save him.'

He reached out, picking a hair from the sofa and letting it drift to the rug. 'The cat is black?'

'Yes. Just do not get too close. He does take a bit of getting used to. The butler claims deep concern that his owner misses him and has sent out servants daily to find his owner. We don't expect success.

'I should tell you…' She forced a smile. 'I might have overspent on the painting. But in time I am sure it will increase in value. Mr Lawrence is quite good.'

'Thomas Lawrence?'

She paused, eyes down. 'I do not believe that was his given name. He said that I can return it and receive the funds back.' She examined the painting, the wistfulness of her own face matching that portrayed in the oils.

'Do you like it?' He wanted to see her eyes sparkle again.

'Not as much as I thought.'

'I am pleased you've made the house comfortable for you.' Easy words to say. 'But please do not select any houses or large properties without discussing it with my man-of-affairs. He has quite a good business sense about him. He purchased the Roubiliac sculpture—which I don't see about.'

'It is gone. The cat toppled it and it landed somehow against the grate and collected a quite unsightly chip.'

He inhaled and exhaled completely before speaking. 'Well, I only bought it as an investment.'

Her brows rose. 'Just how much money do you have?'

'Enough to make you content.'

She put her hands behind her back and moved to him with a swaying motion that reminded him of a wary creature sneaking up on a meal. 'How much funds do you think it takes to make one happy?'

'Happy. I am not sure if that is possible to purchase. But content, I think, can be.'

'Are you content?'

He leaned forward, fingers steepled together, chin down and eyes direct into hers. 'Isabel. We are doing quite well with this marriage. I would like to think we are both content with each other, or will be as the years pass, I will be certain not to cause tales which might distress you.'

Her chin rose. 'Your sister has told me of your parents' deep love. My parents have a—' her eyes became lost '—a considerable amount of love for each other.'

'It is quite unnecessary in our marriage.' He had to make certain they were in agreement on this. He'd already been considering moving out for Isabel's own good. If she were to fall in love with him, and anything were to happen to him, he could not bear the thought of her world turning black.

She tensed. 'My parents find it pleasing.' She had understood that she didn't matter quite so much in her parents' lives as they did to each other, but she'd hoped for that same devotion so many times. She'd thought that once William returned and saw the house with the changes she'd made to make it feel a home, that perhaps he'd realise he'd missed her just a little and he'd like the town house better. She didn't expect as many hugs as the maid had given her upon first returning from the school, but a lingering glance would have been nice.

'Isabel. It's not for everyone and it isn't healthy.'

'Healthy?' She almost squeaked.

'To get so mired in another's life. It's not something I would wish for you.'

'I am willing to take the risk.'

'You shouldn't. You've not seen what it can do.' He stood and his eyes glanced at the doorway. 'I suppose I should let my friends know I am back in town.'

'You've not yet let them know you've returned?'

He shook his head. 'I took each day as it happened, so I couldn't let anyone know of the dates.'

'Then perhaps you could wait just a bit to return to them. I've been wishing so much to see my friend in the country, Joanna. She is with her husband, Luke, visiting his father and has asked if we might like to join them at the Earl's family home. I've always wanted to see Pensum Manor.'

'I've visited it in Hertfordshire once with my parents. It's a fine estate. I'll have my valet return the portmanteau to the carriage and prepare for another trip.'

'You really do not like being in this house much, do you?' She'd thought the extra furniture she'd added might make it more comfortable for both of them, but she'd not been able to fool herself into thinking it the home she wanted and apparently it did no more for him.

'Not more or less than any other. They are all the same to me.'

'No place is really your home. Not even here.'

'If it doesn't leak, one roof is much the same as another roof. If it has a mattress that I can sleep on easily, one bed is the same as another. It doesn't matter much where they are.'

'I like making this my home. I thought you might like it more, too. You had hardly a stick of furniture.'

'It's just because I am practical.'

'Would you not miss me if I were gone?'

'Isabel.' His face clouded. 'We have discussed it. You will not move and change your name. We've agreed on that.'

'I can go to Pensum Manor on my own,' she said. 'I could pretend we are having a quarrel and then…' She forced a smile. 'I will get the butler to send me a post in a few days. I will pen it now. And then I will read it privately and confess that I must return as you are… threatening to throw yourself on a pyre if I do not return. Or something even more eventful.'

'You cannot involve the staff in your—'

'Yes, I can. I have only not considered it before because I didn't think of it. I'm not yet accustomed to having so many helpful people about at my disposal.'

'The pyre is rather dramatic.'

She frowned. 'Well, saying you are going to throw yourself into a candle will not impress anyone.'

'I'll go with you,' he said. 'It's colder out and I could not risk you travelling alone in the winter. Something could happen to the carriage, or the horses, and you would be stranded.'

Isabel clasped her fingers together with an effort to keep herself from twirling about. He was going with her. 'Can you pretend to be quite fond of me whilst we are there?'

He blinked, but his face softened. 'I am fond of you.' Then the stiffness returned to his jaw. 'Very much so.'

The carriage rumbled along on the way to Pensum Manor, springs creaking, jostling the seat, causing Isabel's head to bob a bit and occasionally bumping her against William. The interior of the vehicle blended the scent of William's shaving soap with the remnant earthiness of a brief rain shower. Occasional bursts of wind blew a few faded leaves from the trees and made her feel the path had been created just for that moment.

Even the birds flitted about, seeming more active than she remembered. She turned to ask him if he knew the names of them, then paused. He watched her, eyes twinkling.

'What is so humorous?' She studied him.

'You were humming with the movement of the carriage.'

'I was not.' Her hand fluttered to rest on the side of the window.

He chuckled, reached up and took a strand of her hair that had escaped, wrapping it into a curl before releasing it. 'You were indeed. The moment you started watching the birds you began to hum. I wanted to join you.'

Shrugging, she said, 'I won't do it again.'

He pulled her fingers to his lips, kissed them and released them. Eyes still gentle, lips still smiling, he tilted his head to her. 'You may sing for me any time. The melodies you hum are delightful. I enjoy listening. Please continue.'

She touched her left hand to her throat. 'No. The moment has passed.'

His movements in half-time, he reached out with his left hand, taking her hand from her neck. She'd not realised his right arm rested over her shoulders, until his fingers brushed at her shoulder, cradling her. His eyes, soft and softening her, completed the blanket of warmth. 'You can't leave something so much a part of you behind for ever. It would be like leaving behind...' His arm tensed against her shoulders and his voice roughened. 'A child.'

Even his arm didn't warm her now. She focused on the window, thoughts of the past and the school, and how she'd dreamed many times that her parents had left her at an orphanage and never visited her again.

'Did you dream?' she asked.

He didn't answer, but when she turned to him, his face questioned.

'Of your mother,' she added. 'After she died.'

'No.' A simple word, tossed out, with no emotion in it. And none in his face.

She'd extinguished the warmth, just as if she'd snuffed a candle. She snuggled back and his arm remained at her shoulders and the carriage rumbled along, a boulder of a man beside her. She didn't want to be alone.

She rested her hand on his thigh.

His fingers clasped over hers. 'I didn't dream of her then,' he said. 'Sophia would tell me each time she did and would cry. She dreamed of her every night for months and months. Only recently—have I started dreaming of the past. Of the moments during the first year.'

'I learned a trick that makes the bad dreams stop,' she said. 'It works. I swear by it.'

'What?' He drawled the word.

She pulled her free hand up, making a light fist. 'Right before you go to sleep, you clench your teeth on your knuckle and you think of what you don't wish to dream of. It works.'

His chest vibrated and she looked into eyes that welcomed her back. 'Ah...I don't think I understand. I will crawl into your bed and let you show me just how it should be done.'

Her jaw moved nearer him. 'It only works if you do it. Alone. I distinctly remember. Alone.'

'Alone? I will just keep the dreams then.'

He held her still and dusted a kiss in her hair. 'I've heard that kissing a freckle on a woman works just as well.'

'I suppose it could...' She snuggled against him, and returned her gaze to the window, wishing the trip could last for ever, but it seemed to be over in seconds.

The grounds of the estate came into view and she could hardly believe it. Even being a governess at a mansion so grand would be an accomplishment.

When the carriage rolled to the front of Pensum

Manor, the first thing she saw was her friend Joanna walking hand and hand with Luke in the gardens of his father's home.

The vehicle had hardly stopped before Isabel jumped out, rushing to her friend.

The moments were delightful as William stepped behind her and introductions were completed.

She felt a part of a fable, in which only goodness thrived and no hint of shadows surrounded them— except the brisk air seeped through her coat, chilling her. They walked into the front doors and she tried not to shiver as she left the cold behind.

The first days passed swiftly, but by the third, Isabel sensed an unease in William. He kept watching the other couple as if he disapproved of their affection.

'Stop frowning,' she said, after pulling him away from the other couple as they walked in the garden.

'What are you talking about?' he asked.

At the other edge of the gardens, Luke turned to pick up a...brown leaf. They appeared fascinated by something as simple as a leaf in which its tree had long past lost interest. She couldn't tell what they discussed.

She shaded her eyes against the sunlight and examined the couple. Yes, they were entranced in each other and saw only sunshine in the brown, wintery day.

'It is not so bad, surely, being in love?' she asked, taking her hand from her forehead. He watched her.

'Luke and Joanna seem happy with it. My sister seems satisfied with it.' Just the slightest shrug.

'Sophia's husband is quite thrilled with her.'

He frowned, dismissing the importance of the statement. 'Yes. He throws himself at her feet and is like a puppy begging for her affection.'

'Please don't inform him or Sophia of your opinion.'

'I once told my sister, and she insisted I leave her house and not return.'

'How did you get her to let you go back?'

'I showed up the next morning as always. She saw me at breakfast and was silent for a while and then started telling me how wrong I was.'

'You were wrong. Sophia and I often discuss your errors. Some days it is our favourite thing to speak of.'

His brows gave a quick flick. 'Thank you for informing me.'

She splayed fingertips at her lips and gasped. 'I have besmirched you. I didn't mean such a breach of manners.' She breathed deeply. 'An error.' Then her demeanour became her own. She gave a bow. 'You may challenge me to a duel. We can have a chuck-farthing contest.'

He chuckled. 'I have no spare coins. And lest you forget, Songbird, I have been in many drinking establishments in my day and, on occasion, we test our skills.'

'Lest you forget, I have been to a governess school. In addition to our lessons from our teachers, we also took pride in challenging each other. We played draughts for serious stakes and chuck farthing was the game I preferred.'

'But I only have a few coins with me.'

'You don't need any. I will lend you some. But don't

expect any leniency because you haven't been to a governess school.'

Dashing to the house, she went to her room and found the small pouch the butler had collected for her. Returning outside, she held the bag in the air and shook it. 'I will halve this with you but do not get too attached to the coins, Balfour.'

She untied the string, pulled it open and said, 'Hold out your hand.'

He did and halfpennies tumbled into his grasp.

She stared into his palm, counted and took one back. 'Now we are equal. Do not try to take unfair advantage before the game begins. I assure you, I'm skilled.'

Their eyes met.

'I do not even know how many the bag holds,' he said.

'You will have to trust me.' She smiled. 'Although I would advise against it from this point on.'

'Where did you get coins?' he asked.

'Your butler collected them for me. He is anxious to do my every bidding.' She smiled. 'As we speak, he is having a day of respite with a very nice bottle of your wine.'

'You cannot—he is my servant. I didn't give him permission.'

'I did. I asked him if his loyalty could be purchased and he assured me that was impossible as I had it already because my status as mistress of the house commanded his allegiance second to yours. For such a display of service, I could not help but gift him with a token.'

'You must discuss bribes with me first.' He closed a fist over the coin.

She leaned forward so her side pressed against his hand and her nose tilted so high it nearly reached his. 'Shall we decide that with the coin, Balfour?'

'Songbird, you are out of your league.' He glanced around, grinning. 'We must be private about this. I would not want anyone to think my wife willing to wager away the household funds.'

He took her arm and they darted into the wooded area. At the first clearing they stopped.

'You may be a gentleman and dig the hole.'

'My pleasure.' He took a stick and in moments the freshly disturbed dirt scented the air and he had a small indentation prepared. He stepped back, drew a line in the soil, then tossed the stick to the ground. 'You go first.'

'You will not be able to play by the rules and win against me and I am not certain you can cheat and win.' Isabel held the coin high for his view. 'You see, one of the girls I played against, Grace, was quite good. So please—toss. I want to see what competition you offer.'

'I have wagered against all sorts of men in the tavern.'

'But none as good as Grace, I'd wager.' She smiled. 'Toe to the line and prepare yourself to see how haughty words taste.'

He did and tossed. His coin landed near the indentation.

She pitched. The coins rested side by side.

He took her arm, gently led her back a few steps,

took his boot heel and made another line. Their eyes met. 'It's time to be serious.'

She gathered her coins to break the tie. With her teeth tightened, she toed the line and took aim. Tossing, the coin landed half a width from the hole. She curtsied to it. 'Go ahead, Balfour.' She lifted the edge of her skirt so she could walk delicately by him, then she brushed his shoulder. 'Show me what you can do.'

His eyes widened. 'I shall.'

Toeing the mark, he aimed.

Just as he threw, she called out, 'Concentrate.'

The toss fell short of hers.

She moved beside him and smiled. 'You will have to do better than that.' She collected the coins they'd tossed, made a show of dusting the dirt from them and strutted his way.

She held a coin up, rubbed her fingers over it and aimed.

Just as she moved to throw, he moved so close his breath brushed her ear. 'Concentrate. Take your time and concentrate.'

She took a step away, swallowed to lessen the shivers he'd caused inside her and just tossed. She blinked quickly when the coin landed on the mark. Letting out a pleased murmur, she swaggered. 'I think it's your turn. Aim carefully.'

'Looks like I'll have to,' he said. He pitched and won. He grinned. 'I would like to raise the stakes.'

'Oh?'

He nodded. 'Hairpins.'

She considered it. 'How serious are you?'

'Plenty.'

'A pin equals a knock.'

'What?' he asked.

'A knock on my door before entering my room.'

He shook his head.

'You don't have to play if you fear losing.' She flounced closer. 'I'm not worried about losing.'

'Then I shall raise my stakes,' he said. 'Butler's responsibilities. I want them discussed with me before any changes are made.'

'Hairpins. Staffing. You are asking a lot.'

'We will take it one at a time. Unless you're scared.'

'No,' she said. 'Not at all. Let us begin. For door knocks versus hairpins.' Swirling around, she bit the inside of her lip, aimed and threw. It landed and she gritted her teeth and pinched her eyes shut.

His next throw landed on target.

'Good try,' he said, stepping to pull a pin from her hair and placing it in his pocket. 'Let's try again.'

Brushing at her hair, she said, 'Lucky toss.'

'Do you really believe that?' His voice was soft. 'Then, double the stakes.'

'You're on.'

He won two more pins before she had a run of luck and won three knocks on her door. She was going for a fourth, when he suggested her discussing the butler's duties with him before making changes versus all the hairpins.

She agreed.

She touched his arm, stopping not just the movement in his toss, but in his whole body. Leaning forward, she blew on the coin in his hand. 'For luck.' Then she stepped behind him.

He turned to her, concentration on his face. 'This works better.' Snaking an arm around her waist, he pulled her close for a quick kiss, then he resumed the game. But he missed further than either had done before.

Her toss did no better and went far wide the other direction. Victory was impossible to determine.

'I need more luck,' he said, putting a hand at her waist.

'I think not.' She backed away several steps. 'I plan to win.'

'So do I.' He followed and again soft lips closed over hers. The kiss took her thoughts and, when it ended, his eyes took control as his hands released her.

Then he turned, and pitched, and the coin touched the mark.

'Ah,' he said. 'My mistake the first time was in kissing to give you luck. This last time was for my good fortune.'

His lips met just against hers. Shudders raced in her body as he pulled her close. Her fingers loosened and the purse fell to the ground.

She had no idea how long they'd stood, when he pulled back. It took her a moment before she realised why he'd stopped. Voices. Joanna and Luke calling to them.

'We're here,' William called out. He took her hand and they walked together on the path towards the house. Joanna and Luke strolled up to them.

Joanna's eyes sparkled as she glanced to Isabel's hair. 'Er...we were getting worried when you didn't show up for breakfast, but I see you didn't get lost.'

'We merely lost track of the time while we wandered these lovely grounds and discussed our household,' William said, putting a hand at his wife's back.

'Discussing the household,' Luke said, turning to take Joanna's arm as they moved to lead the way back to the house. 'There's a lot to be said for it.'

William pulled a leaf from Isabel's hair and held it for her to see before letting it flutter to the ground. 'I agree.'

'I know it's a bit cold,' Joanna said, 'but tonight I planned a starlight picnic. I thought we might leave early to enjoy the sunset.'

Horses were readied and Isabel rode with the others to find a bonfire and blankets spread with a feast already laid out. A kettle warmed near the fire, the smell of cider mingling with the burning logs.

As Isabel sat with Joanna, the men trekked about to gather more wood before the night completely darkened.

'Have you heard more of Grace?' Joanna asked, holding a mug in both hands.

'No,' Isabel answered, taking a stick to poke at the edge of the fire.

'I remember when Grace started being ill every morning,' Joanna said. 'You were laughing when you said the same thing had happened to a relative and the family had been gifted with a new baby within the year.'

'Grace turned white, put her hand over her mouth and ran from the room. I didn't even realise what I'd said until I saw her face.' Embers flared as the stick dislodged a log.

'I'll never forget that moment.'

'Without Miss Fanworth, I hate to think what would have happened. She was there the night Grace needed her so much,' Isabel added. 'I held Miss Fanworth in the highest regard before, but after that, I thought her near sainthood.'

'She always seemed to know how to do everything. She made a poultice for your sting when you decided to make a pet of a bee,' Joanna said.

'I thought it a pretty insect. It didn't seem to want to sting me when I picked the flower and I thought it might be happy in my room. Miss Fanworth understood.' Isabel straightened, and then laughed. 'She always understood. But I used to get so angry at Madame Dubois, because she didn't like the songs I made up.'

'Perhaps the two of you would have got along better if you'd not called her Madame Dubious.'

'I didn't realise she was behind me.' Isabel tossed the stick on to the flames.

'Isabel, she was *always* behind you because you were *always* dancing into disaster.'

'Not my Isabel,' William said, dragging up a limb and snapping it into smaller pieces as he talked.

'Have you ever had to keep her from getting herself into a misadventure?' Joanna asked William.

'She's been so reserved since our marriage that I cannot imagine such an event.' Words delivered smoothly. He cracked the biggest part of the limb in two pieces as Luke walked up and placed his bundle of wood on to William's.

William settled beside Isabel. She tried to still the moment in her mind. The stars and firelight, and William beside her.

'Well, when you have children, the daughters might be spirited,' Joanna said.

At that sentence, William's movements stilled momentarily before he answered, though his words were spoken in the same tone as before. 'That will be wonderful.'

Joanna's eyes darted to William's face.

'William can handle high spirits,' Isabel said, knowing Joanna saw too much. 'He has three sisters and they are all splendid.'

'You're right.' The tension of William's posture lessened. In the firelight, his smile looked sincere. 'I can only hope our daughters take after Isabel.'

Isabel didn't move, except for a quick flight of her eyes to William. 'And I hope they have his strength,' she said.

Joanna nodded. 'I feel the same way about Luke.'

Luke gave her a smile and started discussing the times his family had gathered on the property to search for a perfect yule log.

When they finished the meal, Joanna and her husband stared at the stars while the fire crackled behind them. William watched Isabel, sitting alone, staring not overhead, but at the burning logs. The fire's glow lit her face, but gave her a melancholy air.

When he realised she looked cold, he moved his blanket, surprised to notice they'd sat long enough for dew to fall on to the covering. Then he wrapped the covering around her. She started, as if she'd forgotten he was there.

'Could we walk?' she asked.

He reached for Isabel, pulling her to her feet, and away from the flickering glow. Dried leaves crunched under their feet and they left the blanket behind.

Isabel spoke low. 'Did you mean that—about daughters taking after me?'

'Of course.' His voice rumbled and he pulled her into the haven of his arm. 'Oh, Isabel…' An underlying humour lit his words. He pulled her even closer, warming himself more than any fire ever could. 'You should never doubt such a thing. I would even hope our sons have your spirit.'

'That spirit has caused me some trouble. It has caused you some trouble.'

'Oh, it has caused me no trouble, except for my concern for you.' His arms remained around her, cradling. His fingertips brushed a curl back from her forehead.

Only Isabel's presence seemed to ease the barrier he felt between himself and the others, though he didn't think anyone else knew of it. In some ways, he envied the others' innocence. But he didn't have it and never would. He'd lost it long ago. Like a hanging you could never un-see, he'd seen the way loss into another person took hold. The two could become one, which meant the control of one's body was given up to the other and to the whims of fate. Fate had a wicked sense of mischief.

'Do you care for me?'

'How could I not?'

'That wasn't a resounding yes,' she muttered.

'I'm giving a resounding *yes*,' he said.

'Wonderful...' The word trailed away.

'I don't have the innocence of my youth any more.' That had died with his mother and if it could be taken a second time, then it had been drowned by his father's drink.

Isabel's presence lightened the memories, though. She took his mind from them and jarred something inside him that he'd not known remained. Some ember of the past that lingered inside him. The last spark of family left that he could feel.

Even if he had not been forced to wed her, he realised he would have wanted to. He could not stand the thought of her wedding someone else. She deserved the highest respect and the most tender care. He would help her regain her dream.

He pulled her knuckles to his lips for a kiss, savouring the delicate feel of her skin. 'Songbird. The pretence is not doing either of us any good. And I am not sure we are convincing your friend of anything as she keeps studying us. Let's leave tomorrow at first light.' He released her hand.

'I—I don't want to hurt my friends' feelings,' she said.

'I'll explain to Luke. He's newly married, more so than us. I can convince him easily that we wish to spend some time preparing for the holidays.'

'I have enjoyed the pretence.'

'I'm glad you did. But we need to return to London if we don't wish to risk becoming stuck on muddy roads. If the clouds are any indication, we could have rain. I'd like to be in London if the temperature drops.'

'I do want to return that painting before the artist forgets he promised that,' she said.

'The one by the Lawrence no one has ever heard of?'

'Yes. I decided I quite hate it. The wooded glen is nice, but I would like something more fitting to the room. More fitting to the home.'

'What about a picture relating to music?'

She shook her head.

'But you are a songbird,' he said.

'Not any more.'

'You should reconsider that, Isabel. That is the gift I hope for you to give yourself. The return of your desire to become a songstress.' He wanted her to erase the attack from her memory and continue with her desire to sing.

He could see her vision of them as a couple reflected in her eyes. He must stop this togetherness with Isabel before it progressed any further. She could not understand it was for her own good as well. If something should happen to him, he would certainly not want her burying herself in bombazine, covering the large mirror in her old bedchamber and staring at the wall.

William took Isabel's hand, held it high above her head and twirled her, pulling her into a spin until she couldn't keep up and she fell into his arms. He rocked back and forth lightly, his face pressing against her cool cheek, sharing the heat of his body.

'I cannot let you freeze,' he whispered into her ear. 'You are turning into an icicle.'

'I'm not any longer,' she said.

'I suppose you're right. Perhaps I was the one who needed warming.' He spoke the truth. He wished he could feel the warmth of her to his core and the same innocence he saw in her face. But he didn't even remember what it felt like.

'You pulled us away from the fire to get warm?'

'Yes.' His voice was low. 'One can't argue with a successful plan.'

His hands moved to hold her waist. 'Now look at the stars.'

She did and he twirled her again and again, making them spin in her eyes, and stopped by pulling her close, keeping her solid against him while letting the world regain momentum.

'Now,' he said, after raining kisses on her face, 'let us bid your friends goodbye as they do seem to wish to be alone.'

'Are you trying to escape the togetherness of the night?'

He shook his head. 'No. I've seen many other nights like this, but instead of a camp fire, there was lamplight and a book and my mother would read aloud when I was very young. Then my father took over the reading.'

'You must miss her terribly.'

He shook his head. 'She was sick so much at the end.'

He forced a laugh. 'Isabel. I can see by the tilt of your head that you're feeling sad for the boy with no mother, but truly by then I was grown. My sisters were the trial for me. They needed my help.'

'I don't want to feel like another person you need to help.'

He held her in his arms and tried to force his heart to beat for her and pound with love. He waited. Because if he could not love Isabel, then he knew he could never love another person.

Chapter Fourteen

Isabel considered the trip a success. She and William hadn't spoken much during the return home, but the silence had been companionable. William had laughed when he recounted the chuck-farthing game. His smile had sparked something that made her feel treasured. He'd even kept a few of her hairpins as a memento of their game.

She closed her eyes tight, taking time to think of William's tenderness. Then she stared at the blank page of her letter to Grace.

Isabel twirled a wisp of hair which had escaped from her bun, wrapping it into a curl. Surely it would be acceptable to tell Grace about the wonderful moments shared with William at Pensum Manor. If it sounded as if William had fallen in love, well, that was just how the words unfolded.

She wouldn't tell Grace that Miss Fanworth had written, expressing concern over Madame's health. The doctor had been called to bleed Madame, so surely she would recover soon.

The pen scratched as she wrote the salutation, but she stopped while deciding what to say about the marriage.

Isabel nibbled a biscuit when William walked into the room. Her heart jolted, but she distracted him from her gaze by extending her arm to the painting of the wooded glen. 'I hate this picture more each time I see it.' She left her biscuit and stood in front of the art, hands on her hips. 'In fact, I think I should return it today.'

She tiptoed and reached for the painting. In seconds, William was at her back, his shaving soap engulfing her as his arms spread against her and he helped lower the painting. She could sense the individual threads of his coat sleeves against her arms. She could not feel the colour black, but in a way she did—not the sombre dark of mourning but the enveloping warmth of his coat, in the same peaceful manner a pleasant nap might surround one as a dream begins—the moment when the world around fades into fairy tale.

He slipped the painting from her grasp.

'I do not want this ending up like the Roubiliac,' he said.

'If I choose several that I like, would you mind making the final decision? I do not want to keep exchanging them.'

He put the painting against the wall and turned to her.

She could see it in his eyes. The refusal.

'Never mind,' she said, closing the space between them. She patted his elbow, then let her hand drop away.

'I don't know what I was thinking. And, truly...' she grimaced '...it shouldn't be hard for me to select something new. I can have a grand time of it and take the maid along for her opinion.'

'The maid?'

'Bessie. She helped me select this one. It's a pleasant painting, but...' she ran her hand slowly along the gilded wood at the top of the frame, then stopped movement '...not for me.'

'Perhaps Sophia. She has an eye for such things.'

He touched the wood, his forefinger at the edge of hers. From a distance one would not have been able to see the space between them.

'I really wish you would go,' she said.

'Then let us get another picture for you. It will only take a few moments to select a painting. I will attend to it with you and you will have to leave Bessie to her own devices.' He shook his head. 'We should be friends. It will make the rest of it easier.'

Friends to make the rest of it *easier?* She looked up into a face she couldn't read.

'I wish for you to sing again, Isabel. I've listened to you hum. At Pensum Manor, I spoke with your friend Joanna while you weren't in the room and she said your voice is magnificent.'

'I cannot stomach the thought of performing. I cannot. Not again. It...the memories of the knife at my throat. What if someone, anyone, heard me sing and truly thought I was singing for them when I wasn't? What thoughts might someone have? Mr Wren said men

imagined my eyes wanting them. My lips on their body.'
She shuddered.

'Isabel. You must toss that from your mind as the
words of a brothel owner. His life deals in such things.
Men who are like that will not be in the audience—they
will be at Wren's. And if one man thinks such, it is on
him, not you. If he is going to think vulgar thoughts, he
would think them if you were reading a prayer book.'

'I can't sing again around others. I cannot.'

'You'll learn how to again. You must push yourself
into it.'

Stepping to the side, she picked up a piece of evergreen that had fallen from the mantel when they'd
moved the painting. She held it close to her nose before putting it into place. She kept her shoulder turned
in his direction and locked her gaze with his. 'I could
say the same for you. And our marriage.'

'You can't squeeze water out of a rock.' No smile
flashed at her.

'If you are as heartless as you think to be, then
spending a few moments with a new friend at the holiday season shouldn't be too much of a hardship. So let's
select a painting and spend the day at shops.'

'Songbird, that sounds almost as pleasant as listening to a beautiful voice. Since I'm going with you, will
you sing for me?'

She shook her head.

'Very well. I'll go to the shops and content myself
with your speaking voice, and perhaps you'll even hum
a bit. I'd like to spend the day with you.'

She gave herself a moment, then moved so that the

toes of her slippers almost touched the toes of his boots. She put both her palms at his cheeks, the feel of his skin thundering in her body. She tiptoed and, with eyes open, she kissed, moving just so that the barest amount of lips brushed briefly, then she moved away. Neither blinked.

'What are your plans for Christmas?'

'I have not finalised them.'

She covered her confusion by sitting on the sofa and looking to the window. 'Sophia has invited me to Christmas dinner.' She had assumed they would attend together, although Sophia had warned her that William hadn't attended in the past. He'd refused and said he ate with friends, but she suspected he stayed alone.

'Do you wish to travel to your parents?' he asked.

She shook her head. 'No. I would not wish to be on the road in winter and taking the servants from their family. I'm quite happy to be dining with your sister Sophia on that day. We've already been discussing the puddings we might like.'

She splayed her fingers and patted her knees with several quick taps. 'I have made friends with your sisters and have Rambler. I am beginning as I should go on. For Christmas I have instructed the cook that the servants should have a splendid dinner and will be free from their duties except for the absolutely most dire ones on Christmas Day.'

'Do not expect me to be here.'

She ignored the words. 'The time we spent at Joanna's was one of the best times of my life,' she said.

He sat across from her and reached for a biscuit.

'It was enjoyable for me as well.' He moved forward

and tapped the back of her hand. 'You are indeed a delightful woman.'

Bursts of warmth exploded with his touch, but his eyes didn't give her the contentment she had wished for.

She touched the handle of the tea cup, but didn't lift it. Keeping her eyes on the china, she asked. 'Did you not think we shared something—precious in the country?'

'I did.'

The richness of his voice reassured her, until she looked into his face.

'I've not felt quite so since my youth. I felt more alive than in a long time.' His lips pressed into a smile. The kind one formed when not thinking happy thoughts. 'I thought of little else when I returned. Your friends are very absorbed in one another. Much like my mother and father were.'

He pulled back and interlaced his fingers. His gaze drifted to the window. 'I felt compelled into that moment. Different. I had to leave to think about what was happening. I'd thought I might be changing. That I'd see things differently. But I've examined my thoughts over and over and over and I'm not the same as others are. I care for people, but the thoughts of them fade as soon as they are out of my sight.'

He stood, returning to stare at the painting. His back was to her and his voice softened. 'It would be foolish of us to fall into any traps that might cause us regret later.' He stood. 'Our marriage is perfect, Isabel. I am thankful for it. It is not some heart prattle which absorbs and taints the outlook. It is a marriage as successful people have had for centuries. A joining of a man and woman who each continue to follow the path they were meant to follow. It is as near perfect as it could be.'

'I want more.'

His head bowed. 'I am so sorry. Three years ago, one of my best friends was thrown from his horse and died within hours. At the funeral, Sylvester was in tears. Everyone talked of it for days at the club and I did the best I could to commiserate and offer condolences, but I didn't feel the loss. It has been three years and I've had not one moment of sadness.'

'You care for the horses, though.'

'Yes. They're good stock. I've had them for years and they should be treated well—but still, if they were to die, I don't know that I would mourn. I don't believe I would.'

He lifted his head and turned back to her. She'd never seen such compassion—or pity, she wasn't sure which—in the eyes that watched her.

He reached into his pocket, stepped to the table by her reticule and put something on the table. A tiny click sounded when it touched the wood. 'Your hairpins. I know you won them in truth. It was kind of you to make the game longer by letting it play out as it did. But I don't know what I was thinking to keep them, except as enjoyment of our game, the pleasure of your company and a chance to make the wagering last longer.'

He left and his boots tapped down the stairway and she heard him calling last-minute instructions to his butler to have someone prepare the painting for return and ready the carriage.

She moved to the table, picked up the pins, tossed them into the burning coals and left the room.

William stood in the tiniest shop he'd ever been in. It barely contained the three of them, but the paintings were floor to ceiling.

'Another by the very talented Mr Lawww-rence.' The man's footsteps clacked along and he drawled the word out as he showed them the painting. One empty place must have been from the art Isabel purchased.

'It is exceptional.' Isabel examined the painting of a sad child with a sad mother. Isabel's gloved hands clasped. Her coat quite covered her. In the back, the collar came above the bonnet edge and he didn't know quite how they both managed to keep in place. Her bonnet was unlike any he'd ever seen. Darker brown, and circular, but edged all around by a wide row of wispy feathers which never stayed still even when she did.

And yet, the garment didn't overpower her. He surmised that whatever footwear she had on added to her height and the extra fluff of feathers made her appear even taller. She appeared as tall as he stood in his bare feet.

'Very.' William stared at the signature. T. Lawrence. But this was not by Thomas Lawrence although it was similar in style.

'I would prefer to think about it.'

'Ah.' The man's shoulders slumped.

Isabel's actions mirrored the man's. Then she chatted with the proprietor for a few moments. William watched as the man melted under the infusion of blue eyes, siren's voice and something else that he could not quite name.

The man shook his head. William's attention flashed from Isabel to the conversation. The proprietor had just suggested he had a painting in the back which he might show her.

When he brought it out, the aroma of paint lingered around it. A little girl sat alone on a bench in the central part of the picture, her face shadowed by the bonnet. The trees and greenery in the background faded away and emphasised the girl, hands clasped, thinking thoughts a viewer could only guess at.

'It's not finished.' The proprietor smiled, looking at the art. 'I'm Theodore Lawrence Bryant.'

'Perhaps you might sign this one with that name,' William suggested.

The man shrugged. 'I should. But the other sells better even as I tell the people I painted them. I suppose they put it on the wall and hope no one asks too many questions.'

William stepped closer to the art. He looked at Isabel. 'Could you change the hair colour on the little girl to something closer to this?' He held his hand by Isabel's face.

'Most certainly.' The man stood taller.

'And perhaps, in the tree behind her, birds—listening. And a tiny, *tiny* feathery fluff in the bonnet.'

'I'm sure I could add those,' he said.

'Please send it to my home when finished and, if Isabel likes it, we will keep it.'

'Most certainly.' The proprietor looked at William.

'But your friends will be more impressed with a T. Lawrence painting than a Theodore Bryant.'

'I'm not purchasing it for them.' William looked at Isabel and, in one second, he glimpsed something that caused a feeling of his heart rolling down an embankment. He couldn't decipher if the look in her eyes made him need to clasp her tight to be saved or if the gaze was thrusting him into a chasm deeper than his father had been in.

Quickly, he led her from the room and guided her to the carriage, ignoring the howl of the wind and the darkening clouds which dampened the air. But before he got to the steps, something caught the corner of his eye.

He turned to see Lord Robert and his brother, the Duke of Wakefield, trudging towards them. With each step, the Duke's coat beat the air like a raven's wings.

Isabel felt William's pause and turned to see what had captured his attention. Two men walked in their direction and the older one looked up. Recognition chased the sadness from his lips, but not his eyes.

'Balfour.' The older man's thick silvery hair gave him an air of knowledge and his shoulders gave him a fortress of sturdiness.

Isabel sensed William's indecision. Lines of strain appeared at his temples.

In brief sentences, William introduced the Duke of Wakefield and Lord Robert, the Duke's younger brother.

'So pleased to meet you,' Wakefield said, warmth infusing his words to Isabel. 'I played cards with Balfour recently. He is a happier man now that he's married.'

Isabel examined the Duke's eyes for falsehood.

William stilled.

'It does me good to see a young man so in love.' The Duke's smile faded like a snowflake on a warm coat. 'I remember so well…'

William's stance tightened, one foot pointed away, ready to trudge off. 'We must be going. I would not want anyone to catch a chill.'

'Nor would I,' the Duke said.

The only thing appearing cold was William's eyes, Isabel thought. 'Do not worry about me. When I was in Salisbury, one of the other girls at the school challenged me to see who could stand longest in the snow barefoot. I won.'

'A school?' the Duke asked. 'You attended a school?'

The damp air suddenly penetrated Isabel's clothing. She didn't want to embarrass William because of her training to be a governess. 'Yes,' she admitted. 'I am not from London. But my parents wished me to have some education.'

'How wonderful,' the Duke said. 'I am always pleased when I meet women who have had the opportunity to learn. Balfour knows I have long been concerned with education and feel that it is vital to our country's progress.'

'I agree,' Isabel said. 'Although I do not know how the school is faring as I received a letter from one of the teachers, Miss Fanworth, that the owner, Madame Dubois, is ill. She has never been sick before and now she can't seem to leave her bed.'

'Dubois?' The Duke's eyes widened. 'You attended Constance Dubois's school?'

Lord Robert's gaze switched from boredom to an intent perusal of his brother.

'Yes. I attended Madame Dubois's School for Young Ladies. In Salisbury.' Isabel answered.

The Duke reached into his waistcoat pocket and dotted a handkerchief to his forehead, but no moisture shone. 'I once knew the woman you spoke of. In my youth. A fascinating woman.'

'Madame Dubois?' Isabel asked.

'Quite fascinating.' The reprimand in the ducal tone couldn't be missed. 'All these years…' His words faded away. He shut his eyes. 'All these years I have not heard of her.' When his eyes opened, he didn't seem to see his surroundings. 'She… Everything about her was delightful. Full of optimism even when she'd lost so much. Full of laughter.'

'I think you might have mistaken our Madame Dubois for someone else. Our Madame was not—I never saw her laugh.'

He took in a breath.

'She did smile, though. If our lessons were perfect or if we did something well,' Isabel added, not knowing why she felt she must reassure him that Madame was not melancholy. 'But she was quite serious with us.'

'Constance Dubois was one of the most spirted women in the world.' His eyes sparked and his voice commanded. Then the Duke's eyes misted and his tone softened. 'All these years…I have guarded against learning the location of her school. I had made certain

I was never informed. And now I have heard without even asking.' He shut his eyes and shook his head. He reached out, intent on Isabel's answer. 'She will recover?'

'It's said she is coughing constantly and her chest is in pain. The letter said her heart is beating fast and she is chilled, and cannot stop shaking.'

His face paled. Isabel had to give him some respite from the strain in his eyes.

'They have called in a skilled surgeon who will bleed her,' she said, 'so there is hope.'

'My Constance.' Wakefield dotted the handkerchief to his head again and backed away. 'At least she is under a physician's care.' He paused, eyes seeing a long-ago memory. 'The school is in Salisbury, you say? I must beg forgiveness for my abrupt departure, but I must see her again. I must.' He turned to his brother. 'You understand. I have to know.'

He turned, darting down the street.

Lord Robert watched his brother leave. 'My brother has carried the memory of the Dubois woman in his heart since his youth. She was a governess to my sisters. Wakefield is considerably older than us, so he and Dubois were closer in age.'

'The whispers were true,' Isabel murmured. 'It was thought Madame Dubois had had an attachment.'

'I would not have been so noble as he was,' Robert said. He adjusted the patch at his eye. 'My brother tossed aside his own desires and wed for fortune's sake. He didn't care for the funds—only that he might provide for his dukedom and his family. The tenants' houses needed so much.'

Lord Robert chuckled, but it lacked humour. 'Love. I dare say when my brother finds this woman he adored in his youth, it will be too late. Or he will discover she has no memory of him.'

He turned to leave. 'I will find my own way home. Good day.'

Standing silent for a moment, Isabel kept her eyes on the direction the men had gone.

'Madame had warned us that when we were in fine households, never to forget our place,' Isabel said. She studied William and repeated, 'In fine households, we were never to forget our place.'

'Your place is in a fine household, Isabel.'

'I am sure. Of course. You are right.'

'Don't be like Wakefield is.' William guided her to the carriage. 'Rushing off. He has just escaped a mire of grief and now he is rushing back to find it again. I cannot understand someone's wish to touch a fire to see how hot it is.'

The driver spotted them and jumped from the perch to open the door.

'But he has his brother for solace,' Isabel said as she settled and snuggled into her coat.

William snorted. The carriage wheels creaked as they began to roll. 'His brother is a worthless rake.' William brushed the moisture from the window, his leather gloves squeaking against the pane.

'But the two of you are friends.'

'We are,' William agreed. 'That does not mean we

do not know each other, but that we do and tolerate each other.'

'And you wish for us to be friends?' Copper tendrils of hair escaped her bonnet and blended with the chocolate colour of her coat.

He ducked so low that he could look at her eyes. 'Isabel. We will have a completely different type of friendship.'

Doeskin touched his face as she pushed him away. 'I might decide not to be friends with you.'

'I will accept that.' He brushed a kiss at her hand before she slid her glove from him.

She bundled back into the seat, huddling. The sun was lost behind a cloud and the temperature had dropped as the day progressed.

He put an arm around her, pulling layers of coat into his clasp and getting feathers in his nose. He huffed them away from his face. 'You might as well be wearing a suit of armour,' he muttered.

Bright eyes again. 'You do.'

'Where has my sweet bride gone?' He dodged feathers again.

'I don't know who you are speaking of,' she said and straightened. Reaching up, she thumped the carriage top. 'But I am going for a walk.'

The carriage stopped and she darted out. He followed. She shouldn't walk alone and he could not let her. But she'd not liked him holding her tight.

They walked, the carriage wheels rolling behind them, snowflakes beginning their flurry. 'The butler told me it would be bad weather,' he said. 'Claimed his bones were trumpeting it to him.'

She kept her pace, her coat hem kicking up.

'You cannot outrun me, Isabel.'

'I would not try. I am merely keeping my blood flowing in the cold.'

A ragamuffin darted from a shop, shoulders hunched, hands in tattered pockets.

'Boy!' she called. 'Boy.'

He turned, soot on his cheek.

'Can you direct us to Somerset House?'

He nodded, and quickly spoke the directions.

'Thank him.' She nudged William with her elbow.

He reached into his frock coat and pulled out a coin. She coughed. He reached again, pulled out another and gave them to the lad, who took them both, grinned from ear to ear and bowed before scampering away.

'Now it is beginning to feel like Christmas.' She walked again, her pace slower. 'I have never strolled in the streets like this. So different than the Christmases at the school past, and the ones before at my parents' home.'

They walked along, not speaking. An older woman pushed a cart along their direction, followed by a shuffling man.

Isabel almost blocked their path. 'Can you direct us to Somerset House?' she asked.

William reached into his coat before she finished speaking.

As they walked on, he spoke. 'You can only ask direction three more times before my pockets are let.'

She laughed. 'You do have enough for three times?'

'Yes.'

She clasped his arm. 'Is not this more fun than losing the coin at a game of cards?'

'I do not play to lose. But, yes, I am enjoying the pace. You do realise the woman sent us in the wrong direction.'

'Yes. And I think she knew it. But we didn't turn either and she surely noticed. So, it is a game we both played.' She paused. 'If both know the rules, it is a game, not a ruse.'

'Don't let the game trip you up,' he said. 'But one must never forget if the opponent is playing, too. We could have easily turned in the wrong direction there, had we not known.'

'We would have found our way again.'

Neither moved until a burst of wind pelted them with snow, mixed with just enough frozen water to sting the cheeks. He stopped. Putting his gloved hand over her fingers clasped on his arm, he waited until the coachman caught up. 'We need to get the horses to the mews,' he said.

This time in the carriage, the feathers didn't brush against him, but he held her close, letting their body heat melt into one. If not for the horses and servants, he would have kept the carriage going for hours.

He wanted this moment to last because he knew this path would not continue. He'd already discovered another property for sale and it would meet his needs. He had not seen it, but that didn't matter.

'After Christmas, I will be moving,' he said.

The clop of the horses' hooves, the sound of someone shouting for dinner and wind buffeting the world sounded before she spoke.

'Why wait?' Her voice had the coldness of the icicles hanging from the eaves.

'The property won't be available until then.'

She turned in his arms, but he kept her firm.

'Why are you telling me now?'

'The game is too serious. We will work out an arrangement that will suit us both. We'll not be tripping over each other, however, and if you wish to see me not at all, I will agree. Perhaps a few soirées here and there but that, of course, is up to you.'

He could feel nothing except his heart beating.

'I think…' The carriage rolled over a bump, and he cushioned her. 'I think that as you are leaving soon, it will be no rush to decide on the particulars. Perhaps we can meet in the summer some time to decide. Or perhaps it would be best after the weather cools again, as people are returning to town and the soirées begin anew.'

He hugged her tight. He would make this a wonderful Christmas for her and let her know that even if he could not love, she would always be able to count on him in the ways that were most important.

She patted his chest.

He closed his eyes. Relieved. She understood.

And he wished wild flowers truly bloomed from

graves and the sun only shone in Isabel's life. He realised something else. He would have allowed someone else to marry her had the man been able to treat her well and love her as she wished.

Chapter Fifteen

Isabel patted his chest. Warm. Deceptive.

He must have a heart and it must be beating. But that was all the good it did.

She rested her hand against his coat. 'I think when the weather begins to warm, I will visit my parents.'

'Have you written your mother that you didn't trap me into marriage?'

'Did I not trap you? Although it was not my goal.' She paused. 'But, yes, she knows there is not a little one on the way.'

'She should realise that her precious, and only, daughter *is* quite accomplished enough even for a duke and not only a viscount's son.'

'She didn't truly intend that in the letter. It's just the way she writes—and speaks. I resemble my father's family in height and looks, and she still thinks me the gangling little creature who cannot keep from tripping over her own feet. She was uncertain I would be able to secure a post as a governess, so the information that I wed someone of the peerage was a shock to her.'

'Has she ever truly seen the Isabel that you are?'

Isabel didn't answer. She put her arm tight and hugged him close. 'I do thank you so much for rescuing me. Both from Mr Wren and from being a governess.' She took her time with the next words because tiny blades had got loose inside her body and were ripping along from one point to the next, puncturing everything that could cause any pleasure inside her.

'And I don't understand why you cannot stay in the house. I can grasp that you're not in love with me. I can understand that you may never be and I can accept that.'

'I am not meant to live with anyone. To feel trapped—confined—smothers me.'

'Love could be pleasant. In only a few days I fell in love with Rambler and he was underfed, yowled and had a bent tail. It was my good fortune to be able to have a cat of my own. Had I been a governess, I could have loved the family pets, but not my own if the mistress of the house had spoken so.'

'You've only had the cat a short time. How could you love him so quickly?'

'He was shivering and had a crooked tail. He needed me. And perhaps I needed him.'

'I think you're mistaking compassion for love. Compassion and love are not the same. And even if I could feel love, then I don't know that it is always a good thing except for a mother and children.'

'I love Rambler. I looked into his eyes and I saw the sad moments and my heart just wrapped around him.'

His voice rose in tone. 'He's a cat. And you cannot just love instantly.'

She looped her fingers around a button of his coat. 'You are not an expert on love. You are an expert on not loving. I can tell you that I fell in love when I looked into his eyes. It might have been a small little seed of love. But then he walks into my sight again and the little seed grows and grows, until it becomes a full-sized love.'

She pulled at the button and then released it. 'It is his loss if he does not care for me and sometimes I'm sure he doesn't and is just there for the food.' She brushed at his coat. 'He just does not quite understand what it is to love someone.'

His kiss dissolved the chill in her body into sunshine. 'Let us enjoy these precious moments we have together today and not worry about a stray cat who has no home.'

He reached up and pulled at a tiny feather in her hat. Her hand locked on the hat, keeping it in place. He pulled a small wisp of a feather from it and tickled her nose.

She tried to snatch the feather, but he held it away from her.

'The cat has a home,' she said. 'With me.' She swatted for the feather again.

He tucked it at his ear and she laughed to see the wisp sticking from his locks.

'Perhaps the cat is fortunate to have found shelter and your heart. But no cats or dogs will be at my new residence.'

'You are so alone that you cannot make a home with me?'

'I doubt I will even stay in the house where I'm moving very long. It's meant to be temporary.'

'Some things should be permanent.'

'I thought the town house was to be.'

'How long had you lived there before I moved in?'

He spoke the words gently. 'Four years, or thereabouts.'

'Then I started putting furniture and pictures and things to make it a home.' Reaching out, she removed the feather he'd lodged in his hair, but his hand clasped over hers, and with his free hand he took the tuft of feather and tucked it in his waistcoat pocket.

She wanted to pull away, but something deep, deep inside her told her she mustn't. And something else told her it might not be just his feelings for her that he moved from, but from the furniture and fripperies she'd added in hopes of making the town house feel like a home to him.

William saw the downward tilt of Isabel's chin as she moved to the carriage door to alight at the town house. He gave a quick pull to her hand and she stumbled at the last steps, right into his arms.

'My pardon,' he said, giving her a squeeze before righting her to her feet. 'I am fortunate I was able to catch you.'

He leaned forward and sniffed. 'Are you…have you been drinking strong spirits? What will the neighbours think?' He swooped an arm at her waist, causing her to stumble against him. 'Do not worry, I will reassure anyone watching that we are most proper folk.' At the gate, he reached to snap an icicle from its clasp on the iron fence.

Then he crunched the tip of it into his mouth.

'William,' she whispered. 'The coachman is watching.'

His lips almost touched her ear. 'This will not impress him as much as the morning after my fourteenth birthday.' He crunched the icicle again and blew a cold breath at her. 'He stopped the carriage to push my boots back into the door so he could close it again—which I didn't find out about until the night I turned fifteen.'

'Four years younger than I am,' she said.

He nodded, their eyes catching. He saw the moment she realised their true differences in age. She was but five years younger and yet perhaps two lifetimes.

He tossed the icicle aside. Before she could think any more he lifted her into his arms and moved to the door, thumping his boot against the base. The butler opened it.

William spoke in tones suitable to Drury Lane. 'I fear my dear Lady Wife has fainted from the cold.' He whisked her inside. In a low tone, he said, 'Close your eyes, Isabel…'

In two quick strides he was at the base of the stairs. His voice still rang to the rafters. 'I must deposit her by a warm fire.'

'No,' she screeched and clasped her arms at his neck. 'You can't take me up the stairs. You'll kill us both'

'Perhaps you are right.' He put her to her feet. His

tone became formal. 'My pardon.' He bowed and in a flash he'd removed his coat and tossed it to the butler.

Before she could ascend the stairs, he stopped her, twirled her around and bent to grasp her legs and hoist her over his left shoulder. 'This will be safer.'

'No,' she yelped out.

But he trundled her up the stairs and was at the top almost before her protest finished. He didn't set her down, but called down the steps, still performing. 'Wine. My Lady Wife must have wine to be revived.' The acting ceased, but the strength of his voice didn't as he continued speaking to the butler at the foot of the stairs. 'Leave it in the parlour, then see that everyone else in the staff who wishes is also revived with the same spirits. We cannot have anyone expiring from this cold.'

She pounded his back. 'Put me down.'

'But I so like carrying you.' He could not see her head. 'Your bonnet is still attached, is it not?'

'Yes. It is hanging by pins.'

He hefted her a few times. 'I can tell. The feathers are making you light as thistledown. But I will find a place where you can recover.'

He spoke for her ears only. 'And I will help you get warm.' His boots sounded as he took her into his bed-chamber.

He put her feet on the floor. Before she fully righted herself, his hands rested atop her shoulders.

'I didn't want to tell you earlier, but you're about to lose that concoction on your head.'

'No wonder. You have shaken it—'

At the same instant, their hands reached to the hat, but his captured hers and lowered them aside as he took out the remaining pins and slid the bonnet free. He put it on the table at his bedside.

Taking her chin in both his hands, he held her face.

Lips covered hers, tasting. Every sensation but his lips fluttered away from her and she waited, savouring the clasp of his hands and their kiss.

His retreat left her chilled, in a way she'd never noticed before. A sort of aloneness that made her want to follow his lips.

'I liked the hat, though. It suited you, and—' he leaned back into her realm '—it gave me an excuse to touch your hair.'

He pulled a pin free—just the right pin—and her hair fell about her shoulders.

'Even the littlest curl peeking out…' he tossed the pin with the bonnet '…distracts me. And when I sat at the table near you at your friends', everyone kept speaking and talking and I thought, how can they be so absorbed in things so unimportant? Can they not see Isabel has removed her bonnet? Are they not aware of those sparkling eyes?' He untangled more pins from her hair. 'I suppose we ate.'

'You said— You said later it was the best meal of your life.'

The merest nod. 'I told the truth.'

He unbuttoned the coat and pulled it from her shoulders, leaving her feeling lighter. He tossed it to the side, then took her gloves from her hands. 'I'll never forget the dinner. Your laughter.' He brushed the leather against her cheek. 'Innocent eyes. Innocent gaze. And laughter so husky I could not stop trying to bring it to your lips again. You laughed three times.'

Her heartbeats changed. Her whole body insisted she get closer to him.

Her fingertips ran the outline of him, over muscled arms, the curve of his neck and the strength of his jaw. Soft skin at his ear contrasted with the roughness where the day's growth of his beard stopped.

With the precise care of savouring each moment, he reached behind her, unfastening her dress and letting it drop to the floor.

His little finger traced her jaw, swelling the feelings inside her. He trailed down her throat and over her breast, swirling against her peaks.

Tendrils of his hair fell forward, brushing against her cheek, caressing like feather-tips. His lips covered hers again, pulling back enough to whisper her name. When he closed his lips after speaking, he trailed them about her neck, sending shivers deep inside her, melting away all thoughts of any world other than the one in the confines of their fingertips.

Through the darkened room, she could see without using her eyes, aware of each contour where their bodies touched. Aware of his breath, his pulse and his thoughts, because in that moment, they were all the same, combined in a way that only the touch of lovemaking could intertwine two people.

Isabel woke, aware instantly that she lay in William's bed and the space beside her was empty. The room had completely darkened except for the fire. A scraping sound had awakened her. She raised her head.

William stood at the fireplace, holding the poker, pushing the coals, moving them about this way and that, flaring sparks, causing the flames to rise or fall as he moved the fuel around. He held his hand too close to the fire and jerked back. The scent of burned hair confirmed his error.

'That is what happens when one plays with fire,' she said.

He chuckled. 'Thank you for informing me. But I had already realised it.'

'William. You could not be more naked.'

'You could,' he said. He moved to the bed, dashing into the cocoon, his body warm and feet cold. He pulled her close, sliding a leg to hook hers and pull her against him.

'You do not think you will miss this when you move away?' she asked.

'I know I will.' He put a kiss on her lips.

She pulled back. 'You do that to silence me.'

He kissed her again. Soft pulses dragged her words away, but a small bit of thought remained.

She pushed and he rumbled a fake growl into her ear and rained kisses at her cheek and down the curve of her neck into the valley at her collar bone.

'I should go back to my bed or you will get no sleep tonight,' she said. She could not go from the room.

'I want none. Besides…' his chuckle poked humour at himself '…it is not first light, so it is hours until my bedtime. And I have a Christmas surprise I have been waiting to tell you about.'

'What?' she asked.

'I wish for you to sing. For everyone,' he said.

She shook her head.

'Others must hear you. I would like to hear you sing.'

'No.'

'Isabel, you must sing again. For others.' He slipped from the bed and reached for his dressing gown. 'Think about it while I am getting the wine,' he said, after tying the sash. Before he left, he placed a showering of kisses about her face.

She didn't have to think about it. She already knew.

He returned. 'Remember how you enjoyed it, Isabel. When you were at the governess school.'

'Yes, it was fun. To sing for the other girls. Perhaps, only for Sophia and your sisters I might not mind. But not with other people around. I can't.'

He slid into bed beside her.

Thinking back to the governess school, she'd done whatever she could to capture the ears and eyes when she sang. She'd moved about the stage, brought herself to tears with emotion, fell in love with the wall behind the audience's heads and suffered whatever the words spoke of. She supposed she would have jumped to the top of the pianoforte and plunged to her knees and slid headfirst to the floor while continuing the song if it would have kept the listeners' attention. She had tried that on a sofa and the girls had loved it. Once, she had taken the hairpins from Miss Fanworth's hair during a performance and looped and looped the hair into a most towering knot and sang. If an asp had slithered into the room, she would have stepped over it to continue, or sang for it.

She had, in the sense of singing for Mr Wren. She had just not realised it. Now when she thought back to his eyes watching as she sang, she shivered. She'd thought he listened to the song, but instead he'd planned her downfall.

How many other times had she misjudged the eyes on her?

Now she remembered an uneasy feeling when one of the other fathers had spoken to her afterwards. He'd suggested he would have liked to have had a governess like her. Her skin had chilled and she had responded quickly and walked away.

She'd forgotten it in the praise of the next person. Not really believed he'd meant anything unpleasant to her. Had taken it as flattery.

The next time she sang for a group, she'd examined everyone's faces and been certain all was well. But Wren had been in that audience, she remembered. The man who'd spoken to her the first time could have invited him.

Singing was more than just words to her and she could not pour her heart, and show all the emotions she experienced, if a pair of watching eyes devoured her.

When her song began it was not merely being in the centre of the viewers' attention—at that moment her very life rested in their power. Sometimes she didn't recognise the Isabel on stage. Sometimes she could not believe the performance herself. The moments filled her in a way nothing else did, but now she had no wish to ever sing for an audience again. The knife to her neck had cut that part of her life away for ever and she didn't wish for it back.

Before touching the wine, William returned a second time to the windows. Isabel. She did remind him of a bird. She should soar, only returning to earth to enjoy the best of the nature's bounty. He'd purchased some earrings to give her after the Christmas soirée surprise and they matched the sky colour in her eyes. They were nothing like the ring his mother had worn. The ring his father had insisted William take from his mother's hand after she had passed.

He imagined the jewellery on Isabel's hand. The unusual ring with the primitive look of irregular stones would fit the performer's spirit of Isabel.

But he could not give the ring to Isabel.

He remembered the mouldering scent of death. Costly candles, more ornate than any he'd ever seen, had been purchased, filling the house with what he thought myrrh or spices from the past would smell like. Mirrors covered with musty cloths that had been packed away from his grandmother's death—a woman who'd died before William could remember her.

His father had insisted that only the best would do for the day of the funeral, and had had token gold rings quickly made in the style of his wife's so he could present them to the others who mourned. William would have expected his father to have had one ring made for each daughter, but he had not.

The first sign of his father's plunge into the past and unawareness of the world left standing.

He was glad he'd left the ring behind. In fact, he wasn't quite sure where he'd left it, but it wasn't in the town house.

The jewellery wasn't elaborate. The stones could be easily mistaken for glass. The design of it was unpolished. A baroque ring with one central stone and nine of different colours set around it. A family heirloom. Oldest son's wife to oldest son's wife. Only now there would be no child and he just didn't want a son of Sylvester's giving it to someone. Better to be lost in the world, than to be on some bit of frippery Sylvester's offspring would wed.

He couldn't give it to Isabel. The ring had not been on anyone's hand since it had been on the hand of a dying woman. His sisters had never even asked about it. He'd seen Sophia wear a necklace that had been in the family for generations and later his Aunt Emilia had insisted his father give heirlooms to William's other sisters as well. But the ring had been the one piece his mother wore every day. It wasn't even pretty. The jewels were a bit misshapen and he didn't even know what they were.

He poured himself a glass of the wine, wishing his mother could have met Isabel. They would have liked each other, he was certain. His mother would have thought her beautiful enough for a viscount and intelligent enough as well.

Chapter Sixteen

When he returned to the bedchamber, he brought not only the wine, but a lamp.

She sat in the middle of the bed, covers pulled high. He handed her the wine and moved to the chair where he usually sat to don his boots. He observed her in the same way he had once watched the morning dawn and felt it the only brightness in the world.

After she'd finished the drink, he said. 'You once left the school and were willing to risk everything to walk into a disreputable place like Wren's. You already had employment as a governess and you walked from that, and you moved about alone in a town you were unfamiliar with in order to find a stage.'

'I was not thinking. I let my vanity override sense. My mother was right.'

'No. She was not. Many times I have heard others sing. I have heard choirs. I have heard operas. But even as you talk, I can hear the husky siren's voice you have. I am not surprised Wren wanted you to sing in his establishment. I am just surprised he was not sensible enough to help promote you to reputable places.'

'I didn't say I have no skill. I just said I have no wish to perform. It is dead inside me. Just the same as your heart is dead inside you.'

'Don't let Wren take that from you.'

'He hasn't. Before I merely sang because—'

'Because you enjoyed it. It is your gift.'

'Because I knew no better.'

'How many times did you sing for others assembled at the school?'

'I do not remember. I didn't count them.'

'More than a dozen?'

'I am sure, but that means nothing. We didn't have a lot of entertainment. It was either that or embroidery, or watercolours or reading.'

'You bought a pianoforte.'

'Just because of the wood and the way a home feels alive with—'

'With music in it?'

'With a pianoforte.'

One arm folded across himself, he rested an elbow on it and propped his chin on his fist. 'Fair enough. But performance is not dead within you. I know it is not. You walk up the stairs as if you are making a grand entrance.'

'I traipse stairs as I always have.'

'Which proves my point. You were born to sing, Isabel.'

'It doesn't matter. Now I am a wife. This may not be a marriage of the heart, but it is still a marriage and

I have no wish to be anything but a governess now. It will just be one for my own children, as you said. I am quite pleased with the thought. Everything...' she straightened the covers '...has worked out for the best.' She crossed her arms. 'We are both happy in the forward path we have chosen.'

He had stayed home, planning, enjoying the last moments he was to live with her, but he'd already sent a trunk ahead to the new residence and given a few instructions on preparation.

He listened for her humming. But it didn't carry through the walls so he didn't know if she hummed or not.

He'd told Sophia his plans for Isabel to sing at the soirée and he'd asked that it be a surprise.

Tomorrow's performance would give society a chance to see the true talent of Isabel and the true woman she was. In just the short time he had been gone she had transformed herself, although really it wasn't herself she had changed. The woman she was blossomed out even the first night when she wore the ripped and dirty dress. An ache spiralled into him at the memory of what could have happened that night. But Isabel never need be in danger again. And she'd never have to wear torn clothing again.

He was thankful he had enough funds so she could purchase so much. The artwork had been a bit ill advised, but she'd even recognised that later. In truth, his house had never looked better. *Her* home had never looked better.

The songbird had a gilded cage, but she would not be confined into the role of a hidden wife. She would be perhaps the best songstress in the world if she wanted. He would make certain to hire older, burly footmen to accompany her on her travels.

He'd already sent a note to his man-of-affairs explaining the new turn of things, telling him to hire someone well versed in the nature of procuring respectable theatrical venues for a singer. Only at the most refined places would Isabel sing. Any obstacles to Isabel's success would be moved aside.

Isabel would have her dreams. He would place them at her slippers.

But she didn't understand. Rising, he moved down the hallway to her room.

He knocked three times, waited, then heard her call out enter. He walked into the room and she sat at the desk, gazing out the window. One paper, blank, sat atop a stack of others on her desk. The cap was still off the bottle of ink. He walked to the bottle and put the stopper back in place.

'Sophia sent a note that said you have no plans to attend her Christmas Eve soirée.' He picked up the pen from the blotter and touched the tip to his forefinger, leaving a mark.

'I know. We have discussed it.' She reached out and took the pen from his grasp, took the stopper from the bottle and wrote another salutation to her friend Grace at the top of the page.

'It will only stir memories of Christmases past when

I was at my parents or with my friends at the governess school. I wish to start anew, but not that way.'

'She said you almost convinced her.'

She paused, pen in mid-air, and looked up at him. 'But she was polite enough to pretend to accept it. I do like that about her.'

'So do I, Songbird.'

She flicked the pen on to the blotter. 'I do not want to be in a crowd of people.'

He watched as she drew a line over the words she'd written on the page.

'Just a brief song at the soirée.'

'You apparently have not heard the term *no* many times in your life.'

He paused, frowning. 'Now that I think of it, I can hardly ever remember hearing it.' He ran a thumb along the firm jawline pointed in his direction. 'And for good reason. I'm nearly always right.'

She looked heavenward. 'Well, not in this instance.'

'Fair enough.' One hand on the desk, he bent his knees and crouched directly in front of her. 'Songbird. My sister, who thinks the world of you, is having a soirée and it would mean very much to her if we would attend. I've even invited the Duke.'

'William. You're not being fair.'

'No. I have a surprise for you and also I thought you might just try a short song.'

The jaw firmed. 'I will not sing.'

'I wasn't going to tell you and let you discover it yourself, but the surprise is that I have arranged for your friend Joanna and her husband Luke to be there.'

'You…did?'

'Yes. I want this to be a special Christmas for you, Isabel. I know you're sad that your parents were not able to come to London to be with you. But you can still have family about.'

'Are you and I family?'

He stood erect. He'd seen the wistfulness in her eyes. He had to escape that look. 'We took vows of for ever. We are wed.' His voice softened. 'Songbird. Do not set yourself up for unhappiness.'

'I fear it is too late.'

William sat with his man-of-affairs, finishing the plans for opening the new residence, when he heard the door on the lower floor crash open.

He put his hand to his forehead for a second, listening to the stairs take a pounding from boots. Then he stood and met the glare of his father.

One look and William stood. A glance dismissed the man-of-affairs. The man bundled his papers, tucked them under his arm and left.

William's father clasped a small box in his hands.

'I found it. I found what you left behind.' He thrust the box on to the table. The lacquered box that held Will's mother's wedding ring. 'You promised your mother. That Christmas Day.'

'Yes. I did. I said I would give it to a wife some day.'

'I thought when you didn't bring Isabel to my house that she didn't want to visit. I thought there might be a babe on the way and she might not wish to travel. And then when you left, I started thinking about it.

You didn't seem to care enough about your wife or our family to honour your dead mother's last wishes. How could you disgrace your mother's memory?'

'I have done no such thing.'

He picked up the lacquered box and held it in both hands. 'This morning, I thought to look. I don't know why. But I searched your old room and I found this. Just tossed in a drawer as if it were a comb.'

Isabel appeared in the doorway. She didn't speak.

'Why is it not on Isabel's hand?' The Viscount's words blared.

William stared at this father.

'You've never honoured her memory as you should,' his father said.

'You have done so enough for all of us.' William met the red-rimmed eyes of his father. 'Take it back or it goes in the refuse.'

'You will have to be the one to put it there, just as you've put your mother's memory into the dust bin.'

'Father,' William spoke. 'Did you not think that her blood runs through each of your children?'

'I don't want it,' Isabel interrupted from the doorway, her voice whip-crack sharp.

'What?' The Viscount whirled, facing Isabel.

'I prefer this one.' She held up her ring finger. 'That one is too large.'

The Viscount turned back, shooting a glare at William. 'She jumps to your defence.' Keeping his eyes locked with his son's, he said, 'Describe the ring, Isabel.'

'I do not wish to. It is enough that I have said I do

not want it. It is an old ring and I wished for something new.'

'Bah.' One spindly finger pointed at William's chest. 'You didn't have it in your house. You have not shown it to her and I cannot believe you even offered it to her. She would have kept it with the women's trinkets she owns. That is what women do.'

He turned to Isabel. 'A thousand pardons. I didn't make him honour his mother as he should have. I let him carouse about all night, thinking him a youth who needed revelry. Instead, I let him become a man who thinks of nothing but himself. I tried to force him into marriage, thinking he would become the son I wanted. But nothing's changed. Even when he visited the country, he didn't stay at my home.'

'I spent much time at Aunt Emilia's.' William's words slapped the air.

'With that wastrel nephew of mine.' His voice rose. 'The two of you are of the same cloth. But him I can take none of the blame for.'

He turned, walking to Isabel. 'Toss the ring, for all I care. My lineage is dead, except for what my daughters might provide. His son may inherit the title—' his head indicated William '—but I hope he inherits nothing of his own father.'

Isabel shrugged one shoulder and interlaced her fingers. She tightened the fingers of her left hand, the band visible to him. 'If this is the concern you've shown your son all these years, then I want nothing to do with you as well.'

She turned and left.

'So this is the way it is.' He kicked the table legs flying and the box flew to the wall and bounced off. Storming from the room, he slapped the door facing and stomped down the stairs.

William moved to the box and picked it up, but he couldn't open it. The death and the drink. His father had changed so much.

The light of the family had rested in one person's hands and she'd died.

The last Christmas with his mother wasn't just his best memory of Christmas; it was his only memory.

And it was the first time he knew she was ill. Very ill.

His mother had awoken them before dawn, rushing them to get ready, and they'd all bustled into the cold, frosted darkness and travelled to Aunt Emilia's. Their morning meal had been taken in Aunt Emilia's ballroom with small tables spread about and the sideboard covered in platters of food. Children and adults together in a room decorated floor to ceiling in evergreen. The windows faced the sunrise and the sun had bathed them all in gold.

William and Sylvester had trudged outside afterwards, wanting to get away from the conversation of the adults and the bob-apple game the children played. William had found a spear tip while he and Sylvester explored ruins.

Then on the way home from his Aunt Emilia's, his family had bundled together in the carriage and his mother had laughed that there were almost too many children to fit inside, as she held Harriet and brushed the strands of her youngest child's hair from her face.

William had shown them the spear tip and they'd all made up stories about the ferocious knight who'd carried it. Her knight had been named William and he'd given the spear tip to his mother as a token. She'd taken it and said she'd keep it always.

They'd returned home to another feast. His mother had had a coughing spell at Christmas dinner, right after sitting down. She'd said she wasn't hungry and left, insisting they stay. His father had followed her and William and his sisters had eaten, never raising their eyes from the food.

No knight could save her.

William picked up the ring and slipped it on the second knuckle of his smallest finger. It wasn't a pretty ring. Not at all. He'd seen so many more that were more elegant. A daisy shape, and each petal held a small gemstone and the centre a larger one. The biggest gem wasn't perfectly cut and it was more obvious than on the others, almost like a lop-sided face. Even the precious metal holding the gems had a primitive feel, except for the leaves which led around the band.

A seventeenth-century baroque ring worn by his mother. The one his father had asked him to take from her hand after death. William, at thirteen, had wanted it buried with her, because how could his mother be his mother without the ring she'd worn every day of his life.

But it had been his grandmother's and the Viscount insisted it would be for William's wife some day.

He examined the ring, and then touched the stones to his cheek.

Isabel stepped into Sophia's house, lamps shining to make the room bright as day. Taper candles burned, adding a festive air. A red velvet cloth draped at the table beside them. Someone took her pelisse and William's frock coat. Since the night before, he'd not said one word to her other than the most basic of pleasantries on the way. He didn't seem angry, but as if he'd pulled away. Already she'd got used to having him in her life and the distance ate away at her. She pushed the ache in her chest from her body. She would not acknowledge how bleak she felt inside at the thought of spending the rest of her life unloved. Even the thought of seeing her good friend Joanna didn't fill her with the pleasure she'd expected, but increased the emptiness of her heart when she realised she would never have the bond Joanna had with Luke.

They walked past another draped swag of fabric and on a table she noted the bough of evergreen resting on a wooden platter with dried berries and twigs around it, giving the room a holiday scent.

A smiling Sophia, dressed in a yellow-silk gown, and wearing jewels to match, rushed to greet them. 'I am so happy you decided to come. It will be so nice to—it will be glorious to hear you sing, Isabel.'

Isabel instantly stopped. 'But I am not going to perform.'

Disappointment flicked in Sophia's eyes, causing a similar pang in Isabel.

'You're not?' Sophia's eyes took in her brother. 'But I have planned—'

'Leave it, Sophia.' William's voice spoke a gentle command. The warmth of his hand rested at Isabel's back. 'Let's enjoy the evening.'

'Very well.' Sophia smiled. 'It is enough having good friends here. But I was certain you would sing for us. I thought that was why…' Her words faded. First her eyes searched her brother's face, then she gave Isabel a smile.

'I think I hear another carriage,' Sophia said. 'My husband is with the other guests. Pardon me while I greet the newcomers.' She moved away.

Isabel turned, clasping her hand over William's arm so she could pull him close and whisper, 'You told her I would sing.'

'Yes.'

'How could you?'

'I wanted you to have a chance to reach to the skies.'

'You wished to force me into it.'

'No. Well, perhaps. But only because it is right for you.'

'How could you think you know what is right for me?'

One side of his lips quirked up. 'Do you not believe you know what is best for me?'

She paused. 'Well, of course. But I do.'

He took her gloved hand, pulled it to his lips and placed a kiss at the back. 'Sophia gave you a safe place to stay on the night you were attacked. Would it not be a wonderful gift for her to introduce your voice to London, on the night before Christmas?'

'Isabel,' a feminine voice called out.

Upon hearing her name, Isabel turned to see her friend Joanna rushing towards them, with her husband Luke following, adoration for his wife in his eyes.

After a quick greeting, Sophia ushered them into the ballroom.

Isabel clasped her friend Joanna's hands. The chatter of voices rose so loud at the soirée the women had to be close to hear each other.

'William told me last night that you and Luke planned to be here.' Isabel said. 'I am so happy to see you.'

'This Christmas is even more meaningful to me than the last one where we four were together at the school. I can imagine Rachel in Huria living in a palace. It suits her so. The more exotic something was, the more it interested her,' Joanna spoke. 'I hope she is as happy as we are. We have both found love matches.'

Isabel dared not turn to William and see the look on his face when the word love was used. Her smile hurt, but she refused to acknowledge the pain she felt. She would have time for that later.

'Have you heard anything of Madame Dubois's illness?' Isabel asked Joanna.

'No. I haven't.'

Isabel quickly told Joanna of the conversation with the Duke of Wakefield. 'It would be so sad if they are never reunited, but I cannot see Madame falling in love with anyone.'

'But we did. Now we are spending Christmas with our true loves.' She turned. 'Did you imagine we would be so fortunate, Isabel?'

'No. I rather thought I would end up like Madame.' She smiled, but didn't look into anyone's eyes. 'But without the school.'

William's smile took in Lady Howell. He had insisted Sophia visit her house and invite her to the soirée.

His plan on whom to invite had been simple, but was not going as planned. He'd invited Luke and Joanna to give Isabel support, but when Joanna had spoken of love—Isabel's face had paled. He'd invited the Duke of Wakefield—who'd not attended—because the Duke's approval carried a lot of sway. He'd invited Lady Howell and a few of her friends, whose voices just carried. But now that didn't seem to have been a grand idea.

He could not disinvite Lady Howell and he couldn't force Isabel to sing.

William looked at Isabel. 'Please come with me for a moment.'

Before she could respond, he led her out the doorway, securing privacy for them. 'Isabel. Do not let one instance destroy the confidence you should have.'

'How do you know? You have never seen me perform.'

He leaned forward, letting her know with his face that he was not believing her words. 'As we were leaving, Isabel, I told the butler to send the maid to your sitting room and find your music and select songs to send ahead.'

'You cannot—'

He touched her arms. 'One song. Just one. Prove to me you cannot. Or prove to yourself that you can.'

Her eyes fluttered and matching pangs hit his midsection. He didn't want to hurt her. He wanted to give her the dreams she had.

'Never mind,' he said. 'I shouldn't have planned this.' He spoke the truth. He did want her to shine and he wished for her to have her glory, but part of the reason was a salve to his conscience. He wanted to give her something because he could not give her himself and that was what she wanted most.

'I cannot tonight. Not tonight,' she said. 'Lady Howell and her pack of friends are here. And it was not right of you to arrange this without my permission. I will not.'

'Is—'

'You more than anyone else should understand what it is like for something to die within yourself.'

'You're right.' He let his fingers brush hers. 'If it no longer means anything to you, then I agree that you shouldn't sing.'

William stood patiently. She didn't answer. He held out his arm and she grasped it. They walked back into the soirée, moving to Sophia's ballroom, but his sister wasn't visible among the milling people.

Luke called out to William and the two men moved away as they talked.

Isabel heard a voice that could haunt a ghost.

Lady Howell appeared at Isabel's side. 'Good to see you. I was afraid your duties would keep you away.' She cackled. 'I'm Lady Howell, in case you've forgotten. And you're looking quite lovely tonight. This must be quite a treat for you to be among society as you were raised to be a governess.'

'A noble occupation.'

'I'm sure,' Lady Howell said. 'And a good governess is so hard to select as they can be so full of airs.'

'But the important thing is to have someone trustworthy for the children.'

'Yes. Not some upstart who might want to catch the eye of one of the servants or a visiting relative and cause disarray.' She leaned towards Isabel, breathing out the odour of soured milk. 'And how did you and Balfour meet?'

'I was singing at the school.'

'Oh, yes.' Her eyelids half-closed. 'And why was William Balfour at a governess school?'

'He'd heard of my voice and thought to see for himself.' She raised her head straight.

'So, your voice carries? I mean, tales of your voice?' She patted her gloved hands together. 'I'm sure you sing quite well.'

'Well enough.' The milky scent surrounding Isabel made her own stomach feel curdled.

'So why don't you gift us all with a song? I'm sure your husband's sister would be pleased to let you sing at her soirée. I noticed she has the ballroom arranged so that people might sit around the pianoforte.'

'I don't wish to.'

'Well, I can certainly understand that.' She tapped her fan against her cheek. 'But I would think a woman who might have a talent good enough to cause a man to search her out at a school might not be so reserved about it. Of course, Balfour wouldn't have wanted to miss someone like you. Young men get trapped by their affections all the time.'

When Lady Howell said the word *trapped* her eyes glistened with a touch of glee.

And William was going to move from his town house and Lady Howell would hear of it, and it would become quite the chortling contest when Lady Howell talked about it with her friends.

'I think I shall tell Sophia I'd like to sing.' Isabel looked at Lady Howell. 'I have quite the repertoire of songs.'

She just could not remember a single one.

Chapter Seventeen

The instant the people assembled in the chairs, Isabel shut her eyes. Not one word from one song could she remember. At the school, she could not have forgotten them if she'd tried. They bubbled from her.

But never had she felt the eyes on her in such a way. Now it was as if every blink batted her. It was not just the ones who wanted her to fail that caused the clench in her stomach, but the ones who wanted her to succeed as well.

Every time she had performed in the past, she'd been at the school, or in her parents' house. She didn't know why she thought she could sing on a stage when she'd dreamed of singing for others. Nothing felt the same.

William stood at the side, watching. She could feel his wish for her to succeed and that added to her fear that she could not.

Joanna and Luke were sitting front and centre. Sophia sat at the pianoforte.

Isabel looked at the music propped at the piano. She'd

forgotten how to read the words even. She leaned over the piano, concentrating on the words, but it didn't stop the feeling that she needed to run.

'Are you familiar with this one?' Isabel asked Sophia.

'Very much.' The puzzlement on Sophia's face was obvious.

Isabel looked at the song and could finally read the words.

Then Isabel fluttered, adjusting her gloves, taking in a breath and trying to calm herself. One could not sing well when the voice quivered in fear. Sophia stared with concern. Joanna watched with a whisper to her husband and confusion on her face.

Isabel turned, and reached to the music, switching out the songs. The notes wavered so she could hardly read them. She took one and put it on top, then put the others behind, one at a time.

Her breathing would not slow.

She handed the music to Sophia and indicated the first sheet. 'Play this. Over and over.' She had to get alone, away from the eyes.

Then she held her palm up to the audience. 'One moment.' She rushed by William and left the room.

She ran to the red cloth Sophia had put behind the evergreens at the entrance.

Dashing the cloth around her, like a shawl that covered the hair, Isabel let the covering conceal her, drooping over her face and body. Then she began to sing softly to herself.

She heard her voice, heard the quaver dissolve and felt the strength returning. Then she walked into the room as the verse began again, singing, sashaying to the front of the room, not looking at anyone. Just her own too-tight slippers.

She stood front and centre, and didn't move, the upper half of her face concealed except for her lips, as she sang about the loss of her love.

William watched. A spirit began singing. The audience could see her mouth clearly and the words fell into the room, adorned with the same velvet of the covering.

No one moved. William wondered how he breathed. His chest felt too taut to let his heart beat.

She continued and, near the end of the song, thrust the cloth back, letting it fall to the floor, and the volume increased with the sight of her face.

She sang for thousands, not just for the few in the room, and the listeners knew they sat near a woman singing for crowds.

As the notes ended, she didn't wait to begin the next, but turned to the pianoforte, pulled out the music she wanted, and then thrust herself into the rowdy tune, swaggering to and fro, stopping a moment here and there as she walked to William.

William's eyes met hers and he saw the uncertainty. He raised his chin, locking his gaze with hers, silently telling her that she controlled the room.

Her eyes changed and her voice became stronger.

She marched to William and he didn't see Isabel, but an older, wiser version of her self. One who'd lived the words to the song. She reached out gloved hands and while she didn't grasp him, her fists clasped as if she had and her head tilted back, but her eyes roved over the audience and she followed the words of the song, and when she moved aside, her hand flicked and she didn't appear to know he existed any more.

Then she did a song about a country miss who'd lost her beloved and was standing above his grave, only to admit it wasn't truly his grave because she was forbidden to even visit the last vestiges of the only person who had ever cared for her.

Handkerchiefs covered half the faces of the women in the room.

Perhaps, he thought, when one plans an event with an explosive one shouldn't use too much gunpowder.

The song stopped. Isabel turned to Sophia and gave a forceful wave of the head. Sophia slid another sheaf of music into place and her eyes were transfixed on the notes.

A joyous tune erupted, perhaps more suitable to a tavern, but Isabel stood immobile. He could see the governess in her smile. A lady singing a tune not meant to be imbued with polish, but Isabel corrected that, adding a strictness, but making the song a private joke shared with the audience.

Oh, we are oh, so proper now, but some of us have perhaps known where I have substituted very proper words in exchange for less suitable ones, have we not?

If one got the jest, one was a part of it.

Then she sang her last song of the night. For William.

His face became immobile. His arms were crossed. Eyes unfathomable. But she had seen that look before. When men listened to her sing and didn't want their emotion to show on their face. It didn't look valiant to be weeping as a woman sang.

The song ended.

Silence. Perfect silence. She curtsied.

Then gloved hands patted with a vengeance and words of praise erupted. Handkerchiefs flourished, dotting eyes.

'My wife,' William's voice broke through the other sounds and passed through Isabel's ears and wedged in her heart stronger than any words of any song.

She rushed to him, and threw her arms around him.

'Is…' He grasped her elbows and pulled her back. She met his gaze and, for one brown flickering instance, saw black before the smile took hold. Her knees locked in place.

He stepped behind enough to pull her gloved hand out for a kiss above.

'They love each other,' Lady Howell grumbled to the woman at her side. 'But who can blame them? He's got funds and she's spirited. I was sure he'd plucked her out of a brothel, but I found out she's a country squire's daughter and been her whole life at some governess school—' Lady Howell grimaced. 'Bah. Life doesn't know what it's doing half the time, but I'd say you can't beat funds nor beauty with a stick.' She paused. 'Well, you can beat beauty with a stick and if you got coin, it can be a gold stick.' She chuckled, turning her head to search the room. 'Any more of that punch left?'

Isabel turned as her hand slipped from William's grasp. 'Yes. Lady Howell,' she said. 'I believe I could have a drink as well. What more could I ask for as all my dreams have come true?'

'Thank you for gifting us with a song, Isabel.' William spoke and then tucked her hand over his arm.

He retrieved a glass for her and moved them to Joanna, Luke and Sophia.

'Now you know what she was like at the school,' Joanna said. 'She read Mrs Radcliffe's novels and claimed them inspiration for her songs. Madame Dubois despaired of her, but Isabel could sing her way out of reprimands.' She looked at William. 'I must warn you, she can make herself cry when she sings if she wishes, so do not be surprised if you anger her and she returns later with tears in her eyes. It could be a trick.'

'I will keep that in mind.' William's voice rolled over them. 'My Songbird is truly a gift to the world. I fear the performance might have tired her. We should be leaving.' He turned to Isabel. 'Please make your goodbyes to your friends, Isabel. Tomorrow will be Christmas and I imagine you'll wish to spend the entire day with them.'

'I thought we...' Isabel saw the flicker of blackness again. The square of the jaw just beyond the smile.

She turned and bade her farewells to her friends, their happiness bouncing over her like sun's rays.

She had created the exact performance she'd wanted. She had been a success and William's gloved hand over hers kept her close at his side as they made their farewells. William helped her into her coat and she collected the new velvet cape and draped it over her arm.

In the carriage, he shook his head, in wonder. 'You're an excellent singer, Isabel, and an even better actress.'

'I've been performing for the students since shortly after I attended the school,' she said. 'First they were surprised I could sing. But when the new wore off, they might yawn or speak to someone else. I determined to make them take notice while I sang and if their gazes moved I darted about, or swaggered or changed to a different song.' She leaned into the coach seat. 'I could not let them ignore me. I could not. Not in those moments. The moments were mine.'

She crossed her arms over her chest. 'When I sing for people, sometimes my heart beats so fast and afterwards I feel as if I have been running the whole time I was standing, but still, it is delicious.'

'I swear, when you looked at me, I could have believed you were the woman in the song.' He shook his head. 'You'll have people sending you hothouse flowers by the crate, but do not fall for such blather.' He looked out the window, frowning. 'The streets are near frozen. This will not help with my moving.'

'But you'll not want to move now? Surely not? It's almost Christmas. I saw your face while I sang. I saw—'

'Isabel. You saw the same as you gave,' he said.

The words hit her harder than anything Lady Howell had ever spoken.

'Oh.' She huffed at herself. She'd been taken in again during a performance.

'I've paid extra to have the home now,' he said. 'I had the servants begin moving my things while we were out. They were to take the majority of things I need, but leave enough for tonight and we can finish tomorrow.'

'On the eve of Christmas? And Christmas Day.' Her

fingers tightened. 'The servants are working…you could not wait?'

She pressed herself against the opposing side of the carriage and turned to him. 'I thought you cared much more for them than that. They have been with you for years.'

'I do care for them, but it is their employment. We were working tonight as well. This was not all frivolity, Isabel. It may seem like it to you, but your voice will open your way in this town. Lady Howell and her friends will spread the news at their Christmas meals tomorrow as this will give them an *event* to share. The next time I go to the clubs, I will be questioned about it. More will hear of it. Within the space of a few days, everyone who knows of us will know of your voice.'

'Open my way into what?'

'All of what you wish. I've put it at your feet.'

'You have?' The chilled air seeped into her clothing.

'Yes. You wished to move to London to have a stage. I've provided you with one.'

Exerting strength to calm her fears, she said, 'I was the one singing the song. I knew what I was doing. My voice would find a way to be heard once I am at a soirée no matter what. It didn't matter that it was your sister's home. I promise you that I can innocently lean against a pianoforte, trail my hand along the keys and start absently singing to myself and have others listening in a heartbeat.'

'I have speeded the process.'

'You speeded the process so you can tramp out the door of your house and make a sham of a marriage.' She spoke the words, and heard them, and felt them. 'And you have chosen to have a disagreement with me to make the process of your leaving seem more justified.'

'This has been a sham of a marriage since before the vows.' Quiet words, barely stabbing the air. 'We agreed to a marriage with no heart involved. I did so because I knew I had no heart to give.'

She matched her control to his.

'Marriage.' She tapped her chin. 'Tell me, what does that word mean?'

'Nothing to us.'

'Well, you put that more clearly than the signature on your wedding paper. I noticed the grimace on your face when you signed. It was not a death proclamation.'

'It very much felt like one. You cannot know what love does to a person. You have been too secluded with the girls in the school and the countryside. I have seen it first-hand. I have seen it from women who have caught the pox from their husbands and who are dying as the husband is visiting a young mistress. I seen it in the eyes of the men who look at tarts who are fighting for the men's coins. And I have seen what it does to innocent children and people who are merely standing at the side and must suffer because love has grappled someone by the throat and chewed out their minds.'

'Even Mr and Mrs Grebbins knew more about love than you.'

'I don't care who knows more about love than me. I know enough.'

'No. You know nothing about it.' Again she heard her words. They pushed her back into the carriage seat as she struggled with them. It was true. He didn't. If he did, he would not be thrusting hers back into her face. He didn't know of the devotion and the happiness two people could share when looking at the world together.

He spoke to the night. 'Do not care for me, Isabel.'

'Loving you would be the same as loving a gold chamber pot. Rather nice on the outside, but one mustn't get too close or the stink sets in.'

'Thank you. You see, the stink is what happens when one thinks to love.'

'I would quite agree. I am so fortunate we will have a marriage where we are not tripping over each other. But I am very upset that you would expect the servants to work tonight. I will help them crate up your things so you may move sooner. I hope you're taking that hideously arrogant bed with you. I might put something smaller there for guests, or move into it myself.'

'You're completely welcome to do as you wish.'

'I will. Perhaps some dried flowers will give it a fresher smell.'

'You're too kind.'

'Well, it does reek of shaving soap and boot black and leather. Scents that I am quite certain—' She put a hand to her throat. 'They do not do well for me.'

'I agree that they do not. And I quite like them.'

'I hope you are not planning to stay the night at the town house,' she said. 'After all, there is much work to be done moving the things out of the…room. And I can easily direct the servants to send things your way later.'

'I was quite planning to spend the night there as it is still my home for the moment.'

'Please do not forget to leave any instructions you might have for me in the future in such a way as to reach my housekeeper. She will give me all posts and make certain I am kept up to date. Although I do not know how I will make it up to the servants that they are having to work in this season. I will think of something though, no matter how much it costs.'

The carriage rumbled along and Isabel was at the door before the carriage's movement stopped in front of the house.

'If this,' she said, blocking the door and not wanting the coachman to hear, 'is a better state to you than love, then I would wish you a whole lifetime of such bliss.'

She left him behind. He could follow her or not. She didn't care.

When they walked into the house, she said over her shoulder, 'One word with you upstairs, please.'

As quickly as she walked, she could not outpace him. She walked into the windowed sitting room, noting the shutters closed against the cold. She'd seen a crate in the hallway, but no servants in the family chambers. Perhaps they were not too dedicated to be working at the moment either, but she was certain confectionery scents lingered in the air.

'And how are we to handle the addition of children into the house?' she asked.

'I am neither here nor there on the subject. It is not something that must be decided this night or this year for that matter.'

'I wish for them.'

'Then I will do what I can to assist.'

'I somehow knew you would.' She raised her chin. 'I didn't want you to think I would forbid such activities until an heir and a daughter is provided. On the other hand, if a daughter arrives first and second, I will consider myself unable to get the process right and my duty done.'

'We will decide as the time arrives.'

'Very well. Thank you for the wonderful evening.'

'Let us not part on sour feelings. This is for the best, even for you, Isabel. You just do not know it.'

Looking at the floor, she gathered her thoughts. 'You have not dissembled about what you wished for. Not once. I must understand. I suppose I let the dreams I had as a child override the truth.' She raised her face. 'Do not think I am angry at you, William. I am, but I will soon be over it. I am most angry that sunshine does not hide in all dark caves and hungry children do not have fairies to feed them a good meal before night-time. I wish all dreams came true—and simply by writing the words in a song and singing it the world could become clear and all lives be filled with hopes that come true. I have been fortunate because of your intervention. Now I will continue on as planned. I was to remain a spinster for my life and I will always be unwed in my heart. I will not trouble you for a marriage you never wished to have.'

'I wish you pleasant dreams.'

'You as well.' She gave a quick curtsy to him and he left.

She could not quite finish with the untruths. And it had led her into the cave without sunshine.

Chapter Eighteen

A knocking on the door of her bedchamber-turned-into-music-room caused Isabel to sit alert. The lady's maid had already helped her get ready for bed.

William. He simply could not stay away.

Well, he could not stay either, not tonight. She called out to enter. The maid walked in. Isabel's eyes kept trying to make the maid taller and turn her into William, but it didn't work.

'My pardon,' the servant said. 'With the soirée, and the moving and Christmas, I didn't remember to give you this.' She held folded paper in her hand and walked it across to Isabel.

The maid left and Isabel looked at the writing. She knew it was no note from William. It would be from Grace or Rachel, as Isabel had already received a letter from her parents earlier wishing her a joyful Christmas. They would not have time to write again for some time because they would be so caught up in visiting neighbours and sharing the good cheer for the year.

Isabel gazed at the picture she'd had framed. The one Grace had drawn when they were younger. Four smiling faces. Her friends who'd kept her from feeling alone. The other three girls had lifted her spirits even when she'd not mentioned needing a smile. They'd never been further away than a whisper at the school. She'd lost the closeness with them, by distance and circumstance.

She had seen Joanna and Luke, and been able to share in their happiness, but a hollowness had burdened her, until she sang. Then, she'd been enveloped in William's love, but it had been an illusion. A lie. A short-lived lie.

Now the untruths she'd told were settling on her like winter's chill only going deep inside and coating all her feelings in a muck of despair.

She had the servants to keep her company. True, they were paid to be at her home, but surely it was not too terrible to work for her. Or perhaps they simply could not find another post.

Isabel turned the letter to the light and opened it. Rachel had written. The excitement from the words blasted into the room and shot through Isabel's heart. It was all she could do not to stop reading. Rachel was getting married to a prince.

Joanna had Luke.

But not all of them had fared so well.

Isabel didn't know precisely what had happened with Grace and her daughter, except Miss Fanworth said Grace had been satisfied her daughter was cared for. Grace could now continue on, searching out a governess position so she might forget the tragic moments of her past. Isabel imagined Grace keeping the loss deep inside for the rest of her life, the sadness growing greater as the years passed. Much like William's father had mourned.

Nor had Isabel received a post from Miss Fanworth about Madame and she was afraid to write and ask because she might find out something she could not bear. Madame had sounded so ill earlier and Isabel had thought the Duke would return with news, but he'd not attended the soirée.

Isabel continued reading the letter, each swirl of the words dragging like icy drips across the vestiges of her heart. Only, it wasn't vestiges, it was as a big bleeding mess that took up the entire room. She had learned nothing when she caught that bee. Nothing.

Isabel read the words through a blur of moisture. She was invited to the wedding.

She didn't think she should attend. To fall to her knees sobbing as the couple gazed into each other's eyes would not be pleasant. She could imagine the shocked look on faces and herself rolling about the floor in agony.

Looking down at the rug, she sighed. Rolling on the floor would not help. She'd learned to feel things deeply so she could put the emotions into song. That was turning out rather dismally.

A knock again on the door. William. She sniffled. She would forgive him.

But then the door opened slowly and a skirt showed. It would not be him. The maid peeked around. 'I forgot to tell you about Rambler. A boy appeared at the door this morning and was looking for his cat. He'd heard we found one. Rambler ran to him and jumped into his arms.'

Isabel smiled. 'Well, that will make a happy Christmas for the boy.'

She would not cry. She would not. But she did feel all a-sniffle.

'Please tell my husband that I erred when I said I have a cat.'

'I do not believe he is here, but I will see that he is informed when he returns.'

The door shut. Isabel stepped across the room and opened the basket where she kept her sewing. Looking underneath, where she'd hidden them from view, she pulled out the five handkerchiefs. She had not put flowers on them, but simply a strong B with perhaps a few more circles and dots than necessary. For William. She held it to her cheek, and when the soft fabric touched her skin, it was too much.

She took all five and moved to the tiny room and on to the lumpy bed. She sat, her back against the headboard in the small, dark room. She had a whole house, servants, and yet she felt most at home in this room which was the same size as the one at her parent's house.

Even if her mother had been in the same house, Isabel knew she could not have rushed to her and explained. Her mother wouldn't have understood. Her mother had never been anything but the light in the candle in the centre of the room. She'd had six brothers who'd all thought her a gem, then married a man who thought her the whole world of jewels.

Isabel's mother was a good-spirited mother who meant well, but she didn't truly understand tears, or sadness or being alone.

In the darkness, Isabel traced her fingers over the *B*. She was a Balfour now. And probably, in truth, was the perfect wife for her husband. She would learn not to care. She would lock away her feelings in the same way William had. She swallowed. She would find his secret.

If she had daughters, she would teach them to be brave and strong. She would also understand if their hearts were broken and she would give them more comfort than a wadded wet handkerchief.

Singing didn't seem so important now as love. The one thing in the world that she would give up singing for—she could not have.

In the bedchamber, William gave the sleepy-eyed valet the option of waiting to follow until after Christmas Day. The man surely had personal attachments and William didn't wish to disrupt them.

Then the valet examined William's face. That had never happened before. Their eyes had never really met and now the man looked at him as if trying to decipher the back of William's head going straight through from the eyes.

William took the key to the new home. He would not wait until Christmas Day to move. Isabel planned to eat dinner with his sisters, but William would not join the festivities. Spending the day alone would suit him. As soon as Sophia had her own home so she could host his sisters, he'd shut Christmas from his life. He didn't need it.

William marched out the door, letting the cold air blast his face. His fists were at his side and he waited for his carriage. The time seemed eternal until the vehicle approached.

Wind buffeted him. He should have stayed inside to wait for the carriage, but the house had been too warm and the servants not their usual quiet selves. He could hear bustles and taps and hints of disarray. His moving out, along with cooking, had disrupted things.

'Cousin Sylvester's,' William said. He had no desire to go to his new home. He was taking some of the staff to work for him, but they would not begin until the day after Christmas.

'Of course. He will be pleased you're attending his… evening.'

'Wait.' William stopped short, remembering the date. Sylvester always tried to have a particularly ribald dinner party in the late hours and claimed to his friends that it was necessary for them all to attend so they would have something to take the sting out of a pleasant Christmas dinner where one had to sit with elderly relatives and discuss bunions and stuffed gullets and digestive disorders.

But as of late, Sylvester had begun to discuss his own aching head, sorrowful stomach and ingrown toenails more than one would expect. He also discussed hair tonics to excess as he had a deep concern about the thinning spots in his locks.

William would risk the lack of comfort of his body

to protect his ears from a night of Sylvester's slurred words about this remedy or that, and William's necessity of keeping a chamber pot at hand for when Sylvester cast up his accounts.

The moments of solitude would be much better than a night of revelry.

'I wish to inspect my new home and then I will spend the night there.' He didn't wish to speak with anyone.

He placed a boot firmly on the carriage step, aware of the sluggishness and groan of the carriage springs caused by the falling temperatures.

The ride had the spirit of a cortège.

When the carriage stopped, William descended and examined his purchase. A smaller house, further from his club. Further from Sophia's. Closer to Sylvester's. Without the parlour windows and their inside wooden shutters, and the ability to stand at the window looking down over a busy street. The main attraction of this house had been its availability.

He had asked his man-of-affairs to be hasty and, considering all, this was a good selection. He had paid above an expected price to get the residence quickly. Marriage was costly, but he had known it would be so.

William stepped out.

Again the springs in the carriage creaked as the coachman jumped down to give William a lantern. William hurried the man away, knowing he wished to get back to his own family.

When the carriage left, William saw another man, one of his new neighbours, struggling with a wriggling fluff sticking out from where the man held something against his coat. In the other hand, he held a cone of paper wrapped around greenery.

A servant ran out with a lamp and, before the door closed behind him, a little boy, wearing a long-sleeved shirt, rushed from the doorway into the chill.

The father stopped and held out the white barking fluff. The boy took it and hugged. 'Not too tight,' the father said. 'Mustn't squeeze too much or he'll nip your nose.'

The father put a hand on the boy's shoulder, guiding him towards the door while the boy blasted out a selection of names possible for the puppy.

William grimaced. He hoped it would not be a large dog. The barking could quite disturb sleep.

Irritation rumbled through him at the thought he was abandoning his house. Another complication caused by the emotions. The neighbours at the other town house tended to be invisible, but these might not be. The hour was much too late for a little child to be awake.

He raised his eyes higher when a movement at the window caught his eye. The lamps in the house were lit bright as day.

He looked up in time to see a woman, her back to the street, and the man's arm moved into view and held something above her head. Mistletoe. She laughed and moved from view, the mistletoe following.

William turned, trudging into the house, more than ready to put the numbing cold behind him and throw the festivities to the rag-and-bone collectors.

He hated the joyous, wondrous Christmas with all its solitude and bleakness and nonsense.

The cheerful spirit bit into the winter. Each year he looked forward to his favourite day—the day after Christmas. That day he woke up with a smile on his face because normal lives resumed.

The door to the new residence opened without noise. Darkness pressed on each side of him, tomb-like.

The air. The air, instead of seeming warmer from the outside, had captured the chill of the winter and settled into the clasp of the house. Even the scent of lantern oil didn't make it seem warmer.

Above stairs, he saw chairs by a table. Larger pieces of furnishings the owner had left behind as part of the agreement to vacate hurriedly. William kicked a boot heel against the bare floor. No movement. Steady, but not in a comforting way as he'd expected, but in a hard, unforgiving hold.

The fireplace didn't call out to him. The mantel had no engravings, just a wooden structure of average size. He raised the lantern, seeing a pale spot where a picture had once hung on the wall, and at the window, water stains. Shadows flickered like the moments from a bad dream.

He moved through each of the family rooms, seeing the scrapes of life on the walls and the nicks of time about.

Bones, not flesh.

The room with the fireplace and water stains on the wall compelled him to return. William walked to the mantel and put the lantern on it. He found a tinder box and lit the coals in the fireplace, and stood, trying to get the chill from inside himself.

Searching about the house, he found more coals and brought them to the room. The night would be spent sober and he didn't wish to be cold as well.

Again his eyes landed above the fireplace.

The space around the mantel had darkened with the soot and the pale space above indicated a large portrait.

Going to the bedchamber, he saw the trunk he'd instructed sent ahead. On top of it sat a tiny basket, with biscuits, a flask, currants and comfits. Cook didn't want him to starve. He opened the flask and tasted. The water he liked.

He sat the basket aside, opened the trunk and found the box. The box with his mother's ring and the little scrap of feather from Isabel's hat.

He imagined his mother's portrait. The second one. The one started after her death.

His first sight of the completed painting had caused a smothering inside his throat that not even his first bout of drunkenness had cured. His head had ached the next morning—his world had spun, but the picture had remained in the library. Never again had William taken a book from the shelves. The servants had gathered anything from that room he'd wished.

He'd still had to encounter the sight of his father when the Viscount summoned him, shouting out commands that sometimes were nonsense. His father had always been the same—staring at the portrait, an empty glass in his hand. A decanter sat beside him and several others graced the mantel—one container always full.

Above that stone mantel, the picture was not truly of William's mother but a likeness taken from a family portrait completed before her death. The eyes had not been right and yet they had. They'd been dead. He'd never completely erased that image from his mind. Seeing his mother die had not been as hard as seeing the picture of lifeless eyes, staring—every time he entered the room, if he looked in that direction. He learned to keep his eyes from the mantel.

Many times he had contemplated slashing the portrait. But he could not.

Even the room, when he walked by it, door open, and his father inside, had begun to emit some scent of rot.

He'd put a knife into his father's grasp and told him to use it.

His father had stabbed the weapon into the table and sworn to the rafters. William had stood, a brandy bottle in his hand, his cheek cut from a fight he'd been in the night before and his stance defiant.

'Get out of my sight,' his father had shouted.

William had swung the bottle into the door facing as he'd left the room. The shattering crash had resonated. He'd dropped the bottle neck in the hallway on the way to his bedchamber. When the neck hit the rug, he'd looked down the hallway.

Sophia's eyes stared from around her door. Harriet and Rosalind peeped from the other side, all wearing nightdresses. Three wan faces and three sets of eyes looking too large and too old.

He'd begged their pardons, promised them treats for breakfast, suggested a new hair ribbon for Harriet, a book for Rosalind and a new dress for Sophia. He'd said he'd fallen from his horse on the morning ride and was in a foul mood, but his beautiful sisters made his day better.

No one had smiled. At that moment, he had changed. His actions, in his sisters' presence, had become more circumspect. And he'd taken more care when out. He didn't want his sisters losing their only brother and he didn't want to see any more pain in their eyes.

He'd not even realised he must take charge of both the land and the household at first. He'd expected his father to wake any minute and resume the duties to family. Or Aunt Emilia—but her husband had been sick and so had her mother.

He'd waited, but then he'd been able to wait no longer. He'd done the best he could, but he'd not been able to expect everything. One day Harriet had wandered away and he'd been terrified because he'd not planned for it. Not expected it.

William had not wanted to become a parent and particularly not wanted to become a parent for his father. But he'd had no choice.

He raised his head. Nor had his mother had a choice.

His father had, however. William was thankful he'd not realised the tale of him attacking a woman would pull his father from his room or he might have made up the story himself when he was a lad.

Eleven years had passed since his mother had died. He rested his elbow at the mantel and leaned his head on his fingertips, shutting his eyes. His mother had been taken from him and his sisters, and they'd not known what to do. He could understand her being taken from him, but his sisters had needed their mother so much. That made him most angry.

He sat by the coals, watching them as they glowed and then faded away. Several times he moved, raking them around in the same manner he poked about in his head, resurrecting memories of days buried deep in his mind.

Harriet losing her front teeth and thinking they would not grow back. Rosalind stealing a horse from *the stables. Sophia and that rakish soldier. Giving up* on his father. All before he was Isabel's age.

William knew how differently he'd been at nineteen compared to Isabel.

He stopped, realising that his father had been eighteen when he married. Thirty-two when his wife died. Not much older than William.

William's chest thudded. If Isabel had died at Wren's hands… True, he didn't know her then, but still, the thought took his breath.

Perhaps he understood a bit more now. He didn't even want to think of it, and yet, his father had lost the one true love of his life, for ever.

William thought of Isabel again. Alone. What if something happened to her and he was not with her? Wren was not the only man who might want a songbird caged.

He could not live with himself if someone hurt Isabel.

He breathed in and it was as if she touched his skin. She would always touch him, whether she was in the room or not. Whether she was in the world or not. And he could not live without touching her.

He could not bear the thought of her being alone. If she wanted someone to love her, she should have it. Isabel should have whatever she wished for.

And he should give all to her that he could.

He had not known what love was about. He had not expected that a person could fall in love with another person when they were not in the same room. But he fell in love with Isabel at that moment because now when thoughts of her surrounded him, he wanted it no other way.

He no longer cared that it might destroy him if something happened to her. He would be destroyed if he didn't spend his life, whatever remained of it, with her.

William stepped into the house, pleased for the warmth after the long walk and thankful for the plum cake he could tell had been baked. Candles added to the early morning light, giving the entryway a glow he'd never seen before.

The butler stepped up, took William's frock coat and gave a grin and a bow of his head. The bow was usual. The smile unexpected.

'Welcome home, sir.'

William's body lightened. For the first time, he felt the house was more than a place to eat, sleep and gaze out the window. Isabel was here.

'Are you not supposed to be having a day to spend with family, today?' William asked.

He nodded. 'I am spending it with family. Just last month I married Cook.'

William's eyes widened. He'd had no idea of the romance. Cook was the mother of the little boy who'd been tiptoeing about for almost a year.

William nodded and moved up the stairway. He didn't want to wake Isabel.

He looked at his little finger, now wearing the heirloom ring. He touched the band, examining the stone. He slipped it to the second knuckle of his left hand and clasped his fingers closed. Vows might have been said, but this ring was the vow of his marriage. Once the band went on Isabel's finger, they would be married for ever, if she would accept the token.

Chapter Nineteen

The aroma of the burning yule log reminded Isabel of Christmases past, and all that had gone before.

She'd risen well before her usual time and still wore the dressing gown because she'd not wanted to wake her maid early.

But soon she'd have to put on a bright dress and an even more festive face to visit William's sister and pretend everything was well, even though Sophia would know the truth. William not being present would tell too much.

She looked at the crumpled handkerchief in her hand, considering whether to burn it or not. The other had flamed briefly, but hadn't given her the joy she'd expected. She'd had trouble not pulling it back from the fire because it felt wrong to destroy something that reminded her so much of William.

The crumpled handkerchief looked exactly like she felt on the inside.

'Is…' The voice at the door caused her to still, afraid her imagination was deciding to torture her.

She turned, suddenly feeling she sat too close to the flames.

William's hair had been pressed into place by the hat he held in his hand, but he thrust his fingers through the locks, causing it to resume its natural state. He still wore the clothes from the night before.

'Isabel. I am doing the same as my father. The same. I am mired in the past of my mother's death just as he was. He could not go on with his life and I could not go on with my life. I could care for my sisters, but I could not trust myself to have a family.'

She longed to reach for him, but didn't. Looking into William's eyes, she could see flickers of the pain from his childhood.

'After Mother died and the roof began leaking, and the house began smelling of rot, I instructed the man-of-affairs to send workmen to check for a leak from the roof. A leak was found and repairs started. My father complained that his solitude was disturbed, but the men kept working on the roof. I realised everyone would listen to me if my father would not speak to save us.'

Isabel didn't move, but waited.

'The house was rotting away,' William said. 'Father had not noticed. Then I turned fourteen and tossed a bottle into the hallway. I couldn't remember what I'd done that night. I wondered how I could protect my sisters and keep them safe, if I was no more aware than my father.'

Stepping forward, he took her hand and looked to the window. 'After my youngest sisters were skilled at taking care of the estate, I moved where I could visit clubs easier and enjoy myself more. I found this house and had every board checked. Every board had to be solid. The windows had to be tight and the sounds of the outside world diminished. Storms kept at bay. The rooms sturdy. The house shut out the world so I could sleep in the day and be alone when I was here. I do not look out the windows to see what is happening. I look out to see that I know none of the people.'

She imagined his father sitting alone in one house, staring at a portrait, and William alone in another, staring out the windows.

'With my sisters, there are three,' he said. 'It is not as if my heart is solely wrapped around one. But with a wife, my heart would solely be wrapped around her. She would be inside me. How fragile that seems to me and yet—' he touched her cheek '—I cannot risk *not* loving you. That would be even worse.'

At the moment he reached out a hand in her direction, she knew he had made a decision.

He made one step forward. 'I was given the gift of a Songbird almost to my window and I would not raise my head enough to hear the music.'

His eyes searched hers and she threw her arms around him and he tugged her so tight and so close he lifted her off the ground.

When he lowered her to her feet, she asked, 'Have you returned to stay?'

'Absolutely. Wherever you are is where I plan to live.'

Then she looked into his eyes and saw what she'd always wanted to see. Love. For her. If he had not held her, she would have grasped him to remain on her feet. But she didn't even have to tighten her hold. He kept her steady.

He held her away so their eyes could meet. 'I had to step in and care for my sisters and manage the estates when my father was mired in grief. I had to. Perhaps Sophia was old enough to manage, but Ros and Harriet were not. Our family's fortunes would have disappeared. And I had to take the place of mother and father when I felt I had lost my own parents as well. I was so angry and buried it so deep. It wasn't my sisters' fault any more than mine and I didn't want them to suffer.'

'But they didn't, because you took care of them.'

'I did. But not for myself. I had no one to turn to and I accepted it. And I decided I didn't need anyone and I became more and more alone. I lingered at Sophia's house, hoping for a feeling of family, but it wasn't there for me. Then you offered it and it was too good to be true. If I love you, I risk the loss again. But I can't be happy without you. Or even content. Or close to it. I want to have you here.' He clasped her hand, closing her fingers, and pulling her fist over his heart.

'I want to spend Christmas with my wife. This year. And every year for the rest of my life.'

Words she had dreamed of from the man she didn't even know to dream of.

She buried herself against him, the wool scent mingling with the warm earthiness of him.

He stepped back and took a ring from his little finger, and took her left hand, their joined hands igniting a glow of love inside her.

'You're not wearing the wedding ring,' he said, rubbing his thumb over the empty spot where the jewellery had been.

'No. I gave it to some children who were singing at the front door.'

His fingers tightened on her left hand. 'Will you keep a different one? It belonged to my mother.'

'Yes. Your sister told me how a grandfather of yours had it made for the woman he loved.'

Slipping the antique ring on her finger, he moved his hand to cover hers.

'I will be your husband, Isabel, for as long as you will have me, and longer. For you will be my wife in my heart, always.'

She stepped back and sniffed, turning to lift the one handkerchief which was embroidered and put aside to stare at it. The one she'd kept pristine. 'William, you must take this quickly before I cry on it as well.'

He tugged at the corner of the linen, taking it from her hand. 'I'm sorry that I gave you cause to need a handkerchief, Isabel. I will always be here to dry your tears should you cry again, but I hope it is never again because of my actions.'

She sniffed and smiled, reaching for the handkerchief. 'Too late.'

He didn't release the cloth, but pulled her back against him, kissing her tears away.

After Christmas dinner, William turned to Sophia. 'Would you play pianoforte for us? I would like to sing something with Isabel.'

Sophia agreed and moved ahead.

Isabel turned to him. 'You sing?'

'I think I do quite well.' He hugged her close. 'My tone is not so fine as yours, but I would like to sing with you. And tonight, when Ros and Harriet arrive, we'll sing again.'

'They're leaving your father alone?'

'Yes.' He smiled. 'In the message Ros sent to let us know to expect them, she said Father wishes to stay behind, but he is in the best spirits she has ever seen. Apparently after he left my home he came to terms with the past when he realised his children were our mother's legacy. But he won't be alone today. Aunt Emilia's friend lost her husband and he has taken it upon himself to become a confidant. And I sent him a message that you had accepted my ring.'

Isabel reached out, her fingers brushing his knuckles. When their eyes met, she saw a man she'd never seen before—a man at peace with the world around him.

Song bubbled inside her and she wanted to sing for everyone—to give sound to the happiness inside her.

They moved to the pianoforte and Sophia waited while Isabel and William chose to sing *Upon Christmas Day in the Morning*.

Isabel could never stop at one song. She was on the third, her heart filled with sound of William's voice blending with hers, when the pianoforte ended abruptly.

She turned, suddenly aware of another presence in the room. Her mother stood at the doorway, beaming. Her father balanced beside her, a cane in his hand and one foot bandaged with enough cloth to make a small bed covering.

Her mother moved forward, clasping Isabel in a hug. 'We could not miss Christmas without you. We could not,' her mother said. 'And when we arrived at your home the butler directed us here as he was not certain how long you might stay.'

Quick introductions were exchanged and William was hugged as well.

'Although you didn't need to introduce him,' Isabel's mother said. 'I could recognise him instantly from your descriptions in your letters. I was so pleased when you wrote after you married that you had found a matching heart.'

'I didn't mean an exact match, but it is near,' Isabel said, laughing and clasping William's arm to pull them close. 'But how could I not love a man who sings as well as he does?'

'I am so pleased you're happy,' her father said, movements slow as he stood beside his wife.

'Are you well, Father?'

'Never better,' he said. 'To see you has been better than any medicinal.'

Isabel introduced her parents to her new family and as the others talked, William pulled her from the room, took her face in his hands, kissed her soundly and stood back. 'Our voices match so well.'

'So do we,' she said.

* * * * *

THE GOVERNESS'S
SECRET BABY

JANICE PRESTON

To my fellow authors Georgie Lee, Laura Martin and Liz Tyner: it's been a pleasure collaborating with you, ladies, and I hope I've done justice to your characters in the epilogue.

Prologue

Early October 1811

Nathaniel Pembroke, Marquess of Ravenwell, threw a saddle on Zephyr's back, mounted up, and pointed the black stallion's head towards the fell, the words of the letter searing his brain and his heart. As Zephyr's hooves flashed across the ground the tears spilling from Nathaniel's eyes evaporated in the wind and his roar of rage was heard by no man. The fells above Shiverstone Hall were avoided by local villagers and farmers alike, and that was precisely how Nathaniel liked it.

The great black's pace flagged and, reluctantly, Nathaniel steadied him to a trot. The anger and the grief burning his chest had not eased—the hollow place where his shrivelled heart had struggled to survive this past nine years was still there, only now it was cavernous…a vast, stygian void. He should know by now grief could never be outrun. It cleaved to you like lichen clung to the rocks that strewed the dale below.

Hannah. Tears again clouded his vision and he blinked furiously, gazing hopelessly at the gunmetal grey of the sky. Dead. Never again to see his beloved sister's face, or to hear her laugh, or to feel the rare human contact of her arms around him, hugging, reassuring. And David, Hannah's husband of eight years and Nathaniel's loyal and steadfast friend…his only friend. Also gone.

The raw lump in Nathaniel's throat ached unbearably as the words of his mother's letter—delivered as he had broken his fast that morning—reverberated through his brain: a carriage accident; Hannah and David both killed outright; little Clara, their two-year-old daughter, the only survivor.

> *You are named as Guardian to the child, my son. If I can help you, you know that I will, but I cannot, at my age, shoulder all responsibility for her upbringing. Neither will I live in that Godforsaken place you please to call home in order to help you with the task.*
>
> *I urge you to come home to Ravenwell and we shall raise Clara together. It is time you took your place in the world again.*
>
> *If you choose not to, however, then you must come and collect your ward. It is your duty and you owe it to your poor, dear sister to take charge of and care for the child she loved more than life itself.*
> *Your loving*
> *Mother*

Nathaniel turned Zephyr for home, the realities of his dilemma bearing down on him. He could not deny the truth of Mother's words—she was getting no younger and she would never be happy living at Shiverstone Hall—his cadet estate near the border between the North Riding of Yorkshire and Westmorland—nor would it be healthy for her. She lived most of the year at Ravenwell Manor, his main estate in the far more civilised countryside that surrounded the town of Harrogate, on the far side of the Dales.

But…he considered those alternatives, neither of which appealed. Go home to Ravenwell? He shook his head in dumb denial. Never. He could tolerate neither the memories nor the looks of sympathy from those who had known him before. Still less could he stomach the recoil of strangers at the sight of him.

By the time he rode into the yard behind Shiverstone Hall, his decision was made. He had one choice, and one choice only. He must fetch Clara and bring her to Shiverstone to live with him. His courage almost failed at the thought—what did he know about children, particularly one as young as Clara?

'You have responsibilities, Nathaniel. You cannot continue to hide away. How are you ever to produce an heir otherwise? Not every woman will react like Miss Havers.'

Nathaniel bit back a growl at the reminder of Miss Havers. He had suspected how that would end as soon as his mother had told him of the woman who had agreed to a marriage of convenience. Even the lure of his wealth and title was not enough to compensate for his scars. Miss Havers changed her mind after one meeting and Nathaniel had retreated to Shiverstone Hall, resolving to live a solitary life. She hadn't been the first woman to react to his altered appearance with horror: Lady Sarah Reece—with whom he'd had an understanding before he was injured—had lost no time in accepting another man's proposal.

He did not miss his former carefree life as one of society's most eligible bachelors: such frivolous pleasures no longer held any allure for him. Nor did he miss his erstwhile friends. He would never forget the shock on their faces, nor the speed with which they had turned their backs on him after the fire.

He was *happy* with his life, dammit. He had his animals and his hawks—*they* did not judge him by how he looked.

His mother forked a morsel of roast grouse into her mouth and then placed her knife and fork on to her plate whilst she chewed, watching Nathaniel expectantly.

'I am but thirty, Mother. There is more than enough time to produce an heir.'

'Would you pour me another glass of wine, please, Nathaniel?'

He obliged. They were dining alone in the dining room at Ravenwell Manor, the servants having been dismissed by Lady Ravenwell as soon as the dishes had been served. That had prompted Nathaniel to suspect their conversation would prove uncomfortable and his defences were already well and truly in place.

'Thank you.' His mother sipped her wine, then placed her glass on the finely embroidered tablecloth. 'Do not think I am ignorant of your plan, son,' she said. 'You arrive here after dark, at a time you know Clara will already be asleep. What is your intention? To snatch her from her bed before dawn and be away before you need to see anyone, or be seen?'

He hated the sympathy in her eyes but he also knew that behind that sympathy there existed a steely belief in duty. *His* duty: to the estate, to his family, to the memory of his father, and to the future of the marquessate. Her jibe about snatching Clara from her bed sailed too close to the truth.

'I came as soon as I could after reading your letter, Mother. My late arrival was because I did not want to wait until tomorrow to travel, but I *am* afraid I must return in the morning.'

'Must?'

'It will not do to expect a two-year-old child to travel late into the night.'

'Then stay for a few days. At least give the poor child a chance to remember you.'

He had last seen Clara four months before, when she had come up to Shiverstone with Hannah and David from their home in Gloucestershire. They had stayed with him for a week. Thinking of his sister and his friend brought that choking, aching lump into his throat once more. He bowed his head, staring unseeingly at the food in front of him, his appetite gone.

'I could invite a few neighbours for dinner. Only people you already know, not strangers.'

I can't... Bile rose, hot and bitter in his mouth.

He shoved his plate from him with a violent movement. Mother jumped, her fork clattering on to her plate and her face crumpled, the corners of her mouth jerking down as her eyes sheened. Guilt—familiar, all-encompassing— swept through him and he rounded the table to fold his mother into his arms as she sobbed.

'I'm sorry, Mother.' She had lost her precious daughter and he had been concerned only with his own selfish fears. 'Of course I will stay for a few days.' A few days would be all he could endure of his mother's efforts to reintroduce him into local society, he was certain of that. 'But no dinner parties, I beg of you. Do not forget we are in mourning.'

Mother's shoulders trembled. 'You are right,' she whispered. 'But…please…stay with me a short time.'

He dropped a kiss on her greying head. 'I will.'

Poor Mother, left with only him out of her family. He was no substitute for Hannah. Why couldn't it have been he who died? Hannah had so much to live for, whereas he… He batted that wicked thought away. No matter how black his future had seemed, he had never been tempted to take his own life. He was content enough with the life he led. The villagers avoided him and he had his dogs and his horses and his hawks: they provided all the company he needed.

Nathaniel resumed his seat, but did not draw his plate towards him again.

'What about Clara's nanny?' He remembered the woman from Hannah's last visit to Shiverstone. At least she was not a complete stranger. 'I assume she is here and will stay with Clara?'

His mother's gaze skittered past him. 'I am afraid not.

She has family in Gloucester and does not want to move so far away. You will need to appoint a new nanny and then, later, she will need a governess.'

He battled to hide his dismay, but some must have shown, for she continued, 'You must put Clara's needs first. She is two years old. What do you know about taking care of such a young child? Of any child? And Mrs Sharp has enough to do with running the Hall. You cannot expect her to take on more responsibility.'

*She's right. I know she's right...*and yet every fibre of his being rebelled against the notion of not one, but two, strangers coming into his home. He eyed his mother. *Perhaps...*

'And do not think I shall yield if you try to persuade me to raise Clara on your behalf.'

His mother—one step ahead as usual. He must accept that, once again, he had no choice.

'I will advertise for a governess,' he said. One person—surely he could cope with one person. Once she was used to his appearance, all would be well. He need not see much of her. 'Then Clara will not have to adapt to another person in her life later on. She needs consistency after losing her parents.'

Poor little soul. Unwanted by her own mother—an unfortunate girl in trouble—and now losing her adoptive parents. And she was a sweet little poppet. Too young to react with horror to his scars as other children had done in the past, Clara had accepted her uncle and she, in turn, had delighted him with her gurgles and her first attempts at speech. An unaccustomed tingle warmed his chest. She would be his. She might only be two, but she would provide some human contact apart from his servants.

'You must do as you deem right for Clara.' Mother's sceptical expression, however, suggested that she was completely aware of his real reason for choosing a governess rather than a nanny. 'And for darling Hannah.'

A lone tear spilled over and tracked down her lined

cheek. How had he never been aware of those wrinkles before? His mother had aged. Grief, he thought, did that to a person and poor Mother had faced more grief than most.

'I will,' he vowed.

He owed it to his sister, who had tackled her own heartbreak of trying and failing to give birth to a healthy baby with such dignity and grace. She had been besotted by Clara from the very first moment she held her in her arms and impotent anger raged through Nathaniel that she would now miss the joy of seeing her adopted daughter grow and mature. Hannah had been one of the few constants in his life since the fire that had taken his father and changed Nathaniel's life for ever. He would not let her down now. He would write to the editor of the *York Herald*, with instructions to run an advertisement for a trained governess who was willing to come and live at the Hall.

For the first time he felt a sliver of doubt—what sort of woman would agree to bury herself in such an isolated place?

Chapter One

Early November 1811

Grace Bertram breathed easier as she reached the edge of the dense woodland, with its mossy-trunked trees and its unfamiliar rustles and groans, and the barely glimpsed scurrying of invisible creatures through the undergrowth. The track she had followed from the village of Shiver-combe—past the church, across a meadow and a river, and then through that spooky wood—emerged on to the edge of bleak moorland and she stopped to catch her breath, and look around.

Moorland—or, more correctly, fells according to the local villagers who had tried so hard to dissuade her from venturing to Shiverstone Hall—rose ahead of her before merging mistily with the overcast sky. She could just about make out the slate roof and tall chimneys of a house squatting in a fold of land ahead, the only sign of human habitation in that forbidding landscape.

Grace's pulse accelerated in a fusion of anticipation and fear. That must be it. Shiverstone Hall. And there, beneath those glistening black slates, was Clara. Her baby, who now lived in this isolated place with—according to those same villagers—a man who was fearful to behold and who breathed fire and brimstone on any who ventured on to his land: the Marquess of Ravenwell. Grace would not…*could not*…allow those warnings to deter her. She had survived that creepy forest and she would survive Lord Ravenwell's wrath. She would not turn back from the task she had set herself two years ago.

She owed that much to the daughter she had given away at birth.

Grace swapped her portmanteau into her left hand and glanced down at her muddied half-boots in disgust. Her left foot already squelched in her boot and the right felt suspiciously damp too. What sort of *lord* lived out here in the middle of nowhere and did not even take the trouble to build a bridge over the river between the village and his house? An uncivilised sort, that was who, in Grace's opinion. There was a ford for horses and vehicles, but the only place for a person to cross the river was by using huge, wet, *slippery* rocks set in the riverbed as stepping stones. She was fortunate it was only her left foot that had been submerged.

Grace trudged on, muttering under her breath, still following the same track. At seventeen, and a pupil at a school for governesses, she'd had no choice but to give her baby away, but she had regretted it each and every day since then. She had promised herself that one day she would track her daughter down and make sure she was happy and loved and living the life she deserved. And now it was even more urgent that she find her daughter and make sure she was well cared for—and *wanted*—since her discovery that the couple who had adopted Clara as their own had perished in a carriage accident.

But doubts still plagued her as she walked, despite her resolve to see her mission through. She might be bold, but she was not stupid. What if this Marquess would not allow her to see Clara? What reason could she give him for seeking out the child? Not the truth. He would send her packing. No. She must find another reason.

And what if Clara is not happy and loved?

What on earth could she—a nineteen-year-old newly trained governess with no home and little money in her pocket—actually *do*? She pushed the thought aside with an impatient *tut*.

She would deal with that when and if it became necessary.

She plodded on, skirting the worst of the puddles that dotted the track. Finally, she crested the rise ahead of her and there it was. She paused. It was bigger than that first glimpse had suggested, but its appearance—grim and grey with creepers adorning the walls—and location were hardly that of a dwelling in which one might expect a wealthy lord to reside.

A shrill cry echoed through the air and she whirled around.

Nothing.

At least she wasn't still in the forest—that unearthly sound would then indeed have unnerved her. She scanned the bleak landscape, but nothing moved. Another plaintive cry brought her heart into her mouth. She looked up and caught sight of a huge bird—bigger than any she had ever seen—gliding and soaring. It then circled once, before pitching into a dive: a dark blur silhouetted against the low clouds until it disappeared behind the hill that rose behind the house.

Grace swallowed, hunched her shoulders, swapped her portmanteau over again, and soldiered on. Her upbringing at her uncle's house in Wiltshire and, since the age of nine, at Madame Dubois's School for Young Ladies in Salisbury had ill-prepared her for such nature in the raw.

Twenty minutes later the track passed through a gateway in a stone wall, at which point the surface was reinforced with gravel. A broad drive curved away to the left, only to then sweep around and across the front of Shiverstone Hall. A footpath, paved with stone setts, led from this point in a straight line to the house, bisecting a lawn. Grace followed the path until, directly opposite the front door, it rejoined the gravelled carriageway.

She paused, her heart thudding as she scanned the stonebuilt Hall with its blank, forbidding windows, and its massive timber door, just visible in the gloomy depths of a central, gabled porch.

There was no sound. Anywhere. Even the air was still and silent.

It is as though the house is lying in wait for me—an enchanted castle, sleeping until the fairy princess awakens it and frees the inhabitants. Or a monster's lair, awaiting the unwary traveller.

Grace bit her lip, shivering a little, castigating herself for such fanciful thoughts, worthy of one of those Gothic novels Isabel used to smuggle into school and then pass around for her awestruck friends to read. A wave of homesickness hit Grace at the thought of Isabel, Joanna, and Rachel. Her dearest friends. What were they doing now? Were they happy? Grace shook her head free of her memories: the three friends she might never see again and her heartache when the time had come for her to leave Madame Dubois's school. For a few years she had belonged and she had been loved, valued, and wanted—a rare feeling in her life thus far.

Resisting the urge to flee back the way she had come, Grace crossed the carriageway, wincing as the crunch of the gravel beneath her boots split the silence. She stepped through the arched entrance to the porch and hesitated, staring with trepidation at the door looming above her.

I have come this far...I cannot give up now.

She sucked in a deep breath and reached for the huge iron knocker. She would make her enquiries, set her mind at rest and return to the village. She had no wish to walk through that forest as the light began to fade, as it would do all too early at this time of year. She only had to knock. And state her business. Still she hesitated, her fingers curled around the cold metal. It felt stiff, as though it was rarely used. She released it, nerves fluttering.

Before she could gather her courage again, a loud bark, followed by a sudden rush of feet, had her spinning on the spot. A pack of dogs, all colours and sizes, leapt and woofed and panted around her. Heart in mouth, she backed against the door, her bag clutched up to her chest for protection. A pair of wet, muddy paws were planted in the region of her stomach, and a grinning mouth, full of teeth and lolling tongue, was thrust at her face, snuffling and sniffing. A whimper of terror escaped Grace despite her efforts to silence it. In desperation, she bent her leg at the knee and drummed her heel against the door behind her. Surely the human inhabitants of this Godforsaken place couldn't be as scary as the animals?

After what felt like an hour, she heard the welcome sound of bolts being drawn and the creak of hinges as the door was opened.

'Get down, Brack!' The voice was deep and brooked no disobedience. 'Get away, the lot of you.'

Grace turned slowly. She looked up…and up. And swallowed. Hard. A powerfully built man towered over her, his face averted, only the left side of it visible. His dark brown hair was unfashionably long, his shoulders and chest broad, and his expression—what she could see of it—grim.

She could not have run if she wanted to, her knees trembled so. Besides, there was nowhere to run to, not with those dogs lurking nearby.

'You're late,' he growled.

Time seemed to slow. The man continued to not quite look at Grace as her brain examined and rejected all the truthful responses at her disposal.

'I am sorry,' was all she said.

'You look too young to be a governess. I expected some-one older.'

Governess? Are there other children here apart from Clara? The parallels with her own life sent a shiver skittering down her spine. She knew the reality of growing up with cousins who did not accept you as part of the family.

'I am fully trained,' Grace replied, lifting her chin.

Anticipation spiralled as the implications of the man's words sank in. If Lord Ravenwell was expecting a governess, why should it not be her? She was trained. If his lordship thought her suitable, she could stay. She would see Clara every day and could see for herself that her daughter was happy and loved. That she was not viewed as a burden, as Grace had been.

The man's gaze lowered, and lingered. Grace glanced down and saw the muddy streaks upon her grey cloak.

'That was your dog's fault,' she pointed out, indignantly.

The man grunted and stood aside, opening the door fully, gesturing to her to come in. Gathering her courage, Grace stepped past him, catching the whiff of fresh air and leather and the tang of shaving soap. She took two steps and froze.

The hall in which she stood was cavernous, reaching up two storeys into the arched, beamed roof. The walls were half-panelled in dark wood and, on the left-hand side, a staircase rose to a half-landing and then turned to climb across the back wall to a galleried landing that overlooked the hall on three sides. There, halfway up the second flight of stairs, a small face—eyes huge, mouth drooping—peered through the wooden balustrade. Grace's heart lurched. She moved forward as if in a dream, her attention entirely focussed on that face.

Clara.

It must be. Love flooded every cell of Grace's being as she crossed the hall, tears blurring her vision. She was real.

A living little person. The memory—a tiny newborn baby, taken too quickly from her arms—could now be replaced by this little angel. A forlorn angel, she realised, recognising the sadness in that dear little face, the desolation in those huge eyes. Given away by her birth mother and now orphaned and condemned to be raised by—

Grace spun to face the man, who had followed her into the hall. His head jerked to one side, but not before she glimpsed the ravaged skin of his right cheek, half-concealed by the hair that hung around his face. Impatiently, she dismissed his appearance. The only thing that mattered was to ensure her daughter was properly cared for.

'Who are you?'

A scowl lowered the man's forehead. 'I am the master of this house. Who are *you*?'

The master. Clara's uncle. The Marquess.

Well, title or not, scarred or not, you will not frighten me.

Grace drew herself up to her full five-foot-three. 'Grace Bertram.'

'Bertram? I don't… You are not who I expected—'

'I came instead.'

'Oh.' Lord Ravenwell hesitated, then continued gruffly, 'Follow me. I'll need to know something about you if I'm to entrust my niece to your care.'

Grace's heart skipped a beat. This was the moment she should tell him the truth, but she said nothing. Could she…*dare* she…follow her heart? She needed a job and it seemed, by some miracle, there might be a position for her here.

'Clara—' Ravenwell beckoned to the child on the stairs '—come with me.'

Clara bumped down the stairs on her bottom and Grace committed every second to memory, her heart swelling until it felt like it might burst from her chest. She blinked hard to disperse the moisture that stung her eyes.

'Come, poppet.'

The Marquess held out his hand. Clara shuffled across the hall, feet dragging, her reluctance palpable. She reached her uncle and put her tiny hand into his as her other thumb crept into her mouth and she cast a shy, sideways glance at Grace. She looked so tiny and so delicate next to this huge bear of a man. Did she fear him?

'Good girl.'

The Marquess did not sound cruel or unkind, but Grace's heart ached for her sad little girl. At only two years old, she would not fully understand what had happened and why her life had changed so drastically, but she would still grieve and she must miss her mama and her papa. In that moment Grace knew that she would do everything in her power to stay at this place and to care for Clara, her daughter's happiness her only concern.

She felt Ravenwell's gaze upon her and tore her attention from Clara. She must now impress him so thoroughly he could not help but offer her the post of governess.

'You had better take those boots off, or Mrs Sharp will throw a fit.'

Grace glanced down at her filthy boots and felt her cheeks heat as she noticed the muddy footprints she had left on previously spotless flagstones.

So much for impressing him.

'Mrs Sharp?' She sat on a nearby chair and unbuttoned her boots.

'My housekeeper.'

Grace scanned the hall. Every wooden surface had been polished until it gleamed. She breathed in, smelling the unmistakable sweet scent of beeswax. Appearances could be deceptive, she mused, recalling her first view of the Hall and its unwelcoming exterior. Although…looking around again, she realised the impeccably clean hall still felt as bleak as the fells that rose behind the house. There was no fire in the massive stone fireplace and there were no homely touches: no paintings, vases, or ornaments to brighten the place. No rug to break up the cold expanse of stone floor. No furniture apart from one console table—incongruously small in that huge space—and the simple wooden chair upon which she now sat. It lacked a woman's touch, giving it the atmosphere of an institution rather than a home. Grace darted a look at the Marquess. Was he married? She had not thought to ask that question before she had travelled the length of the country to find her daughter.

She placed her boots neatly side by side next to the chair and stood up, shivers spreading up her legs and across her back as the chill of the flagstones penetrated her woollen stockings.

Ravenwell gestured to a door that led off the hall.

'Wait in there.'

Chapter Two

Grace entered a large sitting room. Like the entrance hall, it was sparsely furnished. There were matching fireplaces at each end of the room—one lit, one not—and the walls were papered in dark green and ivory stripes above the same dark wood panelling as lined the hall. On either side of the lit fireplace stood a wing-back chair and next to each chair stood a highly polished side table. A larger table, with two ladder-back wooden chairs, was set in front of the middle of three tall windows. At the far end of the room, near the unlit fireplace, were two large shapes draped in holland covers. Her overall impression of the room was of darkness and disuse, despite the fire burning in the grate.

This was a house. A dwelling. Well cared for, but not loved. It was not cold in the room and she stood upon polished floorboards rather than flagstones, but she nevertheless suppressed another shiver.

Lord Ravenwell soon returned, alone and carrying a letter.

'Sit down.'

He gestured at the chair to the right of the hearth and Grace crossed in front of the fire to sit in it. Ravenwell sat in the opposite chair, angling it away from the fire, thus ensuring, Grace realised, that the damaged side of his face

would be neither highlighted by firelight nor facing her.
His actions prompted a desire in her to see his scarred skin
properly. Was it really as horrific as he seemed to believe?

'Why did the other woman—' Ravenwell consulted the
letter '—Miss Browne, not come? I expected her three
days ago.'

His comment sparked a memory. 'I believe she found
the area too isolated.'

The villagers had regaled her with gleeful tales of the
other young lady who had listened to their stories, headed
out from the village, taken one look at the dark, ancient
woodland through which she must walk to reach Shiverstone Hall and fled.

'And did our isolation not deter you?'

'I would not be here if it did.'

His head turned and he looked directly at her. His eyes
were dark, deep-set, brooding. His mouth a firm line. On
the right side of his face, in a broad slash from jaw to temple, his skin was white and puckered, in stark contrast to
the tan that coloured the rest of his face. Grace tried not to
stare. Instead, she allowed her gaze to drift over his wide
shoulders and chest and down to his muscular thighs, en-
cased in buckskin breeches and boots. His sheer size intimidated her. How furious would he be if he discovered
her deception? Her heartbeat accelerated, thumping in her
chest, and she sought to distract herself.

'Will Mrs Sharp not scold *you* for wearing boots indoors?' she said, before she could curb her tongue.

His shoulders flexed and a muffled snort escaped him.
'As I said, I am the master. And *my* boots,' he added point-
edly, 'are clean.'

Chastised, Grace tucked her stockinged feet out of
sight under her chair. She was in an unknown place with
a strange man she hoped would employ her. This was not
school. Or even her uncle's house, where she had grown
up. She was no longer a child and she ought to pick her

words with more care. She was a responsible adult now, with her own way to make in the world. Ravenwell had already commented on her youthfulness. She must not give him a reason to think her unsuitable to take care of Clara.

She peeped at him again and saw that the back of his right hand, in which he held the letter, was also scarred.

Like Caroline's. One of her fellow pupils had similar ravaged skin on her legs, caused when her dress had gone up in flames when she had wandered too close to an open fire as a young child. She was lucky she had survived.

Is that what happened to Ravenwell? Was he burned in a fire?

As if he felt her interest, the Marquess placed the letter on a side table and folded his arms, his right hand tucked out of sight, before bombarding Grace with questions.

'How old are you?'

'Nineteen, my lord.'

'Where did you train?'

'At Madame Dubois's School for Young Ladies in Salisbury.'

'Where are you from?'

'I grew up in my uncle's house in Wiltshire.'

'What about your parents?'

'They died when I was a baby. My uncle and aunt took me in.'

Ravenwell unfolded his arms and leaned forward, his forearms resting on his thighs, focussing even more intently on her. Grace battled to meet his eyes and not to allow her gaze to drift to his scars. It was just damaged skin. She must not stare and make him uncomfortable.

His voice gentled. 'So you know what it is like to be orphaned?'

'Yes.'

It is lonely. It is being second-best, unimportant, overlooked. It is knowing you are different and never feeling as though you belong.

'I do not remember my parents. I was still a babe in arms when they died.'

Like Clara, when I gave her away.

He sat back. 'I hope Clara will remember her parents, but I am not sure she will. She is only two.'

'She will if you talk to her about them and keep their memory alive,' Grace said. 'My uncle and aunt never spoke to me of my parents. They had quarrelled over something years before and they only took me in out of what they considered to be their Christian duty.'

Silence reigned as Ravenwell stared, frowning, into the fire. Grace knitted the strands of her thoughts together until she realised there were gaps in her understanding.

'You speak only of Clara,' she said. 'You said you will need to know about me if you are to entrust her to my care. Is she not rather young, or do you and Lady Ravenwell have need of a governess for your other children, perhaps?'

Her question jerked Ravenwell from his contemplation of the flames. 'There is no Lady Ravenwell. Clara would be your sole charge.'

'Would a nanny, or a nursery maid, not be more suitable?' The words were out before Grace could stop them. *What are you trying to do? Talk him out of employing you?*

Ravenwell scowled. 'Are you not capable of looking after such a young child? Or perhaps you think it beneath you, as a trained governess?'

'Yes, I am capable and, no, it is not beneath me. I simply wondered—'

'I do not want Clara to grow fond of someone and then have to adjust to a new face in a few years' time. She has faced enough disruption. Do you want the position or not?'

'Yes…yes, of course.' Grace's heart soared. How could life be any sweeter?

Ravenwell was eyeing her, frowning. 'It will be lonely out here, for such a young woman. Are you sure?'

'I am sure.'

Joy bubbled through her. *Real* joy. Not the forced smiles and manufactured jests behind which she had concealed her aching heart and her grief from her friends. Now, her jaw clenched in her effort to contain her beaming smile, but she knew, even without the aid of a mirror, her delight must shine from her eyes. She could not fake nonchalance, despite Madame Dubois's constant reminders that unseemly displays of emotion by governesses were not appreciated by their employers.

'I will fetch Clara and introduce you.'

Grace's heart swelled. She could not wait to speak to Clara. To touch her.

Lord Ravenwell stood, then hesitated and held out his hand. 'Give me your cloak. I will ask Mrs Sharp to brush it for you.'

Startled by this unexpected courtesy, Grace removed her grey cloak—warm and practical, and suitable garb for a governess—and handed it to him. Doubts swirled. Until this moment she had not fully considered that accepting the role of governess to Clara actually meant becoming part of this household and living here with Ravenwell. She thought she had learned her lesson of acting first and thinking about the consequences second, but perhaps, deep down, she was still the impulsive girl she had always been. Her entire focus had been on the lure of staying with Clara. She swallowed. Ravenwell—who had not smiled once since her arrival and who appeared to live as a recluse in this cold, isolated house—was now her employer. This terse, scowling man was now part of her future.

It will be worth it, just to be with Clara. And what kind of life will my poor little angel have if I do not stay?

There was no question that she would accept the post, even if she had not considered all the implications. She would bring sunshine and laughter and love to her daughter's life. Clara would never doubt she was loved and wanted. Grace would make sure of it.

'How many servants are there here?' she asked.

'Three indoors and two men outdoors. We live quietly.'

And with that, he strode from the room, leaving Grace to ponder this unexpected path her life had taken. What would Miss Fanworth say if she could see Grace now? Doubt assailed her at the thought of her favourite teacher. It had been Miss Fanworth who had come to her aid on that terrifying night when she had given birth, Miss Fanworth who had advised Grace to give her baby up for adoption and Miss Fanworth who had taken Grace aside on the day she left the school for the final time and revealed the name of the couple her baby daughter had been given to.

'It is up to you what you choose to do with this information, Grace, but I thought you deserved to know.'

Grace had left school that day, full of determination to find the people who had adopted her daughter, knowing nothing more than their name and that they lived in Gloucestershire. When she eventually tracked them down, it had been too late. They were dead and Grace's daughter had been taken to live with her uncle and guardian, the Marquess of Ravenwell.

Undeterred, Grace had travelled to Ravenwell's country seat, south of Harrogate, where—after some persistent questioning of the locals—she had discovered that the Marquess lived here, at Shiverstone Hall. And, finally, here she was. She had succeeded. She had found her baby.

She could almost hear Miss Fanworth's measured tones in her head: *'Do take care, Grace, dear. You are treading on very dangerous ice.'*

Those imagined words of caution were wise. She must indeed take care: her heart quailed again at the thought of the forbidding Marquess discovering her secret.

I am not really doing wrong. I am a governess and he needs a governess. And I will protect Clara with the last breath of my body. How can that be wrong?

The door opened, jolting her from her thoughts. Raven-well entered, walking slowly, holding Clara by the hand as she toddled beside him, a rag doll clutched in the crook of her arm.

'Clara,' he said, as they halted before Grace. 'This is Miss Bertram. She has come to take care of you.'

A tide of emotion swept through Grace, starting deep down inside and rising…swelling…washing over her, gathering into a tight, aching knot in her chest. Her throat constricted painfully. She dropped to her knees before her little girl, drinking her in…her light brown curly hair, her gold-green eyes—*the image of mine*—her plump cheeks and sweet rosebud lips.

Oh, God! Oh, God! Thank you! Thank you!

She reached out and touched Clara's hand, marvelling at the softness of her skin. How big that hand had grown since the moment she had taken her baby's tiny fist in hers and pressed her lips to it for the last time. She had tucked away those few precious memories, knowing they must last a lifetime. And now, she had a second chance.

She sucked in a deep breath, desperately trying to suppress her emotion. Ravenwell had released Clara's hand and moved aside. Grace could sense his eyes on her. Watching. Judging.

'What a pretty dolly.' Her voice hitched; she willed the tears not to come. 'Does she have a name?'

Clara's thumb crept into her mouth as she stared up at Grace with huge eyes—too solemn, surely, for such a young child?

'She has barely spoken since she lost her parents.'

Powerless to resist the urge, Grace opened her arms and drew Clara close, hugging her, breathing in her sweet little-girl scent as wispy curls tickled her neck and cheek.

She glanced up at Ravenwell, watching her with a puz-

zled frown. She dragged in a steadying breath. She must
not excite his suspicions.

'I know what it is l-like to be orphaned,' she reminded
him. 'But she has us. W-we will help her to be happy again.'

She rubbed Clara's back gently, rocking her and revelling in the solid little body pressed against hers. She was
rewarded with a slight sigh from the child as she relaxed
and wriggled closer. The tears welled. She was powerless
to stop them. A sob shook her. Then another.

'Are you crying?'

The deep rumble penetrated Grace's fascination with
this perfect being in her arms. Reluctantly she looked up,
seeing Ravenwell mistily through drowning eyes. He was
offering her his hand. Grace blinked and, as the tears dis-
persed, she saw the handkerchief he proffered. She reached
for it and dabbed her eyes, gulping, feeling a fool.

She prised her arms loose, releasing Clara. There would
be plenty of time to hold her, as long as Ravenwell did not
now change his mind about employing her. Grace's head
rang with Madame Dubois's warnings on the necessity of
staying in control of one's emotions at all times.

*It's all very well for Madame. She hasn't a sensitive
bone in her body.*

The words surfaced, unbidden, in Grace's mind but,
deep down, she knew she was being unfair to the principal of her old school. If rumour was true—and Miss Fanworth's words on the day Joanna had left the school, as
well as Rachel's discovery of Madame weeping over a pile
of old letters suggested it was—Madame had suffered her
own tragedies in the past. Thinking of the stern Madame
Dubois steadied Grace. The knowledge she had let herself
down set her insides churning.

Would Ravenwell be thoroughly disgusted by her display of emotion? Would he send her away? She pushed herself—somewhat inelegantly—to her feet, hoping she had
not disgraced herself too much. She must say something.

Offer some sort of explanation. Not the truth, though. She could not possibly tell him the truth. She mopped her eyes again, and handed him back his handkerchief. His expression did not bode well.

'Th-thank you,' she said. 'I apologise for giving way to my emotions. I—'

Her heart almost seized as she felt a small hand creep into hers. Clara was by her side and, with her other hand, she was offering her dolly to Grace. Tears threatened again and Grace blinked furiously, took the doll, and crouched down by the child, smiling at her.

'Thank you, Clara. N-now I can see your dolly properly, I can see she is even prettier than I first thought—almost as p-pretty as you.'

She stroked Clara's satiny cheek and tickled her under the chin. She was rewarded with a shy smile. Heart soaring, Grace regained her feet and faced the Marquess, holding his gaze, strength and determination stiffening every fibre of her being. She would give him no opportunity to change his mind. She was staying, and that was that.

'As I was about to explain, I was overcome by the similarities between Clara's situation and my own as a child and also by relief at having secured such an excellent position.' She raised her chin. 'It was an unforgivable lapse. It will not happen again, I promise.'

Chapter Three

Nathaniel felt his brows lower in yet another frown and hastily smoothed his expression, thrusting his doubts about Grace Bertram aside. Would he not harbour doubts about anyone who applied for the role of governess simply because, deep down, he still rebelled at the idea of a stranger living under his roof?

He loathed this sense of being swept along by an unstoppable tide of events, but, from the very moment he had read his mother's letter, he had known his fate was sealed. He was Clara's legal guardian and he must...no, he *wanted* to do what was right for her, both for her own sake and for Hannah's. The familiar ache of loss filled his chest and squeezed his throat, reminding him it was not mere obligation that drove him, but his love for Hannah and David, and for their child. He had vowed to make Clara's childhood as happy and carefree as possible, but the three weeks since his return from Ravenwell had confirmed he needed help.

But is she the right woman for the job?

Those doubts pervaded his thoughts once more.

There were all kinds of very good reasons why he should not employ Grace Bertram as Clara's governess. She was too young and, he had silently admitted as he had watched her with Clara, too pretty. Mrs Sharp would disapprove on those grounds alone—his housekeeper had made no secret of her opinion he should seek a mature woman for Clara's governess. Nathaniel knew her concern was more for his sake than for Clara's and it irritated him to be thought so weak-willed he could not withstand a pretty face in his household. He had learned the hard way to protect his heart and his pride from ridicule and revulsion.

Miss Bertram also wore her heart on her sleeve in a manner most unsuited to a woman to whom he must entrust not only his niece's well-being but also her moral character. And, in the short time she had been here, she had demonstrated an impulsiveness in her speech that gave him pause. Did she lack the sense to know some thoughts were best left unsaid, particularly to a prospective employer? Take his boots off indeed! But, in fairness, this *would* be her first post since completing her training and she was bound to be nervous.

There were also very compelling reasons why he would not send Grace Bertram packing. She was pleasant and she was warm-hearted. With a young child, that must be a bonus. He refused to relinquish the care and upbringing of his two-year-old niece to a strict governess who could not—or would not—show her affection. More importantly, Clara appeared to like Miss Bertram. Besides, if he was honest, there *was* no one else. He had no other option. He had interviewed two women whilst he was still at Ravenwell Manor, hoping to find someone immediately. Neither wanted the job. And that other woman, Miss Browne, had not even arrived for her interview.

He eyed Grace Bertram as she faced him, head high. Despite her youth, he recognised her unexpected core of steel as she threw her metaphorical gauntlet upon the ground. She wanted to stay. Her eyes shone with determination as she held his gaze.

She does not recoil at my appearance.

She had not flinched once, nor stared, nor even averted her gaze. It was as though his scars did not matter to her.

Of course they do not, you fool. You are interviewing her for the post of a governess, not a wife or a mistress.

That thought decided him. They would spend little time together, but her acceptance of his appearance was a definite point in her favour.

'Come,' he said. 'I will introduce you to Mrs Sharp and she will show you around the house.'

He swung Clara up on to his shoulders, revelling in her squeal of delight, and led the way to the kitchen, awareness of the young woman following silently at his heels prickling under his skin. He needed to be alone; he needed time to adjust. By the time they reached the door into the kitchen, his nerves were strained so tight he feared one wrong word from his housekeeper or from Miss Bertram might snap them with disastrous consequences. He pushed the door wide, ducking his knees as he walked through the opening, to protect Clara's head. Mrs Sharp paused in the act of slicing apples.

'Was she suitable, milord?'

Miss Bertram was still behind Nathaniel; he stepped aside to allow her to enter the kitchen.

'Yes. Mrs Sharp—Miss Bertram.'

Mrs Sharp's lips thinned as she looked the new governess up and down. 'Where are your shoes?'

Nathaniel felt rather than saw Miss Bertram's sideways glance at him. He should ease her way with Mrs Sharp, but he felt the urge to be gone. Miss Bertram must learn to have no expectations of him: he had his own life to live and she would get used to hers. He lifted Clara from his shoulders, silently excusing himself for his lack of manners. She was only a governess, after all. He would be paying her wages and providing her with food and board. He need not consider her feelings.

'I'll leave you to show Miss Bertram the house: where she is to sleep, the child's new quarters and so forth.'

He turned abruptly and strode from the kitchen, quashing the regret that snaked through him at the realisation of how much less he would now see of Clara. The past few weeks, although worrying and time-consuming, had also revived the simple pleasure of human company, even though Clara was only two. She'd been restless at night and he'd put her to sleep in the room next to his, needing to know someone would hear her and go to her if she cried. Although the Sharps and Alice, the young housemaid who had travelled back with him from Ravenwell, had helped, he could not expect them to care for Clara's welfare as he did. Now, that would no longer be necessary. A suite of rooms had already been prepared for when a governess was appointed and Clara would sleep in her new room— at the far side of the house from his—tonight.

He snagged his greatcoat from a hook by the back door and shrugged into it as he strode along the path to the barns. The dogs heard him coming and milled around him, leaping, tails wagging frantically, panting in excitement.

'Steady on, lads,' he muttered, his agitation settling as he smoothed the head of first one, then another. His favourite, Brack—a black-and-tan hound of indeterminate breeding—shouldered his way through the pack to butt at Nathaniel's hand, demanding attention. He paused, taking Brack's head between his hands and kneading his mismatched ears—one pendulous and shaggy, the other a mere stump following a bite when he was a pup—watching as the dog half-closed his eyes in ecstasy. Dogs were so simple. They offered unconditional love. He carried on walking, entering the barn. Ned, his groom, emerged from the feed store at the far end.

'Be riding, milord?' Ned was a simple man of few words who lived alone in a loft above the carriage house.

'Not now, Ned. How's the mare?'

'She'll do.' One of the native ponies they kept for working the sheep that grazed on the fells had a swollen fetlock.

Nathaniel entered the stall where she was tethered, smoothing a hand down her sleek shoulder and on down her foreleg.

'Steady, lass. Steady, Peg,' he murmured. There was still a hint of heat in the fetlock, but it was nowhere near as fiery as it had been the previous day. He straightened. 'That feels better,' he said. 'Keep on with the good work. I'm off up to the mews.'

'Right you are, milord.'

The dogs, calmer now, trotted by his side as he walked past the barn and turned on to the track that led up to the mews where he kept his birds, cared for by Tam. There was no sign of Tam, who lived in a cottage a few hundred yards further along the track with his wife, Annie. The enclosures that housed his falcons—three peregrine falcons, a buzzard, and a kestrel—came into view and Nathaniel cast a critical eye over the occupants as he approached. They looked, without exception, bright-eyed, their feathers glossy, as they sat on their perches. He had flown two of them earlier and now they were fed up and settled.

Loath to disturb the birds, he did not linger, but rounded the enclosures to enter the old barn against which they were built, shutting the door behind him to keep the dogs out. Light filtered in through gaps in the walls and the two small, unglazed windows, penetrating the gloomy interior. A flap and a shuffle sounded from the large enclosure built in one corner, where a golden eagle—a young female, they thought, owing to her size—perched on a thick branch.

The eagle had been found with a broken wing by Tam's cousin, who had sent her down from Scotland, knowing of Nathaniel's expertise with birds of prey. Between them, he and Tam had nursed the bird back to health and were now teaching her to fly again. Nathaniel had named her Amber, even though he knew he must eventually release her back into the wild. His other birds had been raised in captivity and would have no chance of survival on their own. Amber, however, was different and, much as Nathaniel longed to keep her, he knew it would be unfair to cage her when she should be soaring free over the mountains and glens of her homeland.

Nathaniel selected a chunk of meat from a plate of fresh rabbit on Tam's bench, then crossed to the cage, unbolted the door, and reached inside. His soft call alerted the bird, who swivelled her head and fixed her piercing, golden eyes on Nathaniel's hand. With a deft flick of his wrist, Nathaniel lobbed the meat to the eagle, who snatched it out of the air and gulped it down.

Nathaniel withdrew his arm and bolted the door, but did not move away. He should return to the house. He had business to deal with: correspondence to read and to write, bills to pay, decisions to make over the countless issues that arose concerning his estates. He rested his forehead against the upright wooden slats of Amber's cage. The bird contemplated him, unblinking. At least she wasn't as petrified as she had been in the first few days following her journey from Scotland.

'I know how you feel,' he whispered to the eagle. 'Life changes in an instant and we must adjust as best we can.'

The turning point in his life had been the fire that destroyed the original Ravenwell Manor. It had been rebuilt, of course. It was easy to restore a building—not so easy to repair a life changed beyond measure. He touched his damaged cheek, the scarred skin tight and bumpy beneath his fingertips. And it was impossible to restore a lost life. The familiar mix of guilt and desolation washed over him at the memory of his father.

And now another turning point in his life had been reached with Hannah's death.

As hard as he strove to keep the world at bay, it seemed the Fates deemed otherwise. His hands clenched, but he controlled his urge to slam his fists against the bars of the cage—being around animals and birds had instilled in him the need to control his emotions. He pushed away from the bars and headed for the door, turning his anger upon himself. Why was he skulking out here, when there was work to be done? He would shut himself in his book room and try to ignore this latest intrusion into his life.

Grace winced as the door banged shut behind the Marquess. She tried not to resent that he had left her here alone to deal with Mrs Sharp, who looked as disapproving as Madame Dubois at her most severe, with the same silver-streaked dark hair, scraped back into a bun. Grace tried to mask her nervousness as the housekeeper's piercing grey eyes continued to rake her. Clara, meanwhile, had toddled forward and was attempting to clamber up on a chair by the table. Grace moved without conscious thought to help her. Clara didn't appear to be intimidated by the housekeeper, so neither would she.

'Well? Your shoes, Miss Bertram?'

'His lordship requested that I remove them when I came inside,' Grace said. 'They were muddy.' She looked at the bowl of apples. They would discolour if not used shortly. 'May I help you finish peeling those before you show me where my room is? I should not like them to spoil.'

Wordlessly, Mrs Sharp passed her a knife and an un-peeled apple. They worked in silence for several minutes, then Mrs Sharp disappeared through a door off the kitchen and re-emerged, carrying a ball of uncooked pastry in one hand and a pie dish in the other. As she set these on the table, she reached into a pocket of her apron and withdrew a biscuit, which she handed to Clara, who had been sitting quietly—too quietly, in Grace's opinion—on her chair. Clara took the biscuit and raised it to her mouth. Grace reached across and stayed her hand.

'What do you say to Mrs Sharp, Clara?'

Huge green eyes contemplated her. Grace crouched down beside Clara's chair. 'You must say thank you when someone gives you something, Clara. Come, now, let me hear you say *Thank you*.'

Clara's gaze travelled slowly to Mrs Sharp, who had paused in the act of sprinkling flour on to the table and her rolling pin.

'Did his lordship not say? She has barely said a word since she came here.'

'Yes. He told me, but I shall start as I mean to go on. Clara must be encouraged to find her voice again,' Grace said. 'Come on, sweetie, can you say, *Thank you*?'

Clara shook her head, her curls bouncing around her ears. Then, as Grace still prevented her eating the biscuit, her mouth opened. The sound that emerged was nowhere near a word, it was more of a sigh, but Grace immediately released Clara's hand, saying, 'Clever girl, Clara. That was nice of you to thank Mrs Sharp. You may now eat your biscuit.'

She glanced at Mrs Sharp, but the housekeeper's head was bent as she concentrated on rolling out the pastry and she did not respond. Grace bit back her irritation. It wouldn't have hurt the woman to praise Clara or to respond to her. But she held her tongue, wary of further stirring the housekeeper's hostility.

Once the apple pie was in the oven, Mrs Sharp led the way from the kitchen. They went upstairs first—Grace carrying Clara—then crossed the galleried landing and turned into a dark corridor, lit only by a window at the far end.

'This is your bedchamber.'

Grace walked through the door Mrs Sharp indicated into a plain room containing a bed, a massive wardrobe and a sturdy washstand. The curtains were half-drawn across the windows, rendering the room as gloomy and unwelcoming as the rest of the house. Grace's portmanteau was already in the room, by the foot of the bed.

'Who brought this up?' she asked, bending to put Clara down. The thought of the burly Lord Ravenwell bringing her bag upstairs and into her bedchamber set strange feelings stirring deep inside her.

'Sharp. My husband.'

'So he works in the house, too?'

'Yes.'

Thoroughly annoyed by now, Grace refused to be intimidated by the older woman's clipped replies.

'His lordship mentioned three inside servants and two outside,' she said. 'Who else is there apart from you and your husband?'

A breath of exasperation hissed through Mrs Sharp's teeth. 'Indoors, there's me and Sharp, and Alice, the housemaid. She's only been here three weeks. His lordship brought her back with him and Miss Clara from Ravenwell, to help me with the chores.

'Outside, there's the men who care for his lordship's animals. Ned is unmarried and lives in quarters above the carriage house. Tam lives in a cottage on the estate. His wife, Annie, spins wool from the estate sheep and helps me on laundry days.

'Now, I have dinner to prepare. I don't have time for all these questions.' She headed for the door. 'Hurry along. There's more to show you before we're finished.'

'I shall just find my shoes.'

Her stockinged feet were thoroughly chilled again, after standing in the stone-flagged kitchen. Ignoring another hiss from the housekeeper, Grace unclasped her bag and pulled out her sturdy shoes, part of the uniform deemed by Madame Dubois to be suitable for a governess, along with high-necked, long-sleeved, unadorned gowns, of which she had two, one in grey and one in brown.

She hurried to put on her shoes whilst Mrs Sharp tapped her foot by the door. As soon as Grace was done, Mrs Sharp disappeared, her shoes clacking out her annoyance as she marched along the wooden-floored corridor. Grace scooped Clara up and followed.

'This is the eastern end of the house,' the housekeeper said, opening the next door, 'which will be your domain upstairs. Your bedchamber you've seen, this is the child's room—there's a door between the two, as you can see. Then there's a small sitting room, through that door opposite, for your own use, and the room at the far end will eventually be the schoolroom but, for now, it will be somewhere Miss Clara can play without disturbing his lordship.'

All the rooms were furnished in a similar style to Grace's bedchamber and they felt chilly and unwelcoming as a result. Clara deserved better and Grace vowed to make the changes necessary to provide a much cosier home for her.

'Is his lordship wealthy?'

Mrs Sharp glared. 'And why is that any business of yours, young lady?'

Chapter Four

Too late, Grace realised how her question might be misconstrued by the clearly disapproving housekeeper.

'No…no…I did not mean…' She paused, her cheeks burning with mortification. 'I merely meant…I should like to make these rooms a little more cheery. For Clara's sake.'

Mrs Sharp stiffened. 'I will have you know this house is spotless!'

'I can see that, Mrs Sharp. I meant no offence. You do an excellent job.' She would ask the Marquess. Surely he could not be as difficult to deal with as his housekeeper? 'Perhaps you would show me the rest of the house now?'

They retraced their steps to the head of the staircase. 'His lordship's rooms are along there, plus two guest bedchambers.' Mrs Sharp pointed to the far side of the landing, her tone discouraging. 'You will have no need to turn in that direction. Alice, Sharp, and I have our quarters in the attic rooms. I will show you the rooms on the ground floor you have not yet seen and then I must get back to my kitchen. The dinner needs my attention and Miss Clara will want supper before she goes to bed.'

Grace followed Mrs Sharp to the hall below, helping Clara to descend the stairs. She bit her lip as she saw the trail of mud from the front door to where she had left her half-boots by the only chair in the hall and was thankful the housekeeper did not mention the mess. The longcase clock in the hall struck half past four as Mrs Sharp hurried Grace around the rest of the ground floor: the drawing room—as she called it—where Ravenwell had interviewed her, a large dining room crammed with furniture shrouded in more holland covers, a small, empty sitting room and a morning parlour furnished with a dining table and six chairs where, she was told, Lord Ravenwell ate his meals.

Grace wondered, but did not like to ask, where she would dine. With Clara in the nursery suite? In the kitchen with the other servants? Clara was flagging and Grace picked her up. The house was, as her first impression had suggested, sparse and cold but clean. She itched to inject some light and warmth into the place, but realised she must tread very carefully where the prickly housekeeper was concerned.

They reached the final door off the hall, to the right of the front door. Clara had grown sleepy and heavy in Grace's arms.

'This,' Mrs Sharp said, as she opened the door and ushered Grace into the room, 'is the book room.'

Grace's gaze swept the room, lined with glass-fronted bookcases, and arrested at the sight of Lord Ravenwell, glowering at her from behind a desk set at the far end, between the fireplace and a window.

From behind her, Mrs Sharp continued, 'It is where— oh!' She grabbed Grace's arm and pulled her back. 'Beg pardon, milord. We'll leave you in peace.'

'Wait!'

Grace jumped at Ravenwell's barked command and Clara roused with a whimpered protest. Grace hugged her closer, rubbing her back to soothe her, and she glared at the Marquess.

'Clara is tired and hungry, my lord,' she said. 'Allow me to—'

'Mrs Sharp. Take Clara and feed her. I need to speak to Miss Bertram.'

'Yes, my lord.'

Grace gave her child up with reluctance, her arms already missing the warmth of that solid little body. She eyed Ravenwell anxiously as the door closed behind Mrs Sharp and Clara. His head was bowed, his attention on a sheet of paper before him.

Has he found me out? Will he send me away?

Her knees trembled with the realisation of just how much she wanted…*needed*…to stay.

'Sit!'

Grace gasped. She might be only a governess, but surely there was no need to speak to her quite so brusquely. He had not even the courtesy to look at her when he snapped his order, but was directing his attention down and away, to his right. Was he still attempting to hide his disfigurement? Grace stalked over to the desk and perched on the chair opposite his.

He lifted a brow. She tilted her chin, fighting not to relinquish eye contact, determined not to reveal her apprehension. After what seemed like an hour, one corner of his mouth quirked up.

'Did you think I meant you?'

'I…I beg your pardon?'

'I was talking to the dog.' He jerked his head to his right.

Grace followed the movement, half-standing to see over the side of his desk. There, sitting by his side, was the rough-coated dog that had jumped up at her when she first arrived at Shiverstone Hall.

'Oh.' She swallowed, feeling decidedly foolish and even more nervous; the dog was very big and she had little experience of animals.

'Now, to business.' Any vestige of humour melted from Ravenwell's expression as if it had never been and Grace recalled, with a thump of her heart, that she might have a great deal more to worry about than a dog. 'I cannot understand how your letter applying for the post can have gone astray but, now you are here, we must make the most of it. You said this is your first post since finishing school, is that correct?'

Grace swallowed her instinctive urge to blurt out that she had written no letter of application. 'Yes, my lord.'

'Do you carry a reference or—?'

'I have a letter of recommendation from my teacher, Miss Fanworth,' Grace said, eagerly. Mayhap she was worrying about nothing. He did not sound as though he planned to send her away. 'It is in my bag upstairs.'

'Go and get it now, please. I shall also require the name of the principal of the school and the address.'

'The…the principal?' Grace's heart sank. 'Wh-why do you want that when I already have a letter from Miss Fanworth?'

Out of the four friends, she had been Madame Dubois's least favourite pupil, always the centre of any devilment. *You are the bane of my life*, the Frenchwoman had once told Grace after a particularly naughty prank. Of course, that was before Grace had Clara—thank goodness Madame Dubois had never found out about *that* escapade— and Grace's behaviour had improved considerably since then. Perhaps Madame would not write too damning a report about Grace's conduct at school.

The Marquess continued to regard her steadily. 'I should have thought that was obvious,' he said, 'and it is not for you to question my decision.'

'No, my lord.'

Grace rose to her feet, keeping a wary eye on the dog as she did so. His feathery tail swished from side to side in response and she quickly averted her eyes.

'Are you scared of him? Brack, come here, sir.'

Ravenwell walked around the desk to stand next to Grace and she quelled her impulse to shrink away. She had forgotten quite how tall and intimidating he was, with his wide shoulders and broad chest. He carried with him the smells she had previously noted: leather, the outdoors, and soap. Now, though, he was so close, she caught the underlying scent of warm male and she felt some long-neglected hunger within her stretch and stir. His long hair had swung forward to partially obscure the ravaged skin of his right cheek and jaw, but he did not appear to be deliberately concealing his scars now and Grace darted a glance, taking in the rough surface, before turning her wary attention once again to Brack. The dog had moved closer to her than she anticipated and now she could not prevent her involuntary retreat.

'It is quite all right. You must not be scared of him.'

There was a hint of impatience in Ravenwell's tone. Grace peeped up at him again, meeting his gaze. He might be intimidating in size, and brusque, but she fancied there was again a hint of humour in his dark brown eyes.

'Try to relax. Hold out your hand. Here.'

He engulfed her hand in his, eliciting a strange little jolt deep in her core. Her pulse quickened. Ravenwell called to Brack, who came up eagerly, sniffed and then pushed the top of his head under their joined hands, his black-and-tan coat wiry under Grace's fingers. The dog had a disreputable look about him, one ear flopping almost over his eye whilst the other was a ragged stump. Grace swallowed. Ravenwell wouldn't keep a dangerous animal indoors. Would he?

'All he wants is some attention,' Ravenwell said, his warm voice rumbling through her.

Grace's chest grew tight, her lungs labouring to draw air.

'Where are the other dogs?'

'Brack's the only one who is allowed inside.' Ravenwell released Grace's hand and moved away, and Grace found she could breathe easily again. 'I reared him from a pup after his mother died.'

Grace stroked along Brack's back, feeling very daring. 'I am sure I will get used to him.'

She imagined telling the other girls about this: how they would laugh at her fear of a simple dog. Then, with a swell of regret and sorrow, she remembered she would never again share confidences with her friends. They could write, of course, but letters were not the same as talking face to face—sharing their hopes and fears and whispering their secrets as they lay in bed at night—or as supporting and comforting each other through the youthful ups and downs of their lives. And those friends, her closest friends—her dearest Joanna, Rachel, and Isabel—had supported and comforted Grace through the worst time of her life. Theirs had been the only love she had ever known.

She longed to hear how they all fared in their new roles as governesses and she knew they would be waiting to hear from her—wondering if she had found the baby she had vowed to trace. But they would not know how to contact her—none of them, no one from her former world, knew where she had been since she left the school or where she was at this moment in time.

She must let them know.

'My lord...if you are to write to Madame Dubois, do you think...might I write to Miss Fanworth too? I should like her to know I arrived safely.'

'What about your aunt and uncle? Will they not also wish to know you are here?'

'Yes, of course.'

She uttered the words, but she doubted they would concern themselves one way or the other as to her welfare, as long as she did not end up back on their doorstep, costing them money. She had visited them before starting her quest to find Clara. They had made it clear their home was no longer hers, now she was an adult.

'I shall write to them as well.'

'You may write your letters in here. Ned rides into the village most mornings with the post.'

'Thank you.'

Grace ran upstairs to fetch her letter of recommendation, deliberating over her strange reaction to the Marquess. There had been a moment…when he had been standing so close…when he had taken her hand… She shook her head, dismissing her reaction as nonsense. It was fear of the dog, that was all. Nevertheless, she would avoid using the book room to write her letters whilst he was present. She would wait until her disturbing employer was elsewhere in the house.

Nerves knotted her stomach when she returned downstairs and handed him Miss Fanworth's letter.

'I must go now and see to Clara.' The words tumbled from her, and his brow rose. 'I shall write my letters later, so they will be ready for the morning. Thank you.'

She did not wait for his response, but hurried from the room, feeling her tension dissipate as she closed the door behind her. She went to the kitchen, where Clara was eating some bread and butter with a bowl of broth. The room was warm, and steamy with a mouthwatering aroma that made Grace's stomach growl in protest, reminding her she had not eaten since her breakfast that morning.

A man with ruddy cheeks, small blue eyes and sleeked-down mousy hair sat beside Clara. He was helping her to spoon the broth into her mouth, in between supping from a tankard of ale. He grinned at Grace, but Mrs Sharp—sitting on the opposite side of the scrubbed table—scowled as she entered.

'What did his lordship want with you?'

Grace tilted her chin. 'I suggest you ask him, Mrs Sharp,' she said. 'If he wishes you to be privy to our conversation, I am sure he will enlighten you.'

Mrs Sharp's eyes narrowed, but she said nothing more.

Grace switched her attention to the man, whose grin had widened, his eyes almost disappearing as his face creased.

'Good afternoon,' she said. 'My name is Grace Bertram and I expect you already know I have come to take care of Clara.'

The man bobbed to his feet and nodded. 'Pleased to meet you, miss. I'm Sharp—husband of this one.' He winked at Mrs Sharp, whose lips thinned so much they almost disappeared. 'I look after his lordship, such as he'll allow, bring in the wood and coal and tend the fires, and do a bit of gardening.

'I'll wager this little one—' he ruffled Clara's curls '—will be happy to have you here. As am I,' he added, with a defiant look at his wife, who huffed audibly and got up to stir a pot suspended over the range.

Sharp's eyes twinkled as he raised his tankard in a silent toast to his wife's back. He tilted his head back, drinking with evident enjoyment.

'Sit yourself down, missy...' he put the tankard down with a clatter, earning him another irritable look from his wife '...and tell us a bit about yourself while Miss Clara finishes her meal.'

Grace took care to tell the Sharps no more than she'd already told his lordship. It was not lying. Not precisely. She merely omitted certain facts. Sharp—as garrulous and inquisitive as his spouse was taciturn—continued to interrogate Grace until, the minute Clara finished eating, Grace shot to her feet.

'I must take Clara upstairs now, so she can become accustomed to her new room before it is time for her to sleep.'

She smiled at Sharp to soften her abruptness and picked Clara up, hefting her on to one hip. She couldn't wait to have her little girl all to herself, nor to get away from Sharp's questions and Mrs Sharp's suspicious looks. Quite why the housekeeper disliked her she could not begin to guess, unless...

'Will Mrs Sharp miss looking after Clara?' she asked Sharp. His wife was rattling around in the pantry and Grace kept her voice low so she would not hear. 'Is that why she does not care for me being here?'

'Bless 'ee, no.' Sharp's words, too, were quiet and he darted a glance at the pantry door before continuing, 'It's his lordship she's protecting. She's worried he'll—' He clamped his lips and shook his head. 'Nay, I'll not tell tales. You'll soon find out, if'n you don't already know.'

'What?' Grace hissed. Why would a housekeeper worry about a marquess? And protect him against whom? Her? That made no sense. 'What were you going to say?'

Mrs Sharp chose that moment to emerge from the pantry and Sharp smirked at Grace. She couldn't question him further now.

'His lordship dines at six,' Mrs Sharp said. 'And we have our meal after he's been served. Do not be late.'

Nasty old crow. Grace left the kitchen and carried Clara upstairs.

'Alone at last, sweetie,' she said, as she shut the nursery door firmly behind them.

She shivered. There was no fire lit and the only illumination was from the single candlestick she had carried up to light their way. The room had bare, polished floorboards, a large cabinet, two wooden chairs and a small, low table.

Grace lowered Clara to the floor. 'We shall have to do something about this, Clara. This is simply not good enough.'

She glanced down at her daughter, who was gazing up at her with worry creasing her forehead and her mouth drooping. Grace's heart faltered and she crouched down.

'Don't look so sad, little one,' she whispered. 'I am not cross with you.'

The enormity of the task she had undertaken dawned on her. What did she know about caring for such a young child? Had she thought, because she was Clara's mother, she would magically know what to do and how to raise her properly? All her training had been about older children. She cupped Clara's face between her palms and pressed a kiss to her forehead.

'We shall learn how to go on together,' she said. 'But first, I shall talk to your uncle and I will make sure you want for nothing. And the first step will be a lovely cosy room where you can play and have fun.'

'Unc' Nannal.'

Grace froze. 'What did you say, Clara?'

Clara—eyes wide, thumb now firmly jammed in her mouth—remained silent. Grace gently pulled Clara's hand from her face. 'Say it again, sweetie.'

'She said *"Uncle Nathaniel"*.'

Chapter Five

Grace's heart almost seized in her chest. She twisted to look over her shoulder, then scrambled to her feet to face the Marquess, who filled the open doorway. How long had he been there? What had he heard? Her thrill at hearing Clara speak faded, to be replaced by anxiety. She could barely remember what she had said out loud and what she had thought.

'I did not see you there,' she said.

'Evidently.'

Her heart began to pound as he continued to stare at her, frowning.

'You shall have a fire up here tomorrow and Mrs Sharp will show you where there is furniture and so forth in storage. You may make use of anything you need to make these rooms comfortable for you and for Clara.'

He does not seem to think of Clara as an unwanted burden. He accepts her as though she is truly his niece.

'Thank you, my lord.'

He looked at Clara and his expression softened. 'You are a clever girl, saying my name. Will you say it again? For me?'

'Unc' Nannal,' Clara whispered.

Ravenwell beamed. 'Well done, poppet. Now, where's
my goodnight kiss?

Clara toddled over to the Marquess, her arms stretched
high, and he swung her aloft, kissing her soundly on her
cheek. Her arms wrapped around his neck and she kissed
him twice, firstly on his left cheek and then—crooning
softly and chubby fingers stroking—she kissed him on his
scarred cheek. Ravenwell's gaze flicked to Grace and then
away. He turned from her, Clara still in his arms.

'Come.' His voice was gruff. 'Let Uncle Nathaniel see
your new bedchamber.'

He strode from the room, leaving Grace to ponder that
scene. She had thought Clara was scared of her uncle but—
picturing again her first meeting with Clara, she now wondered if her daughter's reluctance as she bumped down the
stairs and dragged her feet across the hall was not wariness
of the Marquess, but of Grace. The stranger.

That will teach me not to make assumptions.

A chastened Grace hurried from the room to join Ravenwell and Clara in the child's bedchamber, which adjoined
Grace's.

Grace froze by the door. Here, a fire had been lit—presumably by the elusive Alice—and the room had taken on
a warm glow. A rug lay before the fire and there, stretched
full length, was Brack. He lifted his head to contemplate
Grace and his tail thumped gently on the floor. Twice.

'I do not think…'

Grace's objection drifted into silence as Clara squirmed
in her uncle's arms.

'Brack! Brack!'

The Marquess placed her on the floor and, squealing,
she rushed over to the dog and launched herself on top of
him, wrapping her arms around his neck as his tail continued to wag.

Grace watched, open-mouthed.

'You do not think…?' Ravenwell's voice had a teasing note she had not heard before.

'It does not matter. Clara is clearly fond of Brack.'

'And *she* is not scared of him, despite his size.'

Grace bristled at his emphasis on *she*. 'No, but I did not know he was friendly when I first saw him.'

'That is true. And as you said earlier, you will soon become accustomed to the dogs.'

'I will try.'

Watching Clara with Brack warmed Grace's heart and she could not help smiling at the sight. She turned to the Marquess to comment on Clara's delight but, before she could speak, the good humour leached from Ravenwell's expression and he averted his face. It was only a fractional movement, but she did not miss it.

'Come, Brack.'

He stalked from the room.

Nathaniel sought the sanctuary of his book room. He stood by his desk, staring unseeingly at the surface, tracing with his forefinger the pits and scratches that had accumulated over the years, pondering his gut reaction to Miss Bertram.

Specifically, to Miss Bertram's smile.

Clara needed a governess. That was an irrefutable fact.

Grace Bertram had appeared on his doorstep at a time he was beginning to fear he would never find anyone willing to move to Shiverstone Hall and care for his niece. The alternative—moving back to Ravenwell Manor—had begun to haunt him. So, despite his reservations, he had offered Miss Bertram the post, secured her behind a door marked *Employee* in his mind and banished any thoughts of her as a female. She was as welcome or as unwelcome as any woman taking that post. Her looks were…*must be*… immaterial.

And then she had smiled. And the memories had swarmed up from the depths of his mind, overwhelming him with images from his past: the flirtations, the fun, the laughter.

Memories of how life had used to be.

Unwanted memories of pretty girls who would smile spontaneously at him.

An aggravating reminder of his world before he chose this reclusive life.

With a muttered curse, Nathaniel hauled his chair from under his desk, sat down and pulled a ledger towards him. He flipped it open and forcibly applied his mind to business until it was time to dress for dinner.

He always dined at six and he always—despite dining alone—dressed for dinner. It was the one custom he continued from his former life, allowing him the illusion he was still a gentleman. He contemplated his appearance in the mirror as he wound his neckcloth around his neck and tied it in a neat knot. Would Miss Bertram think he made this effort on her behalf?

And if she does, why should it matter? You are not answerable to her. You are answerable to no one.

The pit of his stomach tangled into knots as the evening ahead stretched before him. Something about the thought of sitting at the table with her, eating and talking, fuelled his vulnerability. But he was sure, once the meal was underway, those knots would untangle. Miss Bertram had already demonstrated a welcome lack of disgust at his scars and that would help him become less self-conscious.

And those memories that glorious smile of hers had awoken? They were just that. Memories. They could wield no power over him as long as he banished them from his mind.

He tugged a comb through the knots in his hair—the winds out on the fells had, as usual, played havoc with it. Should he ask Sharp to cut it? He ran his hand over the side of his face, feeling the now-familiar roughness, as though twists of rope lay beneath the surface. His hair helped to hide the worst of the ravages the fire had wrought, particularly into the hairline where some of his hair had not grown back, but it could not completely conceal it, so it served little purpose.

The sound of his bedchamber door opening jolted him from his musings.

'Sorry, milord,' Sharp said. 'I thought, with the time…'

'No, do not apologise,' Nathaniel said. 'I am late, but I am going down now, so you may continue.'

It was Sharp's custom to tidy Nathaniel's bedchamber and bank up the fire when Nathaniel went downstairs to eat his dinner.

Nathaniel ran down the stairs. The parlour door was ajar and he entered, stopping short on seeing the table was only set for one. He spun on his heel and made for the kitchen. Mrs Sharp was there, ladling food into a serving dish, whilst Ned—who ate all his meals at the Hall—and Alice both sat ready at the table, awaiting their supper, which would be served when Sharp finished upstairs.

'I heard you come down the stairs, milord. Your dinner is ready. I—'

'Why is there only one place set in the parlour, Mrs Sharp?'

The housekeeper frowned. 'I did not think you would want to dine with her, milord.'

Nathaniel bit back a terse retort. This was his fault. He had not specified where Miss Bertram would dine. He had made an assumption.

'A governess would not expect to dine in the kitchen,' he said, 'and it would be too much work for her to dine upstairs in her room. Be so good as to lay another place in the parlour, Mrs Sharp.'

'But…milord…'

'*Now,* please.'

The sound of a throat being cleared delicately behind him had him whirling to face the door. Miss Bertram stood there, hands clasped in front of her, fingers twisting together. She had changed into a dowdy grey dress and the slight blush that tinted her cheeks was the only hint of colour on her person.

'I do not mind where I eat, my lord,' she said.

He did not want a debate. 'I do,' he said. 'You will dine with me in the parlour. Set another place, Mrs Sharp.'

He gestured for Miss Bertram to precede him out of the kitchen. In the morning parlour, he pulled a chair out for her—choosing the place to his left—and then sat in his customary place at the head of the table.

Silence reigned.

Mrs Sharp came in, set a plate and cutlery in front of Miss Bertram and left again, spine rigid.

'Clara went to sleep without any problems.'

He grunted discouragingly.

'I thought you might like to know that.'

Mrs Sharp returned with a tray of serving dishes, saving him from further response.

'It is venison stew, milord.' She placed the first dish in the centre of the table. 'And there are potatoes and some of the pie from yesterday, warmed up.'

Miss Bertram smiled at Mrs Sharp. 'Thank you,' she said. 'It smells delicious.'

'Thank you.'

It was said grudgingly at the same time as the housekeeper darted a worried glance at Nathaniel. The Sharps had been with him since before the fire—had cared for him when the emotional pain had outstripped any physical pain resulting from his injuries, had remained loyal, burying themselves here at Shiverstone without complaint. They clearly worried over the choices he had made for his life.

'Yes, it does,' he said. 'Thank you, Mrs Sharp.'

And he meant for more than just the food. He understood

her concern and the reason why she had not set a place for Miss Bertram in the parlour. She was afraid for him.

Thank you for caring.

She treated him to a fleeting smile before she left the room to fetch the rest of the food.

Nathaniel glanced at Miss Bertram, who was watching him, a glint of speculation in her eyes. He quashed his instinct to avert his face. He could hardly fault her for being curious and he knew he must overcome his natural urge to hide his scars, as he had with his servants. They were impossible to hide; she would see them often enough and, to her credit, her reaction so far had been encouraging. The sooner she accepted his appearance, the sooner he could also forget about it and then his awkwardness would fade.

He reached for her plate to serve her some stew.

As they ate their meal, Nathaniel watched Miss Bertram surreptitiously. Why would such a young, beautiful girl choose to travel all this way north for a post in a bleak place like Shiverstone? She struck him as a sociable sort. It made little sense, but she was here now and he did not doubt she would care for Clara. Whatever the reason, he must count it as a blessing for his niece. He was certain Hannah and David would approve of Miss Bertram.

The thought of his sister and brother-in-law brought the usual swell of anguish, followed by another thought. Miss Bertram had shown no curiosity whatsoever about how Clara had come to be orphaned. She had not enquired once about Clara's parents. Would it not be natural to have some curiosity over how they had died?

Then his conscience pricked him. He had actively discouraged her from conversation, never stopping to consider that if Miss Bertram failed to settle at Shiverstone, she might leave. And then what would he do about Clara? Besides, no matter how he had chosen to live these past nine years, he was still a gentleman and this prolonged silence at the dinner table went against every tenet of his upbringing.

'What made you choose to come to Shiverstone?'

There was a slight choking noise from the woman to his right. His fault, surprising her with a sudden question whilst she was eating.

'Were there no positions closer to where you grew up? Wiltshire, was it not?'

Miss Bertram cleared her throat, then sipped her wine. 'My uncle encouraged me to look for a post outside the county.' She directed a wry smile at her plate, avoiding eye contact. 'He did not want the embarrassment of his niece working for someone he is acquainted with.' There was a hint of disgust in her tone. 'I was the last of my friends to leave the school after our training finished, but when I went back to my uncle's house it was clear I was not welcome. My father had bequeathed me a little money, so I took a room in a lodging house in Cheltenham…and…and I heard about this post and I thought it would be interesting to see the North Country.'

'It is certainly a long way from Salisbury. And Cheltenham. Does it meet your expectations?'

'I…I…no, if I am to be honest. It is wilder than I imagined, but it is very…impressive, also.'

'And do you think you will grow to like it?'

'Oh, yes.' Her vehemence surprised him. 'I am certain of it.'

Nathaniel chewed another mouthful of venison. Was she running from something? Is that why she was content to bury herself out here? He had not yet penned his letter to this Madame Dubois. He would ask her, couching his question in discreet terms.

'If I might ask…' Miss Bertram hesitated. Her head was bent, her concentration still on her plate of food. 'I have no wish to revive painful memories, but I should like to know a little of Clara's parents. So I may speak to her of them.'

Almost as though she senses my suspicions.

'The memories are not all painful.' He closed his eyes, allowing his thoughts to travel back. 'Hannah was a year younger than me and we were very close growing up. There is a portrait of her in the dining room, painted by David, my brother-in-law, if you would care to see it. It is under a dust cover.'

He told himself he covered the picture to protect Clara, but he knew, deep down, it was because he could not bear seeing Hannah's likeness after her death, so he had removed it from the drawing-room wall.

Out of sight, out of mind. Except that did not really work.

'David was a fine artist and painted landscapes for the most part, but he painted Hannah and they presented the result to me when they were last here in June.'

Under the pretence of sipping his wine, Nathaniel swallowed his burgeoning pain. *Concentrate on the happy times.* 'Hannah loved to sing and to play the pianoforte.'

'She sounds a lovely lady. Let us hope Clara will remember something of her and her father.'

'I hope so. She had a fine character and she always remained positive, even in the face of heartache.'

'Heartache?'

The question dropped into the silence. He had said more than he meant to. They had both finished eating and Miss Bertram leant forward, her gaze intense.

'She was unable to bear children. Clara was adopted.'

There was another silence. Miss Bertram pressed her lips together and her lashes swept down, casting a lacy shadow on her cheeks as she fidgeted with the knife and fork she had placed neatly on her empty plate. Her hands were small and delicate, with slender fingers and beautifully shaped oval nails.

She cleared her throat. 'I...I did not know that.'

'As far as Hannah and David were concerned, Clara was theirs. They doted on her. She was such a happy little girl. So very much wanted and loved.'

She raised her head, her large gold-green eyes shimmering as they reflected the candlelight. 'She will be again. I promise you that.'

Chapter Six

Nathaniel's heart lightened at the sincerity that shone through Miss Bertram's words. Here was someone who would help him. The responsibility—he would never call it a burden—of raising Clara and making her happy was no longer his alone. Only now did he recognise the deep-seated worries that had plagued him ever since he read his mother's letter. Only now could he contemplate the coming months and years with a sense of peace and control.

'Thank you.'

Her fine brows drew together. 'Why do you thank me, my lord?' Her eyes searched his.

Nathaniel spoke from his heart. 'I am grateful you are prepared to live out here in order to help me raise Clara. I pray you will remain for a very long time. I do not wish my niece to suffer any more abandonment in her life.'

She stared at him, wordlessly, then dropped her gaze to her plate again. He had to strain to make out her next words.

'I will never abandon her a—'

Her jaw snapped shut and Nathaniel wondered what she had been about to say. Then she hauled in a deep breath, looked up and smiled, driving further conjecture from his mind. The glory of that smile, once again, hit him with the force of a punch to his gut. How long had it been since a woman had smiled at him…genuinely, and not forced or with disgust in her eyes? For the second time that evening, he battened down his visceral reaction. Miss Bertram was his employee. It behoved him, as a gentleman, to protect her, not to lust after her. He made himself imagine her likely reaction to any hint of an approach from him and the thought of her disgust had the same effect on his desire that a sudden squall might have on a summer's day. The resulting chill chased over his skin and his insides shrivelled, as though by shrinking away from his surface they might protect him from the result of his momentary lapse.

The door opened and Sharp ambled in, bringing with him the smell of a brewery. Nathaniel did not grudge him his weakness. At least the man did not overindulge through the day and he deserved some compensation for moving to Shiverstone and leaving his friends and his favourite alehouse in Harrogate behind. Normally garrulous in the evening, Sharp cleared the dishes in silence and, shortly after he left the room, Mrs Sharp came, carrying a warm pie—apple, by the smell of it—and a jug of cream.

Nathaniel took advantage of the distraction to study the newest member of his household even further. So very delicate and pretty, with fine cheekbones and clear skin and silky, blonde hair…no wonder he had been momentarily attracted to her. Familiarity would help. He would cease to notice her appearance, much as she would cease to notice his scars. At least Clara would be cared for and happy.

'I am pleased to hear you say that,' he said, resulting in a swift sideways glance from Mrs Sharp, whose long nose appeared to twitch, as if to say, *What are you talking about?*

Miss Bertram pursed her lips, her eyes dancing, as she watched the housekeeper.

'Mrs Sharp—' amusement bubbled through her voice '—the stew was delicious and the pie smells wonderful. I can see I shall have to restrain my appetite if I am not to increase to the size of a house.'

'Hmmph. I am sure it matters not to anyone here if you should gain weight, miss.'

Miss Bertram's gaze flicked to meet Nathaniel's and this time he was certain she was biting back a smile. A conspirator's smile. He had talked overmuch. Given her the impression they were allies. Even that they might become friends. Every instinct he possessed told him to beware.

'When you have finished your dessert, you may use the book room to write those letters we discussed,' he said.

He steeled his heart against the hurt that flashed across her face. Better she did not get the wrong impression. He was not here to be her friend.

'Mrs Sharp, please be so good as to serve tea to Miss Bertram in the book room. Shall we say in fifteen minutes? And tell Sharp to bring my brandy here.'

'Yes, milord.' Such satisfaction communicated in just two words.

They finished their meal in silence.

What to write?

Grace brushed the untrimmed end of the quill pen against her cheek as she pondered how much she should reveal to Miss Fanworth.

The letter to her uncle had been easy: an enquiry after his health and that of the rest of the family, the news that she had obtained a position as governess to the niece of the Marquess of Ravenwell and her address, should they wish to contact her. She decided, with an inner *hmmph*, that it would be unwise for her to hold her breath waiting for that last to occur.

But… Miss Fanworth… She bent her head and began to write.

My dear Miss Fanworth,
I hope you will be happy to know that I found my
child. She is happy and loved, and I am reassured

that she is well cared for, so I am content. Thank you so much for trusting me with the names of her new parents. I shall be in your debt for ever.

I must also acquaint you with my good fortune in securing a position as governess for the Marquess of Ravenwell. He has the intention of writing to Madame for a reference—despite your letter of recommendation—and I am hopeful that she will find it in her heart to dwell less upon my early escapades and more upon my later years at the school when she pens that reference!

My new address is at the top of this letter and I would count myself fortunate if you might write to me once in a while to tell me how everyone at school fares. Please, also, should you write to them, communicate my address to my dear friends Rachel, Joanna, and Isabel. Might I also request that you send on any letters addressed to me that may have arrived at the school?

Please convey my most sincere regards to Madame and to the other teachers and staff.
Your very grateful former pupil,
Grace Bertram

Grace read and reread her effort anxiously. No, she had not lied, but she had successfully masked the truth. If Madame was to discover the actuality of her new position, she would surely inform his lordship and he would banish her immediately.

She could not fathom the brusque Marquess. His initial reluctance to converse over their meal had disappointed, but not surprised her—no one would choose to live such a reclusive life if they craved company. But the man was not shy and, in Grace's opinion, it was plain bad manners not to make the smallest effort at civilised conversation. Although—she had told herself as she concentrated on her meal—she must remember she was only the governess and not a guest to be treated with due deference.

But then he began to talk and she had relaxed, thinking he was merely unused to company. And her thoughts had raced ahead and, in her imagination, she helped him to overcome his awkwardness and taught him to enjoy socialising, for Clara's sake, and the house would be filled with light and laughter...but then Mrs Sharp—that wicked old crow—had come in and jerked her back to reality and Ravenwell had pokered up all over again.

The prospect of the evenings to come filled her with dismay, but at least she would not lack company entirely at Shiverstone Hall. Sharp was as affable as his wife was hostile, Alice, the newly arrived fourteen-year-old housemaid, was a plump chatterbox and Ned, although he had little to say, did not appear unfriendly.

And there was always Clara. A warm, comforting glow spread through Grace. Her child. The days ahead would be filled with Clara, and the Marquess and his moodiness, and Mrs Sharp and her meanness could go to... Grace squashed that thought before it could form into the word in her brain. She was a mother now, with responsibilities. She was no longer a rebellious girl with a penchant for trouble.

Her letter would suffice. She would leave her letters with his lordship's, on the console table in the hall, for Ned to take to Shivercombe village in the morning.

She leaned back in Ravenwell's chair, her lids heavy. It had been an exhausting day, both physically and emotionally. The homesickness for her school days and for the companionship, laughter and love of her friends welled up, and hot tears prickled. She blinked furiously. Life had taught her that self-pity was not an option. It achieved nothing. She and her friends were grown women now. She'd wager *they* were not wallowing in nostalgia, but embracing their new lives with hope and confidence.

Well, she was sure Isabel and Rachel would be doing just that, but what of gentle, reserved Joanna, abandoned on the doorstep of Madame's school as a baby? She had been taken in and brought up by Madame and the other teachers and it had been a lonely existence until the age of nine, when other girls her age were taken in as boarders. Grace, Isabel, and Rachel were the closest to family Joanna had ever known and she prayed the family who had employed her would be kind.

As for Rachel, there was no doubt in Grace's mind her independent, self-sufficient friend would be in her element with the opportunity to travel to exotic places after she had been employed by a sheikh, in the kingdom of Huria. The girls had found the country on the map—beyond the furthest reaches of the Mediterranean Sea—and Grace had marvelled at the distance Rachel must travel. Journeying as far as Shiverstone Hall had been quite far enough!

And Isabel—a momentary disquiet sneaked through Grace. There had been something about Isabel and her insouciance when she left the school. Her meek acceptance of her future as a governess had seemed out of character, when they all knew her great ambition was to become a famous singer. Would she settle in her new life? Or would she risk everything in her bid for excitement?

She longed to hear all their news and hoped that, as promised, they had written to her care of the school as she had not known where she might eventually find employment. Selfishly, she was relieved she had mislaid her friends' addresses during her travels for, even if she *could* write to them today, how much of the truth would she dare reveal? Could she admit the reality of her new situation? She had never kept secrets from them before, not even the greatest secret of her life, when she discovered she was with child, but…would they understand what she had done, or would they condemn? They would worry about her, of that she was certain.

* * *

That brief interlude, when Lord Ravenwell had reminisced so movingly about his sister, might never have happened. Over her first few days at Shiverstone Hall, Grace barely saw her employer. He only appeared at dinner, dressed in his black tail coat and meticulously knotted neckcloth, adorned with a ruby pin. He remained distant and, after another few abortive attempts at conversation, Grace gave up. Her days were long and full, and by the evening she was exhausted, so she followed her employer's lead and ate in silence.

The quietness and calm of their meals gave her time to think. Time to wonder why he lived as a recluse, what had caused his scars, why he had talked that one time on her first night and then clammed up. He was a puzzling man.

The silence also gave her time to observe. He had been a handsome man. Still was, if one ignored the scarring. The skin of his jaw and up the side of his face on the right-hand side was uneven and pale in contrast to the rest of his face, which was lightly tanned, no doubt from exposure to the sun and the wind out on the fells.

Then, one evening when he was in his cups and his wife was out of earshot, Sharp had told her how his lordship had been burned nine years ago in a fire at Ravenwell Manor. A fire that had killed his father. Before that Ravenwell had been one of society's most eligible bachelors and had led a carefree life filled with fun and pleasure. The fire had scarred more than his skin, Sharp had slurred. It had scarred the very essence of the man. Grace's natural sympathy had been stirred, but she knew the Marquess would not wish for pity and so she said nothing. But still she wondered at the reclusive life he led. He must be lonely.

His size no longer intimidated her, but his silence did. And his dogs—other than Brack, to whom she was slowly becoming accustomed. Ravenwell spent much of his time outside and, although Grace and Clara ventured into the fresh air almost every day, they remained close by the house and they saw nothing of Clara's uncle. Grace's heart bled for Clara. For all his lordship's fine talk about not wanting his niece's life disrupted, what did he think he was doing now by avoiding all contact with her every day? He might just as well not live here, for all Clara saw of him.

Grace kept her counsel. For the time being. For now, she was content to expend her energy in making their upstairs rooms more homely and in coaxing smiles and more words from her daughter.

Chapter Seven

'Good afternoon.'

It was the fourth day of her new life at Shiverstone Hall. Grace and Clara had been playing on the lawn in front of the house and now Clara was chirruping away to herself as she gathered pretty stones from the carriageway, piling into a heap. Grace tore her attention from Clara, shielding her eyes against the low-lying sun. A young man, clad in a black coat and black, low-crowned hat, stood a few yards away, smiling at her.

'Good afternoon. Mr...?'

'Rendell. Ralph Rendell.' He raised his hat, revealing a mop of curly light brown hair. 'I am the curate at St Mary's.'

Grace's ignorance of the existence of St Mary's must have shown in her expression for Mr Rendell laughed, and said, 'The church in Shivercombe village.'

'I am pleased to meet you, Mr Rendell. Are you a frequent visitor to the Hall?'

The curate's smile broadened. 'And that, I surmise, is a delicate way of enquiring the purpose of my visit.'

Grace bit her lip against her answering smile.

'My visit,' he continued, 'appears to have already achieved its purpose.'

'Which was?'

'To satisfy myself as to your safety, Miss…?'

'Oh, I am sorry. I am Miss Bertram. Miss Grace Bertram.'

Mr Rendell bowed. 'I am delighted to make your acquaintance, Miss Bertram. Am I correct in assuming you are the young lady who enquired for directions to the Hall in Shivercombe last Tuesday and has not been seen since?'

'Yes, indeed,' Grace replied. 'I came in response to an advertisement for the post of governess.' She felt her face heat and, unable to meet his eyes after such a blatant lie to a man of God, she lowered her gaze to Clara, who now stood watching them, her thumb jammed in her mouth. Grace bent and gently tugged at Clara's hand. 'No, sweetie. Your hands are dirty.'

'To this little one? So the rumours *were* true. I did not know the Marquess had a child.'

'Clara is his lordship's niece. She is an orphan.'

Except she still has me, even though she will never know it. Poor Clara: her adoptive parents dead, her father killed at the Battle of Bussaco and me, her real mother, never able to tell her the truth.

Grace buried the sorrows of the past as Clara crouched down again to continue piling up stones. She was here now. That was all that mattered.

'Why should you have a concern for my safety, sir?'

'There was a certain amount of disquiet in the village after you failed to return. Lord Ravenwell is something of an enigma to the good folk of Shivercombe and—in the nature of filling the vacuum resulting from his servants' most unsatisfactory refusal to gossip about him—the villagers have developed their own theories and stories about this place and its master.'

Grace laughed. 'Yes. I recall. When I asked for directions, I was earnestly advised not to risk coming here. But I am pleased I did.'

Those tales had strengthened her resolve to find her daughter.

'And I am pleased to discover you safe and well, Miss Bertram.' Mr Rendell smiled, his hazel eyes creasing at the outer corners. He squatted next to Clara and handed her an attractively veined stone to add to her pile. 'And to make the acquaintance of this little treasure.'

Clara smiled at the curate. 'Fank 'oo.'

'She has beautiful eyes,' Mr Rendell said. 'A most unusual colour.'

Grace strived to sound nonchalant. 'They are lovely indeed.' She bent to take Clara's hand. 'Come, sweetie. It is time we went indoors.'

Mr Rendell stood up and brushed at the hem of his coat, before smiling at Grace. 'And it is time I took my leave of you. I have achieved what I set out to accomplish.'

Guilt over her abruptness prompted Grace to say, 'Would you care for a cup of tea, Mr Rendell? Did you walk all the way here?'

'No, I drove. I left my gig at the stable yard with Tam.' He stared up at the Hall, scanning the frontage, then returned his gaze to Grace. 'Yes, I should welcome a cup of tea, Miss Bertram. Thank you.' His reply was laced with determination.

Grace puzzled over the curate's tone as she led the way to the front door. He had given the impression of a man waging an internal battle…no doubt he was fully aware her enigmatic employer discouraged visitors. But good manners dictated she should offer her visitor some hospitality. After all, he had come all this way, merely to assure himself of her well-being.

Conscious she might be violating an unwritten rule that strangers were not to be invited inside the Hall, Grace lifted the latch and, straightening her spine, marched into the entrance hall. Mrs Sharp was descending the stairs and Grace's courage almost failed at the sight of the hostile housekeeper. Almost, but not quite, for Clara must meet and socialise with others if she was not to grow up shy and awkward in company. And did not she… Grace…deserve to have some friends outside the Hall?

'Mrs Sharp,' she said, 'this is…' Her words faded into silence as Mrs Sharp smoothed her hair back with both hands before hurrying down the remaining stairs, a welcoming smile on her face.

Well!

'Mr Rendell, how very good of you to call. Miss Bertram, please show our visitor into the drawing room and I will bring you refreshments.'

'You have been here before?' Grace asked the curate as she sat down.

'No, never. Mrs Sharp is a regular at church, however, so we are acquainted, although it must be a month since her last attendance. I confess I am a little bemused by her welcome—such visits have been positively discouraged in the past.'

'Does Lord Ravenwell attend church as well?'

'No. We have never seen him in the village. All the servants come to church, when the weather permits, for the track between here and the village can become treacherous in inclement weather. They do not mix with the villagers, however. That fact, in itself, spawns even more speculation about his lordship.' He leaned forward, suddenly intense. 'You are happy here, Miss Bertram? You must know you can rely upon me to help if ever you need it.'

'I am…content enough, sir.'

Was she happy? She was thrilled to be with Clara and nothing would tear her away. But happy with the rest of her situation? With her brusque employer and the taciturn housekeeper—although Mrs Sharp had been surprisingly helpful with Grace's efforts to refurbish the nursery wing upstairs once she accepted there was no criticism of her housekeeping skills. Or with the regularly tipsy Sharp and friendly but unsophisticated Alice? It was too soon to say. And yet, what choice did she have? She had nowhere else to go. And Clara needed her.

'But I thank you for your concern and you may rest assured you will be the first person to whom I shall apply should I ever need help.'

'Then I am satisfied. And I shall look forward to seeing you on the morrow in church, together with this little one.' He reached out and ruffled Clara's curls and she tilted her head to stare at him from her seat on the rug. 'It is never too early to educate a child in the ways of the Lord.'

'I shall be there.'

Grace's heart lifted. It might only be a church service, but it would break the monotony of life at the Hall. So far, she had ventured no further than the kitchen garden to watch Sharp digging the soil in preparation for planting in the spring.

'If not this week, then next,' she continued, 'for I have no idea how we might get to the village. Clara cannot walk that far.'

'You may ride in the carriage with Annie and me.' Mrs Sharp had returned and was pouring the tea. She passed a cup to Mr Rendell and then one to Grace. 'Ned usually drives us and Sharp sits with him up on the box whilst Tam rides.'

Grace stared at the change in the housekeeper—was this all to impress the curate with her good Christian values?

Before she could respond, the sound of boots on the flags of the hall floor rang out.

Clara scrambled to her feet. 'Unc' Nanniel,' she said.

Nathaniel strode through the hall, Brack at his heels. A morning out on the fells, flying Amber, had given him a raging appetite. He was delighted with the eagle's progress. Her wing was growing stronger and she was becoming accustomed to hunting again, in preparation for her release back into the wild.

A scuffle from the direction of the drawing room distracted him. He stopped, then forgot his hunger as a beaming Clara erupted from the room, arms aloft.

'Unc' Nanniel!'

'Clara!'

He bent to catch her up in his arms, then swung her in a wide circle, revelling in her giggles. He hugged her close and kissed her cheek. How he had missed her.

Your fault, came the silent riposte.

It was true. He had deliberately avoided Miss Bertram—and thus, by association, Clara—since her arrival. That first evening, he had found himself relaxing...talking too much...*revealing* too much. He did not want a friend. The danger of becoming dependent upon her company, upon *anyone's* company, disturbed his sleep. What if she did not stay after all? He could not bear to become accustomed to her company and then lose it, leaving him to endure the agony of readjusting to his self-imposed exile.

It was bad enough having to dine together every evening. The silence—yet again, his choice—gave him too much time to think. And to remember. Miss Bertram, with her delicate lily-of-the-valley scent, her prettiness and her femininity was a constant reminder of what he had given up and an ever-growing challenge to his male instincts, kept suppressed for so very long. Not that he would ever risk an overture towards her. A beauty like Miss Bertram would be disgusted by the mere thought of intimacy with a man like him. Besides, the standards he expected of himself would not allow him to take advantage of an innocent woman in his employ.

But...he was increasingly irked by his own behaviour. It smacked of cowardice. If Miss Bertram should decide to leave, then he would simply have to deal with it. He had dealt with worse things. Hannah's face floated into his mind, and his heart clenched. *Far worse.* He would put his caution aside and accept Miss Bertram's presence in his household. He could not run away for ever. He strode towards the drawing room. Clara had come from there. Ergo, Miss Bertram must be in there.

It was time he changed.

He walked in through the door and slammed to a halt as he took in the three faces turned towards him. Of the three, both Mrs Sharp and Miss Bertram wore identical expressions of consternation. The third—a young man—smiled as he rose to his feet and extended his right hand.

'I beg you will forgive my intrusion, sir. Ralph Rendell, curate of St Mary's, at your service.' The young man did not approach Nathaniel, but remained standing with his hand thrust out, a confident smile on his face. His clear-skinned, handsome face.

Nathaniel put Clara down and walked towards the young curate, fighting the urge to twist his neck to shield his scars from Rendell. He shook the proffered hand, steeling himself not to flinch as the other man's fingers closed around his hand, touching the scarring on the back of his hand, even though it gave him no physical pain. The curate showed no flicker of reaction and some of Nathaniel's tension dissipated.

'Ravenwell.'

He gestured to the other man to sit, aware he now had two choices. He could stalk out. It was common knowledge visitors were not welcome at the Hall and no one would be surprised. Or he could be a gentleman. Only moments ago he had accepted it was time to change. Out of the corner of his eye he saw Miss Bertram chew at her bottom lip, worry creasing her brow. Her clear unease settled the matter.

'Mrs Sharp, be so good as to bring another cup, will you?' And he sat down.

Clara immediately clambered on to his lap and settled into the crook of his arm, sighing contentedly.

'Clara is happy to see you, my lord.'

He caught the hint of reproach. 'I have been busy these past days,' he said. It was true. Gradually accustoming Amber to flying and to her new freedom had taken much of his time. He bent his head, rubbing his cheek against Clara's. 'I am happy to see you too, poppet.'

Clara pulled her thumb from her mouth with a pop. 'Unc' Nanniel,' she whispered.

Nathaniel turned his attention to Mr Rendell. 'It is seldom we get visitors to the Hall, Rendell.'

'Indeed.' Light brown eyes regarded him steadily. 'I came to ensure myself of Miss Bertram's well-being.'

Nathaniel heard Miss Bertram's stifled gasp and felt his brows snap together in a frown.

'Well-being?'

Rendell continued to hold his gaze. 'Yes. She was known to have come out to Shiverstone on Tuesday last. I came to make certain of her safe arrival.'

Tactful wording. Nathaniel could not but be impressed by the young man's courage in braving Nathaniel's carefully nurtured reputation to ensure the safety of a stranger.

'Most commendable.'

Mrs Sharp bustled in with another cup and a plate piled with slabs of fruit cake. Nathaniel's stomach growled at the sight, his hunger pangs resurfacing with a vengeance. He accepted a slice of cake and bit into it as Mrs Sharp poured him a cup of tea.

'I have promised Mr Rendell that Clara and I will attend the church service tomorrow,' Miss Bertram said. 'That is, if you are happy to give your permission, my lord?'

With his mouth full of cake, Nathaniel could not immediately reply.

'I am sure his lordship will not stand in the way of your moral enlightenment, Miss Bertram,' Rendell said.

Nathaniel swallowed his food. 'I would not dream of objecting to your attendance at church, Miss Bertram.'

'And,' Rendell continued, 'I would deem it an honour if you would call upon us at the rectory if you can spare the time to visit Shivercombe, Miss Bertram. The rector's daughter is a similar age to yourself, and...' he leant over to tickle under Clara's chin, causing her to squirm with delight '...we have a litter of kittens this young lady might enjoy meeting.'

'Kittens, Clara! How exciting.' Miss Bertram switched her attention from Clara to the curate. 'I am sure she would love to see them, sir. She already takes great delight in his lordship's dogs. But will you not be too busy, with tomorrow being Sunday?'

'Oh, I did not mean tomorrow. You will surely welcome an excuse to visit your neighbours on occasion. After all, living in seclusion is not everybody's choice.'

Nathaniel bit back an angry retort. How dare Rendell chastise him in his own house, and back him into a corner like this?

Outmanoeuvred, by God...and by a man of God, at that.

Then his exasperation subsided, to be replaced by an impulse to laugh. What was he thinking? Was it his intention to keep Miss Bertram a prisoner at the Hall? He had chosen not to mix with his neighbours, but had no justification for forcing her to do likewise. And it would be good for Clara.

'You are right,' he said. 'Can you drive?' he added, to Miss Bertram.

'No.' It was said with regret. 'My uncle did not think it worth having me taught. I thank you for your offer, Mr Rendell, but I am afraid I am unable to accept your invitation.'

'Your man rides or drives in most days, does he not, my lord? Surely Miss Bertram and Clara could come in with him?'

'They could, but he normally leaves here very early and returns immediately. It would not be long enough for a social visit.'

The stubborn tilt of the curate's chin suggested he would

not easily give in, prompting Nathaniel to add, 'You may drive yourself to the village in the gig, Miss Bertram. Our old cob, Bill, is perfectly safe.'

She gasped, pink infusing her cheeks, her green eyes sparkling with excitement. Was she so very eager to get away from the Hall? No sooner had the question formed in his mind than he realised its absurdity. Of course she would be eager to meet other people. What fun was it to be isolated out here with a two-year-old, an employer who barely spoke to her and a bunch of servants?

'That would be...but no. I...I do not know if I could. I am not used to horses.'

'Nonsense. Bill is an old hand. He knows the way to and from the village with his eyes shut and he never gets above a slow trot. I will teach you. You will cope admirably, I am certain.'

As he spoke, Miss Bertram smiled at Rendell with such pleasure Nathaniel's stomach twisted tight. He eyed the curate's clear, handsome countenance and experienced a sharp pang that no woman would ever again look at him in such a way.

No woman or Miss Bertram, specifically?

He surged to his feet and handed a dozing Clara to Miss Bertram, goaded by that snide voice in his head.

I am not jealous of Rendell. I merely do not want people here, in my house.

His reputation had kept visitors at bay for almost nine years and yet, less than a week after Miss Bertram's arrival, his home was already invaded. It was more than a man should have to bear.

See the effect of a pretty face on a man? You do right to keep your distance. Would Rendell be here if the governess was an old harridan?

He thrust aside the thought he was being unfair to Rendell. He was in no mood to be reasonable—he did not

want people here. He preferred his animals and his birds
for company.

'Thank you for calling.' He forced a pleasant tone. 'I
apologise, but I have urgent matters needing my attention.'

Rendell stood and Nathaniel shook his hand.

'I am pleased to have made your acquaintance at long
last, my lord. Dare I hope we might see you in church one
of these Sundays?'

Nathaniel stared at him, then turned on his heel and
stalked from the room.

Impudent devil!

Chapter Eight

'Mrs Sharp.'

The housekeeper paused in the act of serving the evening meal. 'Yes, milord?'

'On Monday morning I shall require you to set aside an hour or two to watch Clara, if you please.'

'Yes, milord.'

He waited until Mrs Sharp left the room before saying, 'On Monday I shall instruct you on harnessing and driving Bill, Miss Bertram.'

He was tempted to relegate the task to Tam but, once the idea of teaching her himself had taken hold in his head, he could not relinquish it. She finished chewing her mouthful of food, then turned to look at him, her green eyes glittering. She was so beautiful, whereas he…he fought his usual battle not to move his head to hide his scars. Stupid, mindless reaction. She knew he had scars so what point was there in turning away?

'I am grateful, but there is no need for Clara to stay with Mrs Sharp. She can come with us. She will not be in the way.'

'Clara likes Mrs Sharp. You need not think she will be unhappy staying in the kitchen with her. Besides, it will do Clara good to be watched by someone other than you, in case—'

'In case what? In case I leave her?'

Nathaniel put down his knife and fork to give himself time to think. Why had she almost bitten his head off? Her head was bent, a muscle twitching in her cheek as she pushed her food around her plate with her fork.

She flicked a glance at him. 'I apologise. I did not mean to interrupt.'

'If you had allowed me to finish my sentence, I was about to say in case you are ever ill or indisposed,' he said. 'Mrs Sharp may be a little…sharp, for want of a better word, but she is fond of Clara.'

'I am aware of that. It was not for that reason I spoke as I did. I should not have done so, but…'

She had begun speaking with such resolve, but now she hesitated, her eyes searching his, the golden flecks in her irises reflecting the light of the candles. Nathaniel's nerves jangled a warning that he might not care for what she was about to say. He waited for her to continue.

'When I first came here, you said Clara had faced enough disruption in her life.'

'You cannot believe that staying with Mrs Sharp constitutes disruption.'

'No, of course I do not. But…your inference was that Clara should not have to cope with losing anyone else from her life.' Her head tilted and she raised her brows. 'What about you?'

'Me?' His voice deepened into a growl. 'What the dev… deuce do you mean by that?'

Her indrawn breath sounded loud in the silence. 'Her parents died. She has been here only a few weeks, getting used to you, and then I arrive. Other than this afternoon, she has not set her eyes on her Uncle Nathaniel since last Tuesday.'

He liked the way she said his name. *Nathaniel.* He thrust

that wayward thought aside and concentrated on her meaning. And, with a sense of shame, he realised she was right. That afternoon he had accepted he must change, but he still had not recognised the effect of his behaviour on Clara.

He recalled Miss Bertram's gentle rebuke: *'Clara is happy to see you, my lord.'*

In his efforts to shield himself he had failed to protect Clara from the very thing she must fear—losing someone else she loved. No wonder she had been so delighted to see him earlier and no wonder she had clung to him later, when he had said goodnight to her as she was about to go upstairs to get ready for her bedtime.

Miss Bertram continued to eat her meal, but her attention did not waver, stirring…what? Not discomfort. Not any more. Already he was becoming accustomed to her presence. And he wasn't annoyed by her presumption. Rather, he was intrigued by her pluck and determination. He could not condemn her concern for Clara's happiness.

'I stand chastised,' he said. 'And I thank you for pointing out my dereliction of duty.'

Her eyes blazed, shooting golden sparks. *'Duty?'*

He stiffened. 'You forget yourself, Miss Bertram.'

She took no notice. 'A child does not require *duty* from those upon whom she is entirely dependent. She requires… needs…love. And…and *time*. And—'

Nathaniel held up his hands, palms facing her, fingers spread. 'Enough! I concede. It was poor phrasing on my part and you are right. I shall ensure I spend more time with Clara in future. In the meantime, I hope you can accept she will not suffer if Mrs Sharp cares for her on Monday. Bill is docile, but I do not think harnessing a horse to a carriage should be undertaken with a young child underfoot. She will be much better off in the warm kitchen.'

Miss Bertram bowed her head. 'Agreed.'

They finished eating in their now customary silence but, as Sharp brought in the brandy at the end of their meal and

Miss Bertram stood to withdraw, an unexpected yearning for company beset Nathaniel.

'I shall take my brandy in the drawing room tonight, Sharp. And please tell Mrs Sharp to send in an additional cup with the tea tray.'

'Very well, milord.'

'Do you play chess, Miss Bertram? I have a fancy for a game.'

'I do not, my lord.'

'Would you care to learn?' He easily interpreted the doubt in those gold-green eyes of hers. 'There is no compulsion. I shall not dismiss you from your post if you refuse. We could as easily play a hand or two of cards.'

'I should like to learn the game. I have been told in the past that chess is a game the female mind cannot comprehend.' Her lips firmed, then she smiled, raising her chin. 'I viewed that as a challenge, but had no opportunity to discover whether he spoke the truth.'

'He?'

Grace did not immediately respond. They walked side by side to the drawing room and a sideways glance revealed a frown line between her brows and a wash of pink across her cheeks.

'He was an old friend.' There was the slightest tremble in her voice. 'He went away to be a soldier.'

A suitor, perhaps?

She had told him the barest of bones of her life before she had come to Shiverstone Hall. Would she ever reveal the flesh of her past? He would not ask. Why would he need to know about her life before? She was a governess. That was all he needed to know. That, and how well she cared for his niece.

They entered the drawing room.

Ah. He halted.

'The chess table,' he said. 'I forgot. It was stored away.'

There had been no need to keep it out: gathering dust,

creating work for Mrs Sharp, reviving painful memories for him. David had been his only opponent since he had moved here after the fire. And now...with David gone...

He tamped down the stab of pain and regret, turned on his heel and strode towards the dining room, grabbing a candlestick from a table as he passed. A patter of feet followed him.

'I can manage,' he said.

'It will be easier with two of us,' she said, sounding a touch breathless.

Nathaniel shortened his strides and a gurgled laugh reached his ears. He glanced down at Miss Bertram, now by his side.

Her eyes twinkled. 'It is hard work to keep stride with you, my lord. You have very long legs compared to mine.'

Nathaniel grunted at that naïve remark, his imagination delving under her ugly brown dress to the slim legs he suspected were hidden beneath. It took no effort to recall that glimpse of shapely ankle on her first day here. He tried to empty his mind of such thoughts the second they surfaced, but it was too late—his pulse had already accelerated. And the picture his wayward mind painted was not easily dismissed.

He directed his thoughts to the whereabouts of the table in a room filled with numerous unrecognisable items draped in holland covers.

'There.'

He pointed to a shrouded shape near the window. He tugged at the sheet covering it, revealing the chess table, a gift from Hannah and David. He smoothed his hand across the cool surface of the chessboard, created from sixty-four squares of attractively veined Italian marble set into a fine rosewood surround. Memories of a very different kind flooded his brain, dousing that inappropriate surge of lust.

'It is beautiful.'

He started as she copied his action, stroking the table

with reverence. The sight of her elegant hand, with its slender fingers and perfect oval nails, next to his ugly skin churned his stomach and he snatched his hand away.

He sensed her quick glance, but kept his eyes averted.

'How can you bear to hide such craftsmanship away?'

He bent to lift the table. 'It is not heavy. I do not need your help.'

'Where are the chess men?'

'Inside the table. The top is hinged.'

He carried it to the door, then hesitated, looking back. Miss Bertram stood stock still, gazing around the room, a speculative look on her face.

'Do not forget the candle,' he said.

She snatched up the candlestick and hurried after him.

He set the table near the window and dragged the two wooden chairs close so they could play. As he did so, Miss Bertram lifted the top of the table and peered inside.

'Draughts! We used to play draughts sometimes at the school, my friends and I.' At first delighted, her tone became wistful. 'Isabel taught us.'

'Isabel?'

'One of my best friends at school. There were four of us.' Her head snapped up, her eyes sparkling. 'May we play draughts? I do know how to play that game.'

'Are you backing away from that challenge you spoke of, Miss Bertram?'

She blushed. 'No, of course not.'

'Good. I shall teach you the basics tonight: what the pieces are called, how they may be moved and the aim of the game, which is to trap your opponent's king in such a way he has no safe square to move to.'

'And then you can kill him?'

She said it with such relish, he was startled into laughing.

'I trust you refer to the king and not your actual opponent?'

'For the moment.' She peeped saucily at him through her lashes, triggering a tug of response deep inside him.

How long was it since he had enjoyed a joke? He concentrated on keeping their conversation to the rules of chess.

'No, the king can never be removed from the board. It is sufficient to have surrounded him. Your opponent then surrenders his king and you have won the game. It is called checkmate.'

Her fine brows gathered into a frown. 'That seems very odd to me. I should rather kill the king. Then there would be no room for doubt.'

Nathaniel listed the different pieces on the board, explaining how each man could be moved and how important it was to plan several moves ahead and guard against losing the most valuable men.

'So…this one…' she reached out and picked up the black knight '…can move like so?' She put the piece on the wrong square.

'No, no. The knight's movement is the trickiest of all the moves to remember. He can move in an "L" shape. So—' he used his left hand to demonstrate '—from this square, this knight can move to here…and here…and…'

'And here!'

Her hand darted out and, before he could withdraw his own, she grasped his hand and tugged, sliding hand and knight together across the board to the fourth possible position. Her skin was warm against his, her fingertips soft. Fierce concentration creased her brow as she studied the board.

She pulled his hand again. 'And here!' She looked up, beaming. Then her mouth opened. 'Oh!' She snatched her hand from his. 'I am sorry. I…' Her cheeks bloomed beet-root red.

'You were carried away with enthusiasm?'

'Yes!' Her lips stretched in a tentative smile. 'Do you think I am ready?'

Nathaniel swallowed hard. She was so young. Naïve. 'Let us leave all that information to sink in,' he said. 'If you have time tomorrow, you might come in here and try to remember what each man is called and how he moves and then, in the evening, we will play.'

Her face clouded.

'And now...I shall challenge you to a game of draughts,' he said.

Her expression cleared. 'Oh, yes. That will be fun.'

Fun. An alien word to use in connection with himself and his life. He cleared the chessmen away and set out the draughtsmen whilst Miss Bertram poured the tea, brought in several minutes since by Mrs Sharp.

'You talked of your school friends earlier.' Nathaniel moved his counter in his opening gambit. 'Are they also governesses?'

What happened to your 'I don't want to know'? Or does that only apply to former beaux? Nathaniel dismissed that sneering voice as Miss Bertram played her opening move and he replied. He owed it to Clara to know more of the woman who would be raising her.

Didn't he?

'Yes. I am longing to hear how they go on.'

Miss Bertram studied the board, the tip of her tongue playing with her top lip, stirring long-suppressed needs deep inside Nathaniel. He forced his gaze to the board, but time and again it drifted back to the woman sitting opposite him.

'I asked Miss Fanworth to pass on my address to them so I hope they will soon write to me.' She moved another man, before adding, 'Although Rachel's letter might take a long time to reach England.'

'She has gone overseas?'

'Yes. She went to be the governess to the children of a sheikh, in the Kingdom of Huria. It is in the desert.'

'That does sound exotic. Did you not hanker after a similar adventure?'

She hesitated. 'No,' she said, finally. 'I think the North Country is enough of an adventure for me. Rachel's parents travelled much of the time, leaving her behind, and I think that is where her dream of travelling to faraway places began. She loves teaching children, so I am sure she will be happy.'

Silence fell whilst Miss Bertram again studied the board. She reached out and moved a man, jumping one of Nathaniel's, and grinned triumphantly as she made great play of removing it.

The devil. He would have to pay more attention to the game and less to his beautiful opponent.

'Isabel,' Miss Bertram said, as Nathaniel contemplated his next move, 'was the only one of us who spent much time with her parents as a child. Her papa taught her to play draughts and she taught us. She has gone to a family in Sussex, and Joanna, my other friend, has gone to a place in Hertfordshire. She is…she has no family and was brought up by Madame at the school.'

'You must miss your friends.'

'I do.' There was a pause. 'Do you not miss yours?'

'No.' Nathaniel kept his gaze on the game during the ensuing silence. Finally, he looked up. 'I no longer yearn after that frivolous way of life and my former friends crave nothing else.'

Irritated as much by his compulsion to explain as by her question, he studied the board again. There. A move he had overlooked. He moved one of his men, putting two of Miss Bertram's under threat. She peered more closely at the board.

'Hmmph. I cannot save both but, equally, you cannot take both. So I shall do this.' With another triumphant smile she moved a third man, reaching Nathaniel's side of the board and earning a 'crown' to turn her man into a king. 'Now I can move it forward *and* backwards.'

Nathaniel secured one of her men and they played on, the conversation on the safer territory of the game. When they finished, Nathaniel found himself the target of a pair of accusing green eyes.

'You allowed me to win.'

He had not. He had been too distracted to give the game his full attention.

'I thought it only fair to give you a taste of what you will be missing once we embark upon our chess challenge,' he said, looking down his nose at her. 'I want you to re-call the taste of victory even as the memory of it fades on your tongue.'

Miss Bertram laughed, revealing pearly white teeth. Nathaniel responded, but the stiff pull of the skin at the side of his face soon jerked him back to reality. What the hell was he doing?

'Come. The hour grows late.' He pushed to his feet and scooped the draughtsmen from the board. 'Open the top, if you please, Miss Bertram.'

She did as he requested and he returned the pieces to their place inside the table.

'Will you…will you be joining us at church tomorrow?'

Nathaniel reined in the temptation to snap a reply. She meant nothing by it. She was young and new to his house-hold. She would come to accept his decisions and Shiver-stone Hall would settle into a new routine.

'No.' He had no need to explain. He crossed the room to the door and opened it. 'Goodnight, Miss Bertram.'

He held the door wide as she passed through with a mur-mured, 'Goodnight, my lord.'

Chapter Nine

On Monday morning Clara sat happily at the kitchen table, helping Mrs Sharp knead dough.

She barely looked up when Grace said, 'Goodbye, sweetie. Be a good girl for Mrs Sharp.'

Despite the wrench of leaving Clara, even for so short a time, anticipation for the morning ahead fizzed through Grace's blood. She hurried from the kitchen and promptly collided with a wall of solid muscle. She teetered backwards and two hard hands gripped her arms as the scent of shaving soap and musk weaved through her senses. Her heart leapt and her pulse skittered.

'Oh!'

'Steady.' A finger beneath her chin tilted her head up and two deep brown eyes studied her, provoking a flush of heat through her body and into her cheeks. 'I had not thought you quite so eager to commence with your driving lesson, Miss Bertram.'

'I am sorry, my lord.'

Her voice sounded shaky. She cleared her throat and stepped back, tugging her upper arm free of his other hand. His hand fell away and her pounding pulse steadied.

'I did not want to keep you waiting.'

He held her gaze for a long moment, then smiled. 'Well, you have not, so you may relax.'

They left the house and, as they walked to the stables, a howl rent the air. Grace stopped, scarcely daring to breathe. 'What was that?'

'Brack.' Ravenwell kept moving. 'He objects to being shut up with the other dogs. I thought you might concentrate better with only Bill to worry about.'

Grace hurried to catch him up. 'It is not my fault I am unused to animals. I shall become accustomed to them, I promise you.'

It was the Marquess who stopped this time. 'I am sure you will. And to the human inhabitants also, I trust.'

'Everyone has been welcoming. Except—'

'Except Mrs Sharp. Yes, I am aware and I have spoken to her. It is not that she dislikes you but, as you must accustom yourself to the animals, so she must become accustomed to new people.'

Grace darted a look at him. It was not only Mrs Sharp who must grow accustomed to newcomers.

Inside the barn, Ravenwell entered a stall, slapping at the huge, rounded quarters of a grey horse who obligingly stepped sideways.

'Miss Bertram...' Ravenwell untied the horse and backed him from the stall '...meet Bill.'

Grace pressed back against the wall. Bill was not as tall as some horses, but he was wide and looked very strong. The head end was not as intimidating as the rear and Bill eyed her with a gentle eye and stretched his nose out, whiffling through his whiskers.

'Take off your glove, so he can learn your scent,' Ravenwell said.

Grace removed her glove, reached out a hesitant hand and stroked Bill's nose.

Ravenwell presented a chunk of carrot on his palm and

Bill picked it up delicately with questing lips and then crunched, eyes half-closed in contentment.

'Here.' Ravenwell passed Grace another piece of carrot. 'Hold your hand flat, like this.'

He supported her hand underneath with one hand and with the other he straightened her fingers. A pleasurable shiver darted through Grace, and she had to force herself to concentrate on his words.

'Never bend your fingers or thumbs. He would not mean to bite, but he might easily mistake them for a carrot. And horses have strong teeth.'

Ravenwell showed Grace the harness and how to tack up Bill, who stood patiently whilst she fumbled with straps and buckles and struggled with the notion she must open his mouth to put a metal bit between those long, yellow teeth.

'You may never need to harness him on your own but, if you should wish to go out and the men are out on the fells, it will be useful for you to know how to do it.'

They led Bill from the stable and backed him between the shafts of the gig, Grace gaining confidence all the time. Bill was so docile, how could she be scared of him? But she took care to keep her feet away from his huge hooves.

'Why does he have such hairy legs?' she asked as Ravenwell handed her into the gig and passed her the reins.

'They are called feathers. They protect the horse's legs against water and mud.'

He climbed into the gig and settled beside her, his thigh warm and solid next to hers, producing, once again, a shiver of awareness. He was so big, so male. She felt safe by his side.

'Now...' he reached for Grace's hands '...you hold the reins like so and Bill just needs a small shake to get him moving.'

Bill walked forward and the gig jerked into motion.

'Keep a light contact with his mouth—that is how you steer him—but you will find he is so familiar with the way to the village, you will hardly need to do anything. We will drive as far as the ford, so you can drive across the river, and then we will return home.'

Grace's confidence increased as the lesson continued. Her nerves dissipated and she began to enjoy both Ravenwell's company and the scenery. The weather was mild for the time of year: the sky a bright blue with white clouds scudding across it, although there was little wind at ground level. This was now her home. The isolation and wildness of the landscape fascinated her and she was surprised by a sudden impulse to take up her paints and attempt to capture its grandeur. At school, her skill and talent had been in portraits and miniatures and the art master, Signor Bertolli, had often despaired of her lack of aptitude in executing landscapes. Affection warmed her at the memory of her messy and disorganised but always encouraging teacher. It would be hard to find the time to paint, with Clara to care for, but she would enjoy the challenge of improving her skill and Clara would benefit in time, when Grace could use her knowledge to help her daughter acquire the accomplishments expected of a young lady.

'Thank you for teaching me to drive,' she said, on impulse. A skill was a skill, whether it was painting or driving. 'It will be agreeable not to have to rely on anyone else if I wish to visit the village.'

'Did you enjoy the church service?'

'Why, yes. As much as one ever enjoys being preached to.'

'I doubt Mr Rendell would appreciate hearing you say that.'

'Oh, he is not at all prosy, I assure you. He is just like any other young man. I told him you were teaching me to play chess and he said he might challenge you to a match one day.'

Silence. Grace peeped sideways. Ravenwell was frowning, his brow low and his mouth tight. She had thought he might be pleased—he must be lonely, living out here with no friends.

He has chosen to do so. You know he will not appreciate your interference.

She had spoken without thought and now the easy atmosphere between them had changed. She could not unsay those words, but she could smooth the moment with inconsequential chatter to distract him from his thoughts. From his fears. Although why such a powerful and wealthy man should fear anything was beyond Grace.

'Miss Dunn has invited me and Clara to call at the rectory next week. With your permission, of course, and if you think I can safely drive Bill?'

He glanced down at her, his frown lifting, to Grace's relief.

'I am sure you will cope, but I shall send Ned with you the first time to make sure.'

'Can you spare him from his duties?'

'Yes. Your and Clara's safety must take precedence. It will be pleasant for you to have a friend in the village.'

'Thank you.'

She sensed reservation behind his words. Was he concerned her visits to the village might result in callers at Shiverstone Hall? She could find no words to reassure him without openly mentioning his dislike of strangers. She still did not understand his choice to live this way. Was it embarrassment over his scars? He was a grown man and a lord. Could he not just brazen it out? Or was there something else. Something deeper? Sharp had hinted as much on her first night at the Hall. She vowed to find out more.

They had reached the river—Shiver Beck—and Grace drew Bill to a halt.

'Why do you not build a bridge? I got wet feet using those stepping stones on the day I arrived.'

She glanced at Ravenwell as she spoke and caught him biting back a grin.

'It is *not* funny.'

'Of course not.' His eyes danced, giving the lie to his words. 'No one normally *walks* from Shiverstone into the village. Drive on, Miss Bertram. You will not get wet feet in the gig.'

Grace shook the reins. Bill crossed the ford without hesitation but, as soon as they emerged on to the far side, Ravenwell showed Grace how to turn the gig for home. It was clear he had no intention of going anywhere near the village.

Grace drove back to Shiverstone and Ned emerged from the barn to unharness Bill and rub him down.

'Should I not learn to do that as well?' Grace asked.

'Very well. Ned, you may leave him to us.'

When they had finished, Grace looked up at Ravenwell to see him studying her with an amused smile. He removed one glove and reached to rub gently at her cheek.

Grace stilled at his touch, a *frisson* of awareness skittering down her spine and setting her insides a-flutter.

'You have a smudge,' he said.

His eyes wrinkled at the outer corners as he smiled and Grace's knees seemed to weaken, causing her to sway towards him. Horrified by her involuntary response, she braced her spine, even as every nerve ending in her body tingled and her breathing quickened.

'Now, as you have proved such an able pupil, I have another challenge for you.'

Grace swallowed. Hard. It was not the thought of a challenge that so unnerved her, but his intimate gesture and the way her pulse had leapt when he touched her, and her sudden awareness of how lovely and kind his eyes were when he smiled—not at all what one would expect from this normally terse man. Her response scared her a little. He was so very…*male*.

Ravenwell, in contrast, appeared oblivious to both his gesture and to Grace's reaction.

'I shall introduce you to the dogs,' he said.

Those words vanquished her embarrassment. A horse was one thing. Bill had stood obligingly still most of the time—he had been either tethered or in harness and thus under control. The dogs... She backed away a step.

'Come...you must not fear them or they will sense it. How shall you manage with Clara when she wants to visit the kennels?'

'Are they shut in? They will not be...' she swallowed, trying to quell her fear '...jumping around?'

Ravenwell laughed. 'I will not allow them to jump around.' He crooked his arm, proffering it to Grace. She hesitated and he raised one brow. 'The track up to the kennels is stony. I should not like you to turn your ankle. Come, you may meet them one at a time. They will make a noise, but they will not harm you.'

It felt odd, placing her hand on the arm of her employer. It was rock solid under her fingers and, again, she was reminded of his powerful build as his aura of masculinity pervaded every sense. She felt vulnerable and yet protected at the same time. A peculiar mix, but not unpleasant. Side by side they followed the path to the kennels.

'How many dogs do you have?'

'Nine, plus Brack. They are an assorted bunch—I use them mostly for hunting, except for Fly and Flash. They are collies and they work the sheep out on the fells. You can meet them first.'

Ravenwell and Grace headed back to the Hall some time later, Grace's head spinning with the names and purposes of the various terriers, spaniels, and the one pointer as well as the sheepdogs. Brack, sulking after being shut in the kennels, was at their heels.

'Why is Brack allowed indoors and not the other dogs?'

'I cannot imagine the chaos of living with that lot under one roof. No, they are happy enough in the kennels; they have known no different from when they were pups. Brack...his mother was a terrier—a big lass and a total hoyden she was. She went missing once for two weeks and, when she came home, she was in pup. Tam reckons she'd been visiting over towards Kendal. There's a pack of otter hounds out that way and when the litter came the pups had that look about them. And Brack certainly loves water. It might be hard to believe it now, but he was the runt of his litter. He failed to thrive and his mother rejected him. So I took him in and hand-reared him and he's lived in the Hall ever since. Eight years now.'

Grace reached out and patted Brack's rough head, aware that most men, given those same circumstances, would have destroyed the weak pup.

'What happened to his ear?' She fingered the ragged stump on the left side of his head.

'His mother bit it off when she rejected him. He may not be the most handsome dog in the world, but he is loyal and trustworthy.'

'Looks are not everything,' Grace said, opening the door to the kitchen, 'and he is very patient with Clara.'

A warm fug of air, filled with delicious smells, assailed them as they entered the room. Clara looked up, then scrambled from her chair as Grace removed her hat and her cloak.

'Ma Berm. Ma Berm,' she shouted, arms lifted as she ran to Grace.

'Miss Bertram,' Grace corrected, even as her heart skipped. It had sounded so like Mama. But she must never allow her guard to waver. She was Miss Bertram. Not Mama. She dropped her outer garments on a nearby chair as she lifted Clara and hugged her close. 'What have you been doing, little one?'

Alice looked up from her task of peeling potatoes.

'She's helped us with the baking, ma'am, and now Mrs Sharp has gone to the parlour to set out refreshments. She said as you'd both be famished after all that fresh air.'

'Uncle Nanniel!'

Clara squirmed in Grace's arms and then launched herself towards her uncle, arms outstretched. Grace, caught unawares, staggered with the shift of weight in her arms and found herself for the second time that day pressed up against the Marquess. His arms came around her, steadying her, whilst Clara's arms encircled her uncle's neck, hugging him tight, locking them into a three-way embrace. For a few wonderful moments Grace leant into Ravenwell's solid, muscular body. Her lids fluttered closed as his musky scent enveloped her and she relished the sensation of being held...of feeling safe. Then, aghast at the yearning such feelings invoked, she wriggled. After a couple of failed attempts, they eventually parted. Grace sneaked a glance at his lordship, to find him regarding her with laughter lighting his eyes.

'You will no doubt wish to refresh yourself before eating, Miss Bertram.'

A teasing note warmed his words, conjuring a silent *hmmph* from Grace. Whatever her instinctive response to his lordship, he clearly did not see her as anything other than an amusing diversion. Without volition, her hand lifted to her hair which had, she discovered, fallen from its pins. At that moment Mrs Sharp returned to the kitchen.

'There you are, milord. I have been to—'

Her mouth snapped shut and she raked Grace with a look of such suspicion Grace's cheeks fired up all over again. Then she raised her chin. She had done nothing wrong. What right did the housekeeper have to look at her as though she'd caught her in some misdemeanour?

'Alice was just telling us about the luncheon,' Ravenwell said into the sudden fraught silence. 'Thank you, Mrs Sharp. I am afraid Clara was a little over-enthusiastic in her welcome, so Miss Bertram is about to go and attend to her hair.' His lips twitched and Grace suspected him of holding back a laugh.

'You may leave this little miss with me, Miss Bertram, and we shall see you in the parlour when you are ready.'

Ten minutes later, having hastily washed her hands and face and brushed out and repinned her hair, Grace came downstairs, her steps slowing as an unfamiliar shyness at the thought of facing Lord Ravenwell came over her. She pressed her hands to her fluttering stomach as she reviewed the morning. What would his lordship think of her foolish reaction whenever they touched?

You are being ridiculous. He cannot know what you feel.

A high-pitched squeal sounded, quashing any remaining awkwardness, and she hurried to the parlour, where she stopped dead at the sight of Ravenwell crawling around the room, Clara perched on his back like a monkey, giggling as she wrapped her small fists in his hair, clinging tight.

Brack stood aside, tail wagging furiously.

'Ride Brack!'

'Ride Brack?' Ravenwell laughed, reared up on to his knees and reached behind to swing Clara from her perch. 'As you have asked so nicely, Miss Clara, you may ride Brack once around the room.'

He sat her on the dog's back, holding her and—Grace could see—supporting much of her weight.

'Miss Bertram, would you please lead Brack around the room?'

Grace started; she had not thought him aware of her presence. She came forward and took Brack's collar.

'Come, Brack.' She was thrilled when he moved at her command.

They completed the circuit, and Clara shouted, ''Gain! 'Gain!'

Ravenwell laughed, scooping her from Brack's back.

'You will tire Brack out and Miss Bertram and I are hungry.' He pulled a chair out for Grace. 'I shall think about buying a small pony for Clara next year. I am certain she will enjoy learning to ride. And you can learn at the same time.'

A simple statement to give so much pleasure. For the first time since she arrived at the Hall she truly felt she belonged. She had a settled place in the world and a family, of sorts. She sat, murmuring her thanks, her emotions welling as she resolutely ignored her earlier disquiet over the feelings stirred by his lordship.

Ravenwell plonked Clara on the chair next to Grace, handing her a slice of buttered bread.

'This will keep madam quiet whilst we eat,' he said. 'Oh, by the way...' he reached into his pocket '...Mrs Sharp gave me this after you left the kitchen.'

Grace took the letter from the Marquess and read her name on the front in a familiar hand. Isabel. It had been addressed to her at the school and the address scratched out and readdressed to her at Shiverstone Hall. She turned it over and on the back was a short note from Miss Fanworth, thanking Grace for her letter and promising to write very soon. Excited, Grace began to break the seal, but then stopped. She should not read the letter at the table. Besides, she wanted to savour every word in private, with no one watching and able to interpret her thoughts and feelings from her expression.

Grace spent much of the next half an hour trying to deter Clara from snatching a sample of every morsel of food upon the table and then discarding it after one nibble.

Ravenwell watched her efforts with a sardonic lift of his brow.

'And this illustrates perfectly why children should take their meals in the nursery.'

Grace bristled. 'She is just excited by being in here and eating with us.'

He laughed, holding his hands up, palms facing her. 'There is no need to leap to her defence, Miss Bertram. It was merely an observation. I am not about to chastise her for doing what children do.'

Grace bit her lip. She should not speak so boldly to her employer. 'I am sorry. And I concede your point. It does not make eating my own luncheon particularly easy.'

'At least you will not have to fret about the effect of Mrs Sharp's cooking on your waistline.'

Grace relaxed at the teasing glint in Ravenwell's eyes, then grabbed at Clara as she stood on her chair and prostrated her torso across the table in her determination to reach a plate of macaroons, despite the half-eaten one already on her plate.

'That is true.' Grace stood up, hoisting Clara on to her hip. Clara squirmed, protesting vocally but unintelligibly. 'Now, this little girl appears to have eaten her fill so I shall take her upstairs for her nap.'

Ravenwell had also risen to his feet and a warm tingle flowed through her at his gentlemanly gesture to a mere governess.

'And you, Miss Bertram? Have you satisfied your appetite after your exertions?'

She smiled. 'I have had sufficient, thank you, my lord. Thank you for teaching me to drive—I shall be sure to take advantage of my new skill.'

He cocked his head to one side. 'And dare I think you are becoming used to our countryside? You appeared to derive some enjoyment from the views.'

Grace untangled Clara's fingers from her hair. 'Oh, yes. I confess I found it somewhat bleak and intimidating at first, but I very much enjoyed it today. In fact, it has awoken a desire in me to get out my sketchbook, although I doubt I have the talent to capture its full glory. I have also resolved to take Clara for a walk every day, weather permitting.' She smiled at him. 'I might even take Brack.'

'Well! Today has been a success already and it is only half over.'

Grace headed for the door.

'Do not forget your letter, Miss Bertram.'

Isabel's letter! How could I forget?

Grace turned and Ravenwell was there, very close, the letter in his hand. She looked up, past the broad expanse of his chest, into his smiling brown eyes and awareness tugged deep in her core as, again, her pulse leapt and her breath quickened. His eyes darkened and grew more intense, then Clara pressed her cheek against Grace's and the moment passed.

'Thank you.' Grace took her letter, forced a quick smile and left the room, the meaning of that exchanged look teasing her brain.

Chapter Ten

Clara eventually dozed off and Grace escaped to her sitting room to read her letter.

It was concise, almost terse, and the news it contained shocked Grace to the core. Isabel, married? Her happy, joyful friend—who had loved to sing and had long dreamt of the passionate love with which she would one day be blessed—trapped in a marriage of convenience with the son and heir of a viscount?

Her marriage to William Balfour was, Isabel wrote, a joining of *'two sensible people in exact understanding of each other'*.

How Grace's heart ached for her friend. The letter sounded totally unlike the lively girl Grace loved like a sister. How she wished she lived closer and could offer her support and comfort. The date at the top of the letter told her it had been written way back in August. Poor Isabel. Wed over two months and Grace had not even known. She wondered how Isabel had fared since.

She would write back immediately and hope Isabel would be bolstered by her support. Although…her burst of enthusiasm faded. How could she write and burden Isabel with the truth about Shiverstone Hall and Clara?

Isabel asked in her letter if Grace had tracked down her baby and, if Grace wrote a reply, she must lie.

But to lie would be a betrayal of their friendship.

She would wait. She would write to her friend later—after a few more weeks, when she was more settled here at the Hall and hopefully Isabel would be in a happier frame of mind and Grace would have come to terms with her own deception.

That decision—really no decision at all, merely a putting off of the inevitable—fretted at Grace for the remainder of the day.

'You have been remarkably quiet this evening, Miss Bertram,' Ravenwell said as they sat opposite one another at the chess table after dinner. 'I hope your letter did not bring bad news?'

Grace's attention jolted back to the drawing room in which they sat. 'Not bad news, precisely. But unsettling.'

She gathered her thoughts and tried to focus on the game. She studied the board, then leaned towards it, peering at the chessmen as though a closer perspective might conceivably improve her position.

I know I'm a beginner, but how have I ended up in such a predicament after so few moves?

The Marquess was watching her, a small smile playing around his lips.

'Quite,' he said, as though she had spoken aloud. 'Your attention is clearly not on our game.'

'I am sorry.'

'No need to apologise. It takes practice, and one's full attention, to play well.' Ravenwell began to move the pieces back to their starting positions. 'We will play another night, when you are not so preoccupied.'

He pushed back his chair and stood up, brandy glass in hand. He was going. Probably to his book room to work on his ledgers. Her surge of disappointment shocked Grace as she anticipated a long evening alone with her thoughts.

Ravenwell, however, did not move away from the table.

'Would you care to talk about whatever is bothering you?'

Grace recognised the effort it must cost this private man to make such an offer—she had seen and appreciated his efforts to change since she had pointed out that his avoidance of her was punishing Clara. She was no longer intimidated by his brusqueness, which she now knew concealed a gentle man who loved his niece and was kind to his animals.

'Isabel's news seems to be all I am able to think about. Mayhap saying it out loud will help me make sense of it.'

He gestured to the chairs by the fire. 'Come, then.'

Where to start? But the Marquess was—or once was—a man of the world in which Isabel now found herself. He might be able to ease some of Grace's worries.

She told him about Isabel and her arranged marriage with William Balfour.

'Balfour… I know of the family, but I cannot recall a William. He is no doubt younger than I. But why you are so worried for your friend? She has made an excellent match. She will be set up for life.'

'You do not understand.'

How could he possibly understand when he had never met the free spirit that was Isabel?

'Isabel's parents doted on her…she dreamt of singing in the opera and she thrives on being adored. How will she survive with a husband who does not love her?'

Grace cringed at Ravenwell's huff of amusement. *He thinks me a romantic ninny now.* 'You do not believe love is necessary in a marriage?'

'I do not. You, on the other hand, expose your youth and naivety in believing such poetical nonsense.'

If only he knew...

The veil had been swept from her eyes long ago. In her mind's eye she saw Clara's father, Philip, tall, lean and handsome with his ready smile, charm personified, who had flirted with her sixteen-year-old self and persuaded her of his love—Philip, whose immaturity sent him fleeing to join the army when Grace had told him she carried his child. Philip, who had been dead nigh on fourteen months, killed in action.

She felt the familiar wash of sorrow over Philip's death on the battlefield, but she had long since accepted that what she had felt for him had been infatuation, fed by his flattery and her foolish pride that such a handsome youth should take notice of her and make her feel important. Every trace of her naïve, youthful love had been wiped from her heart as she saw him for precisely what he was: a self-serving youth who thought sweet words were a sufficient price to pay to get what he desired.

And he was right, wasn't he?

A shudder shook Grace at the memory of that terrifying period in her life when she had succeeded in concealing her condition from everyone other than her best friends but, despite everything, she would not allow her experience with Philip to sour her.

'I cannot accept that love can be dismissed as mere poetical nonsense.'

'You make my point for me. You have no experience of the real world. Indeed, how could you have? You have been secluded at your school since the age of...what...ten?'

'Nine.'

'Nine. Precisely. Naïve nonsense. You should do yourself a favour and rid your brain of such romantic drivel.'

He could not hide his bitterness. Was it because of his scars, or had he unhappy experiences of love? Well, she would not allow him to sully her opinion of the world. She had always—like Isabel—believed in true love.

'Your friend will do very well in her marriage,' he continued, 'and it is a waste of your time to be fretting about her.'

'That is—' Grace stopped.

'That is what, Miss Bertram?'

His eyes were dark and unfathomable. His jaw set.

Sad. But she did not dare say that. She must not be lulled by this new, friendlier Ravenwell. He still paid her wages and he could still dismiss her if she forgot her place.

'That is no doubt wise advice,' she said instead. 'There is nothing I can do to help Isabel. Besides, she has a strength and determination that I am sure will help her cope.'

Ravenwell stood. 'Now your mind is at rest, I have work to do. I shall bid you goodnight.'

He strode from the room, leaving Grace staring after him.

What is going on inside his head? He cannot be happy, living like this.

She switched her gaze to the fire, watching mindlessly as the embers glowed red, emitting an occasional tongue of flame and sending intermittent sparks up the chimney. Her heart went out to the Marquess. How lonely he must be. She would love to see him smile more often and relax. There and then she swore to do all she could to bring more light, life and laughter to his life.

'What have you been saying to put his lordship in such a tear, missy?'

Grace started. She had not heard Sharp come in.

'I am not sure. We were talking about love and marriage…concerning some news I had from a friend,' she added hastily, in response to Sharp's smirk. 'He told me to rid my mind of romantic drivel and thoughts of love, then said he has work to do and left.'

Sharp tidied their empty cups on to a tray, then picked

up Ravenwell's abandoned brandy glass—still half-full—and drained it with a single swallow and a wink at Grace.

'Ah.' He placed the empty glass on the tray and shook his head. 'No wonder.'

'Why do you say that?'

Sharp tapped his finger against the side of his nose. 'I'm not one to gossip.'

'You are admirably discreet, Sharp, but you *understand* his lordship and that is why I ask you rather than any of the others—'

'The others? They do not know the half of what I know.'

'I'm certain *they* do not know the real reason his lordship cuts himself off from his friends and family.'

'No, they don't.' Sharp sat in the chair opposite Grace and leaned forward. 'Only me and Mrs Sharp know the whole truth. We was all at Ravenwell then, living at the Dower House while the manor was being rebuilt. His lordship had been courting Lady Sarah before the fire, but when he went to London to see her, she'd have nothing to do with him. She wed someone else soon after.

'He came home, and never went down south again. Even at Ravenwell, the stares and the whispers were so bad he'd barely leave the estate, but he still suffered from the guilt.'

Guilt? Grace longed to probe, but feared if she interrupted Sharp now he might clam up.

'And then his mother took it into her head to arrange a marriage. To Miss Havers. Desperate for a title and money, she was. But the little bi—beg pardon, *witch*—took one look at his lordship and swore that neither title nor wealth were sufficient to entice her to wed a monster. 'Course, that was soon after the fire. His scars were still raw then. They look better now.'

Ignorant women! Scorning an injured man in that way, destroying his faith in love. If I could get my hands on them...

Sharp's gaze rested on Grace's hands—curled into fists

on her lap—and he smiled. 'Now you see why my missus is so protective of his lordship,' he said softly.

'After that—' his voice was brisk again '—we came to live here and we've been here ever since.'

It was as Grace suspected. Ravenwell had cut himself off from society to protect himself from rejection. And yet...that didn't really explain it. A man such as he...if he wanted to mix with others, surely he was strong enough to withstand a few stares and pitying glances?

'And the guilt?'

Sharp's eyes narrowed. 'I've said too much. Never you mind, missy, 'tis none of your business.'

Grace halted the gig and tied off the reins, as Ravenwell had taught her, delighted and proud at having successfully accomplished her first drive to Shivercombe. They were in the lane outside the rectory and she looked round as the front door was flung open.

'Miss Bertram!'

Mr Rendell—tall, slender, and handsome—hurried down the path to the front gate, beaming. There had been a time, Grace realised, when the attention of such a man would have set her heart soaring but now, although she was pleased to see the curate again, her heart remained stubbornly unmoved.

In her mind's eye an image of a very different sort arose—dark, brooding, attractive in an altogether different way—the difference between a boy and a man. She tried hard to ignore the *frisson* of desire and need that trickled down her spine.

'Good afternoon, Mr Rendell.' She accepted his hand to assist her from the gig and then lifted Clara down. 'As you can see, I have braved my first drive to the village, albeit with Ned in attendance to ensure Clara and I come to no harm.'

Ned had ridden behind the gig and now came forward to take charge of Bill.

'In that case, I shall congratulate you upon the success of your first outing and express my delight in finding you both unscathed by the experience. The weather is currently kind and it would be wasteful not to take advantage.'

'It would indeed. Miss Dunn did invite us to call upon her, but—because of the weather—we did not specify a day. I do hope this is not an inconvenient time? We shall not stay above half an hour, but having a purpose for my drive made it all the more enjoyable.'

'Alas, I am on my way to visit a parishioner, but Miss Dunn is at home and I make no doubt she will be delighted to see you. With your permission, I shall escort you to her and then I must be on my way.'

'Thank you, sir. Ned, we shall not be long.'

'Go round to the kitchen door when you have secured the horses, Ned,' Mr Rendell said, 'and Cook will find you some refreshments.'

The curate picked up Clara and led the way into the square, stone-built rectory. He showed Grace into a smart drawing room and went in search of Miss Dunn.

The first person to come into the room was the Reverend Dunn, his twinkly eyes creased into slits by his cherubic smile.

'Miss Bertram, what a pleasant surprise. Elizabeth asks if you will join her in the parlour where there are some little friends young Clara might like to meet.'

He winked at Grace, held his hand out to Clara, who took it without hesitation, and ushered Grace before him, indicating a door at the end of the passageway.

'It is not as grand as the drawing room and we would not normally entertain visitors in here, but I am sure you will take us as you find us.'

Grace pushed open the door and stepped into a much cosier, if somewhat shabbier, room. The thought flashed through her mind that here was a home in which one could feel comfortable, in stark contrast to the dark, unwelcoming reception rooms at the Hall. The idea of effecting some changes—sparked initially by the beauty of the chess table—grew stronger.

'Good afternoon, Miss Bertram.'

The voice shook her from her thoughts and she gazed around what appeared to be an empty room.

'Go on in,' urged the Reverend Dunn from behind her.

Grace walked forward and there, shielded from the door by a sofa, was Miss Dunn, sitting on a rug before the fire with two kittens scrambling over her lap whilst a third pawed at a length of string being dangled in front of its nose. A large tabby-and-white cat sat to one side, assiduously washing itself whilst keeping one eye on the youngsters.

Grace laughed as the kitten pounced on the string and tumbled on to its back.

'Good afternoon, Miss Dunn,' she said. 'I had forgotten about the kittens you mentioned on Sunday. They are very pretty.'

'Please, call me Elizabeth, for I am sure we are destined to be bosom friends.' She gestured to a chair and bade Grace sit. 'I hope you do not object to being received in our family parlour, but Mama has banned these little ones from the drawing room. Quite rightly, given the havoc they wreak. Please forgive me for not rising but, as you see, I am serving the useful purpose of providing a soft lap for their play.'

'Of course. And you must call me Grace.'

Her spirits rose. How lovely it would be to have a friend so close to her new home; it would help to ease the pain of missing her school friends.

'Look, Clara. See the kittens? Are they not sweet?'

Clara ran forward, all eagerness, and the kittens scattered.

'You must take care if you are not to frighten them, Clara,' Miss Dunn said, gathering her on to her lap. 'Sit here with me and we shall see which of them is bold enough to come and meet you.'

An hour later, Grace tapped the reins on Bill's broad back and they set off on the drive to Shiverstone Hall, Ned riding behind. Grace waved goodbye to Elizabeth and to Mr Rendell, who had not long before returned from his visit and joined them in the parlour, along with Mrs Dunn and a tea tray. Watching her new friend and Mr Rendell together—catching the occasional shared glance and the resulting pink tinge of Elizabeth's cheeks—Grace suspected there was more to their friendship than they might wish anyone to suspect.

As they left the village, Grace glanced at Clara, sitting quietly for once, one hand clutching tight at the handle of a covered wicker basket wedged on the seat between them. Doubts surfaced. Had she presumed too much, accepting this gift for Clara? Then Clara looked up at her, shining eyes huge in her beaming face, and all doubts shrivelled.

Ravenwell loved Clara.

He would not begrudge her a kitten.

Would he?

Thinking about the Marquess set up those peculiar nervy sensations deep in the pit of Grace's stomach once again. They had plagued her ever since the moment he had wiped that smudge from her cheek. Ridiculous thoughts and longings flitted in and out of her mind, no matter how hard she tried to quell them. She did not need to concentrate on driving. Bill, as Ravenwell had promised, needed no guidance to find his way home. Instead, she diverted her wayward thoughts by admiring the beauty of the day and of the surrounding scenery, imagining in her mind's eye how she might capture it on canvas.

Chapter Eleven

Nathaniel trotted Zephyr steadily down the track that led through the forest towards the village as Brack ranged through the trees, nose to the ground. He was concerned about Clara's safety. That was the only reason he couldn't settle to anything this afternoon, after he learned that Grace had driven them both in the gig to Shivercombe. Never mind that Ned was there to keep them safe. That was his role. He would only go as far as the river and he would await them there, if he did not come upon them beforehand. Sharp had assured him Miss Bertram only intended to stay at the Rectory for half an hour before returning and they had already been gone an hour and a half.

He emerged from the forest and followed the track as it curved towards the ford in the river. Here, large slabs of rock—smoothed by centuries of erosion by the flowing waters of Shiver Beck—had been laid across the riverbed to create a place for carriages to cross. The only time it became impassable was after heavy rain when—although not very much deeper—the swiftness of the current rendered the ford treacherous. At least the water level fell as quickly as it rose, so they were never cut off from the village for long.

Nathaniel reined Zephyr to a halt as they reached the

ford and slid from the saddle, pulling the reins over the horse's head so he could crop the grass whilst they waited. Brack, as usual, could not resist the lure of the water and swam into the deeper water, downstream of the ford. It was a beautiful, crisp November day, but Nathaniel was in no mood to appreciate either the weather or the natural beauty of his surroundings. He crossed his arms and tapped his foot, his attention fixed on the track that led from the ford and soon disappeared from view as it wound into the village.

Finally, as he was beginning to think the unthinkable— that he must go into the village and make certain they were safe—he heard the *clip-clop* of horses' hooves and the rattle of wheels. His heart returned to its rightful position in his chest as Brack exploded from the river and shook himself thoroughly, sending sparkling drops of water arcing through the air. Nathaniel mounted Zephyr, sending him splashing through the ford as Bill plodded into view, towing the gig, and he heard Miss Bertram say, 'Look, Clara. There is Uncle Nathaniel.'

'Uncle Nanniel! See kitty!'

Bill halted beside Zephyr. Clara bounced up and down on the bench seat whilst Miss Bertram…he focussed on the governess. Miss Bertram did not quite meet his gaze. She looked sheepish. Guilty, even. What had happened in the village?

'Ned, you may ride on ahead,' Nathaniel said. 'There is no need for us both to accompany the gig.'

Even while he was speaking, he was chewing over the meaning of her expression. Had she met with Rendell? Did she feel guilty for meeting him whilst she was meant to be looking after Clara? He tamped down the spiral of anger that climbed from deep in the pit of his stomach, knowing he could not begrudge her some independence or the opportunity to make friends. He might choose to live the life of a recluse, but he could not insist that others—even if they worked for him—follow suit.

Besides—he took in Clara's joyous expression—it was good for Clara.

He reined Zephyr around, called Brack—who appeared strangely eager to clamber into the gig—to heel and nudged the stallion back into the river. A glance behind showed Bill following behind, splashing through the crystal water that reached halfway to his knees as he negotiated the ford with the ease of long familiarity. Once they reached the other bank, Nathaniel rode alongside the gig.

'Did you visit Miss Dunn?' She had said they would visit the rectory, to call upon the vicar's daughter.

'Yes, indeed, and we agreed we are to be friends and I am to call her Elizabeth and she will call me Grace.' She threw a huge smile in his direction, but it did not distract him from the tinge of anxiety in her eyes or prevent him from noticing her hurried speech. 'We had an exceedingly pleasant visit and then Mrs Dunn joined us, and Mr Rendell, and—'

'Kitty!' Clara half-stood in her effort to interrupt Miss Bertram and gain Nathaniel's attention. 'Kitty!'

'Hush, Clara. Sit down. It is dangerous to stand up.' Miss Bertram scooped Clara's legs from under her and plonked her back on the seat. 'And it is rude to interrupt.'

'Uncle *Naaaaaanniel*.' Clara's appeal was a whine of frustration.

Miss Bertram shot him a wary look from under the rim of her bonnet, then reined Bill to a halt, her expression resigned.

'I had better confess this now, for you shall discover the truth soon enough.'

Every beat of Nathaniel's heart thundered in his ears. What was she about to tell him? Sudden fear gripped him, clenching his stomach. He couldn't lose her. Clara would be inconsolable.

Miaow.

Brack reared up on his hind legs, his front paws on the step as he thrust his head on to Miss Bertram's lap, whining.

'Brack! Get down, sir! My apologies, Miss Bertram, I cannot think what has possessed him.'

'I can.' She brushed at the damp patch on her brown pelisse with a rueful smile.

'Kitty!'

Miaow.

'Oh, heavens! There is no help for it. My lord, Elizabeth... Miss Dunn...gave Clara a kitten.' Her tone rang with defiance, but her expression was wary. 'I know I should have asked your permission first, but—'

'*Kitty.* Uncle Naffaniel. Kitty!'

A kitten! He forced down the relieved laugh swelling his chest. And he had feared—he did not allow that thought to develop. It did not matter what he had feared. He was in danger of allowing his imagination too free a rein when it came to Miss Bertram. Their conversation the other night about romance should be enough to convince him to keep his distance. If she *had* developed a *tendre* for Rendell, so much the better.

'No wonder Brack is so interested in the gig. I assume it is inside the basket?'

Grace nodded.

'See kitty?'

'Not now, poppet. If he runs away we shall never find him. Besides, Brack might eat him for supper.'

'Oh, no. I did not think...might Brack hurt him?'

'Come, let us get home.' The horses began to move again. 'And I do not know, is the honest answer. We have never had cats at the Hall, but he is a hunting dog, so...'

Her face was stricken. 'What have I done? Clara will be devastated if he should get hurt.'

'Then we shall make sure he stays safe.'

'Thank you.'

Her face, as always, lit up with her smile, her mercurial eyes shifting from green to gold and back again. They were as changeable as the play of sunlight through the first leaves of spring, the colour always shifting, reflecting the light, and… Nathaniel tore his gaze from hers.

'It remains to be seen what Mrs Sharp will say.'

Their gazes clashed again—this time with a conspiratorial mix of amusement and trepidation.

'A cat? *Indoors?*' Mrs Sharp propped her hands on her hips. 'It will run riot, up and down the curtains, scratching the carpet. And the *mess…*'

'I am sorry, Mrs Sharp, I did not think of that. But… look at Clara's face…how could you deny…?'

Miss Bertram cast an anxious look at Nathaniel.

'The decision is made, Mrs Sharp. How hard can it be for five adults to keep control of one small kitten?' Nathaniel set the basket on the table as he spoke and unbuckled the strap that held the lid in place.

'My lord! Not on the *table.*'

'I shall not put the cat on the table, Mrs Sharp. I am merely removing it from the basket.'

Sharp—who had jumped guiltily from his favourite chair in the corner as Nathaniel, Grace and Clara had come into the kitchen—peered into the basket as Nathaniel lifted the lid. A reedy *miaow* issued forth, followed by a black-and-white face, whiskers quivering.

Sharp reached in and picked up the kitten. 'You look like you've been a-sweeping the chimneys.' He grinned at Grace. 'Is that his name? Sweep?'

'Sweep!' Clara reached up for the kitten.

'There, little miss.' Sharp put the kitten down and it shot across the room and underneath the large dresser at the far end.

'Causing havoc already,' Mrs Sharp grumbled as Clara let out a wail and toddled after the kitten.

'Oh, dear. I am sorry, Mrs Sharp.' Grace went to the dresser and knelt down to peer underneath.

Nathaniel's eyes were immediately drawn to the shapely round of her bottom, suggestively outlined by her woollen dress. He wrenched his gaze away, irritated he should even notice.

'Allow me, Miss Bertram.'

He crossed the kitchen to kneel beside her and reached under the dresser. Needle-sharp claws raked his hand and he bit back his curse as he scooped up the kitten and dragged it from its hiding place.

'Take the kitten up to the nursery where it is quieter.' He thrust the kitten at Miss Bertram. 'It will be your responsibility to clean up after it and to train it. Is that understood?'

'Yes, my lord,' she said, her eyes downcast.

He felt an ogre, snapping at her like that, but at least no one would suspect the truth of his wayward thoughts—they would blame his sour mood on the kitten.

He hoped Brack would accept it—he made a mental note to introduce them as soon as possible. It was a pretty little thing, with a fluffy coat that was mostly black, with white on its face, stomach, paws, and tail. Sweep. The name suited it, with its white face marred only by a black smear across its upper lip and another around one eye.

He watched Miss Bertram leave the kitchen, the kitten cradled in her arms. Clara bounced alongside, clearly delighted with her new friend.

She would not be intimidated by him. She had moved beyond that stage. She could see past his brusqueness. He would grow to accept Sweep as soon as he saw how much Clara loved her kitten. He would do anything to make Clara happy. Grace brushed out her hair and twisted it into a chignon as she prepared for dinner. Clara was already asleep, exhausted with all the excitement of the day, and Sweep sat on Grace's bed, watching her from wide green eyes.

'You will have to stay in the kitchen at night,' she told him.

She'd thought long and hard about it, but she could not have Sweep disturbing Clara at night, neither did she want him in her bedchamber. Cats, she knew, were often active at night and likely to disrupt her sleep. Now she had only to persuade Mrs Sharp to agree. She smoothed her dress over her hips and scooped Sweep off the bed.

'Mrs Sharp…' she said as she entered the kitchen.

'What is that cat doing here?'

'Now, now, missus.' Sharp came to Grace and took the kitten from her. 'Miss Bertram can hardly leave Sweep upstairs with Miss Clara asleep, can she? And you were complaining about mice only t'other day.' He winked at Grace. 'He'll do grand in here of an evening and Miss Clara can play with him during the day.'

'Hmmph. Just you keep it from under my feet. I'm too busy to have to watch where I'm stepping all the time.'

Grace handed Sweep to Sharp, smiling her thanks, and headed for the parlour. That was her first challenge accomplished and more easily than she had anticipated. Now for the second.

She waited until they had withdrawn to the drawing room, and Mrs Sharp—still grumbling under her breath about *that cat*—had delivered the tea tray. The Marquess, as was now his custom, had carried his brandy glass through from the parlour. Grace poured tea for herself and, ignoring the chess table, she settled into one of the two fireside chairs. Ravenwell hesitated, raised a brow and then joined her.

'Do I detect a desire to talk rather than play?'

'Yes, my lord.' She was committed now. She must do this, for Clara's sake. The worst he could do was refuse.

'When I first came, you said I might make changes to the nursery wing.'

He inclined his head. 'I did indeed. And have you done so?'

'I have, with help from Alice.'

'And did you find everything you need?'

'Yes…'

Grace sucked in a breath, but before she could continue, he said, 'I sense a question coming.'

Grace bristled at the smile teasing the corners of his mouth. He thought her amusing. Someone to be indulged.

'I am only asking for Clara's sake,' she said stiffly. 'I want her to have a home here.' She waved her arm, indicating the room in which they sat. 'The nursery and her bedchamber are now comfortable and cosy, but what about here?'

His brows snapped into a frown. 'Here? This is a drawing room. Not a place for children.'

'Children?' She leant forward. 'We are speaking of your niece. Do you intend for her never to come in here?'

'She does come in here,' he growled.

'Precisely.' Satisfied she had made her point, she sat back. 'Look around you. I am sorry if I speak out of turn, but there is nothing welcoming or homely about this room. And what about Christmas?'

'Christmas?' His brows shot up. 'What about Christmas?'

How could she explain without sounding full of self-pity? She did not want Clara's memories of her childhood Christmases to echo hers.

'What did Christmas mean to you as a boy?'

Understanding dawned in his eyes, and he smiled. 'Stir-up Sunday, delicious smells from the kitchen for days on end, gathering greenery and bringing in the Yule log, going to church on Christmas morning, exchanging gifts.' He gazed into the flames, a wistful look on his face, as he listed his memories. 'Twelfth Night and the Lord of Misrule. Family gatherings with pantomimes and charades…'

He fell silent. He looked…lost and vulnerable. It was the only time Grace had ever seen him with his guard down and her heart went out to him. It had been his choice to live this isolated life but he had been forced into it by the reactions of others. He had only been twenty-one. Such a young man.

He appeared to recollect her presence and his lips firmed. 'It is not the same now. I am happy with the house the way it is.'

'You may be content and you may not relish the thought of celebrating Christmas, but…do you not see? It is our responsibility to make sure Clara's childhood memories are as happy as yours.'

Ravenwell tilted his head as he focussed on Grace. 'And as happy as yours?'

'Some of them,' she admitted. 'The later ones. The Christmases I spent at school, with my friends, are some of my happiest memories.'

'And were your early Christmases *un*happy?'

'Not unhappy, precisely, but then I knew no different. My uncle and aunt were extremely devout and they eschewed anything that smacked of pagan tradition. For them, it was all about church and charity. Laudable, I know, but… for a child…'

She rose to her feet and walked away from the fireplace, away from the warm glow of the flames and the candles on the mantelshelf, to the dark end of the room, then stopped and faced him.

'This room should be the heart of the home and the focus of Christmas.' She waved her arm, encompassing the unlit fire and the bareness of the rest of the room.

Ravenwell looked around the room as if seeing it for the first time. 'I see what you mean. For Clara's sake.'

She smiled. 'For Clara's sake.' She returned to her chair.

'I should like to move some of the furniture back in here, with your permission.'

'I shall not object, as long as Mrs Sharp is agreeable. We kept the furniture to a minimum to lighten her chores. It has never bothered me in the past.'

'She has Alice to help now. And if the work should still be too much, I am sure Annie would be happy to earn a little extra.'

'You may do as you think fit.'

She had not expected enthusiasm; his grudging approval was a step in the right direction. She had vowed to turn this bleak house into a happy home for Clara. Now that vow had widened to include Lord Ravenwell.

Chapter Twelve

Three days later, Clara woke with a runny nose and a sore throat. She was listless and touchy all morning and Grace could do little other than sit and cuddle her next to the nursery fire. Even Sweep was unable to raise a smile or a spark of interest and the morning dragged as Grace remained on tenterhooks, constantly alert for signs of a fever developing. The only bright point was a letter from Rachel, sent all the way from Huria—via Miss Fanworth—which Ned brought back from the village.

Rachel's letter described a very different world to Shiverstone Hall. She wrote of the luxury of the palace she lived in—*a palace!*—the vastness of the surrounding desert and the beauty of the verdant oasis. She had three children in her care—eight-year-old Aahil, his sister Ameera, six, and his brother, Hakim, four—who were slowly growing to trust her. Grace could read her love for the children in the words she had penned. About her employer, the majestic-sounding Sheikh Malik bin Jalal al-Mahrouky, she said but little. There was caution in her words and Grace thought he must be most intimidating.

A little before eleven Mrs Sharp sent Alice upstairs to offer to sit with Miss Clara for a spell whilst Miss

Bertram went to the kitchen for a cup of chocolate. Grace took Sweep with her, putting her next to Brack who, unusually for this time of day, was curled up near the kitchen range. After a hesitant beginning, the two animals had become friends.

'How is she?' Mrs Sharp handed Grace a cup of warm chocolate.

'Tetchy. And most displeased at being left with Alice,' Grace said, sitting at the table. 'Thank you.'

'It is to be hoped you do not succumb to the cold as well. You look pale.'

The housekeeper's concern was unexpected, endearing her to Grace, who cradled the cup between her hands and sipped, then tipped her head back, heaving a sigh, watching mindlessly whilst Mrs Sharp chopped carrots.

'I cannot believe how exhausting it is, sitting and doing nothing other than nursing Clara.'

'Has she slept at all?'

'Not yet.' Grace finished her chocolate and stood up. 'I must return and relieve Alice. Poor Clara, she is so miserable. She does not know what she wants, but she wants it *now*.'

'I have mixed up a remedy for her, to help ease her throat.' Mrs Sharp often treated common ailments within the household with her remedies. 'Give her a spoonful and then, when she does fall asleep, I will sit with her. You'll be bound to have a disturbed night with her and you have missed your walk today. You should go outside for some exercise whilst you are able to. It is a beautiful day.'

Startled by the housekeeper's unusual solicitude, Grace thanked her and, when Clara dozed off shortly after luncheon, Grace took her up on her offer.

Ravenwell had been out since first light, according to Sharp, sitting in his favourite overstuffed armchair in the corner as he sucked on his pipe. Grace lingered, hoping to learn a little more about her puzzling employer.

'Likes to keep himself busy, see. Stops him from brooding.'

'Brooding?' Grace busied herself folding Clara's freshly laundered clothes, as though any answer was of no consequence and she asked merely to be polite. The best way to wheedle information from Sharp was to pretend disinterest.

'Oh, aye. He exhausts himself every day, to stop him thinking about his father. It's the guilt.'

Guilt. Sharp had mentioned guilt before, but always refused to explain.

'Oh, I cannot believe his lordship has anything to feel guilty about.'

'Well that's just where you'd be wrong, missy.' Sharp tilted his head back and, eyes half-closed, blew a perfect smoke ring into the air. 'So you don't know ever'thing, for all yer education.

'No,' he went on after a pause. 'He'll never forgive himself. Feels it here—' and he thumped his chest in the region of his heart '—he does. He ain't the hard man you think he is.'

I don't think him a hard man at all. But she had more sense than to say so to Sharp.

'We tried to stop him going back into the fire, but three of us couldn't hold him back, he was that determined.'

'Was that the fire at Ravenwell Manor?'

'If'n only we could've stopped him, but he were like a man possessed. And his mother. It fair curdled the blood to hear her screams.'

'But…' she had to ask and hope Sharp wouldn't clam up '…why did he go back into the fire? Is that when he got burned?'

'Aye. 'Twas his father. He couldn't walk so well and he was upstairs when it broke out. His lordship…the Earl of Shiverstone as he was then…tried to rescue him. He got as far as the bedchamber, but then the roof caved in and his father was gone. Lord, the nightmares he suffered afterwards. Not to mention the pain. If'n you've ever burned your hand with a candle flame, missy, you'll know the agony. Only multiply that a hundred...a thousand...fold, and you might get nearer the truth.'

Poor Nathaniel. A hard lump of misery lodged in Grace's throat as she imagined his suffering, at only twenty-one years of age. Two years older than she was now. Another piece of the puzzle that was Lord Ravenwell slotted into place. The guilt, as well as the scars, must have been an intolerable burden to one so young.

She donned her pelisse and set off to walk up the hill behind the Hall, her sketchbook under her arm, hoping to capture the wildness and beauty of the landscape with her pencil. She had never ventured up on to the fells before— it was too far for Clara to walk—and she looked forward to exploring this area of her new home.

Her breath grew short as she plodded up the path, determined to reach Shiver Crag, jaggedly silhouetted against the blue of the sky, but she found she had to stop long before then to catch her breath.

She gazed back the way she had come. The day was clear and sharp, and the land fell away below her to flatten into the dale, with its woods and pasture. There was the river she had to drive across to reach the village and... she searched, her hand shielding her eyes...yes, there was the church tower, jutting out amongst the jumble of rooftops. Her chest swelled as she breathed in the cold air, refreshing her lungs and making her blood sing with energy.

She would walk a little further and sketch a little before going back. And she would hope that somehow, miraculously, her nap had restored Clara to full health. Her attention was caught by a huge, golden-brown bird circling lazily in the sky. *Good heavens.* She had thought the bird she saw when she first arrived at the Hall was big, but...this one was gigantic. She watched its mesmerising, effortless glide and marvelled at the span of its broad wings, tipped by feathers that resembled splayed fingers.

She looked back up to the crag. It was further than she first thought. She would have no time to reach it today, but it would be an imposing focal point for her sketches if she walked just a little further, to where the terrain levelled out ahead.

She trudged on until she reached the grassy plateau and there he was.

Ravenwell.

He had not seen her—he stood to her right, half-facing away from her as he delved inside a bag on the ground. What was he doing up here, all alone? Was he…as Sharp had said…brooding? It was odd there were no dogs with him. Nor was there a horse in sight. Did he come up here to this wild, solitary place to think about his father and the night of the fire? Would he welcome company, or would he send her away? The temptation to retreat before he saw her was powerful. She could disappear back down the path and he would never know she had been there.

But…this was her first opportunity to sketch this stark but beautiful landscape and she was loath to waste it. Making her mind up, she tucked her sketchbook more securely beneath her arm and headed towards the Marquess, picking her way across the springy tussocks of grass.

As she drew near to Ravenwell, he raised his left arm, clad in a massive gauntlet, straight out in front of him and let out a shrill cry. Grace's steps faltered. Was it some sort of ritual? A movement caught her eye. The bird—that monstrous bird—had stopped circling. It swooped purposefully and then flew straight at Nathaniel.

It's attacking! No!

Grace ran towards Ravenwell, waving her arms and her sketchbook, shouting as loudly as she could. The bird—surely as big as Grace herself—veered at the last minute, beating its powerful wings as it rose up into the air, its curved claws just missing Nathaniel's head.

Grace grabbed Nathaniel's hand in both of hers, her sketchbook dropping unheeded to the ground.

'Are you all right?' Her breath came in short, heaving bursts.

'What the *devil* do you think you're doing?'

Grace quailed at his fury. He tore his gaze from her and followed the bird's flight.

'Have you any idea how long I…?' He paused.

Hauled in a deep breath.

Looked back at Grace.

Narrowed his eyes.

'Did you ask if I was *all right*?'

Before she could reply, he threw back his head and howled with laughter.

She glared. 'What is so amusing?'

'You!' He gasped for breath. 'Were you trying to *save* me?'

'Well, I did, did I not? That monster attacked you. I frightened it away.'

His chest heaved as another peal of laughter rang out. 'That monster, as you describe her, is an eagle. And she has enough power in those talons of hers to do you some serious damage. And you thought to…'

Their gazes fused, and his words faded. Grace trembled as longing curled through her body and she lost herself in the molten depths of his eyes.

'I…'

At that single word, his gaze, soft as a caress, drifted down to settle on her lips.

Nathaniel's initial burst of rage was, within seconds, quashed by his mirth that this dainty, feminine girl had thought to rescue *him*. Her eyes, glinting in the sunlight, flashed her annoyance and he was drawn into their gold-green depths. And his laughter died. And then her lips parted and, without volition, his gaze dipped to trace their delicate shape and admire their soft, pink fullness. And to wonder how they would taste…

'I…' she whispered again.

Then he was jolted from his entrancement as shock flashed across her face and red infused her cheeks, and he felt the wrench deep inside as she released her grip on his hand. His right hand. His damaged hand, with its coarse and ugly puckered skin. He snatched it away, thrusting it behind his back, out of sight.

'I…I am sorry, my l-lord.' She would not meet his eyes now. 'W-was it meant to fly at you like that?'

She was so pretty. Too pretty, too delicate, for a beast like him. He found the strength to thrust aside his humiliation in order to smooth over their mutual embarrassment.

'Yes, but it is not your fault.' He occupied himself pulling the leather gauntlet from his left hand. 'You meant well.'

He conjured up the image of Ralph Rendell. Now there would be a suitable pairing: the same station in life, both of them young and attractive. Unscarred. That thought had the same effect on his lust as falling in Shiver Beck on a winter's day—something he had done once and never wished to repeat.

'Will it come back?'

He scanned the sky. Amber was very close to being fit enough to return to the wild. Would she return after her scare?

'There. See.' He pointed at the bird. 'She has not gone away. Not yet.'

'How…? Is she tame? Is she yours?'

He told her the tale of how Amber came to his care.

'Her wing is healed now. I've been releasing her for longer each day to strengthen it. She comes back for food, even though she has begun to hunt for herself. One day, she will simply not return and hopefully she'll head north, back to the Highlands where she was born.'

'It sounds so romantic, the Highlands.' Her voice was wistful.

'More romance, Miss Bertram?'

Her lips compressed and a light flush crept over her cheeks. Not the most sensitive comment, following their difference about romance the other evening, and that interlude just now, when he had thought...

What had he thought? For one moment, he had forgotten who he was. *How* he was. He had been a man, looking into the eyes of a pretty girl. It had been a mistake, not to be repeated.

'Have you ever been to Scotland?' he asked.

'No, but I have seen paintings. It is like this but...more so.'

Nathaniel looked around. More so indeed. Very much more so.

'Where is Clara?'

'She is unwell. I have left her asleep, with Mrs Sharp watching over her, whilst I take some exercise.'

'Does she need a doctor?'

'No. We both agree it is only a cold; there is no sign of fever. But she is very miserable, poor mite.'

'I shall come and see her when I go home.' Something caught his eye and he bent to pick it off the ground.

'Is this a sketch book?'

'I thought I might have time to capture the view. I have never been up here before. It is too far for Clara.'

Nathaniel riffled through the pages. 'There aren't many landscapes here.'

'No.' She put out her hand and he whisked it out of her reach so he could continue to look through it.

'They are mostly portraits,' she said repressively, 'and they cannot possibly be of interest to you as you do not know any of the subjects.'

'Oh, I don't know. Here.' He held up a watercolour of three young women and grinned. 'I could be interested in these three beauties. Are they the friends you told me about?'

A light flush stained her cheeks. 'Yes.'

He looked at the painting. It showed skill. 'This is very good. Which one is which?'

She named the three and he said, 'Would you paint Clara for me, when she is better? I should like to have a portrait of her at this age.'

'Yes, of course.'

'Thank you.' He handed her the sketchbook. 'Perhaps you would like to sketch whilst we wait to see if Amber returns?'

Grace perched on a rock and Nathaniel stood behind and off to one side, watching her work. He could watch her all day: her frown of concentration, the pull of her bottom lip through her teeth, the blonde strands of hair that had blown loose and glinted in the sunlight. Rendell was a lucky man, if she had set her sights on him.

All too soon, it seemed to Nathaniel, she closed her book and stood up.

'I must get back to Clara. Oh!' She pointed. 'Amber has come back.'

Sure enough, the eagle was circling out over the dale. Nathaniel hadn't even noticed.

'Stand back,' he said, pulling the gauntlet on to his left hand. 'And for God's sake stay still this time. We don't want to spook her again.'

He waited whilst she retreated several paces, then took a morsel of rabbit from his bag and called as he turned his left side to Amber and extended his left arm, the meat held between his forefinger and thumb. There was the swish of wings, the jolting impact of the landing and the squeeze of the eagle's talons through the stout leather of his gauntlet.

'May I stroke her?'

Nathaniel took a hood from his pocket and slipped it over Amber's head. 'You may now.'

He glanced down at her profile as he spoke. Her brows were bunched across the bridge of her perfect little nose as she stroked Amber's feathers.

'But she would not hurt me. You laughed at me when I thought she was attacking *you*.'

'I laughed at your bold conviction that *you* might protect *me*. I probably should not have laughed, for you showed courage, but please take more care in future, particularly if you have Clara with you. The hood is to keep Amber calm. She is still a wild creature at heart—can you imagine the damage that beak could inflict on a person's face?'

Grace peered at Amber and shuddered.

'It looks so cruel.'

'It is efficient. It helps her survive. Cruelty does not come into it. But she is a powerful predator and should be treated with respect. Come. It is time I returned her to her mew.'

They headed down the hill, to the stable yard.

'Would you care to see my other birds? They are smaller than Amber, but tame. I use them for hawking, as men have done for centuries.'

She hesitated before saying, 'I should love to see them, but maybe another day? I must return to Clara.'

'I shall come and see her once I've put Amber away.'

Nathaniel watched Grace walk away, conflicting emotions churning his insides as he thought back to that moment up on the fell.

That look.

It had fired all sorts of longings deep within him. And she responded—her eyes had not lied. She had been all too aware of that *frisson* that passed between them.

It had been so very long since he'd experienced feelings for a woman—not just the physical need for a woman, but the longing for…more. That most dangerous of random thoughts had taken root in his heart: *What if…?*

She had held his hand without flinching, without even seeming aware… With a harsh sound, he quashed the bud of hope that formed deep inside his heart before it could begin to unfurl.

A beautiful girl like Grace would never want someone as damaged as him.

This yearning inside…it had been stirred up by Hannah and David's deaths…by the realisation that, now, apart from his mother, he was truly alone.

I will adjust to this new reality. I still have Clara. No one can take her from me.

He returned Amber to her enclosure, working without conscience thought, his heart heavy, aching with the burden of loss.

When he reached the house, he found Clara inconsolable—the only place she would settle was on Grace's lap and consequently he saw little of either of them for the rest of the afternoon or the evening. Bored with his own company, Nathaniel went to the book room to work on his ledgers, but he could not concentrate, his wandering thoughts returning again and again to that moment on the fell when their gazes had clashed. Finally, he admitted defeat and, as the clock in the hall struck eleven, he climbed the stairs to bed.

On the landing, a whimper and a cough reached his ears. Praying Clara had not taken a turn for the worse, he headed for her bedchamber.

It's a cold. Nothing to fear. She will recover.

But cold dread gnawed at him. Childhood was precarious; so many died in infancy. He could not bear… Clara was all he had left of his beloved Hannah. He could not lose her as well.

He must set his mind at rest. He entered her bedchamber

quietly, his gaze drawn to the bed, dimly visible in what remained of the firelight.

Clara was asleep, spreadeagled on her back, mouth open as she snored gently. Love for the tiny girl filled his heart. So very precious. A pale shape on the far side of the bed caught his eye—a hand, resting on the coverlet, mere inches from Clara. He tiptoed around the bed, his wavering shadow preceding him, and gazed down at Grace, fast asleep in a chair by the bedside, her head tipped back, the white curve of her throat both seductive and vulnerable. Even in sleep, she was graceful, her lashes fanned against her delicate cheekbones, her honey-blonde hair lying in a loose plait over her shoulder.

Grace. The name suited her to perfection. Ever since that afternoon, Nathaniel had found it impossible to think of her as Miss Bertram.

Grace.

She was clad only in a thin white nightgown that clung to her, softly draping petite breasts and clearly outlining the hard buds of her nipples. Blood surged to his loins. He forced his gaze from her breasts, quelling his inappropriate lust.

She was cold.

A blanket pooled around her feet. He crouched to gather it up and then softly settled it over the sleeping woman. A faint line creased her brow and she turned her head against the back of the chair and shifted her hips. She murmured… a soft, indistinct sound…and then stilled, her brow smoothing over, her lips relaxing, as she sank once more into sleep.

Nathaniel—breath held—tucked the blanket around her so it wouldn't slip again and then carefully, silently, refuelled the fire.

Then he tiptoed from the room and quietly closed the door.

Chapter Thirteen

'What do you think, Alice?'

The young maid stood back. 'They look better, miss. They make the room lighter. More…more happy, somehow.'

'I think so too,' Grace said, admiring the new curtains at the windows of the drawing room.

She had found them in a huge old linen press in a spare bedchamber during one of her searches for items to bring a more homely touch to the Hall. The original heavy deep green curtains had deadened the room, sucking the light from it. These, in contrast, were patterned in white and gold and instantly brightened the room. The gold echoed the yellow veining in several of the 'white' squares on the chessboard and in the marbled panels set into the doors of a small decorative cabinet Sharp had carried into the room at her behest.

Thinking about chess set Grace's thoughts in the direction they had taken ever more frequently since her chance meeting with Lord Ravenwell up on the fells three days before. He *had* changed since her first week at the Hall, when they had only met at dinnertime in the evening. Now, he regularly visited Clara in the nursery—where yesterday he had surprised them both with a dolls' house he'd had sent from York—and he spent every evening after dinner with Grace in the drawing room: playing chess or cards or reading, sometimes aloud, whilst Grace applied herself to mending or embroidery. However much Grace adored spending time with Clara during the day, she anticipated the evenings, and Ravenwell's company, with increasing pleasure.

She hoped he would approve of the changes she was making today. She had uncovered the pianoforte and also a pale gold sofa, which she had grouped with the two wing-back chairs near the fireplace, and Sharp and Ned had brought in two more upholstered chairs that she had found stored under covers in the dining room. All it needed now was a few ornaments on the mantelshelves and it would be done.

'There's another rug, miss,' Alice said, eyeing the small rug set before the fire where Clara—still a bit snuffly after her cold but with her energy restored—sprawled with Sweep. 'It's nicer than that dull thing, so Mrs Sharp says, with pretty colours in a pattern.'

'Clara. Take care with Sweep's claws, sweetie.' Grace cocked her head at Alice. '*Mrs Sharp* told you that?'

The housekeeper was slowly warming towards Grace, but her reaction this morning when Grace told her she was moving some furniture into the drawing room had been unpromising. Grace had feared a return to their former frosty relationship.

'Yes, miss. She came in when you was out with that cat.'

The entire household, apart from Grace and Clara, referred to Sweep as 'that cat'. Clara was besotted with her kitten, who was running the household ragged, and Grace tried to forestall as much of his mischief as possible. She took him outside several times a day to keep the house clean and in the vain hope of wearing him out. As he grew, he would become easier to cope with. She hoped.

'Did Mrs Sharp tell you where the other rug is?'

'No need, miss. Sharp's gone to fetch it.'

With that, the door opened and Sharp staggered in, a rolled-up carpet—for it looked too big to be called a rug—on his shoulder. They moved the furniture, rolled up the old dingy rug and unrolled the new one, with its symmetrical pattern in white, yellow and green.

'I've given it a good beating,' Mrs Sharp said.

Together, the four of them heaved the furniture back into place, then stood back to admire the effect.

'It looks beaut—' Grace stopped, her heart plummeting. 'Where is Clara?'

She had moved Clara to the other end of the room whilst they were busy, but now there was no sign of her. Or of Sweep. The door was ajar and, cursing herself for getting distracted, Grace dashed out into the hall.

'Oh, no!' Mrs Sharp clutched at Grace and pointed wordlessly up at the landing, her face ashen.

Nausea welled into Grace's throat, her stomach clenching in violent denial of the tableau on the galleried landing above: Clara, standing on a wooden chest and leaning over the balustrade, arms waving as she stretched to reach Sweep, who was strolling nonchalantly along the handrail.

'Sweep! Sweep! *Bad* kitty!' she shouted. 'Danjous!'

Before Grace could move, or speak, a dark shape streaked past the group clustered in the hall. Brack reached the landing, reared up on his hind legs and grabbed Sweep in his mouth. Clara's howl galvanised Grace into action and she tore up the stairs. By the time she reached the landing Brack was back on all fours and had retreated to the far side of the landing, the kitten clamped in his jaws, and Clara had clambered off the chest.

She ran towards Brack, shrieking, 'No! No! No bite!'

Grace swept Clara into her arms before she could reach the dog and turned away, pressing her face, eyes tight shut, into the sweet-scented skin of her daughter's neck, sickened by what had so nearly happened and also by the sight she might see if she looked at Brack. Clara would be devastated if Sweep was injured. The others had followed her—she had heard them pounding up the stairs behind her. Let them deal with the tragedy.

A hand gripped her shoulder, and tugged her around.

'It's safe to look,' rumbled a deep voice.

His lordship. Nooooo. I'll lose my job...no more than I deserve... Clara could have been killed! But, oh, how can I bear...?

Her panicked thoughts steadied. *Safe.* He said it was safe to look. Gingerly, she lifted her head and opened her eyes. A squealing Clara was plucked from her arms. Her gaze darted to Brack, lying by the wall, forelegs outstretched. And Sweep. On his back, between Brack's legs, paws waving in the air as he tried to bat the dog's nose. As Grace watched, Brack lowered his head and swept his tongue along the kitten's exposed stomach.

No blood. No disaster.

Her heart slowed from its frantic gallop to a trot and she breathed again. There was no one else on the landing. Those feet she had heard behind her had been Ravenwell.

'How...?'

'I was in the hall. You dashed past without even noticing me. It was I who sent Brack to fetch the cat.'

Grace dropped her chin to her chest. Sucked in a shaky breath. 'I am sorry. Clara should not...I allowed myself to be distracted.'

'By what, may I ask?'

How could she admit she had been distracted by making changes in his house? How could this be worse?

It would be worse if Clara had fallen. Her knees trembled at that thought and she squeezed her eyes shut again, her neck and shoulders tight with the effort it took not to collapse in a wailing heap.

I have made a mess of everything.

'Well?'

That single harsh word forced her eyes open and her gaze to his. His dark eyes bored into her.

'Alice?' His voice rose, calling down to the hall below. 'Come up here. Take Miss Clara to the nursery. And take that infernal cat with you.'

He raised a brow. 'I'm waiting.'

Grace gripped her hands together. 'We were making a few changes in the drawing room.'

His brows snapped together. 'What changes?'

She forced herself to hold his gaze. 'You did say I might.'

A look of scorn crossed his face. She could not blame him. What happened was inexcusable. Clara had been in her charge.

'I am sorry,' she said. 'I am not trying to excuse myself. We were moving furniture. One minute Clara was playing at the other end of the room with Sweep, the next she was gone.'

Fear shivered through her as she relived the terrible moment when she had run out into the hall and seen her little girl... She bit back a sob.

'We?' That quiet voice bristled with menace. 'You mean to tell me my entire household was present and not one of you noticed Clara leave the room?'

'It was n-nobody's fault but mine, my lord.'

'At last something we can agree upon.' His eyes flashed with anger.

'Wh-what will you do?' Her voice wobbled as the next sob broke free. 'P-please...do not dismiss me. I l-like it here.'

'You cry at the thought of losing your position here, but what of the fact my niece could have been *killed*?'

'I d-do not cry for myself! That picture is burned into my mind...she's so small...so vulnerable... I cannot forget the horror of seeing her...'

Her hands twisted painfully as she tried to interpret his expression through blurred vision.

'The only reason you are here is to look after my niece.' His voice was harsh and uncompromising. 'Yet it appears to me you are more interested in altering your surroundings—*my home*—into your idea of suitably luxurious surroundings for yourself than in Clara's welfare.'

Stung, Grace glared at him. 'That is unfair. And untrue. You *know* my reasons for those changes. You *agreed*.' She hauled in a breath. 'I only wish to make a comfortable and happy home for your niece. She is a *child*. You may choose to live in these cold cheerless surroundings, but Clara deserves better! She deserves a home and a loving family.'

'Instead of which she has me. And a houseful of servants.'

Bitterness infused his words and shame coursed through Grace. She had not intended to wound him but, before she could try to repair the damage, Sharp called urgently from the hall below.

'Milord! Milord!'

'What is it?'

'It's her ladyship, milord. Her carriage is coming up the track.'

Ravenwell's jaw clenched. He shot a hard look at Grace. 'This matter is not resolved.' He reached into his pocket and pulled out a letter. 'Here. Ned brought this back from the village. It is a happy chance that brought me indoors to give you your letter immediately. Had I delayed, Clara might well be dead by now.

'Go. Make Clara presentable and bring her down to greet her grandmother in twenty minutes. And, for God's sake, keep that cat out of the way.'

He ran down the stairs, Brack at his heels, and Grace turned to walk slowly towards the nursery wing, her eyes burning with shame.

'Had I delayed, Clara might well be dead by now.'

He was right. She had never seen him so furious, nor so scathing. What if he persuaded his mother to take Clara home with her? If he did not think Grace a fitting person to care for her, he might very well do that. She must work hard to impress her ladyship. If *she* thought Grace suitable, she might persuade Ravenwell to keep her as Clara's governess.

Before she went to the nursery room to get Clara ready, Grace slipped into her bedchamber, needing a moment of quiet to settle her nerves. She perched on the edge of the bed, still shaken, sick dread swirling through her.

She opened her letter, seeking distraction. It was, she saw with a glad heart, from Joanna. Eager to find out how her friend was faring in her role as governess to the Huntford family in Hertfordshire, Grace began to read, her jaw dropping at Joanna's amazing news: the newborn baby who had been abandoned on the doorstep of Madame Dubois's School for Young Ladies was, in reality, the granddaughter of a marquess. And not only had her grandfather publicly acknowledged her and introduced her into society, but Joanna had also met and fallen in love with Luke Preston, the son of the Earl of Ingham, and they had recently married.

Her happiness shone through every word she had penned.

Pleasure for her friend warred with envy in Grace's breast. Yes, she was excited and thrilled for Joanna, for she knew how Joanna had longed to know about her real family, but she could not help but compare Joanna's happy future to the uncertainties of her own. She did not want to leave Shiverstone. She *would* not leave Shiverstone. She did not know how but she must, somehow, persuade his lordship that he could not manage without her.

Putting the letter aside, she hurried to the nursery to make Clara presentable to meet her grandmother.

Ten minutes later, Grace drew in a deep breath, smoothed a nervous hand over her hair and tapped on the drawing-room door before entering, Clara's hand firmly in hers. The Marquess stood before the fireplace, hands clasped behind his back. His eyes were hard, anger still simmering. She swallowed and crossed the room, surreptitiously towing Clara, whose steps had suddenly lagged. An elderly lady—stoutly built, with the same deep brown eyes as her son—watched them cross the room.

Grace bobbed a curtsy.

'Mother, this is Miss Bertram. Miss Bertram, my mother, Lady Ravenwell.'

'Good morning, Lady Ravenwell.'

Every inch of Grace passed under her ladyship's inspection before, finally, she inclined her head. Her expression indicated neither approval nor disapproval. It was hard not to squirm under such scrutiny, which revived uncomfortable memories of various summonses to Madame Dubois's study for some infraction of the rules.

Her ladyship's expression softened as she switched her gaze to Clara. She held out her arms. 'Come to Grandmama, Clara.'

Grace urged the little girl forward, worried she did not remember her grandmother, but Clara's initial reluctance turned to eagerness and she rushed forward, releasing Grace's hand.

'Ganmama.' Clara allowed herself to be hugged and kissed, then wriggled free. 'Ganmama. I got Sweep.'

'Oh! She is talking again. Oh, Nathaniel, you have worked wonders with her.'

The Marquess cleared his throat. 'I believe you must credit Miss Bertram with Clara's progress.'

'Then I shall. Thank you, Miss Bertram.'

Grace smiled at her ladyship and was once more subjected to a sharp appraisal. Had Ravenwell told his mother about Grace's dereliction of duty? A glance at Ravenwell's rock-like expression revealed no clue. She hovered a moment, unsure for the first time of what was expected of her. She had begun to feel like part of the family, with an established position in the household, but Lady Ravenwell's arrival had underscored her true position. She was neither family nor servant, but somewhere in the middle, and she now felt awkward and out of place. She retreated to a chair by the window whilst Clara remained by her grandmother, pleading with her to come and see her kitten.

The same thought bombarded Grace's head without pause: she had forgotten her place and had crossed that boundary between staff and family. Lord Ravenwell was right to be furious. Furtively, she scanned the room. Her changes might have improved the room, but she understood how they must appear to him. She had been presumptuous, both in accepting the kitten without consulting him first and in initiating changes in *his* home. She was meddlesome and an irritant and she had compounded her error by embroiling the rest of his staff in—

'Miss Bertram!'

His voice, exasperated, penetrated her silent scold. She jerked to her feet. He stood directly in front of her and she was forced to crane her neck to meet his gaze.

'You had better go and fetch that infer… Sweep,' he growled. 'Clara will not rest until Mother has made its acquaintance.'

Chapter Fourteen

Dinner with Lady Ravenwell was an ordeal. Her ladyship—resplendent in a green satin gown, a matching turban and emeralds—barely acknowledged Grace's presence, talking to Ravenwell about mutual acquaintances in whom he clearly had no interest. It was a relief when the meal was over but, before Grace could excuse herself and disappear upstairs, Lady Ravenwell made clear her expectation that Grace would join her in the drawing room whilst her son remained in the parlour with his brandy.

'You may pour the tea,' the Marchioness commanded as she swept from the room.

Grace glanced over her shoulder at Ravenwell, hearing the scrape of his chair on the floor. It had become his habit to drink his brandy in the drawing room, over a game of chess or a hand of cards, but he had merely pushed his chair away from the table. He leant back, stretching his long legs straight. He caught her eye and, for the first time since that afternoon, she caught a glimmer of humour in his expression. She pressed her lips together and stalked from the room. She had no trouble interpreting his amusement.

She was the lamb to be sacrificed on the altar of his mother's chatter.

It was worse than she feared. His mother did not wish

to converse with Grace. Neither did she wish to talk at her, as she had talked at Ravenwell throughout their meal. Her intention became clear as soon as Mrs Sharp had deposited the tea tray and left the room. Grace had barely begun to pour when the interrogation began.

Where was she from? Who were her family? *Where* had she gone to school again? What were her qualifications…if any? Lady Ravenwell's tone clearly expressed her doubts on that last one. And the question that recurred time and again: how, precisely, had Grace found out about the position of governess at Shiverstone Hall?

'The post was advertised in the *York Herald* which is not, to my knowledge, read in Salisbury. How did *you* discover it?'

'My teacher at the school, Miss Fanworth, was told of the vacancy by a friend of hers.'

Grace's hand was tucked down by her side with crossed fingers. A lie was not really a lie if you had your fingers crossed—or so she and her friends had told each other when they were young. Besides, it was very nearly true. It was Miss Fanworth who had arranged Rachel's position in Huria—she could quite easily have done the same for Grace.

'What is the name of this friend?'

'I do not recall.'

'Have you ever been to Harrogate, Miss Bertram?'

'No, my lady.' That, at least, was no falsehood. The stagecoach in which she had travelled to Ravenwell Manor had put her down before they reached Harrogate.

By the time the Marquess came through, close to an hour later, Grace's nerves were in shreds and, as her ladyship's focus shifted to her son, she begged to be excused.

'Do you customarily retire at such an early hour?'

'I am concerned Clara may have trouble sleeping tonight with all the excitement of your arrival, my lady, particularly after her recent cold. From my sitting room upstairs, I shall hear if she wakes.'

Visions of Clara wandering out on to the landing—even though she knew that chest had been removed—had plagued Grace all evening.

'Very commendable, I am sure. I believe in bestowing praise where it is due, Miss Bertram, and I confess that, despite your youth, you have impressed me with your attention to duty. I thank you for taking good care of my granddaughter.'

Grace blushed as, without volition, her gaze flicked to Ravenwell and fused with his. They both knew that to be a lie.

As she mounted the stairs, the certainty he would now tell his mother the truth churned her insides until she felt sick. Lady Ravenwell's clear suspicions about Grace were troubling enough, but if she should learn of Grace's neglect, Grace would surely be dismissed and then what would she do? She peeped into Clara's bedchamber. Her daughter was sound asleep, on her back as usual, with the blankets kicked askew and her thumb jammed into her mouth. Grace crept in and stood by the bed, love for her child flooding her. Finally, she straightened the covers, bent to kiss Clara's forehead and then retreated to her sitting room.

Grace pondered her uncertain future as she stared into the flames. That future was entirely in the hands of Lord Ravenwell and never had she felt more keenly the divide between her station and his world—a world to which, she realised, both Isabel and Joanna now belonged. She did not begrudge them their good fortune, but how she wished a small piece of their luck might rub off on her.

What could she do? What power did she have?

The answer was none.

She could only wait, impotently, for his decision and then, if he decreed she must go, she must be prepared to fight. For one thing was certain: she would *never* leave her daughter.

We could run away. I could take Clara and go.

For a few minutes, she indulged that fantasy, before reality crashed over her. It was not even remotely possible. Snatch the ward of a nobleman? And how could they live? And then an even greater truth struck her—an insight so startling it near stole her breath. With a gigantic thump of her heart, she understood she would not leave even if she could.

Because taking Clara away from Shiverstone Hall would mean leaving Lord Ravenwell.

Nathaniel.

And not only could she not bear it if she were never to see him again, but she would never, ever—*could* never, ever—hurt him in that way.

Shaken to her core by that revelation, Grace stumbled to her feet and returned to Clara's bedchamber. She stood and gazed at her beautiful daughter, battling against the sick realisation that, somehow, she had fallen for Nathaniel. She had seen beneath the scarred, irascible and reclusive façade he presented to the world to his kind, loving, intelligent heart.

But... Caution screamed through her head. *Remember Philip. You thought you were in love with him and you were wrong. Don't make the same mistake. Nathaniel is a marquess, far above your touch. And right now he does not even like you.*

Finally, lids heavy and stifling a yawn, she knew she must go to bed. She bent over Clara and smoothed her curls gently from her forehead.

'Sleep well, my beloved little girl, and sweet dreams,' she whispered. 'Mama is watching over you.'

A sudden sound from behind her sent her spinning to face the door.

* * *

Nathaniel froze.

All he could take in was the guilt written all over Grace's face.

Mama?

He pushed away from the doorjamb, against which he had stumbled when he heard her words. Her eyes were huge and he saw the movement of her throat as she swallowed. And then she moved, gliding towards him, one finger to her lips, her eyes…her beautiful, gold-green eyes—the image of Clara's, and how hadn't he seen the resemblance before?—stricken.

He barely moved aside and she brushed past him, out into the passageway. The hairs on his forearms rose at her touch and her clean, sweet lily-of-the-valley scent pervaded his senses.

Mama.

He followed her out of Clara's room on to the landing.

'Explain yourself.'

Anger flared, boosted by the vision of Clara in danger that afternoon, and his panic when he had seen her. How very precious she had become to him. What would he do… how would he survive…if he lost her too? His very vulnerability terrified him. And now…what would this new revelation mean for the future for all of them?

Grace had paused to close Clara's door.

'Well?'

She was trembling. He hardened his heart and strode to the door of her sitting room. He held it wide and beckoned. Inside, he stoked the fire and added more wood, willing his temper under control before trusting himself to look at her.

Grace stood inside the door, fingers interlaced, knuckles white. 'Why did you come to Clara's room?'

'Am I not allowed? She is *my* ward. I needed to ensure she is safe after the danger she was put in this afternoon.'

She flinched. 'You cannot know the guilt I feel over my neglect.'

'I am still awaiting an explanation. Do not make me ask again.'

'Clara is my daughter.'

That simple statement crushed any residual hope that he had misheard. The agony in her voice wrenched at his heart, but he could not quash his anger, or his hurt, over her betrayal. He had begun to trust her. Since her arrival, his evenings had changed from something to dread to a time keenly anticipated. How, and when, had the barriers he had built against the rest of the world been breached?

'Why are you here? Did you intend to snatch her away from me?'

Her mouth fell open and yet her gaze skittered from his. 'No! I would never do that.'

'But the thought crossed your mind.'

He watched her intently, noting a blush creep up her neck to her face.

'Only once. You were so angry with me...earlier...but I would never do such a thing. It was a fleeting thought, soon exposed for an idle fantasy. I could never take her from you, nor you from her. I am not so cruel.'

'You said this afternoon that Clara deserves a home and a loving family. You said she deserves better than me and a houseful of servants.'

Her eyes flashed and she crossed the room to glare up at him.

'You twist my words, my lord. It was you who said she only has you and a houseful of servants.'

'But you believe it is the truth.' He grabbed her, his fingers biting into the soft flesh of her upper arms. 'You think she deserves better. That I am incapable of giving her a happy childhood.'

'No!'

She squirmed to free herself and he released her, taking a step back, ashamed he had allowed his anger to prevail. Yet she did not retreat. She moved closer, her gaze searching his.

'Clara adores you.' Her scent enveloped him and her breath was warm upon his skin. Her fingertips caressed his cheek with a featherlight touch. 'You do not see how her eyes light up when she sees you. She has settled here. She is happy.'

Her eyes darkened and her hand slipped to rest against his chest. Without volition, his head lowered and he brushed her sweet, silken mouth with his. His blood quickened, together with the compulsion to sweep her into his arms and taste her again. And again. But doubts nipped at the heels of that compulsion.

Why now?

She must be desperate indeed to contemplate seducing a man like him—desperate to stay with her daughter.

Nathaniel spun away and faced the hearth, propping both hands against the mantel, gripping the wooden edge, grounding himself. She sounded sincere, but could he trust his instincts? He silently berated himself for a fool. He should dismiss her immediately. There was no excuse for her deceit. But he could not utter the words. God help him, he *wanted* to understand. More, he wanted to forgive. He did not want her to go. His very neediness infuriated him, but it was a fury directed against himself, not her.

'That should not have happened.'

'I am sorry.' He had to strain to hear her whispered response.

'Why *did* you come here, if not to reclaim your daughter?'

'I p-promised myself, when she was born, when I gave her away that, one day, I would find her and make sure she was loved and wanted.'

'She was. My sister and her husband doted on her. And now—'

'And now, you dote upon her.'

'Yes,' he said gruffly. 'So why this charade?' He turned to face her. 'Why did you apply to be her governess?'

She hung her head. 'I did not. Not precisely.' A puff of air escaped her and her shoulders slumped. 'I shall tell you the whole story. M-may I sit?'

'Of course.' He waited until she sank on to the armchair by the fire, then dragged over a wooden chair to sit opposite, swinging it around to straddle it, resting his arms across the back.

She told him a tale that was not unique. It happened too frequently: a young girl, her head turned by romantic words and enticing kisses, and a green youth who did not consider the repercussions of his persuasions.

'Seventeen years old.' If such a thing happened to Clara, when she was so young and innocent, he would be after the culprit with a horsewhip. 'What did your uncle have to say about it?'

Her head jerked up, her expression one of horror. 'My uncle did not know. He and my aunt are very devout…they would not…nobody knew, only my three best friends, and I swore them to secrecy.'

'But…surely your teachers must have realised.'

'I managed to hide the change in my shape. My clothes were always loose on me—my cousins are bigger than I and Aunt refused to alter the dresses too drastically. She said I would grow into them and it was not worth altering them twice.'

Compassion blossomed for the child unwanted by her own family. No wonder she needed to ensure Clara was loved and wanted.

'When the babe came…' She fell silent, leaning forward, her elbows propped on her knees, staring at the floor. 'Well…' She hesitated again, then she looked up at him, a blush staining her cheeks but with a look of resolve. 'It was worse than any of us thought it would be. My friends went to fetch Miss Fanworth and afterwards she…'

Her voice had started to wobble and tears brimmed. Wordlessly, Nathaniel passed her his handkerchief.

'Thank you.'

She mopped her eyes before resuming her tale.

'Miss Fanworth thought it best to find a family who would adopt the baby. She knew my own family would not stand by me, so they were never told.'

'But…the principal of the school. Madame Dubois. She must have known. I am surprised she did not expel you.'

'I have no doubt she would have, but she never knew either.'

'And you knew Clara had gone to Hannah and David?'

'No. I did not know who her new parents were until my last day at school. Miss Fanworth told me their name and that they lived in Gloucestershire. That was all I knew. By the time I tracked them down, it was too late and Clara had gone. I was told you were her new guardian and I was even more determined to make sure she was happy. And that you wanted her here with you.'

'Unlike you, with your uncle and aunt.'

'Unlike me.'

She paused, staring down at the handkerchief she kneaded in her fingers, nibbling at her bottom lip. Then she shook her head and looked up, a mischievous glint in her still-watery eyes.

'Those stories I was told about you, in the village… well, suffice it to say they were wild enough to drive me on to come here. I even braved walking through that horrid wood. And then, when I arrived…I was so petrified by the dogs…and then you growled at me that I was late and before I knew it the idea of staying on…of seeing Clara every day…'

She choked on her words, then hauled in a ragged breath.

'Don't send me away. *Please* don't. I know I let you down today and I still feel sick at what might have happened, but I swear I shall take more care in future, only

I *cannot* go…I simply cannot. I'm sorry I did not tell you the truth but, once I was here…how could I?'

Nathaniel held up his hand, hating to hear her beg. Although she had lied, he could not condemn her. She had been driven only by concern for Clara's welfare.

But what about that kiss? She ought to go.

I know. But I do not want her to go.

Then you must confront it. Now.

'I cannot condone what you have done, but I shall not send you away. I, too, am not so cruel. There was no need to try to entice me with…with…'

Dammit. I can't even say the words.

'Understand this, Miss Bertram. If you stay, you stay on as Clara's governess. Nothing more. And no one—ever—must know the truth. Were the truth to get out, it would be too shocking. You must realise the damage such a scandal would do to Clara in the future.'

'Yes. Of course. I understand.' Grace slumped back in her chair, hand to her face, still clutching Nathaniel's handkerchief. 'Thank you.'

Her voice was muffled, her shoulders quivered and he heard a distinct sniff. He suppressed his urge to comfort her. Instead, he stared into the fire, waiting for her to regain her composure. The wood had caught well and tongues of orange, yellow and occasional green reached for the chimney. Eventually, from the corner of his eye, he saw her hands leave her face and she straightened in her chair.

'So,' he continued their conversation, 'the secret will remain between the two of us. No one else must know. I—' A thought struck him. 'Have you told your friends?' He could not recall franking a letter for her, other than the two she wrote on the day she arrived. 'Or your teacher?'

'No. I was too ashamed to admit what I had done and neither do I wish to lie, so I have not yet written to them. I merely told Miss Fanworth that I had tracked Clara down and that she was happy and that I had secured a post here as governess. She does not know the truth.'

Relief, doubt and the still-present anger combined in a stomach-churning mix.

'And, most particularly, my mother must never know.'

'D-did you tell her what happened this morning?'

'No. I did not wish to worry her.'

'That is a relief.'

Her lips quivered in a tremulous smile, prompting a surge of blood to his loins. How he craved a further taste, but he could not take that risk—a beautiful woman like Grace could never truly desire a damaged man such as him.

What about when you met on the fell? There was a spark between you then.

He dismissed that thought with a silent curse. He had not known at the time that Grace was Clara's mother, but Grace knew the truth and she would know the one certain way of remaining with her child was by making herself indispensable to her employer by whatever means necessary. No wonder she felt entitled to alter his home to suit her own needs.

'Where is her father now? Are you still in touch with him?'

'He is dead.'

'I am sorry,' he said.

'I have no need of your sympathy. What I believed to be love was, in truth, infatuation. I was filled with longing for romance and I fell for his sweet words. I am older and wiser now.'

He raised a brow. 'You are? Our recent conversations suggest otherwise.'

Her cheeks bloomed pink. '*I* have not allowed *my* experience to sour me, or to turn me into a cynic about love, if that is what you mean.'

Touché, Ravenwell!

There was nothing to say that would not sound defensive. What if he was a cynic? Did he not have good reason?

'I bid you goodnight, Miss Bertram.' He bowed and left.

Chapter Fifteen

'I have concerns about that young woman, Nathaniel.'

Nathaniel took a second to compose his expression before looking at his mother, ramrod straight on the other side of his desk. He laid his pen aside, rose to his feet and rounded the desk to pull a chair forward for her. Then he crossed the book room to shut the door.

'What are your concerns, Mother?' he asked as he settled back into his own chair, elbows on the armrests and fingers steepled at his chest.

'I am far from convinced of the reason she has come this far from her friends and family to take up a position as a governess. Why would she not choose to stay—?'

'Mother, please do not interfere in my domestic arrangements. Miss Bertram is good with Clara. I do not want to lose her.'

'But it makes no sense, quite apart from the recklessness of a young woman travelling *alone*, from one end of the country to the other, to attend an interview with no guarantee of employment at the end of it. She is hiding something. I am convinced of it.'

'You are allowing your imagination to conjure up unwarranted suspicions.' It was hard to allay his mother's doubts and suspicions when Nathaniel was still plagued by his own. 'I understand her teacher knows someone in the county who read my advertisement.'

'I have a mind to write to this Madame Dubois and—'

'There is no need. I have already done so and have received a satisfactory report of Miss Bertram's time at the school. There is nothing for you to worry about.'

'I am your mother. I am allowed to worry about you.'

'About me?' Nathaniel felt his brows bunch in a frown. 'I thought this conversation was about Clara's governess?'

His mother ignored him. 'I cannot be easy in my mind about Miss Bertram. Fish heard gossip in the village that a young woman had been snooping around, asking questions about Hannah and David and what had happened and whether Clara was at the Manor. What if it was Miss Bertram?'

'Fish should mind his own business.' The butler at Ravenwell Manor had always been a busybody. Nathaniel pushed his chair back and went to crouch by his mother's side. 'There is nothing to worry about. Miss Bertram is good for Clara and she has settled in here well. Why, even Mrs Sharp is warming to her and that in itself is a miracle.'

'Mrs Sharp worries about you too.'

Nathaniel surged to his feet. 'It is neither her place nor yours to worry about me. I am a grown man and I am perfectly capable of managing my own household.'

He stalked back around his desk and threw himself on to his chair, furious he had allowed his mother to rattle him.

His mother's lips thinned and her nostrils flared as though in response to a bad smell.

'She is very young. It would surely be better for Clara if her governess was a more mature woman. Someone more experienced.'

'Better for whom? I believe Clara will benefit from having someone young and lively. And Miss Bertram is schooled in all the accomplishments required for a young lady. She will be an excellent teacher for Clara as she grows up.'

'She is also exceedingly pretty.'

Ah. So now we get to the crux of the matter.

Nathaniel met his mother's scrutiny with a raised brow. Lady Ravenwell sighed.

'Very well, I shall say no more for the time, but I shall keep a wary eye on Miss Bertram whilst I am here.'

Heaven forbid his mother should discover the truth. Or that she might suspect his growing attraction for Grace, or that they had kissed—albeit just a brush of the lips— last night. Nathaniel had lain awake half the night fretting over whether he was right to allow Grace to stay but, in the end, he accepted he could do nothing else. He could not part mother and daughter. And he did not want to lose Grace for his own sake as well as Clara's. He enjoyed her company. She had brought light and hope into his life, just with her presence.

That kiss had been a moment of madness, when both of their passions were roused.

It must not happen again.

'There is no need but, if it will help set your mind at ease, then by all means do so,' he said. 'I am confident you will see that Miss Bertram is very fond of Clara and has her best interests at heart.'

'If you say so, Nathaniel. Now, I must also speak to you about Christmas.'

'Christmas?'

First Grace, now his mother. How he wished the festive season would pass Shiverstone by without any fuss. He'd had no appetite for celebrating since the fire but, last year, Mother, Hannah, David and, of course, Clara, had come to Shiverstone for the full twelve days, refusing to allow Nathaniel to spend another Christmas alone. Now, the happy memories of last year were yet another painful reminder of his beloved sister.

'I wish you and Clara to come to the Manor for the Christmas season as I find I am unable to come here.'

'May I ask why you are unable to come to the Hall?' Would Mother, like him, find the memories of last Christmas too painful?

His mother grimaced. 'Uncle Peter has invited himself and his family to stay at the Manor. He stopped for a few nights on his way up to Scotland and, before I knew what had happened, it appears it was all agreed.'

Her obvious vexation made Nathaniel smile. His father's younger brother was a slippery fellow and, as the years passed and Nathaniel showed no sign of marrying, his uncle's sense of entitlement to the Ravenwell title and estates had grown.

'Oh, no. Poor Mother. What a sorry Christmas you will have, with that flock of vultures eyeing up the furniture. I've a mind to marry simply in order to put his nose out of joint.'

'Oh, how I wish you would, Nathaniel.' Mother leant forward in her eagerness. Then she visibly subsided. 'But I fear you will never give yourself a chance of happiness. I could throttle both Lady Sarah and Miss Havers for the way they behaved.'

'They did me a kindness. Would you really want such shallow sorts as either of them to become my Marchioness?'

'I would like *someone* to have the opportunity. I fear you will never meet anyone out here in this wilderness. Please say you will come to Ravenwell for Christmas, Nathaniel. We could have a Twelfth Night party as we used to.'

He hated to deny her, but he simply could not face it. He did not have to say so; his expression must make his refusal plain.

'Please, Nathaniel? I cannot bear to think of you here, all alone—'

'I am not alone,' he said, more sharply than he intended. 'I have Clara.'

And Grace.

'And do you not think Clara would benefit from seeing her relations?'

'No, I do not. Hannah told me about the first time my uncle saw Clara. He called her a…well, you may guess what term he used. He made no attempt to disguise his disapproval. No, I shall not subject Clara to my uncle's insults. I am sorry, Mother, but we will spend Christmastide at Shiverstone Hall.'

His mother stood. 'Do not think this is the last word on the subject, Ravenwell, for it is not.'

Blast, he'd annoyed her now. She only ever called him Ravenwell when she was angry with him.

His mother stayed a week. By her last day, Nathaniel's patience was stretched to breaking point. Every day had seen a repeat of their conversations about Grace and about Christmas. Finally, his mother had accepted he meant what he said. He would not send Grace away and replace her with an older governess and he and Clara would not be going to Ravenwell Manor for Christmas. The only good part of his mother's visit was that her presence masked the inevitable awkwardness between Grace and him and made it easier to avoid being alone with her.

His final conversation with his mother took place in the drawing room—which, if he was honest, *had* improved beyond all recognition since Grace had changed it. Even his mother had commented on its pleasant appearance in comparison with her last visit. Lady Ravenwell had already visited the nursery to kiss Clara farewell and Nathaniel and his mother were alone, awaiting her carriage.

'Nathaniel.'

His heart sank. He knew that look. 'Yes, Mother?'

'Do not look so hunted. Even I must accept defeat at

some point. I shall not mention Christmas, nor try one last time to persuade you to appoint a different governess.' She crossed the room to peer from the window, then returned to stand in front of him, her expression resolute. 'I hope you will take what I am about to say in the spirit in which it is intended, son. I only ever have your best interests at heart. You do know that, don't you?'

He took her hands. 'Of course I do.' There was no escaping it. Let her say what she must. She would be gone soon. 'What is it you feel honour-bound to say?'

'Nathaniel! There is no need to take that tone of voice.'

'My apologies, Mother.' He deserved that rebuke. 'Please, do go on.'

'I urge you to take care with Miss Bertram. You already know my concerns about her and I shall not repeat them. But you are a wealthy man. A nobleman. You are a good catch for a scheming miss and what better way to inveigle her way into your affections than through your niece?'

Nathaniel's muscles turned to stone as his mother placed a gentle hand against his scarred cheek. Every instinct screamed at him to pull away, but he knew that would hurt her and might even lead her to believe there was some truth in what she said. He released her other hand and folded his arms across his chest.

'I am a grown man, Mother, not a green youth. I can take care of myself.'

'I have seen the way you look at her, Nathaniel, when you think yourself unobserved.'

He struggled to control his dismay as her words sank in. Was he so transparent that even his mother could see through him? What if the servants could see the truth? What if *Grace* could tell? He must take more care.

'Living out here, all alone…take care, darling. Please.' Her voice became urgent as the sound of wheels on the gravel outside heralded the arrival of her carriage. 'She is exceedingly pretty, but no good can ever come of getting embroiled with an employee. I make no doubt she is well aware of the luxuries and comforts that await the woman who ensnares you. From governess to marchioness would be quite an achievement for one such as Miss Bertram.'

No suggestion that Grace might like him for himself and not merely for what he could provide. Even his own mother thought him unlovable. He thrust down his pain.

'You have nothing to fear, Mother.'

Quite apart from the fact a beauty like Grace would never look twice at someone like me, she still visits the village regularly to see Rendell. If she is interested in anything other than being with Clara, it is not me.

'Miss Bertram is here solely to care for Clara.'

Grace put her lips to Clara's ear as she hugged her tight to her chest.

'Shh…' she breathed, willing Clara not to speak.

After Lady Ravenwell came to the nursery to say goodbye to Clara, Grace had made the mistake of saying that Grandmama would be travelling in her carriage. Clara's eyes had widened.

'Wanna see horsies.'

She'd been adamant and Grace had finally succumbed. Although Lady Ravenwell had clearly not taken to Grace, surely she would be pleased her granddaughter had come to wave goodbye.

Now, Grace stood frozen outside the drawing room, absorbing what she had heard, her heart racing. The thud of booted feet approaching the door from within sent her scurrying to the front door. She would think about what she had heard later. For now, it was imperative Nathaniel had no inkling she had overheard his mother's words. The past week had been awkward enough, since that incident with Clara and since he had discovered she was Clara's mother.

And that kiss—she could almost cringe when she recalled how she had invited it.

It had been he who had resisted deepening that kiss. Not she.

Oh, but was her ladyship right? Did Nathaniel watch her? Did he think of her as a woman and not merely a governess?

But then why had he avoided being alone with her since that night unless he, too, suspected her of planning to ensnare him into marriage.

'Miss Bertram.'

She turned, willing her expression not to give her away. Nathaniel, his mother on his arm, approached across the hall.

'I did not expect to see you down here.'

Grace stretched her lips in a smile. 'I made the mistake of telling Clara that Lady Ravenwell was going away in a carriage. Clara is most eager to see the horses.'

'Ah.' He tweaked Clara's cheek, then smiled at his mother. 'Your granddaughter has developed a healthy obsession for horses. Here…' he reached out '… I will take her. You may go about your duties, Miss Bertram, and I shall send Clara to you later.'

Send. Not bring. It is not my imagination. He does avoid being alone with me.

There was nothing Grace could do but relinquish her daughter, drop a curtsy and return upstairs. She tidied the nursery, the conversation she had overheard repeating in her head until she could scream her frustration.

That Lady Ravenwell suspected her of having designs on Nathaniel was no surprise. His mother clearly thought the worst of Grace and her motives in coming to Shiverstone. Grace searched her conscience, but she could honestly say that, despite her own burgeoning feelings, she had never… *never*…dreamed of *catching* Nathaniel or of inveigling her way into his affections as his mother had so vulgarly put it. She had only ever followed her natural urges, inviting his kiss because she wanted him to kiss her, not because she planned to lure him into marriage. And now, with his mother's suspicions planted in his head, would Nathaniel also suspect her of being a scheming miss, out to seduce him for mercenary reasons?

But...his mother's words echoed again: *I have seen the way you look at her when you think yourself unobserved.*

Did he look at her in such a way? Or was it lust his mother saw? Would any red-blooded man not, on occasion, find his baser instincts come to the fore, such as happened that day out on the fell? Surely that was merely a man tempted to succumb to the moment? There had been other instances of tenderness—such as when he had wiped the smudge from her cheek—but his action had been that of a brother, not an admirer.

Images from the past darted through her memory and her stomach clenched. She must not repeat the mistake she had made with Philip. Now, more than ever, she wished her friends were here to talk to or that she could write to them and ask their advice. They would help her make sense of this tangle of emotions: Joanna with her calm good sense and her ability to accept whatever life threw in her path, fun-loving, independent Rachel with her healthy scepticism about love, Isabel, with her love of the dramatic, always ready to distract and entertain whichever of her friends was feeling blue.

Deep down, though, she knew what her friends would say. They would tell her to banish any dreams of Nathaniel as a man. He was her employer.

Nothing more. Two words that prompted an echo from that fateful night.

If you stay, you stay on as Clara's governess. Nothing more.

He could not have been more clear.

She must forget that overheard conversation. Clara would be her focus, no one and nothing else. She would fight her feelings by keeping busy. There was plenty to do with Christmas less than four weeks away. She had used her spare time during Lady Ravenwell's visit productively: knitting mufflers for Sharp and the outdoor men and mittens for Alice and Clara, as well as embroidering handkerchiefs with initials and edging them with lace for Mrs Sharp and Annie.

She had racked her brains for a present for Nathaniel and could think of nothing more interesting than also embroidering his initials on a handkerchief, but her brain was full to bursting with ideas for making Clara's Christmastide a time to remember. There were doll's clothes to sew, a bonnet to knit to match her new mittens and, best of all, a painting of Sweep to hang on Clara's bedchamber wall. Tam—who had a talent for carpentry—had agreed to frame it and Sharp had promised to paint the frame with gilt paint.

A soft knock at her sitting-room door drew her attention and she tucked the handkerchief she was currently embroidering down by her side, out of sight.

It was Alice, holding Clara by the hand. Brack had followed them upstairs and, with a flash of inspiration, Grace knew what she could give Nathaniel for Christmas. He had already requested a portrait of Clara but she could include Brack in the portrait, too, as a surprise.

He might not return her love, but that did not stop her from wanting to make him happy and to brighten his life. His smile would be her reward.

Chapter Sixteen

It did not take Grace very many days to realise that coaxing a smile or, indeed, any indication of pleasure, from Nathaniel was a task beyond her meagre efforts. Clara was the only person who could tease a pleasantry from her increasingly taciturn uncle on the very few occasions he visited his niece whilst she was in Grace's care. Most days, though, upon his return from a day spent outside, Nathaniel sent Alice to bring Clara to him in his book room, leading Grace to the conclusion that, knowing the truth of their relationship, he simply did not want to see her and Clara together.

Their former easy friendship was no more and Grace mourned its passing. After overhearing his mother's warning, Grace had feared she would analyse Nathaniel's every word, look and gesture for his true feelings but, in actuality, there was no mistaking his opinion of her. His rejection of her—even as a friend—resurrected all her old insecurities. Her uncle, aunt and cousins had not wanted her. Philip had not wanted her. Now Ravenwell could barely stand being in the same room as her. Clara's very existence confirmed Grace's lack of moral character and she supposed she should be grateful Nathaniel hadn't cast her out on her ear immediately.

Her life at Shiverstone Hall would be lonely indeed if not

for Clara. Clara was a constant joy: the shining star around which Grace's life revolved. She gave Grace the strength to endure the shards of pain that pierced her heart every time Ravenwell looked right through her.

A week after his mother's departure, Grace and Clara returned from a visit to Elizabeth and, after handing Bill to Ned to unharness, Clara spied Tam.

'Doggies?' She ran up to him, her eyes beseeching. 'See doggies?'

He tweaked her cheek. 'Might I take Miss Clara to the kennels, Miss Bertram?'

'Yes, of course, Tam. I believe I might wait here for her, if you do not mind.'

Tam grinned. 'We'll not be long.' He knew very well Grace's dislike of facing the dogs all at once.

Grace could hear Ned whistling in the barn as he rubbed Bill down. She leaned against the barn wall, her mind drifting, thinking of nothing in particular. The ring of a boot heel on stone jerked her back to awareness and she straightened just as Nathaniel strode around the corner, coming from the direction of the mews where he kept his birds.

He stopped short, his brows bunching, and Grace's heart sank even as her breath caught at the mere sight of him. She could not bear this. How was she ever to mend this distance between them? It was as though he hated her. His mother could not have been further from the truth if she had tried. She stretched her lips into a smile.

'Good afternoon, my lord.'

'What are you doing here? Where is Clara?'

'She has gone with Tam to the kennels. I am waiting for them to return.'

'I see.'

He began to move away. There was a time when he would have teased her about her nervousness around the dogs. Now he could barely look at her. Rebellion warred with caution in her heart and won. How dare he treat her like a pariah?

'My lord, you did offer to show me your hawks. Might we go and see them now?'

He stared at her, expressionless. 'I am busy.'

She'd risked thus far. She would not back down. 'When might I see them, then?'

'When I invite you, Miss Bertram.' He lifted his hat. 'Good afternoon.'

He strode away before she had any chance to reply.

Following that encounter, Grace made no further attempt to break through his reserve. She could not afford to alienate him. She was here, with Clara. That was the most important point of all. Any further tension between herself and the Marquess could only jeopardise her future at the Hall—a risk she must not take.

Her trips to the village—whether to visit Elizabeth or to attend church—provided some respite to the increasingly fraught atmosphere at the Hall, but even those were lost to her when day after day of heavy rain confined them all to the house.

Almost two weeks after Lady Ravenwell's departure, Grace pulled open the curtains in Clara's bedchamber and folded back the shutters. At last! The rain that had fallen incessantly for the past week had stopped and given way to the sun: pale and weak, maybe, as it hung in the washed-out blue of the sky, but without doubt the sun.

'Look, sweetie,' she said to Clara. 'Ned was right. It *has* stopped raining. We shall be able to go out today.'

And what a relief that would be. With everyone confined indoors, unable even to attend church on Sunday, tempers had begun to fray, with snapped remarks and frowning faces on everyone. She turned to Clara, who had scrambled from under the bedcovers and was jumping up and down on her bed.

'Clara. Do not bounce on your bed. I have told you before.'

'Sweep! Sweep!'

'Yes, we will go and find him, as soon as you are dressed and have eaten your breakfast. Come, quickly now, or your porridge will be cold.'

She dipped the washcloth in the warm water Alice had brought up and washed Clara's hands and face, then dressed her in a warm, woollen dress. She then uncovered the serving dish of porridge and served up a bowl each for herself and for Clara. They would need something warming inside them if they were to drive to Shivercombe today, as she planned. The thought of visiting Elizabeth buoyed her spirits.

Hand in hand, Grace and Clara went to the kitchen.

'Sweep!' Clara ran to her kitten, who promptly disappeared under the dresser—his favourite refuge.

'Clara. I have told you. You must move slowly and not shout. You have scared him.'

Grace laughed, looking at Mrs Sharp to share her amusement. She was busy slicing ham from a joint and had not even glanced up when they came in the room. There was a large basket on the table, half-full, and the set of her mouth suggested she was not in a good mood.

'His lordship wants food sent out,' she grumbled. 'I told him, I did, Ned'll have to come back after it. I haven't got time to spend traipsing all over the fells a-looking for them and Sharp's rheumatics are playing him up, with all the wet weather.'

'Could I take it for you?'

Mrs Sharp paused, then shook her head and resumed slicing. 'No. You've got Miss Clara to watch and I can't have her under my feet today. Alice is helping Annie with the laundry. Got to make the most of the weather while there's a chance of drying them sheets.' She shook her head. 'His lordship's got no idea. He can only think about them animals. Setting that bird to fly today, they are, then seeing to the sheep. He doesn't understand what it takes to keep this place running. And with Christmas just around the corner, too.'

She wrapped the slices of ham in a clean cloth and put the bundle into the basket, then wrapped thick slices of bread and some hunks of cheese and piled them on top.

Grace watched her in silence, chewing at her lip. 'Is there anything else I can do to help?'

She got the answer she hoped for. 'No. You're better off taking Miss Clara out for a breath of fresh air. And take that wretched cat out of here too. Although...' she paused again to wipe her brow on her sleeve '...he did take after a mouse this morning. Didn't catch it, mind, but I dare say he'll get better when he grows. At least then he'll be some use.'

Grace ignored the housekeeper's grumbles. It was plainly one of those days and the less said the better. 'I thought I might drive to the village and call upon Elizabeth,' she said. 'If you are sure you do not need me.'

'That is a...oh, drat! I forgot to put in the pickles.'

The housekeeper rushed to the larder, returning with a jar of pickled beetroot and a bowl of apples. Grace didn't linger. Mrs Sharp was clearly preoccupied. She put on her cloak and bonnet, then helped Clara with hers and then they headed for the barn where Bill was stabled.

Some time later—hands chilled following her struggle with stiff straps and buckles—Grace climbed aboard the gig and gave Bill the office to proceed. She felt inordinately proud of herself. It was the first time she had harnessed Bill to the gig without help. She had checked and double-checked each fastening and she was confident nothing was amiss. She smiled down at Clara, tucked in by her side, a blanket around her legs.

'This is fun, is it not, sweetie? We are off on an adventure, after being stuck indoors for so long. It will be nice to see Miss Dunn again, won't it?'

'More kitties?'

Grace laughed, tilting her face towards the sun and breathing deeply of the clean, fresh air. 'No more kitties,' she said. 'I think one is enough, don't you?'

She drove the gig down the track and into the forest. It still gave her the shivers, but she felt much braver driving the gig than she had when she had walked through it all alone, scared of every sound and terrified of what might await her at Shiverstone Hall after the villagers' lurid stories.

Her confidence soared. She had been a town girl through and through, but now she had learnt about the countryside and the animals. She had climbed the fell and touched an eagle. She could harness a horse and drive a gig. She had even grown to like the dogs. Well... She liked Brack on his own. She was still wary when they all ran loose at once, leaping and barking. How her friends would stare at what she had accomplished and how brave she had become.

The only dark cloud in her life was Nathaniel.

She no longer deluded herself that he harboured feelings for her and she could only pray they might soon regain their former easy-going companionship, with its games of chess and cards, and accompanying smiles and laughter. Since his mother's visit all of that mutual ease had fallen away and, at dinner every evening, they each fumbled for the right words to say.

Heartsore. She had heard the word before, but hadn't known such pain could be real.

Bill plodded placidly on through the wood and, very soon, they emerged from the cover of the trees and followed the curve of the track down to the ford. Bill stopped. Grace frowned.

'Get up, Bill.'

She shook the reins. Bill took two steps, then jibbed

again, his front hooves at the water's edge. Grace slapped the reins on his back, clicking her tongue in imitation of Ned, but Bill would not budge. The ford was wider than usual, but the water—murky and brown instead of its normal crystal clarity—did not look much deeper. Grace doubted it would reach Bill's knees, let alone swamp the body of the gig.

She flicked the whip across the horse's broad back. He laid back his ears and shook his head, setting his bit jingling.

Stupid animal, frightened of a bit of water.

'Stay here, Clara, and do not move. I shall be back in a minute.' Grace tilted Clara's chin so she could look her in the eyes. 'Promise?'

The little girl nodded and tugged the blanket tighter around her legs. Satisfied Clara would stay put, Grace climbed from the gig and walked to Bill's head.

Nathaniel scanned the sky to the north. He had set Amber free as soon as he had reached the high fell. She had circled above him and his men for a long time, waiting, he knew, for him to call her in with a reward of food, but he had ignored her. Instead, he and his men had concentrated on locating their sheep after all the rain, rounding them up ready to drive them off the fells to the lower pastures for the remainder of the winter. Finally, Amber appeared to give up and she flew north in a steady line until now she was a mere speck in the distance.

Even though it was the right thing to do, Nathaniel was sad seeing the giant bird go. He hoped Amber would soon regain her mistrust of man—she had already successfully hunted for herself, so hopefully she would have no reason to seek out humans.

'Your lordship.'

'Yes, Tam?' Nathaniel answered absently, still watching

that increasingly faint speck. They had stopped for a brief rest, on the edge of the fell above Shiver Dale.

'My lord!'

His interest caught by Tam's urgent tone, Nathaniel joined him on the edge, where he gazed out over the dale to the south.

'Look.'

Nathaniel followed Tam's pointing finger, down the slope to the dale where the beck flowed. A horse and gig had emerged from the wood, heading down the track that led to the ford.

'That's Bill,' Nathaniel said. 'And Miss Bertram.'

Grace. Off to visit that damned curate again.

Jealousy flooded through him, turning him rigid with anger even as his common sense reminded him he had done everything possible in the past two weeks to keep her at arm's length. Then his brain caught up with what his eyes were seeing.

'What on earth does she think she's doing? The river isn't safe to cross after all that rain.'

'Ay, but will *she* know that?' Ned said, from where he held their three horses. 'That's Miss Clara in the gig 'n' all.'

'Bill's sensible; he won't attempt to cross.' Nathaniel tried to believe it, but he knew how deceptive the beck was after rain. What if she persuaded the cob to go forward? The power of that current... Sick anxiety twisted his gut and he walked across to Ned and took Zephyr's reins, pulling his head up from the grass. 'I'll go down and turn them back.'

He tightened Zephyr's girth and mounted before looking down the hill again. Sure enough, Bill had planted his feet on the edge of the river and was refusing to walk on. He headed Zephyr down the slope, in a direct line to the ford, leaning back to help the horse with his balance. The ground was slippery and, more than once, Zephyr's hooves slipped and only the stallion's great strength prevented them tumbling. It took all of Nathaniel's concentration to pick out a safe path.

Then he heard a shout from behind him. He looked up and a spasm of fear clutched his belly. Grace had climbed from the gig and was pulling at Bill's bridle, trying to persuade him into the river. Nathaniel swore loudly and, heedless of the danger, he dug his heels into Zephyr.

The stallion responded gallantly and they bounded down the slope, his hooves skidding perilously as Nathaniel offered silent prayers for the surefootedness of the stallion and the continued stubbornness of the cob. They reached gentler ground and Zephyr transitioned into a gallop, but it was heavy going across the sodden ground. Then time appeared to slow as Nathaniel saw Grace try once more to tug Bill forward. Bill threw his head up, knocking her off balance.

'Noooooooooooo!'

Nathaniel crouched low over the stallion's neck, urging him ever faster, but there was nothing he could do to prevent the tragedy unfolding. He could only watch, helpless, as Grace toppled backwards, arms windmilling, into the water.

Chapter Seventeen

Five seconds later Nathaniel reined Zephyr to a halt as a black-and-tan shape streaked past and launched itself into the river. Bill again stood, statue-like, facing the water. The river swept on. No sign of Grace. Or Brack.

I must find them. He looked at Clara: eyes huge, huddled in a blanket in the gig. *I can't leave her alone.*

He wheeled Zephyr around, staring back across the dale. Tam had already reached the bottom of the hill; he would reach the gig in a matter of minutes. Nathaniel waved at Tam, then pointed to Clara. Tam raised his hand in acknowledgement, then leaned forward over his horse's neck, urging him faster.

'Do not move,' Nathaniel called to Clara.

No time for more. No time to stop and reassure her. Heart in mouth, he kicked Zephyr into a canter, following the beck downstream. He trusted the stallion to pick a safe path as he scanned the river, trying not to despair at the speed and strength of the roaring, churning mass once they left the comparative calm of the ford. They weaved around bushes and trees, always sticking as close as possible to the riverbank. Finally—he hauled on the reins—a flash of white, a face, two arms wrapped around a sturdy branch protruding from the beck.

Nathaniel leapt from the saddle and raced to the water's edge.

'Grace!' Her eyes were screwed shut, lips drawn back to bare clenched teeth. 'Grace!'

A tree had toppled into the beck, its trunk disappearing under the surface some ten feet before that branch emerged from the swift rush of mud-coloured water. Nathaniel shrugged out of his greatcoat, pulled off his boots and clambered on to the trunk. He cursed freely at the rough bark that cut into his knees as he crawled along and again when he reached the place where the trunk sank from sight under the frigid water. The tree's bulk helped steady the rush of the beck at this point, but it was still fierce enough to knock him off balance. Nathaniel manoeuvred around to sit astride the submerged tree, then steadily pulled himself closer to Grace.

'Grace! Hold on, sweetheart. I'm coming.'

Her eyes opened. *Thank God.* They stared uncomprehendingly. Her lips were blue and now he could see her teeth chattering. He must get her out of this and fast. He pushed himself to go quicker, aware—even as he neared her—that she was rapidly weakening. Her head lolled on her neck and her arms were losing their hold, gradually slipping.

'Hold on! Think of Clara! You can't leave her!'

She made a visible effort to rouse, forcing her head up and opening her eyes. Nathaniel dragged himself along the submerged truck, ever closer.

You can't leave me.

His father's face... Hannah's... David's...they floated through his mind's eye and his throat thickened.

'Stay with me, love. Hold on. I'm coming.'

I cannot lose you as well.

A sob erupted from his chest. He clamped his teeth against the next.

No time to fall apart, Ravenwell. Get on with it. Get her.

She was so close. Just like his father. He had seen him, through the flames, but he could not save him. He had failed his father. Left his mother a widow. He would not fail Grace and leave Clara an orphan. As if in a nightmare, he saw Grace's head slump and in a final, desperate lunge, he reached her at the moment her hold on the branch slipped. He hauled her into his chest with one arm and snatched at that same branch with his free hand. Immediately, the power of the flow lifted him and tugged at his legs until he was stretched out, feet pointing downstream. He fought the greedy suck of the river, gritting his teeth against the screaming agony of his arm and shoulder, hauling them both against the current until he was close enough to link his arm around the branch.

Gasping, he stared at the bank. So near and yet so far. But failure was not an option. Clara needed them both. He kicked out with his legs, struggling to bring them back under him until, at last, he could feel the trunk beneath his feet. He could not risk turning to face the bank. Sending a heartfelt prayer heavenwards, he shifted Grace into a more secure hold and dropped into the water, one leg each side of the trunk again, gripping it with muscles honed from years of riding. He inched backwards along the trunk, desperation fuelling him, until he reached the bank. Near-exhausted, he dropped to the ground, Grace's inert form cradled in his arms, and staggered away from the river.

Six feet from the water's edge, his knees buckled and he collapsed, cushioning Grace against the fall. He set her down and she immediately rolled to her side and began to cough, water dribbling from her mouth. He rubbed and patted her back, scraping wet strands of hair from her face.

I must warm her. He forced his stiff muscles to move, turning to scan the riverbank upstream. *Surely Tam or Ned will come soon.*

He struggled to his feet, juddering with the cold, stripped off his wet jacket and shirt, picked up his discarded greatcoat and rubbed it briskly over his chest and arms. Then he fell to his knees next to Grace and pulled her into a sitting position. He must warm her and he could not do that whilst she was clad in soaking wet clothes. Her cloak had already gone. She moaned as he struggled to remove her dress.

'What…?'

'Help me, my love.' He placed his cheek against hers and rubbed skin against skin. 'We need to get you warm.'

She scrabbled at his arm with weak fingers. 'Clara!'

'Hush. She is safe. The men are with her.'

Her entire body was shaking as he tugged again at her dress.

'Wha…no! You…you…'

Her words were slurred and weak, but still she managed to struggle as he worked the sopping woollen dress up her body and over her head.

'Miss Bertram!'

She stilled momentarily at his command, then thrashed her head from side to side. 'No, no. *Noooo…*'

Grimly, Nathaniel continued to disrobe her, until she was clad only in her shift. He lifted her to his lap and reached for his greatcoat, wrapping it around her, pulling her wet hair out from the collar. He rubbed her with brisk movements, praying the friction would warm her, talking to her to keep her awake.

'Stay with me, my darling. Don't leave me. Think of Clara.'

The welcome thud of hooves eventually sounded and Tam appeared. He slid to the ground.

'Thank God, milord.'

'Miss Clara?'

'Ned's driving the gig back to the Hall. Is Miss Bertram…?' He paused and peered more closely. 'I don't like her colour, milord. We need to get her home.'

'We do, Tam. I'll take Miss Bertram on Sammy and you can ride Zephyr to the Hall.' The stallion would never tolerate a double burden. 'Tell Mrs Sharp what's happened and to heat plenty of water ready for us.'

He wrapped his coat more securely around Grace and handed her up to Tam before regaining his feet and pulling on his boots. It took him two attempts to mount Sammy. His legs were about as much use as lengths of string and agonising pain ripped through the muscles of his right arm and shoulder as he dragged himself into the saddle.

'Where's Brack?' Tam asked.

A hard lump lodged in Nathaniel's throat. 'I've not seen him since he went into the water after Miss Bertram.'

Tam hoisted Grace up in front of Nathaniel, then he stripped off his own heavy coat.

'Here, milord. No good you coming down with the ague on top of all else. We'll come back out and search for the dog once Miss Clara's safe and I've spoken to Mrs Sharp.'

He swung up on to Zephyr and galloped away. Nathaniel blinked back hot tears, then muttered yet another curse. He was getting soft. But… Brack had been with him a long time. A loyal companion.

Grace stirred and he wrenched his attention back to the matter in hand. He flung Tam's coat around his shoulders, blessing the immediate warmth as it blocked the chilly December air from his still-damp skin, and then shifted Grace into a more secure position on his lap.

She was so very delicate. How would she survive? He pressed his lips to her temple, willing her to keep fighting. Her shivers were ever more violent. He must warm her. He loosened the coat around Grace and pulled her close into his bare chest, skin to skin. They would warm each other. He rearranged the coats around them and nudged Sammy into a walk, leaving the reins lying slack on his neck. He could not risk going faster and cause either of the coats to slip off.

His arms encircled Grace beneath the tent of the coats and he rubbed her slender limbs in turn. The delicate bones of shoulders and hips, elbows and knees revealed the lack of flesh beneath her skin. She weighed little more than a child.

'Stay with me, my darling. We will soon be home.'

Home.

Her presence had changed the Hall into a home for him after nine long years of it being nothing more than a roof over his head. She belonged there, with Clara and with him, and yet he had done everything in the past fortnight to make her feel unwelcome and unwanted, using his anger to hide from reality. He had seen the pain in her eyes and he had ignored it, more concerned with protecting his own heart and peace of mind.

They settled into a rhythm, with Grace huddled against his chest, his chin resting on the top of her head, his thoughts ranging free. He had not failed this time, as he had with his father. He relived his terror when he had seen her tumble into the river. His muscles tightened without volition, nestling her closer into him, willing the heat of his skin to warm her.

Cold killed. He saw it happen every spring, when an ewe lambed earlier than expected. If the weather was unkind and the lamb couldn't get dry and warm, it would soon succumb, the cold numbing it, slowing everything down until it sank into death.

He would not allow that to happen to Grace. That terror he had felt...he knew, with heart-stopping certainty, that it had been more than the horror he would have experienced had it been Tam or Ned who had fallen.

A low moan reached his ears and again his arms tightened reflexively. He could not lose her now. She felt so frail in his arms, but she had a strong will. She would survive.

She *must* survive.

For Clara's sake.

For his.

'Stay with me, my darling Grace. Stay with me.'

He had thought that by keeping her at bay his growing

feelings might wither and die, but he had been wrong. They had continued to twine around his heart until he could no longer ignore the truth.

He was in love with Grace Bertram.

Fool that he was.

He needed to say the words. If the worst should happen, he needed her to know.

'I love you,' he whispered and pressed his lips to the cool skin of her forehead.

He had fallen in love with her, even though he knew she could never love a damaged soul such as he, and even though she deserved all the things in life he could not provide: friends, fun and laughter, parties and dancing.

It seemed the heart did not respond to logic.

He cringed at how he had treated her since his mother's visit.

God, please. Let her live, and I promise to change my ways. Even though I can never tell her how important she is to me, I will show her. I will make her happy. Every single day. I swear.

He rode right up to the back door. Everyone piled out, faces creased with worry, and Mrs Sharp and the other women carried Grace off to get her warm and dry.

'Tam's gone out to look for Brack,' Sharp said, as Ned took charge of Sammy.

'I must go, too. I need to find him.'

His legs buckled as he turned to follow Ned and he stumbled. Sharp was by his side in an instant, tugging Nathaniel's arm across his shoulders.

'Yer in no fit state to go anywhere, milord. There's a tub of warm water a-waiting in your chamber—best you get yourself warm and dry and some food inside you before you think about that. There's nothing you can do that Tam can't.'

'I'll go out, too, once I've settled Sammy, milord,' Ned called over his shoulder. 'Don't 'ee fret. We'll find 'im.'

Sharp helped strip Nathaniel, who could not even summon the energy to shield his scars as he normally would.
Sharp took his wet clothing away, leaving Nathaniel to his
thoughts. He closed his eyes and rested his head against
the rim of his bathtub, feeling the heat of the water seep
through his flesh and thaw his chilled bones. He had nearly
lost her. Grace. She smiled in his imagination, her clear,
soft skin radiant, her expressive gold-green eyes warm and
sparkling, her blonde hair as fine and delicate as strands of
silk. Then another picture took its place—river-drenched
hair straggling across her face in dirty strands, lips blue
and pinched, pale eyelids, fragile as a moth's wing, closed
in utter exhaustion.

He exploded from the bathtub, unheeding of the water
that sloshed on to the floor. A towel was draped over a
chair near the fire, warming. He grabbed it and scrubbed
at himself, then pulled the waiting shirt and trousers on to
still-damp skin. He shrugged into his banyan and strode
from the room towards the nursery wing.

He tapped at Grace's bedchamber door. Annie—Tam's
wife—answered.

'How is she?'

'Sleeping, my lord. She—'

'Stand aside. I want to see her.'

He must see her. He needed reassurance. He needed to
know she was safe. That she would survive.

'But—'

'You will be here the entire time. There can be no impropriety.'

He pushed the door wide, leaving Annie no choice but
to move out of his way. He crossed to the bed and stood
staring down at her.

So small. So fragile. But her cheeks were pink, as were
her lips, and her breathing was even and regular. The fear
that had seized him loosened its hold and the tight band
around his chest eased.

'Has the doctor been sent for?'

'No, my lord. She is bruised and battered, but Mrs Sharp is certain she will recover.'

He had faith in Mrs Sharp's experience in treating injuries and illnesses.

'She said Miss Bertram's chest sounds clear,' Annie continued, 'so she doesn't think she breathed in any water.'

'That is good. Has she regained consciousness at all?'

Nathaniel laid the backs of his fingers against the silken skin of her cheek. It was warm. As it should be.

Reassurance.

There was a graze on her forehead that had begun to swell, but otherwise she appeared unscathed.

'She came round when we bathed her, as she warmed up,' Annie said. 'But she didn't make much sense. She was gabbling about Miss Clara. And Brack.'

At her words, a crease appeared between Grace's eyebrows and her lips pursed. 'Brack.' Her voice sounded hoarse. 'Where's Brack?'

Annie came to stand beside Nathaniel. 'We told her Miss Clara was safe. Alice brought her before Miss Bertram went to sleep,' she whispered. 'But we didn't know about Brack.'

Grace's lids slitted open and she fixed her gaze on Nathaniel. She ran her tongue along her lips.

'Is he safe?' She pushed her bedcovers down and held her hand out to Nathaniel.

Annie tutted and pulled the sheet and blankets up, tucking them around Grace, but she resisted the woman's efforts to fold her arm back under the covers.

'Nath…my lord.' She spoke with urgency. 'He saved me. Brack.' Her lids drifted shut, then she sucked in a deep breath. He could see the effort it took to force her eyes open again. 'Tell me. Is he all right?'

He could not lie, not when those green eyes were fixed on him so beseechingly. He took her hand in both of his, resisting the urge to press his lips to her skin. Never, by word or deed, would he embarrass her by revealing the extent of his feelings for her.

'I do not know. Ned and Tam are out looking for him now.'

Her fingers clutched at his. 'He saved me. He pushed me towards the bank and I grabbed a branch, but he...he was swept away.'

She gulped, her eyes sheened with tears and her anguish wrenched at his heart. He wanted nothing more than to protect her from anything and everything bad in this life. He stroked her hand, cursing the inadequacy of his efforts to comfort her. Unbidden, an image of Ralph Rendell arose in his mind's eye and a silent growl vibrated in his chest.

'I saw him...I could not...' Her voice trembled.

'Hush.' Nathaniel smoothed her forehead. 'We will find him.'

Somehow. Alive or dead, we will find him.

'You must sleep now. Please, do not worry.'

'You will tell me the truth?'

'I will.'

That image of Rendell would not go. Nathaniel knew he should only care about what was best for Grace, but still he hesitated. He did not want the man here. But...the curate had the right to know what had happened. He must set aside his feelings for Grace's sake.

'Shall I send for Mr Rendell?'

Her eyes widened. 'Am I dying?'

'No!' He gripped her hand. 'Of course you are not dying.'

'Then why...?'

'He is your...friend. I thought you might want to see him.'

Her lids lowered. 'No. There is no need.'

His spirits rose. Was she not as smitten as he thought?

Grace stifled a yawn. 'I am so very weary.'

'Sleep then. I shall see you later.'

After I have found Brack.

He headed for the door.

Chapter Eighteen

Nathaniel rode out on his bay hunter, Caesar, dread clogging his throat and that tight band once again clamped around his chest. He was afraid of what he might find but, at the same time, he could not rest until he knew what had happened to Brack.

The sun was low in the sky, the shadows lengthening and he reckoned he had an hour before it would become too dark to search. He aimed straight for the place where he had found Grace, and began to follow the course of the beck, scouring the bank and the undergrowth for any sign of his faithful dog. The failing light did not help his search. Brack's black-and-tan colouring would be easily camouflaged by the dark earth and fallen leaves under any bushes, unless he was out somewhere in the open. That was not likely. He would hole up somewhere, as long as he had an ounce of strength when he got out of the water. Nathaniel refused to accept the dog might not have succeeded in getting out.

After five minutes of riding Nathaniel muttered an oath, reined Caesar to a halt and slid from the saddle. He'd not been thinking straight. From a nearby hazel he cut a long, straight stick and, pulling the reins over the horse's head to lead him, he began to walk. His entire body ached, but he ignored the pain. There would be plenty of time to re-cuperate after he found Brack. He trudged on downriver, poking the stick into and under every bush, whistling and calling from time to time, ears straining for any reply.

He had searched maybe a quarter of a mile of bank when two figures on horseback materialised out of the gloom.

'Well?'

'Nothing, milord.' Ned touched his finger to his cap. 'Sorry.'

'We've ridden up and down this stretch twice, as far as the bridge, and we've seen no sign, milord.' Tam said. 'But we did meet Gil Brown from the Braithwaite estate and he promised to alert their men to keep an eye out. I doubt there's more we can do tonight.' He cast a meaning-ful look at the sky, darkening by the minute. 'It's going to be a cold one, by the looks of it.'

It felt hopeless, yet Nathaniel couldn't give up. Not yet. Not while there was still light to see by.

'You two get off home,' he said. 'I'll just walk on a bit further.'

The two men exchanged a look.

'We'll stay and help.' Tam started to dismount.

'No!'

Tam slowly swung his leg back over the saddle.

'Sorry. I did not mean to snap.' The men's stares burned into Nathaniel, shaming him. 'Thank you both for your efforts.'

He knew the men were concerned about him, but he needed to be alone. Hope had faded. If the worst *had* hap-pened…he wanted to face that alone.

'You have ridden this stretch. I'll walk it, until it gets too dark. It will not take more than one of us to do that.'

Their hoofbeats faded into the distance and Nathan-iel resumed his lonely search, praying silently even as he called Brack's name. He needed to know. He could not bear to imagine his faithful Brack injured and in pain. He would rather he was already dead than lying somewhere alone, hurt and slowly dying.

Finally, the night had drawn close all about him. He knew he must abandon the search. Heart a lead weight in his chest, throat aching with unshed tears, he flung the stick away into the darkness, threw the reins over Caesar's head and put his left foot in the stirrup. He had bent his right leg ready to propel himself into the saddle when Caesar threw up his head, his ears pricked as he stared at something off to their right, away from the river.

Probably a fox. Or a rabbit. He had nothing to lose, though, so he took his foot from the stirrup and walked towards whatever had caught the horse's attention. Caesar followed without hesitation. Nothing too strange then, or he would plant his hooves in the ground and refuse to move. Nathaniel swallowed, nerves playing havoc with his insides. *What if...?*

Feeling foolish for that sudden upwelling of hope, he called, 'Brack? Are you there, boy?'

He strained his ears. Nothing. He glanced round at Caesar, still on high alert, staring...staring...not wild-eyed, but focussed and intent. Nathaniel walked in the direction of Caesar's gaze. Ten yards. Fifteen. Caesar halted, snorting quietly, soft nostrils vibrating. Nathaniel stroked his nose, looking around, trying in vain to see...something.

He whistled.

The barest scuffle sounded from the undergrowth in front of them. He dare not drop the reins, for fear Caesar might finally take fright. He pulled the reins over the horse's head again and moved towards the sound. When his arm and the reins were at full stretch, he stopped, trying desperately to penetrate the darkness, wishing he had not discarded his stick.

Then he heard it. A low whimper. Heart in mouth, he cast around for somewhere to tie Caesar. If it was Brack he would need the horse—well accustomed to carrying deer carcasses—to get him home. He tied Caesar to a sapling and then ran back to where he had heard that sound.

'Brack?'

A rustle. He honed in on it and moved forward with care. A bush loomed in front of him. Dropping to his knees, he felt beneath. His fingers met with damp, matted fur and another whimper.

'Thank you, God.'

With both hands, he felt along Brack's body, eliciting several whines. Hopefully they were bruises and not broken bones. He was horribly aware that Brack—stretched full-length on his side—had not even raised his head. He could not leave the dog here all night; he had no choice but to move him. He eased Brack from under the bush, closing his ears to his whines and one weak yelp. Dogs, unlike horses, were always vocal at the slightest hurt; he must trust that was the case this time. Nathaniel stripped off his coat and wrapped it around Brack, who was now panting in distress. Nathaniel's nerve almost failed him. What if he caused lasting damage?

I must. He can't survive out here. And I can't see to examine him properly.

'Sorry, old lad,' he muttered, 'but I've got no choice.'

He lifted Brack as gently as he could, then carried him to Caesar. Mounting was awkward—he had to search for a fallen tree first, to make it possible—but they were soon on their way home, Brack's inert form lying across Nathaniel's lap.

He'd found Brack but would his faithful friend survive?

When Grace roused, the house was quiet and her room dark, just a residual glow from the banked fire to penetrate the gloom. She shivered, closed her eyes again and wriggled around, snuggling deeper under the covers, vaguely conscious of aches and pains in various parts of her body. Eyes still shut, she lay cocooned in the warmth, her mind scrambling its way from the depths of sleep, remembering her sense of achievement in harnessing Bill to the gig, and—she sat bolt upright, the covers falling unheeded to her waist.

Oh, dear God! Clara! She is safe... I'm certain she is safe. I saw her...they brought her in to see me.

Didn't they?

She threw back the covers and—*ouch*. What had started as a leap from her bed turned into a crawl. She had never felt so battered and bruised. She gritted her teeth against the pain and felt around for her slippers. She slipped them on and then found her chamber candle on her nightstand and took it to the fire to light it with a spill. Her shawl was draped at the end of the bed. She snatched it up, flung it around her shoulders—it was so large it almost reached the floor—and went to the door that connected her bedchamber to Clara's. She raised the candle to light the room and her terror subsided at the tiny form sleeping peacefully. Her pulse steadied. A movement caught her eye and she realised someone else slept in there, on a truckle bed. It was Alice, presumably to attend to Clara if she woke, so Grace wouldn't be disturbed.

Grace stood watching her daughter, digging into her memory for what she could recall of the day before. She remembered Mrs Sharp giving her a dose of laudanum to help her to sleep. She relived the moment she had tipped backwards into the icy water and the unexpected strength of the flowing water that swamped her clothes and tumbled her along until she was beyond the ford and in the deeper water. She shivered, nausea squeezing her throat as she remembered swallowing mouthful after mouthful of filthy water, desperately gasping for air every time her face broke the surface, and Brack...

She backed out of Clara's room. Had they found him? She frowned, the action prompting a pain in her temple. She touched her forehead, feeling the swell of a lump and the rough soreness of abraded skin. She should return to bed and yet, even as that thought crossed her mind, her stomach rumbled. She would give anything for a warm drink and something to eat. She would go down to the kitchen—the range would have been banked for the night, but there would be enough heat to warm some chocolate and, besides, she could not sleep without discovering Brack's fate. If they had found him, he would be in the kitchen, where he slept every night.

Grace left her bedchamber and descended the stairs, wincing as she put her weight on her left leg. As she crossed the hall to the door that led to the servants' domain at the rear of house, the longcase clock struck two, making her jump, thereby setting the shadows cast by her candle to dance across the panelled walls. She shivered, pulling her shawl tighter around her.

She followed the passageway to the kitchen and lifted the latch, pushing the door open to reveal the soft glow of a single candle on the dresser. Stepping lightly, Grace rounded the table. There, stretched out on a folded blanket before the range, was Brack. His ear flicked and he thumped his tail gently against the floor, but did not lift his head, his neck being pinned down by a loudly purring Sweep, who was draped over it.

'What are you doing out of bed?'

The soft query came from the gloom at the far end of the kitchen. A tall form unfolded from Sharp's favourite overstuffed armchair, leaving a huddle of blanket behind. Nathaniel stepped into the light. The sight of him…the memory of what he had done for her… Grace shook her head, mutely, swallowing down the surge of emotion that threatened to overwhelm her.

'What is it, G… Miss Bertram? Are you unwell?'

He was by her side in an instant. Large, safe, comforting. Heat radiated from him and his scent—citrus soap with an undernote of warm male—invaded her senses. He slipped his arm around her waist, supporting her weight.

'You should not be down here. Come. Sit down.'

He urged her towards the chair. She resisted.

'No. I am well, I promise you, apart from a few bruises. It was only that I…' She turned within the circle of his arm and tilted her head, capturing his gaze. 'Thank you. From the bottom of my heart, I thank you.'

His eyes darkened as they searched hers. His lips parted as his head lowered, but then his shoulders jerked and he raised his head, breaking eye contact. She searched his expression. His lips were now a tight line. A frown creased his brow and a muscle bunched in his jaw.

'You have no need to thank me.' His voice was gruff as he removed his arm from her waist and shifted a fraction, putting space between them. 'Anyone would have done the same.'

She knelt by Brack, stroking him to cover the slap of humiliation.

'And you, handsome, steadfast Brack.' She leant over to press her lips to his domed head. Her eyes blurred with tears. 'Without you, I would certainly not be h-here.'

She gulped back a sob. Giving way to her emotions would achieve nothing other than to embarrass both her and Nathaniel. She would not have looked up at him so… so *invitingly*…but…had she imagined those tortured pleas? Those endearments? She brushed those unanswered questions aside. Whether she remembered truly or not could make no difference. She had acted without thought and Nathaniel's rejection was plain. And painful.

She would focus on the reality. She had survived. Her terror would fade and she would continue with her life. Much as she had after she had given up Clara. Grace had learned the value of resilience then and she would use that lesson now. She would survive Nathaniel's rejection.

Grace smoothed Brack's head, giving her time to compose herself. Sweep had by now roused, seeking some of her attention, and Grace tickled him under the chin.

'Is he injured? Will he recover?' she asked.

'We think that, like you, he is battered and bruised and shocked, but nothing broken. He should be back to his old self within a few days.'

Sweep set himself to wash Brack's ear and then moved on to his eye. Brack seemed not to object. Grace patted him.

'Where did they find him?'

'About half a mile down river from where you were.'

'I am so relieved.'

Grace regained her feet, stumbling slightly. Nathaniel cupped her elbow—no supporting arm around her waist this time.

'I came down to find out if Brack was safe,' she said, keeping her gaze on the dog and the kitten, 'but I am a little hungry. Do you mind if I—?'

'Sit down and I will find something for you.' Nathaniel ushered her, again, towards the chair in the corner.

Weariness settling in her bones, Grace sank into the chair, folding her legs and tucking her feet under her as she snuggled into the still-warm, still-smelling-of-Nathaniel blanket. Nathaniel watched her until she was settled, an unfathomable expression in his dark eyes. She heard the vague noises of food preparation and soon found a plate with a slice of Mrs Sharp's fruit cake thrust into her hands.

'Thank you.' She nibbled at the cake, the plate balanced on her legs, until Nathaniel returned with a cup of chocolate. She drank it gratefully, her lids growing heavy with the effort of trying to stay awake. Vaguely she felt the bowl and plate being removed and then she remembered no more.

'Ooh, miss! Such goings-on yesterday.'

Alice was wide-eyed as she lit the fire in Grace's bedchamber. Grace winced at the protest of her sore muscles as she rolled over.

'How is Miss Clara? Is she awake yet?'

'Not yet. She was awake in the night for a while, so she is making up for it now.'

Which meant Alice, too, had been awake but she was as cheerful as ever this morning, despite her disturbed sleep, as she cleaned her hands with a damp cloth and dried them on her apron. Grace felt like nothing more than snuggling back down and sleeping the day away, but it was time she got up. Clara would wake soon, wanting something to eat… Grace sat up abruptly, her hand to her mouth.

'What is it, miss? Have you got a pain?'

'No. No, I am all right. I had a recollection of something…' *Or was it a dream?* 'Alice. Did the men find Brack yesterday?'

'No, miss.'

Oh, no. Poor—

'But his lordship did.'

'His lordship?'

He had brought her home and then gone out again for his dog? Her heart swelled with admiration for his loyalty and courage.

'Yes, miss. Half-dead he was. The dog, I mean, not his lordship, although he didn't look much better.' Alice bustled over to the bed and handed Grace her shawl. 'I've never seen him so…so…*anguished*. Nothing would do for him but to sit up all night in the kitchen in case Brack took a turn for the worse.'

So it wasn't a dream. She *had* gone down to the kitchen and talked to Nathaniel. And invited him—albeit wordlessly—to kiss her. An invitation he had refused. Nausea churned her stomach. But how had she got back to her bedchamber? She had no memory of anything after drinking that chocolate…

Alice walked to the door and opened it, then paused to look back at Grace. 'That's the trouble with animals, isn't it, miss? They can't tell you what hurts. Not like people.'

Not like people... Grace flopped back against her pillows. *But people can choose not to tell you what is wrong. And not all pain is physical.*

Nathaniel...

Alice was still speaking.

'I beg your pardon, Alice. I'm afraid I missed what you said.'

'I said, Mrs Sharp said you must stay in bed and she will bring you some breakfast directly.'

'But...' Grace levered herself up to a sitting position.

'Now, miss, you'd best do what Mrs Sharp says, or...' Alice rolled eyes, then laughed. 'I'll look after Miss Clara. Mrs Sharp said to take her to the kitchen for her breakfast today.'

'Bring her in to see me first, Alice. Please? I need to see she is all right.'

'Oh, bless you. Miss Clara's bright as a button. It's you that needs looking after.' And with that Alice bustled from the room, shutting the door behind her.

Grace relaxed back into the pillows again, picking over the events of the day before, her thoughts circling and circling...avoiding...too afraid to confront the truth...too terrified to admit, even to herself, the awful thing that *could* have happened yesterday as a consequence of her actions when Bill had jibbed at the water's edge.

What if...?

The sound of the door opening dragged her from her thoughts. She plastered a smile on her face. But it was not Clara, or Alice, who appeared.

It was Nathaniel.

Chapter Nineteen

'Good morning, Miss Bertram.' His dark brown eyes were filled with concern. 'Alice said you were awake. How are you feeling this morning?'

'Sore.' Her burgeoning guilt forced her to admit, 'And ashamed.'

He came closer. 'Why ashamed?'

She sat up, hugging the covers to her chest. 'For the trouble I have caused. For the danger I p-put you in.' Her eyes swam as she finally confronted her worst fear. 'When I think…if you had not been there…what might have happened t-to…Clara…'

Her daughter's name strangled in her throat as she choked back a sob. This was the first time she dared to put that dread into thought, let alone words. Until this instant, it had remained a black spectre hovering around the edge of her consciousness. She had put her precious daughter in danger through her own stupidity. Tears burned her eyes and stung her nose.

Nathaniel perched one hip on the bed, facing her. 'You are not to worry about something that did not happen. It was an accident.'

'But she might have…she could have…' The tears spilled from her eyes, and she covered her face with trembling hands. 'I was so proud of myself,' she muttered through her fingers. 'Stupid! Stupid! I had proved I could harness Bill without any help and I did not want to turn back. My own pride almost cost my life. And yours. And Brack's. And Clara's...'

She ended on a wail. Strong arms came around her and she was hugged close to his solid chest, the steady thump of his heart in her ear as she cried out her guilt and her distress.

'Do not blame yourself. The fault was ours.' The rumble of his words vibrated through her, soothing her. How she wished she could stay cocooned in his arms always. 'We should have warned you the current is treacherous after heavy rain, even though the ford appears shallow enough to cross safely. We all know you are not used to country ways.' His hands cupped her shoulders and he moved her away, ducking his head to peer into her eyes. 'If it will make you feel better, Mrs Sharp is, even now, in her kitchen worrying herself sick that she had said nothing.'

'Mrs Sh-Sharp? B-but she does not even l-like me.'

A handkerchief was pushed into her hands.

'She is becoming accustomed to you.' There was a wry note in his voice. 'I thought you knew that.'

'I had begun to hope it was true.'

Grace dried her eyes and blew her nose, then tucked the handkerchief under her pillow.

'I might have need of it again,' she said in response to Nathaniel's raised brow.

'I can see I shall have to replenish my store of handkerchiefs. I recall you promised me at your interview that you would not succumb to your emotions again.'

Grace's heart lurched. 'You cannot...do you mean to send me away?'

'For crying? Or for depleting my stock of handkerchiefs? It was but a jest, Miss Bertram, albeit a poor one.'

I no longer even recognise a joke at my expense. I am useless.

The vague recollections that had plagued her since waking suddenly came into sharp focus. She could not contain the gasp that escaped her as she remembered Nathaniel carrying her from the river. Disrobing her...

'My dress.'

The words blurted out before she could stop them. Better she had waited to ask Alice, but it was too late and Nathaniel waited for her to expand that comment with raised brows.

'I...that is... I wondered...I remembered...' The sick feeling in her somach invaded her throat as she felt her face burn.

All the planes of his face seemed to harden. 'You remember correctly, Miss Bertram. Please understand that you were dangerously cold when I pulled you from the beck. You needed to be warmed and that was impossible with your clothing sodden with icy water.'

'Oh.' She plucked at the fringe of her shawl. 'I see. I do understand. Is... Did you... Are my clothes here? At the Hall?'

'Ah. No, they remain where I discarded them. On the riverbank.'

'But I will need—'

'You will not wear those garments again. Not whilst you are in my employ. I do not wish to be reminded of—'

He fell abruptly silent, a scowl upon his face, and Grace's heart sank. Of course he did not wish to be reminded of her stupidity and how it had almost killed him and Brack, not to mention the risk to Clara. But she needed her dress and her cloak.

'But I only have—'

'Enough.' He raised his hand, palm facing her. 'I will replace your clothing. There are lengths of fabric stored somewhere—you may choose whichever takes your fancy and make…or, no. Speak to Mrs Sharp. I believe there is a seamstress in the village who will make up some dresses for you. You will hardly have the time, with Clara to care for. And, for God's sake, do not choose brown or grey or any of those other dull colours you are wont to wear.'

Grace stared, flummoxed. 'But, my lord, I am a governess. I should wear clothing suitable to my—'

His gaze snapped to hers. 'And I, Miss Bertram, am your employer. If I choose to order my employee not to wear dresses that transform her into a drab, then I expect to be obeyed. Without question. Is that clear?'

The warmth in his voice belied his harsh words. Her heart lifted; he was not so very angry with her after all.

'Yes, my lord.'

She smiled tentatively. Truthfully, it would be no hardship to accept his offer. Dark colours always drained her complexion. She should not really care about her appearance, but she was woman enough to want to look her best, especially in front of Nathaniel.

'Thank you. And—and I am pleased Brack is safe. I did not know, last night, that it was you who found him.'

He raised a brow. 'Does it matter who found him?'

'I meant…that is…you went out again for a dog when you must have been as exhausted as me.'

'Not quite,' he said, with the glimmer of a smile. 'And Brack is not just *a* dog. He is *my* dog. I look after my own.'

'And you love him.'

'You think it strange that I care for my animals?'

'No! I think it admirable.'

It was not only his animals he cared for. He cared for Clara and for the people who worked for him too.

For her.

'Thank you, again, for saving me yesterday, my lord. And for looking after me last night.'

His eyes crinkled at the corners. 'You are very welcome, Miss Bertram.'

A suspicion suddenly struck her. 'Did you put laudanum drops in my chocolate last night?'

A bubble of laughter rose inside her at the face he pulled, reminiscent of a small boy caught out in mischief.

'Guilty as charged. I apologise, but you needed to sleep, not lie awake fretting, so I thought you could use a little assistance.'

'No wonder I could not remember returning to my bed.' She willed her cheeks not to grow pink. 'I... Did you...?'

'I carried you upstairs, if that is what you are wondering. You did not stir. And you cannot—' he fleetingly brushed her cheek with one finger '—be embarrassed after the events of yesterday afternoon. I was the perfect gentleman, I can assure you.' A faint smile stretched his lips and was gone.

'I did not doubt it, my lord. Thank you.'

The bed rocked as he stood up. 'I am relieved to find you on the road to recovery and will leave you in peace. Mrs Sharp has prescribed rest for you today, so please ensure you do as she says.'

He turned on his heel and left the room, leaving Grace to ponder her growing feelings for a man who did not return them.

Or does he?

His mother had seen enough in his behaviour to prompt her to warn him off Grace and most successfully, too, to judge by his behaviour since her visit. There was a definite softening in his attitude today, though, and she would swear she had not misremembered those frantic endearments when he rescued her.

But...her doubts about her own judgement were still powerful.

Look what happened last time I believed a man cared for me.

She conjured up the memory of the night before when she had gazed up at Nathaniel. He *had* been tempted to

kiss her, but then he had ignored her silent invitation. H
was her employer. A marquess.

Miss Fanworth's warning against dalliances with em
ployers whispered in her memory. The teacher had joine
the four friends as they waited in their shared bedroom fo
the carriage that would whisk Joanna away to her new lif

It never ends well, she had said. *Look at poor Madame.*
and then she had blushed, pursed her lips and shaken he
head when urged to tell the girls more.

Grace and her friends had often speculated about wha
had happened to Madame in the past. Rumours—passe
down from each generation of schoolgirls to the next—tol
the tale of a newly qualified governess who had fallen i
love with her high-ranking employer's heir. It was said tha
Madame had been paid off with the school in Salisbury
but that she had been left broken-hearted.

Grace struggled to believe the stern Frenchwoman ha
ever been so ill-disciplined as to allow her heart to rul
her head—a trait of which she had accused Grace on mor
than one occasion—but then, the night before Rachel ha
finally left the school, she had discovered a little more o
the truth. Unable to sleep, Rachel had gone downstairs an
happened upon Madame reading a pile of old letters wit
tears in her eyes.

'*Surtout, garder votre coeur,*' Madame had said, befor
sending Rachel back to bed with a warm drink. *Above al
guard your heart.*

Rachel had told Isabel and Grace—Joanna had alread
left the school—and they had come to the conclusion th
rumours about Madame's lost love must be true.

With a sigh, Grace wriggled down under the covers an
rolled on to her side. Henceforth, she would make sure
was her head that ruled her heart. Madame had spoke
wisely. At least she would still see Nathaniel every da
Perhaps now they could return to their chess games an

their former, more comfortable relationship and forget the cold, unhappy atmosphere of the past fortnight.

She would encourage him to spend more time with Clara and she would focus on making them both happy.

It was four days since Grace's accident. Sunday morning. Everyone had gone to church, taking Clara with them, but Grace had declined to go, unable to face the inevitable questions about her ordeal.

As soon as the carriage disappeared from sight, Nathaniel said, 'Would you care to see the hawks today? The weather is perfect. We can fly one if you would like to.'

Grace beamed her pleasure, causing Nathaniel to burn with shame at the memory of his brusque rebuttal the last time she had asked to see the birds.

As they soon reached the top of the fell—the place where Grace had thought the eagle was attacking him—Nathaniel said, 'Are you certain this is not too much for you?'

Grace laughed, her eyes sparkling, her cheeks flushed with their walk. She wore an old black cloak of Mrs Sharp's—he had ordered her a new cloak, but it was yet to arrive—and a serviceable brown bonnet, but Nathaniel swore he had never seen any fine lady as beautiful as Grace Bertram.

'I am not tired. How could I be when you have walked up here at a snail's pace to accommodate my woefully short stride?'

He stopped anyway. 'Here is a good place. There is no need to go further.'

His kestrel, Woody, was on his arm. Next to the other birds of prey—the buzzard and the peregrine falcons—he was dainty and colourful and Grace had fallen in love with him, admiring the black-spotted, chestnut-brown plumage on his back and wings, and his slate-grey head and tail.

Nathaniel removed Woody's hood and set him free to

fly. Grace watched, awe and delight on her upturned face
and Nathaniel watched Grace.

'He is staying in one place now,' Grace said.

'He is hovering. It is how kestrels hunt. They have sharp
eyesight and they watch for the movement of mice and
voles, or for small birds. It is hard to see it, but if you watch
very carefully you can see that his head stays perfectly still
whilst his wings and his body absorb the currents of air.'

'Will he come back to you?'

'Yes, of course. I've had him from a chick. He could not
survive out here on his own. Here, we will call him in.'

He stripped the gauntlet off his left hand and passed it to
Grace. 'You are right-handed so you must wear the glove
on your left so you can replace his hood and change his
jesses over without fumbling.'

'What if I hurt him?'

Anxious eyes searched his and his heart flipped in his
chest. How he resisted the impulse to take her in his arms
there and then he did not know.

'Do not worry. I am here. I will do it.'

Her trusting smile set his blood on fire.

'Stand like this…' with his hands on her shoulders, he
moved her so she stood sideways to where Woody flew
'…hold your arm out in front of you, like so, with your
fingers straight…' he raised her left arm '…and stay still.'

He stood close, his hand behind hers, holding a sliver
of fresh meat. He let out a call to the bird, who, knowing
there would be food as a reward, flew in, straight as an
arrow, and landed on the side of Grace's hand. She gasped.

'I did not think I would feel him through the leather
but I can feel his grip.'

Nathaniel gave Woody his reward and folded Grace's
fingers around the thin strip of leather—the jess—which
was secured to the kestrel's anklet.

'There,' he said, Grace's lily-of-the-valley scent fill

ng his senses, she was so close. 'Now you have control of when he flies again.'

They flew Woody several more times, then Nathaniel lipped on his hood and they started for home.

'Thank you, N…my lord,' Grace said.

He bit his tongue to stop himself from giving her permission to call him Nathaniel. How could that help in his efforts to keep her from his heart?

'I am pleased you enjoyed it, Miss Bertram.'

'Do you think…might I come with you again? I should like to see the bigger birds fly as well.'

As she spoke, she stumbled against him and he caught her, pulling her close. He looked down. She looked up. He was so tempted to succumb to the desire sizzling through his veins, but he could not. He stiffened his resolve and, with a pang of regret, he put her from him. She had accepted the scars on his face and his hand, but she was young…naïve…she could not possibly realise the full extent of the damage that damnable fire had wrought. Imagining her horror at the sight of his naked body sent shudders of dread rippling through him. How could a beautiful woman like Grace ever accept—be intimate with—a ravaged man like him?

'Thank you for catching me,' Grace said, after a few seconds of uncomfortable silence. 'I should take more care.'

She sounded completely unconcerned and relief flooded Nathaniel that he hadn't followed his desire to kiss her.

'I should like to ask you about the Christmas decorations,' she then said.

'Yes?'

'I should like to cut some evergreens in the woods. Mrs Sharp said there is holly and ivy, and…and…well, some other trees, that I could use to make garlands to decorate the Hall.'

'You mean such as laurel and juniper?'

'Yes.' She didn't sound sure. 'I think she said thos
sorts.'

Nathaniel suppressed his smile, love filling him at th
effort she was making to fit into this alien—for her—place

'You do not need my permission to cut branches in th
woods.'

'No. But I do need your permission to ask Ned or Tan
to help cut them. And carry them home.'

Home. He liked the way she said home.

'Of course you may ask them. And I will help, too
When is it you wish to start?'

'A few days before Christmas. And then we shall mak
garlands and decorate the Hall on Christmas Eve. It woul
be nice…' her voice became wistful '…if we might have
Yule log, too. Do you think—?'

'The wood has all been cut for the winter. I doubt w
have anything big enough.'

But he would move heaven and earth to find one, jus
for Grace.

Chapter Twenty

Two days later, Nathaniel appeared in the doorway of his book room as Grace descended the stairs carrying Clara—already dressed to go out—and her own new cloak and bonnet. She put Clara down when they reached the hall and the little girl ran straight to Nathaniel, arms aloft. Love, tinged with melancholy, laced her veins as she wished the three of them were a real family.

'You are going out?' Nathaniel swung Clara up and kissed her before putting her down again.

'Yes.' Grace avoided his gaze, draping her cloak over the newel post whilst she donned her bonnet. 'We are going into Shivercombe to consult with the seamstress and take her the fabric I have selected for my new gowns. I shall also visit Miss Dunn.'

'Are you sure about driving, so soon after your accident?'

Grace paused in the act of tying her bonnet ribbons under her chin. She adopted a light tone. Nathaniel didn't need to know the full extent of her nerves. 'I have to cross the beck again sometime, so why not today? I *must* replace my dress and I long to see Elizabeth.'

She had missed attending church on Sunday and Elizabeth had sent a very concerned note, via Mrs Sharp, en-

quiring after her health and inviting her to visit soon. Grac
swung her new cloak around her shoulders and fastene
the silver clasp at her neck.

She hesitated. She had already thanked Nathaniel fo
her new cloak, but this was the first time she had worn it
And she was very conscious of him watching her, his gaz
sending shivers dancing across her skin.

'Thank you again for this beautiful cloak.' She stroke
the fur trim.

'The colour suits you.'

His voice was gruff, as though he were embarrassed
The cloak was emerald-green velvet, lined with fur, an
Grace had gasped with delight when she opened the pack
age Ned had brought back from the village yesterday. I
was the finest garment she had ever worn.

On impulse, she said, 'You could come with us, if yo
are worried.'

He stared. 'To the village?'

'Indeed. We will not stay above half an hour with Eliza
beth and if it will set your mind—'

'Take one of the men.' He pivoted on his heel and shu
the book room door firmly behind him.

Grace bit her lip. It had been a foolish thing to suggest
Of course he would refuse.

'Come, sweetie.' She took Clara's hand. 'Let us go.'

Her bravado lasted until the final part of the track tha
led down to the ford. As it came into view, her heart bega
to thump and she clenched the reins, inadvertently pullin
Bill to a halt. How she wished Nathaniel was by her side
but no sooner had that thought surfaced than she quashe
it. She glanced down at Clara, sitting quietly on the benc
seat beside her. A pair of solemn green eyes gazed bac
at her, giving her the strength to overcome her nerves an
drive on. The water was back to its normal level and flow
and Bill did not hesitate to plod across the ford, but stil

Grace held her breath the whole way and only breathed easily again once they were safely through.

She called upon Mrs Campbell, the seamstress, and was measured for two round gowns, before calling at the rectory where a grand fuss was made of her. All the Dunns were present, as was Mr Rendell, and they demanded every detail of her accident, exclaiming with horror at her ordeal.

'I am grateful for your concern,' she said, finally, after the Reverend and Mrs Dunn had left the room. 'But I wish now to put it behind me. I know now not to attempt the ford when there has been heavy rainfall, so it was a valuable lesson.'

'A lesson? My dearest Grace, you have no need to put on a brave face for us.' Elizabeth reached down to pluck Clara from the floor and sat her on her knee. 'Your Miss Bertram is *very* brave, is she not, Clara?'

Mr Rendell flashed a sympathetic smile at Grace. 'Eliz...er... Miss Dunn, I believe Miss Bertram means to convey the message that she does not wish to be continually reminded of her ordeal.

'Let us instead discuss Christmastide, for it is a week tomorrow, and I have traversed the length and breadth of Langthrop Wood this morning in order to discover where the best holly berries grow, only to return somewhat disheartened.'

'It is a little early to cut greenery.' Elizabeth spoke somewhat absently, engrossed by now in a game of pat-a-cake with Clara. 'We do not decorate the church until Christmas Eve as a rule.'

'I know, but last year it took us so long to locate the best berries, we were decorating the church until well after dark, if you remember. I thought to save us time on the day if I knew their location, but now it looks as though we shall have to be content with nothing brighter than green leaves.'

'But I noticed an abundance of berries on my drive into

the village today,' Grace said. 'I may not recognise man
trees, but I do know holly.'

An image flashed through her mind of Isabel, the previ
ous Christmas, a sprig of holly with bright berries tucke
into the red ribbon she had tied around her best bonne
A wave of nostalgia hit her. How different this Christma
would be from last.

'But that is Shiverstone Woods, Grace. It is on Lor
Ravenwell's land, and we could not…he does not…' Eliza
beth's voice drifted into silence.

'I shall ask his lordship for permission,' Grace said. 'H
may choose not to attend church, but the rest of us do an
I am sure he will not object—'

'I do not need you to petition his lordship on my be
half,' Mr Rendell said, firmly. 'I shall ask him myself. I
fact, with your permission, Miss Bertram, I shall accom
pany you back to Shiverstone Hall today in order to settl
the matter.'

'But Ralph… Mr Rendell…what if Lord Ravenwell i
angered?' Elizabeth's voice rang with fear. 'Why do yo
not allow Grace to—?'

'Hush, Elizabeth.' He leaned over and patted her hanc
'There is no need to upset yourself. The village rumour
are built on fear of the unknown. His lordship was per
fectly civil when last I called at the Hall and I have no fea
of him. It is only right, as it is for the church, that I as
him myself. He can only refuse, but I hope he will find
harder to refuse me face to face than through the mediur
of an employee.'

Ralph? Elizabeth? Grace barely paid attention to thei
words—she was too busy speculating over the meaning c
her two friends calling one another by their given name:
How romantic it would be if they were in love, and the
married, and had a baby…

She came back to the present with a start, her own nam
having penetrated her thoughts.

'I beg your pardon?'

'I said, I shall saddle my mare and then, when you are ready to leave, I shall ride back to the Hall with you. You can point out the hollies on the way. I am aware this must seem a trivial matter to you, but it is important to our congregation that the church be festively decorated to celebrate Our Lord's birth day. And, traditionally, the villagers use any leftover greenery to decorate their cottages.'

'I do not think it trivial, Mr Rendell, and I shall welcome your company on the journey home.'

'That is settled then.' Mr Rendell rose to his feet. 'I shall leave you ladies to your gossip and I shall be ready whenever you are, Miss Bertram.'

He bowed and left the room. Elizabeth's gaze followed him, lingering on the closed door as though he were still in sight until, with a visible start, she appeared to recall her visitors. She glanced at Grace, a becoming flush colouring her face, and then she ducked her head, burying her face in Clara's curls.

'Mr Rendell is a very pleasant young man, is he not, Elizabeth?'

'Oh, he is. He is so…oh! I simply must tell someone, but I must swear you to secrecy, Grace, for Ralph has yet to speak to Papa, but…we have an *understanding*.'

Grace clasped Elizabeth's hands. 'I am so happy for you. I hope…do you believe your father will give his permission?'

Elizabeth beamed, her dark eyes sparkling. 'I do hope so.' Then her smile faltered. 'But until Ralph gets a living of his own, we will have to remain here. It would be so wonderful to have a home of our own,' she concluded in a wistful tone.

'I am sure it will not be long before he is able to progress.'

'You will not tell Ralph—or anyone—that I told you?

We did agree we must keep our love to ourselves until he
speaks to Papa. I only hope it may be soon.'

'I will not breathe a word, Elizabeth, but I am delighted
for you.'

'Ralph.' Clara looked from Elizabeth to Grace and back
again. 'Ralph.'

'He is Mr Rendell to you, sweetie.' Grace tickled Clara
under the chin, then held out her arms. 'Come, Clara. It is
time to go home.'

'You call that place home, Grace, but does it truly feel
like home to you? I heard it was—oh! I am sorry, that was
most indiscreet of me.'

Grace did not need to think about it. Despite the occasional longing for her old friends, she could not imagine
living anywhere else.

'Yes, it does feel like home. I make no doubt Mr Rendell told you the house is sparsely furnished and dark, but
his lordship has allowed me to make a few changes and I
think it is an improvement.'

'Well, I think you are very brave, living there.'

Anger stirred. 'Lord Ravenwell is not an ogre and I have
no need of bravery, I can assure you.'

'I did not mean—'

'And I did not mean to snap at you.' Elizabeth's stricken
expression roused Grace's remorse—she was only reacting
to the stories that circulated about Nathaniel. 'His lordship
is kind to me and he loves Clara; how can people say such
cruel things about him?'

'They tell their stories to fit the facts as they see them,
Grace. If his lordship came into the village on occasion
they would base their opinions on what they see, not what
their imaginations conjure forth.'

'If only they knew him as I do—'

Grace bit her tongue, her cheeks scorching as understanding dawned in Elizabeth's eyes.

'Oh, *Grace*… I did not suspect you had developed feelings for him. Please, do take care. You are a lovely young woman, but even if he did return your…your *affection* you surely would not wish to spend the rest of your life in such an isolated spot, cut off from everyone.'

'I have no expectations beyond my present position.' Grace stood up, preparing to depart.

'Now I have angered you. I am sorry for speaking so bluntly. It was unforgivable in me.'

Grace had no wish to leave Elizabeth on bad terms. 'No, it is I who must apologise. You spoke out of concern for me. And I truly have no expectations, Elizabeth, but… people can change, can they not?'

'Only if they truly want to, my dear. Do not forget, his lordship has lived his chosen life for several years now and therefore must be content. If he did crave a more sociable existence, do you not think he would have shown some signs of change by now?'

Grace hesitated. How could she put into words what she wished for, deep in her heart? She longed to cry: *Love can conquer all*, but she knew such a sentiment would worry Elizabeth and embarrass them both. No, she would keep her own counsel. And hope she was right and Elizabeth wrong.

'We must go now, Elizabeth. Goodbye.'

It was pleasant to have Mr Rendell's company on the drive home. He tied his horse to the back of the gig—much to the delight of Clara, who spent the entire journey on her knees, facing backwards, and chattering to the animal—and rode in the gig with Grace and Clara. They pulled up in the stable yard, handed the horses over into Ned's care and walked to the house.

'I will go and find his lordship,' Grace said, showing Mr Rendell into the drawing room.

'This room is much improved since my last visit.' He

turned a circle. 'Is that your doing, Miss Bertram? You have an eye for colour, I see.'

Grace felt her cheeks heat with pleasure at his compliment.

'She certainly does.'

Grace spun round. Her heart gave a tiny lurch at the sight of Nathaniel, his brown hair windswept, filling the open doorway.

Nathaniel scowled. That delicate blush told its own tale. Her beau had escorted her home and Grace could not disguise her pleasure.

'I was up on the fells and I saw you driving up the track.' The eruption of jealousy when he had seen them had threatened to overwhelm him. It was contemptible. He must learn to be pleased for her—for them both. 'Good of you to see Miss Bertram safely home, Rendell.'

'It was my pleasure.' Rendell strode over to Nathaniel, his right hand thrust out.

From the corner of his eye, Nathaniel noticed Grace's gaze drop to his hand. It was gloveless and her expression revealed her qualms as clearly as if she spoke.

She is afraid I will snub him.

As she lifted her gaze to his, he raised a brow, stepped forward and clasped Mr Rendell's proffered hand, conscious of the whisper of relief that escaped her lips as he did so. When had she become such an important part of his life he was constantly aware of her and what she was feeling?

His instincts urged him to leave now, but his pride forced him to stay.

'I have asked Mrs Sharp to send in refreshments. You will take tea with us before you leave, Rendell?'

Nathaniel gestured towards the cluster of seating around the fireplace. 'Please, take a seat.'

He followed the curate across the room, but did not sit. Instead, he poked at the fire, stirring the flames into life. Mrs Sharp carried in the tea tray and departed again. Grace then poured the tea whilst Rendell made a fuss of Sweep—who had jumped on his lap—exclaiming over how big he'd become. Nathaniel accepted a cup from Grace and finally sat down.

The minute he did so, Rendell spoke, as though he had waited for the right moment. 'I had an ulterior motive in escorting Miss Bertram home, for I have a request to make of you, my lord.'

Random thoughts and suspicions darted through Nathaniel's head. Chief amongst them was that Rendell meant to ask his permission to court Grace.

Nonsense. Why would he need my permission? I am not her father.

But there was Clara. Nathaniel swallowed. Hard.

What if he knows the truth? What if he wants them both? What if...?

He slammed a door in his mind against those increasingly frantic conjectures.

'Go ahead.'

Clara bustled over to Rendell. 'Ralph,' she said, gazing up at him. ''n Sweep.'

A punch to the gut could not have stolen Nathaniel's breath more effectively. *Ralph?* He stole a glance at Grace, who was struggling not to laugh.

'Clara! This is Mr Rendell. You must not call him anything else. Can you say Mr Rendell for me?'

'Mr Wendell.'

'Good girl. That is better. I apologise, Mr Rendell, I fear Clara must have overheard something she should not have done.'

The curate's cheeks had bloomed red. 'It is of no matter, Miss Bertram,' he said hurriedly. 'Now, your lordship, if I might move on to the purpose of my visit—I am here to request permission for myself and some of the villagers to gather holly in Shiverstone Woods.'

'Holly?'

'Er...yes. I have searched the woods on the other side of the village, and the holly there has barely any berries and—'

'And the berried holly is needed to decorate the church for the Christmas services,' Grace said. 'You should blame me if Mr Rendell's request has angered you, for it was I who told him of the abundance of berries in Shiverstone Woods.'

Nathaniel hastily smoothed his frown away. If only he could admit to them it had been incredulity that creased his brow, not anger. Holly...he had worked himself into a panic, and all Rendell wished to discuss was holly? Although there was still the small matter of Clara calling him by his first name. She had heard that somewhere.

'Yes. You have my permission.'

Grace beamed. 'Thank you.'

'We will gather it over the next few days,' Rendell said. 'And we will then decorate the church on the afternoon of Christmas Eve. It is quite an occasion. Most of the village helps and then we have a short service, with carols.'

'It sounds magical.' Grace's eyes shone with enthusiasm. 'Might we... It would be lovely to take Clara, if you will allow it, my lord?'

'Your entire household would be welcome to come along, my lord.'

'I understood it was your intention to decorate the Hall on Christmas Eve, Miss Bertram?' She had told him of her plans over dinner the night before.

'It is, but we shall collect the greenery in advance, to give us time to make garlands, and then all we need do on Christmas Eve is bring them indoors and decorate the rooms. We should be finished in time to help at the church.'

He could not resist the plea in her eyes. He had sworn not to stand in the way of her having friends in the village, even if those friends did include the handsome curate.

'Of course you may attend. I am sure Clara will enjoy it.'

She beamed again—a smile that tore at his heart. If only she might always smile at him like so. He did not want to lose her, even though it seemed inevitable. His mind shied away from the complication of Clara. He would not let her go. But could he part mother and daughter? Clara, he knew, could be the means to keeping Grace at Shiverstone Hall even if she fell in love with another, such as Rendell. But... could he be so cruel? So selfish?

Loving Grace meant he wanted her to be happy. Always.

Impatiently, he thrust aside his conjectures. He would deal with these issues if...when...they arose. In the meantime, he would do everything in his power to keep Grace and Clara happy and content. And if that meant throwing himself into preparations for a Christmas he saw little point in celebrating this year, then so be it.

Chapter Twenty-One

'Not one, but two letters, Miss Bertram. You *are* popular.'

It was four days before Christmas and Ned had been to the village as usual to collect the post. Spying them on the table in the hall, Nathaniel used them as an excuse to pay a visit to his niece and her governess in the nursery.

'Two?'

Grace held out her hand and he gave her the letters before swinging a clamouring Clara up into his arms and spinning around with her.

'Oh, how lovely.'

Grace's cheeks were pink with pleasure and Nathaniel found his thoughts wandering in a completely inappropriate direction: Grace…hair wild and unrestrained…beneath him…pink with a completely different kind of pleasure. He forced his attention from Grace and to Clara, bending to tickle her face with his hair.

'They are from Joanna and Isabel,' Grace said. 'Is it not kind of them to write again, even though I have not yet replied to their letters?'

Her pleasure from something so simple humbled him. She had been through a difficult childhood, a heartbreaking experience, and she was in effect all alone in the world—he had not failed to notice her uncle had not replied to her letter—and yet still she saw the good in people and remained full of positivity. Was that due to her youth? Would she, like him, grow more cynical over time? Or was it simply in her nature to see the goodness and kindness in everything? Her attitude was contagious. It had changed his household, and for the better. Even Mrs Sharp had shed her misgivings about Grace.

Grace placed the letters, unopened, on the mantelshelf.

'Are you not going to read them?'

She shook her head, her blonde hair escaping from her pins in delightful tendrils that caressed her neck. 'I shall wait until I may give them my full attention, when Clara is asleep.'

'Read them. I shall play with Clara, so you will not be distracted nor feel you are neglecting her.' He sat on the floor next to his niece and began to stack brightly painted wooden blocks one on the other.

Grace smiled her thanks and reached for the first letter. From the corner of his eye he watched the expressions chase across her face. When she had finished, she looked thoughtful.

'I hope it did not contain bad news?'

'I beg your…? No. No, not bad news. It was from Isabel. Do you recall…my friend who married William Balfour, Viscount Langford's son?'

Clara, crowing in delight, dashed Nathaniel's tower of blocks to the floor.

'Indeed, I do.' Nathaniel scooped the scattered blocks into a heap. 'You were worried about her, I remember.'

And we disagreed about the need for love in marriage.

'I need worry no more, it seems. They have been to stay with Joanna and her new husband, Luke, at his family home in Hertfordshire. Isabel seems much happier than last time she wrote. Indeed, she talks of her husband in glowing terms…and, yet, still it feels as though there is something she is hiding. Oh, how I wish I could see her face to face and know that everything is all right.'

'If the other letter is from Joanna, could that shed some light?'

Nathaniel grabbed Clara and tickled her. She squirmed, giggling. When he released her, she scrambled to her feet and ran to the other side of the nursery. Nathaniel promptly started to rebuild the tower.

After a silence whilst Grace read Joanna's letter and during which Clara charged at Nathaniel and demolished the tower once more, Grace set the second letter aside with a sigh and a look of longing on her face.

'You miss your friends, don't you?'

She started. 'Yes. But it is not that. It is…they have both moved on with their lives. That, somehow, more than anything, brings it home to me that there is no going back. Our childhood is over and two of the four of us are already wed. And Joanna is so very happy, I—'

She fell into silence. Had her thoughts drifted to Rendell? Was she envious of her friends' happiness? Did she hope…wish…the curate would speak and give her the same joy?

'Again! Again!' Clara hopped from foot to foot and Nathaniel began to gather the blocks once more.

'Joanna says Isabel and William have settled into their marriage,' Grace continued after her pause, 'and they are happier than they were at first.'

'See. I told you a successful marriage has no need of love or romance.'

She frowned, lips pursed. 'She *also* believes that Isabel has fallen in love with William, but not he with her. Or, at least, he is denying his feelings.'

Nathaniel found he could not hold her gaze and he focussed on Clara.

'Now, Miss Bertram, I shall build my tower again and, this time, woe betide any young lady who tries to knock it down.' He wagged his finger at Clara, who squealed excitedly from the far side of the room.

Miss Bertram, it appeared, was not to be deflected. 'I cannot believe that will make a happy life for Isabel.' Her lids lowered, as did her voice, and he had to strain to catch her final words. 'Unrequited love, surely, must be the most painful cross of all to bear.'

This conversation needed to end. It was drifting too close to reality for Nathaniel's comfort.

'There is nothing you can do about it,' he said, 'so I suggest you put it from your mind.

'Whooooaaaaa!' Clara had launched herself across the nursery, straight at Nathaniel, landing with full force on his chest, knocking him backwards. He used her momentum to lie on his back and swing her up above him, face down. 'Clara is flying, like a bird.'

He happened to glance across at Grace and he caught her watching them with that same look of longing. If it wasn't for Rendell, he might think...but no. To complete that thought would lead to madness. He had only to look at her and then at himself in the mirror. No, that yearning expression was no doubt a wish that it was Clara's father playing with her. Not him.

He sat up, standing Clara on her own two feet, and then stood up, brushing his hands over his breeches and coat. Again, Grace watched him, following the movement of his hands and Nathaniel's pulse quickened, stirring his blood. If only...

'I must go,' he said.

Grace also rose. 'We are due down in the kitchen,' she said. 'I said I would help Mrs Sharp make mince pies and gingerbread, and I promised Clara she might play with Sweep.'

'Sweep? Play Sweep?'

'Yes.' Grace picked Clara up and kissed her cheek. 'We shall go and see Sweep now. He has taken to staying in the kitchen,' she added to Nathaniel. 'I suspect Sharp feeds him titbits and Mrs Sharp is happy, now he is keeping the mice at bay. But Clara is not so happy, because she wants to play with him.'

'Let us hope her new toys at Christmas will help take her mind off the cat,' Nathaniel said as they left the nursery, side by side.

Tam had made Clara a wooden Noah's Ark and he and Ned were busy whittling animals to go inside it. Grace, too, had been busy making gifts. Some—her knitting and embroidery—he had seen, for she had taken to bringing it to the drawing room after dinner and working on it whilst he read aloud. But her painting, for the nursery wall, she said, was allowed to be seen by no one until Christmas Day. Her busyness had prompted him to set aside a little of his indifference for Christmastide and to purchase gifts for Clara and for Grace. In accordance with custom, the servants would receive their Christmas boxes on Boxing Day.

They were at the head of the staircase. 'Here, let me carry her downstairs. She is getting heavy; I have the bruising on my chest to prove it.'

He reached to take Clara and his hand brushed against Grace's. A faint gasp reached his ears, even as they jerked apart, Grace quickly relinquishing her hold on the child. Nathaniel's heart pounded and heat flooded his veins even as the hair on his arms and the nape of his neck stood to attention.

Grace's cheeks had taken on a tinge of colour. He saw her swallow as she raised both hands to lift her hair and repin it. Then she smoothed her hands down the skirt of her gown and finally she looked at him, with a strained smile.

'Thank you.'

Nathaniel rode Caesar into Shiverstone Woods and yelled Tam's name.

A faint shout came from deep within the trees and he

turned the horse in that direction. Five minutes later he rode into a small clearing and reined Caesar to a halt with a vicious but silent curse.

There were others here. Strangers.

Tam, Ned and Grace were watching him and all he wanted to do was wheel the horse about and gallop away. He regretted riding Caesar. Had he been on Zephyr, he could have excused himself on the grounds the stallion would not wait quietly whilst he helped to cut and gather branches for Grace's garlands. As it was, he had no excuse.

Caesar sidled beneath him, tossing his head, reacting to Nathaniel's tension. He could not leave, not with Grace's eyes upon him as she walked towards him with such a welcoming smile. He gathered his courage and dismounted. How many others were here? How many eyes to gawp? How many fingers to point? How—

'Thank you for coming to help.'

She was by his side. She laid a tentative hand on his sleeve. He resisted the urge to shake her off.

'The villagers are here today to gather decorations for the church as well.'

'So I see.' What else could he say? It mattered what Grace thought of him.

He scanned the clearing and the nearby trees. Most of the people continued with cutting and bundling holly, ivy and other evergreens. There were a few surreptitious glances but, in the main, the villagers were getting on with the task in hand.

His heartbeat slowed. It would take an hour or so of his life. He could do that for Grace. He need not speak to anyone else and, if he did not speak, he knew they would leave him alone.

'Where do you want me to start?'

Christmas Eve dawned bright and cold. Clara woke Grace early, so she took her down to the kitchen for her

breakfast. It would be warmer there. She went in, Clara
on her hip, to find Sharp in his chair, sucking on his pipe,
Sweep curled on his knee. Mrs Sharp was nowhere to be
seen.

'Good morning, Sharp. Do you think it will snow?'

Sharp removed his pipe. 'Don't 'ee go wishing for snow,
missy. It makes life very hard way up here.'

Grace sighed, knowing Sharp was probably right, but
today she did not wish to be practical. She wished today
and tomorrow to be fun-filled and romantic and beautiful,
and a covering of snow would be perfect. It had snowed
last Christmas in Salisbury. It had covered the ground and
painted the rooftops and the bare branches of the trees glistening white, turning the school and its surroundings into a
magical place for the four friends who had remained at the
school for the Christmas holidays—their last Christmas as
schoolgirls and their last Christmas together.

Grace pushed down her memories and the yearning that
arose in their wake. She was here now. She had Clara.
Surely she was worth any sacrifice? And if her love for
Nathaniel must remain unrequited, then she must learn
to accept it.

Madame had survived *her* lost love,

Isabel's recent letter, in addition to writing about her
marriage, had also contained extraordinary news about Madame who, sadly, was gravely ill with pneumonia. During a
conversation about girls' education with the Duke of Wakefield, Isabel happened to mention Madame Dubois's School
for Young Ladies, and the Duke had been quite overcome.
The tale that emerged was of two young people who had
fallen in love but, out of duty to his poverty-stricken estates and his family, the Duke had put aside his own desires
and married for money. He did finance the school—just as
those old rumours had always claimed—but he told Isabel
he had made sure he was never told its location.

The Duke had then rushed away, to travel to Salisbury and visit Madame in her sickbed.

Poor Madame. Grace hoped she would recover and that she and the Duke were now reunited. No wonder she had warned her pupils against forgetting their station and falling for the seductive wiles of employers, or employers' sons. But Madame had never mentioned the danger of falling in love. Grace did not even have the excuse of being seduced. She had succumbed to the man himself—not to whispered compliments, adoring looks or tempting kisses.

'You are very quiet, missy.'

Grace started. She had pulled out a chair and sat at the kitchen table as though in a dream, a still-sleepy Clara on her lap.

'Sorry. I was thinking about decorating the rooms. The garlands—'

'The missus and Alice have already fetched them indoors.' With Mrs Sharp adamant that not one sprig of greenery should cross the threshold until Christmas Eve, they had made up the garlands in the barn, with a brazier to keep them warm. 'They're in the dining room, ready to be hung up after breakfast.'

Later that morning, a shadow fell across Grace as she placed the final candle in the garland that swathed the huge carved stone fireplace in the hall.

'The house looks very festive. Well done, Miss Bertram.'

She smiled at Nathaniel, the little leap of her heart at the sight of him now so customary as to barely register. 'Thank you. I have enjoyed it, but it has been a joint effort.'

'I know. Come…' he crooked his arm '…I have a surprise for you. Outside.'

He led her to the front door, which was rarely used. They stepped out into the porch and Grace gasped. Bill stood solidly in front of the house, a massive log attached with rope and chains to his harness.

'A Yule log?' She beamed up at Nathaniel. 'But...yo
said...'

'It would not have been a surprise if I had told you m
plan, would it? And there is something else.'

He pointed to the side of the porch. There, on th
ground, lay a bundle of green, forked branches festoone
with white berries.

'Mistletoe!' Grace felt a blush build in her cheeks. Sh
could make a kissing bough. Would Nathaniel...? She cov
ered her sudden embarrassment by saying, 'Where doe
that grow? I could not see any in the wood.'

'There is a lime tree in the park at Ravenwell. I sent Ne
over a few days ago to fetch some.'

'He certainly brought a large bundle.'

With lots of berries...that is a lot of kisses. Grace knev
all about the tradition of kissing beneath the mistletoe an
plucking off a berry for each kiss. A swirl of anticipatio
tightened her stomach. *Will he kiss me? If I stand beneat.
the mistletoe, later, when there is no one else there, wi.
he kiss me?*

She sneaked a look at Nathaniel as he directed Ned an
Tam in unchaining the log. The three men heaved the lo
off the ground, but Grace had eyes for no one but Nathan
iel as his shoulders bulged with the effort and his stron
thigh muscles, clearly outlined by his breeches, flexed.

In no time, the log was positioned in the huge, open fire
place and Tam and Ned left, closing the front door behin
them, leaving Grace and Nathaniel alone.

Grace had carried in the bundle of mistletoe. Nathanie
turned and she saw his eyes smoulder, like a banked fir
and she felt again that tug of anticipation deep inside her
Her blood quickened and, certain she must be blushing
she moved away, putting the mistletoe on to the floor b
the round mahogany table that now graced the centre o
the large hall.

Then Sharp came into the hall, followed by Mrs Sharp, Alice and Clara.

'I've brought the kindling, milord.'

Sharp set to work laying the small, dry twigs and split logs around the Yule log whilst Nathaniel disappeared towards the kitchen. He soon emerged again with a smoking lump of charred wood on a shovel.

They all gathered round as he placed the wood on to the twigs already laid and piled more on top. They soon caught and flames began to lick around the Yule log. There was a cheer, and then the Sharps and Alice—with Clara, who wanted to play with Sweep—retreated to the kitchen, leaving Grace and Nathaniel alone again.

Chapter Twenty-Two

'Why did you light the fire that way?' Grace asked Na
thaniel.

'It is tradition,' Nathaniel said. 'Every year, a piece o
the Yule log is saved and then, the following year, it i
used to light the new one. That was a piece we saved fro
last year.'

'I thought you never celebrated Christmas?'

Grace felt absurdly let down. Nathaniel had shown n
enthusiasm for Christmas and she had congratulated herse
on changing his mind about celebrating this year.

'I do not,' he said. 'Not since…well…' He touched hi
cheek, fleetingly. It was the very first time he had eve
referred to his scars and Grace was touched by this ev
dence of his trust. 'Then my family came to Shiverston
for Christmas last year and it was almost like old time
But…this year…I've been dreading…the memories…with
out Hannah and David…it did not seem…' His voice fade
into silence, a muscle bunching in his jaw.

Poor Nathaniel. Any festivities would be bound to rais
painful comparisons with last year.

'This Christmastide will not be the same, but I hope yo
will enjoy it in a different way.' Grace silently vowed tha
she and Clara would help him make new happy memorie

'I will. You have helped me see the importance of enjoying the Christmas season, for Clara's sake.' He indicated the mistletoe. 'Where shall I hang this?'

Grace eyed the mass of green. 'In here?' She indicated the hall. 'I shall tie a bunch with red ribbon. I doubt we will need all of it, however.'

She looked up and their gazes fused, sending heat spiraling once again through her body, making her skin tingle. Then, because it was nearly Christmas, and because she had offered a kiss—more than once—and been resisted, and just because she felt a little like the rebellious Grace Bertram of old, she bent, snapped off a branch and then straightened, holding the sprig of mistletoe above her head.

He stilled. Not a muscle twitched as he looked deep into her eyes. No smile. No frown. He could not refuse this time. Could he?

His eyes flared and then, with a heartfelt groan, he crushed her to him, his mouth covering hers: hot, hard, demanding. Her lips parted and he took possession, exploring every inch of her mouth. She clung to his shoulders as their tongues entwined, shivers of desire racing through her as he pressed close, the evidence of his arousal hard against her. Even as she melted into him, however, she sensed his change: like someone slowly awakening, as though his brain was catching up with the actions of his body.

He lifted his mouth from hers. She clung closer, but it was no use. Gently, he eased her back, then took her hand—the one that still clutched the mistletoe—and plucked a berry, holding it up between thumb and forefinger.

'You are right,' he said. 'Such a large bundle will be wasted here. Tell Mrs Sharp and Annie they may take what they need before you dispose of the rest.'

Grace loathed this confusion of emotions. How could he kiss her as though his soul depended on it, then dismiss her as easily as he would the leftovers of a meal once his hunger was assuaged?

'I shall take what is left over to the church this afte
noon. I am sure there are plenty of men in the village wh
will be pleased to make use of it.'

Goading him was a risk, but she was cross and sh
wanted to provoke a reaction.

He scowled. 'You still intend to help decorate th
church?'

'I do.' She raised her chin. 'You should come too.
would not hurt you and Clara would be thrilled.'

His eyes narrowed as a low growl rumbled deep in hi
chest. 'I never said it would hurt. Be ready at two.' And h
stalked into his book room and slammed the door.

He did not want to go into the village, but that challeng
was a provocation too far after that kiss. Until then, he ha
successfully carried the moment: breaking their kiss, de
spite the insistent clamour of his body for more, and fak
ing a detachment so far from the truth it was ludicrous. H
had goaded her. And she had goaded him right back. An
then his pride stopped him backing down. Now, as the ca
riage rumbled across the ford and followed the lane to th
village, it was too late to change his mind. He would no
appear a coward in her eyes.

He could not believe it when she had snapped off tha
mistletoe and tempted him to kiss her. It was tradition: a b
of fun, a quick kiss under the mistletoe. And he, poor de
luded fool that he was, had lost control and kissed her lik
a starving man at a feast. But…she *had* kissed him back
He had not imagined that. And now, he was more confuse
than ever. He thought her heart belonged to Rendell, bu
then why would she return his kiss with such…*passion*?

Grace sat opposite him, with Clara. She was beauti
ful, wearing her emerald cloak and, beneath that, the ne
blue-sprigged muslin dress that Mrs Campbell had mad
for her. Her eyes had shone when Ned had brought he
two new gowns back from the village. She made the bes

of the hand life had dealt her. Unlike him. Her courage humbled him: she had travelled hundreds of miles to find Clara, for no reward other than to ensure her daughter was happy and loved.

Was *that* why she kissed him in return? Was her love for her daughter the motive for everything she did? Was she acting a role, intent on securing her future with Clara?

They walked up the cobbled path to the church door, the murmur of voices within getting louder with every step. As they entered, there was a sudden hush from the occupants. Nathaniel stiffened as he felt every eye upon him, but took courage from Clara's tiny hand in his. A symphony of whispers reached his ears, but how could he blame them for their curiosity when it was he who had fostered his own reputation?

A familiar figure emerged from the throng. Ralph Rendell strode down the aisle, hand outstretched.

'My lord, Miss Bertram—how good of you both to come. And little Miss Clara too.'

Despite that kiss, Grace showed no trace of awkwardness on greeting the curate, who appeared unsurprised by Nathaniel's presence. The villagers, one or two of whom Nathaniel recognised from collecting greenery, soon returned to their tasks. Such an enormous step for him seemed of scant importance to everyone else.

Nathaniel's head ached.

'Good afternoon, Rendell.' He made himself smile. 'We had some greenery left over from decorating the Hall: holly, mistletoe and so forth. We thought you might find a use for it.'

They were joined by a fleshy, older man, dressed in black with a white stock, and an attractive, dark-haired young woman.

'Thank you, that is most generous,' Ralph said. 'Now, Lord Ravenwell, might I introduce the Reverend Dunn and his daughter, Miss Elizabeth Dunn?'

Nathaniel shook hands with the clergyman and bowed to his daughter, who dropped a curtsy, tensing under the latter's open appraisal.

'The additional greenery is most appreciated, my lord,' Reverend Dunn said, 'but I must request that you do not bring mistletoe into the church.'

Nathaniel raised a brow. 'You have some objection to mistletoe, sir? I recollect seeing it in York Minster in the past.'

'That is an old tradition and the Dean there might do as he pleases. *I* do not believe it has any place in the House of God, with its links to the druids and paganism. However, it will prove most welcome in the Rectory.'

The vicar grinned and Nathaniel relaxed somewhat.

'Papa! May I tell Grace our news?'

'Rendell?' The vicar looked to his curate, who smiled. 'I have no objection.'

Elizabeth took Grace's hands. 'I am bursting with happiness.' Her cheeks bloomed pink as her dark eyes sparkled. 'You must be the first to know. Mr Rendell has spoken to Papa and he has given his consent. Our betrothal will be announced tomorrow.'

Shock reverberated through Nathaniel. His gaze flew to Grace, but she revealed no hint of distress as she hugged her friend and congratulated the curate. When the others at last moved away, Nathaniel placed his hand briefly at the small of her back. She stiffened. He dipped his head.

'That was unexpected. Are you all right? We can leave if you wish.'

Her puzzled frown seemed genuine. 'I was not surprised, for Elizabeth confided in me on my last visit. Come, let us fetch the greenery from the carriage.'

They brought in the branches of holly and ivy, laurel and juniper, and helped to decorate the church. Then the Reverend Dunn donned his vestments and read a short service before leading the congregation in singing carols. Clara, too young to know the words, warbled away happily and Grace's sweet voice rang out.

Hark the Herald Angels Sing... Nathaniel sang by rote as his mind wandered.

Not by a single word or look had Grace shown anything other than pure delight for her friends, but she *had* been forewarned. She'd had time to prepare for the announcement. Grace was resilient and self-reliant, but Rendell's choice of another woman must surely open the wounds from her unwanted and unloved childhood, and from Clara's father's rejection. Nathaniel recalled his own despair when, despite the understanding between them, Lady Sarah Reece had accepted another man's proposal after Nathaniel's disfigurement.

He knew the pain of rejection.

Without volition, he rubbed at his right cheek. Two women—Sarah and Miss Havers—had rejected him on the strength of his facial scars alone. He'd never had the courage to reveal the rest of the damage wrought by the fire. He'd spent his life since then alone, apart from his servants and his family.

Until now. He looked around the congregation: happily singing, the odd few meeting his eyes with a smile. They already seemed to accept his appearance. Had his experiences as a young man—newly injured and facing the shocked stares and unkind remarks of strangers and the avoidance of former friends—driven him to wrongly believe all people would react in the same way?

He turned his gaze to Grace. She glanced up, smiling, her eyes warm. There was no one he would rather be beside, he realised, but that insight terrified him. He could never expose himself to rejection again. Those past memories were too strong; they still held the power to hurt. As, no doubt, Grace's memories of her lonely, unloved childhood could still hurt her.

Had Rendell's betrothal to Miss Dunn revived those

childhood insecurities? Could that be why she had returned his kiss under the mistletoe? Had she been seeking comfort? Did she crave assurance that she belonged and was capable of being loved? Was that why she had fallen so readily for Clara's father's sweet words?

Well, he could offer comfort, he could provide a home. He could offer no more and, sooner or later, a woman such as Grace would want more. He had seen her pleasure as she interacted with the Dunns and the rest of the villagers and, although the danger posed by Rendell had passed, there would be other men.

She needed people around her, and happiness and laughter, and that he could not offer.

The singing ended.

'My lord. Miss Bertram. Would you care to join us for a bite of supper?' The Reverend Dunn stood before them. 'It will not be very grand, but I know Elizabeth and Ralph would welcome the opportunity to celebrate with their friends.'

'I am not sure,' Nathaniel said. 'It will be dark soon...'

From the corner of his eye, he saw Grace's smile fade and he was helpless to resist.

'...but...on the other hand, the sky is clear and, although not a full moon, there should be enough light to see us home.'

Ralph Rendell joined them. 'It would mean a lot to us if you can stay a while.'

'Very well. We shall accept. Thank you.'

Grace looked thrilled. And he was happy to make her happy.

Chapter Twenty-Three

It was late by the time they arrived home. Ned drove the carriage away from the front of the Hall with a rattle and a clatter of hooves, and then there was silence. The landscape was frosted, sparkling like a hundred thousand diamonds in the moonlight. The night air was still, scented with wood smoke, and Grace—pleasantly light-headed from the combined effects of the mulled wine, the infectious joy of the newly betrothed couple and the intimacy of that slow carriage ride in the dark, with Nathaniel and Clara, like a proper family—was convinced there was magic in the air.

It was a night when anything seemed possible. Nathaniel had visited the village and met his neighbours for the first time in nine years. He had helped decorate the church and he had accepted the vicar's invitation to supper at the rectory. He had already begun to change, thanks to her. How much further might he change, with her help?

Her future suddenly seemed full of promise and boundless possibilities and, for the first time, settled.

She had found a place to call home: a place where she belonged and a home where she was not only wanted, but where she was valued and valuable.

Clara was already asleep, cradled in Nathaniel's arms, and Grace opened the front door to allow him to carry her through. Brack, tail whipping back and forth, was there to greet them, as was Sharp. Grace put her finger to her lips and pointed to Clara.

Sharp nodded, sliding the bolts home quietly as he secured the front door.

'Will you be needing me for anything else tonight, milord?'

'No. You may go to bed, Sharp. Thank you.'

Sharp disappeared towards the back of the house. Nathaniel turned to Grace and her stomach flipped. Surely she was not imagining the heat in his gaze.

'I will carry Clara to bed,' he whispered.

Clara barely stirred as Grace undressed her and put her in her nightgown, then tucked her into her ready-warmed bed, after removing the warming pan with its load of hot coals. She kissed her little girl's forehead, smoothing her unruly curls, and then Nathaniel, too, kissed her goodnight. They left the room, Nathaniel holding the door for Grace and then closing it softly behind her.

Nathaniel hesitated. 'Shall you retire immediately?'

She shook her head, mute. She wanted to be with him. She longed to surround him with her love and to heal him and to help him return to the life he should be living.

If only he would take me in his arms.

She felt emboldened—by the night, by the hush of the house around them, by the wine—but not so emboldened that she could take the first step towards the intimacy she craved. She was sure the desire that smouldered deep in his eyes every time he looked at her was not mere wishful thinking on her part, but still she could not risk making the first move.

She played a little game in her head: *If he does not care for me, he will send me to my room. But...if he does care...*

'I am not tired,' she said, 'but if you do not wish for company, I shall retire to my sitting room.'

He half-bowed. 'I shall enjoy your company.'

They walked downstairs side by side, Grace's stomach dancing with butterflies. Was she wilfully allowing her imagination to lead her into the wrong decisions? Was it just because she longed for him that she imagined he felt the same? She, of all people, knew what the outcome of this night might be. She had Clara to prove it. And yet, her heart was so full of love for Nathaniel, so full of the yearning to take him in her arms and soothe away the years of hurt and loneliness, that she would face that risk with her eyes wide open and no regrets.

In the drawing room, the fire was still alight. Grace sat on the sofa whilst Nathaniel poured two glasses of wine from a decanter. He sat on a chair. Grace stared at the crystal wine glass in her hand, fiercely concentrating on the play of firelight through the ruby red of the wine, quelling her disappointment. She had been so sure he would sit by her side. Doubts now dominated, where only moments before she had been so full of hope. She sipped the wine, the spicy, fruity tang teasing tongue and throat, and cautioned herself not to get this wrong...not to make a fool of herself.

Her lips tingled with the effects of the wine. She glanced up as she soothed them, saw his gaze follow the movement of her tongue and her pulse leapt in response.

She had to break the silence—had to say something, no matter how inane, before she blurted out the truth she held in her heart.

'Thank you for coming with us today.'

He lifted his glass in salute, but said nothing.

'It must have been hard for you.'

A faint line etched between his brows and then was gone. If she hadn't been watching so closely, she would have missed it. He placed his glass on the side table and leaned forward, reaching to capture her hands. She stilled, her heart racing as their gazes locked. Her head whirled. She could drown in the brown depths of those beautiful eyes.

'It *was* hard, but not as hard as I anticipated.' His fingers firmed around hers. 'And I have you to thank for that. You have helped me face my fears.

'Before today I would have let the stares and the whispers of those strangers bother me and I would have walked away from those that stared. I have allowed my fear to dictate my life, but you have taught me to give others the chance to accept me for myself and not judge me by how I look.

'You have taught me there are more important things in life, such as Clara's future.' He hauled in a breath. His eyes darkened. 'I owe you so much, Grace.'

Grace turned her hands within his grasp and curved her fingers around his.

'You owe me nothing. Allowing me to stay here with Clara is reward enough. I am happy here. This is my home, now, for as long as you will allow me to stay.'

'Then that will be for ever, for I have promised you I will never part you from Clara.'

'Thank you. I cannot tell you how much that means to me.'

She willed him to kiss her, striving to communicate her love and her desire by a look alone, but that smouldering heat still did not flare into passion.

Why does he hesitate? Does he fear I will reject him?

Could she, by loving him, banish the pain of the past and show him the way to a brighter future? She could not be mistaken…this lost soul in front of her needed her. She had it in her power to heal his hurts and to restore his pride. She must find the courage to take the first step…

'Grace…I…'

'Hush.' Holding his gaze, Grace slid from the sofa to her knees before Nathaniel. She placed her fingertips to his lips, then slowly, gently, she stroked her hand over his face, caressing his damaged cheek, registering the uneven texture, as though knotted pieces of rope lay beneath the surface of his skin: tangible evidence of the fire that had changed his life for ever.

He stilled, every muscle tense, his eyes haunted.

She could not put into words how proud she was of him, for facing the villagers and for his willingness to change; such words would surely injure his masculine pride. No, she could not tell him, but she could *show* him all those things, and she could show him, by her actions, that in her eyes he was both beautiful and lovable.

She leaned into him, pressing her body between his muscled thighs as she placed her lips on his.

It was akin to kissing a statue. Hard lips, rigid jaw. She pressed closer still, raising her other hand so she cradled his face, her lips soft as they moved against his mouth. Every muscle appeared to wind a notch tighter, if that was possible, until, with a groan and a gasp, he took her in his arms, moulding her to him, as he angled his head, his lips softening and moving under hers. His mouth opened and their tongues met, igniting a fire deep inside.

She poured her heart and her soul into that kiss, molten fire sizzling through her veins until she could no longer tell where she ended and he began. Her body had melted, sinking into him like honey on warm toast. A strange ache spread through her, rendering arms and legs heavy with need.

She wound her arms around his neck, pulling his head closer, fingers threaded through his hair, losing all sense of place and time. He slid to the rug, holding Grace close to his chest as he lay on his back, hands roaming freely over her back, bottom and thighs, stoking her passion.

She fumbled at the knot in his neckcloth. His hands covered hers in a vice-like grip. Grace raised her head, studying his tight expression.

'What is wrong?'

'I…I cannot…'

She covered his lips with hers. 'Yes, you can,' she whispered. 'For me.'

His grip tightened momentarily, and then, with a growl, he released her wrists to tear the cloth from around his neck and cast it aside. Grace had no need to see his neck to understand his sudden doubt. Her fingertips, and then her lips, discovered the same bumpy texture as on his cheek and she feathered the entire surface of his neck and jawline with tiny, butterfly kisses: the soft, lightly stubbled undamaged side as well as the tight, uneven, stubble-free area that bore the scars of the fire.

She pulled away, raising her upper body by bracing her hands on his chest.

'Can you feel my lips on your neck?'

His hands tightened at her waist. 'No. Your touch is too gentle.'

He groaned then, as she lowered her body to his once more and pressed her lips more firmly to his neck.

'Can you feel that?'

'Yes, but only as pressure. It is like eating food without being able to detect the nuances of taste.'

She arched her upper body away from his again, capturing his gaze. 'Then tell me what gives you pleasure.'

A wicked light crept into his eyes. Large hands stroked over the globes of her bottom and squeezed as he rocked his hips, pushing the hard ridge of his erection against her.

'This.' He rocked again. 'This gives me pleasure.' He raised his head from the floor and captured her lips again in a slow, drugging kiss. 'Infinite pleasure.'

In one swift movement that wrung a gasp from her, he rolled her on to her back and settled on top. His weight on her sent delicious swirls of anticipation throughout her body and her thighs parted of their own volition, the sensitive flesh between a yearning, hollow ache. She sighed, closing her eyes, succumbing to pleasure as gentle hands skimmed her neck and body and questing lips followed.

She clutched his shoulders with urgent fingers, arching beneath him as he nibbled the exquisitely sensitive bud of her nipple through her muslin gown.

A hand skimmed up her leg, then pushed her stocking and garter down to caress her bare flesh even as he seized her lips in another scorching kiss. In feverish anticipation, Grace reached for the buttons of his waistcoat, then slid her hands inside, stroking his broad back, revelling in the play of honed muscles through the fine linen of his shirt. He was so big, so male...*all* male...and she wanted him with an urgency she could barely contain. She squirmed beneath him, vaguely aware that she moaned as she did so, and then his weight was no more. Her eyes flew open. He had propped himself up on his arms.

'Are you sure, Grace? You will not be...my appearance...' His uncertainty was tangible.

'Hush.' She pressed her fingertips to his lips. 'I am sure.'

She dared not say more. More words might turn into a plea, she wanted him so much.

He rose to his feet in one fluid motion and then gathered her into his arms, carrying her much as he had Clara earlier. He hugged her tight to his chest.

'I will not take you on the floor,' he said, before taking her lips again.

He strode for the door and they were up the stairs and in Grace's bedchamber in a flash. He placed her on the bed and immediately followed her down, pushing the neckline of her dress low to free one breast. He drew her beaded nipple into his mouth, sucking and nibbling until she was on fire.

Their clothes were gone—she barely noticed how and when—and finally they were flesh to flesh and he was moving over her and inside her, and she was arching to meet him, the urgency building, digging frantic fingers into his back...snatching at the sheet beneath her...clutching his hair as he dipped his head again to her breasts—

striving for—reaching for—and then finally…finally…she was there and soaring free, her body pulsing with pleasure as Nathaniel withdrew and, with a heartfelt groan, spilled his seed.

Panting, Nathaniel drew her close to his chest and hooked the blankets up to cover them. He pressed his lips to the top of her head and—happy, contented and replete—Grace sank into a satisfied sleep.

Chapter Twenty-Four

Grace opened her eyes to the vague awareness that a new day had dawned and there was a moment when she could not fathom what was different. Her mind felt—not unpleasantly—fuzzy and she lay still, warmly cocooned, fleeting images of the day before darting through her memory, like butterflies flitting in and out of patches of sunlight.

The day before... Christmas Eve...which meant today was—her idle thoughts stuttered to an abrupt halt. Those wavering memories steadied and coalesced as she became conscious of a slight soreness between her thighs and the presence of a large, warm body in her bed, nestled into her back. Panic flowed and then ebbed and her lips relaxed and stretched in a spontaneous smile. Nathaniel. Her dream had come true. Carefully, she wriggled around until she faced him. She watched him sleep in the dim light of the early morning, love flooding her heart.

They could be a proper family now. Her and Nathaniel and Clara. And even, in the future, maybe they could have more children. Brothers and sisters for Clara. And he would no longer feel the need to isolate himself here at Shiverstone Hall. And—

Nathaniel's eyes opened. He blinked and she leant over and kissed him, tracing the sculpted muscles of his hair-roughened chest. She breathed deeply. He smelled wonderful and she snuggled closer. He smoothed her hair away from her face and kissed her, a wonderful, slow, drugging kiss. His hand skimmed her breast, then settled, and the flesh between her legs leapt in response.

'Good morning, Grace,' he murmured as he bent his head.

He circled her nipple with his tongue, then drew it deep into his mouth. She gasped and bit his shoulder.

'Do you like that?'

A wicked smile hovered on his lips and then he trailed his tongue down her body to the apex of her thighs. She sighed her pleasure, opening for him, giving herself up to the wonderful sensations spiralling through her body as Nathaniel loved her.

'We will be so happy, the three of us as a family,' she murmured later, as Nathaniel rolled off her and lay on his back.

He stared up at the ceiling, a deep line grooved between his brows. 'Family?'

'Why…yes. You and me and Clara…' Grace propped herself up on one elbow, and traced his lips with her fingertip. 'Just think how she will benefit as she grows up. You will no longer have to bury yourself here at Shiver—'

He turned his head to stare at her. 'I *like* it here at Shiverstone.'

'Well, yes, of course. I know that. But, with me by your side, it will be different. We could live some of the time at Ravenwell; we could invite friends to stay—'

'I *have* no friends.' He sat up, scrubbing his hands through sleep-tousled hair.

Grace's spirits floundered for a moment before she rallied. If only she could make him see how much better his life could be. How much happier.

'Maybe not, at the moment, but you will love Joanna

and Isabel when you meet them and I am sure their husbands are—'

'No!'

He leapt out of bed, keeping his scarred side facing away from her. He snatched his discarded shirt from the floor and tugged it over his head.

'But... I will help you. You must not fear—'

He stared at her, his eyes cold. 'I do not need your help. Nor your pity. I must go. Clara must not see me here.'

'No, of course not, but...she will know eventually, w-won't she?' She could not prevent disquiet threading through her voice.

'Know that we slept together? That would hardly be appropriate for a two-year-old. Last night should never have happened.'

Instinct leapt to the fore; Grace knew intuitively what he was doing. He was retreating into himself. He was so used to protecting himself he did not see he no longer need do so. Grace flung the covers back and rushed to him, heedless of her nakedness.

'Nathaniel.' She grabbed his arms. 'Do not say so. Last night was...do you not see? We can be a family now. Think of Clara, how lovely it will be for her to have a new papa and mama.'

With every word she said, his expression hardened. How could she get through to him? Make him see how wonderful their future could be?

'With us by your side, you can take up your rightful place in society again.'

He shook her hands from him. 'I do not want to take my rightful place in society again. Last night was a mistake. We were both under the influence of too much wine. We were two lonely people seeking comfort. Nothing more.'

Grace snatched her shawl from a chair and flung it around her.

'It was *not* just the wine. That was not the only reason

you made love to me.' Tears crowded her throat, choking her voice, and she kept swallowing in an attempt to contain them.

'I never offered anything other than comfort. I cannot be what you want me to be. I have no wish to change my life. I want you to go.'

The breath left Grace's lungs in a whoosh and her legs went to jelly. 'Go? What do you mean?'

'Leave. I don't want you here. I cannot bear to see you or to have you under my roof.' He tugged on his breeches, gathered the rest of his clothing and stalked to the door.

'But…you cannot mean that. Nathaniel…my lord…you *promised* you would never send me away.'

He spun to face her, his lips curled in a snarl. 'I do not want you here. I want you gone. Today.'

'But…I have nowhere to go.' Grace hauled in a ragged breath. She must stand up to him. This could not be happening. 'No. I won't go. I will not leave you and I will not leave Clara.'

He stilled, his brown eyes hard as they raked her. 'Go to Ravenwell. Take Clara. It is her you really want and, God knows, you have more right to her than I.'

Hot tears scalded her eyes. 'But—'

'Take her. I do not want you here. You presume too much, Miss Bertram.'

Fury now rose up, overwhelming her misery. 'Presume?' She all but spat the word. '*I* presume too much? And you, my lord? What of your presumption? Did you presume that, because I made a mistake once, I would be content for my body to be used to slake your lust? Do you now presume that your two-year-old niece's needs are of no account when they do not happen to coincide with your own whims?'

'I will never neglect Clara's needs. I will provide you with a house on the estate at Ravenwell and an income. Neither of you will ever want for anything.' He opened the door.

'Except love!' Grace tried one last time. 'What about my heart? How can I be happy without you?'

'Love? You already know my view on that, Miss Bertram.' His bitter laugh was cut short as he slammed the door behind him.

Grace's anger sustained her all through the soul-destroying packing of her belongings and the leave-taking of the staff, telling them she was taking Clara on a previously arranged visit to her grandmother. There was no way on earth Grace would leave her daughter with that heartless monster.

Nathaniel was conspicuous by his absence—riding out on Zephyr over the fells, according to Sharp, who handed Grace a pouch containing coins.

'His lordship said to take it to cover your expenses.'

Grace resisted the urge to throw it in Sharp's face. This was none of it Sharp's fault. Besides, she would have need of the money. A plan, born of desperation and fury, had begun to form in her mind. Her heart was in pieces, but she hid every hint of despair, concentrating instead on efficiency and practicality as she packed Clara's clothes and a few toys in a bag, including all the presents Grace had so lovingly made for her. She distributed her gifts to the servants and received some lovely scented soap from the Sharps and Alice in return, and then—the very last thing before she left—she went to the empty guest bedchamber where she had concealed the picture of Clara and Brack she had painted for Nathaniel. Her first impulse was to burn it, but she carried it to Nathaniel's bedchamber and left it lying on the bed. She hoped he would suffer every time he looked upon it. She had poured her heart and soul into making love with him and he had flung it back in her face.

She had been taken for a fool. Again.

Ned had agreed to drive Grace and Clara to Ravenwell and by eleven they were on their way, a lengthy drive ahead of them. Grace waited until both Shivercombe village and the Hall were behind them, then called to Ned to stop.

'Yes, miss?'

'There has been a change of plan, Ned. Please drive me to Lancaster.'

'Lancaster? But, miss, I were told—'

'Who told you, Ned? His lordship?'

'Why, no, miss. You did.'

'I instructed you to drive to Ravenwell, Ned, and now I am instructing you to drive to Lancaster instead. It is quite all right. I have merely changed my mind about visiting Ravenwell…that is all.'

They would stay tonight in Lancaster and then head south. She felt guilty hoodwinking poor Ned, but she flatly refused to be sent off to Nathaniel's disapproving mother. With the money in the pouch she had calculated there would be just enough to get her and Clara to Salisbury. She did not much care what might happen to her after that, but what she needed now was a familiar place and a friendly face.

Miss Fanworth would know what to do.

Four days later, after a tortuous journey of jam-packed, rackety coaches and of further overnight stops at dubious coaching inns in Manchester, Birmingham and Bristol, Grace and Clara were set down in Cathedral Close, outside the stately façade of Madame Dubois's School for Young Ladies. Grace gazed at the familiar surroundings with a painful lump in her throat. Here were such memories. She had not expected to return so soon, nor under such circumstances.

The sheer obstinacy that had kept her going through the last four days faltered. Miss Fanworth might well be sympathetic, but she would not condone what Grace had done. As much as she had told herself Nathaniel deserved to lose Clara, she knew, deep down, she was wrong to bring her here without his knowledge or permission. And what of

Madame? Her heart sank at the likely reception she would have from the formidable principal of the school.

A whimper from Clara triggered renewed resolve. They had come this far. They were both exhausted. She tightened her hold on Clara's hand, picked up their bags with the other and mounted the front steps to knock on the door. Many of the pupils and staff would have gone home for the Christmas holiday, she knew, but she also knew some would remain. Neither Madame nor Miss Fanworth had any other home.

The door swung open, its hinges well-oiled as ever, to reveal the sombre features of Signor Bertolli. His eyes widened above his magnificent moustache.

'Miss Bertram!' He gestured for Grace to enter and to sit on one of the sturdy chairs set against the walls of the spacious, brightly lit entrance hall, with its classical cornices and stately staircase. 'I will tell Miss Fanworth you are 'ere.'

He hurried across the hall towards the closed door of Madame's office and a sudden fear hit Grace, remembering Mabel's last letter which had said Madame was ill.

'Wait! *Signor!*'

The art master paused, looking back over his shoulder.

'Where is Madame?'

'She 'as been unwell with the pneumonia, but she is getting better. Miss Fanworth 'as been running the school.'

Two waves of relief hit Grace, the first at the news of Madame's recovery and the second at the realisation she would not yet have to face Madame. Could she and Miss Fanworth, between them, concoct a story to explain Clara's presence? Her little girl's wan appearance tore at her heart. The journey had been tiring for Grace, let alone for a two-year-old who did not understand why she had once again been uprooted from familiar surroundings and taken from the people she loved. The guilt had nearly overwhelmed

Grace at times during that interminable journey when Clara had asked for her *'Uncle Naffaniel'*, but it had been too late to turn back and, besides, Grace could not summon the courage to face him again.

Thus, by the time Signor Bertolli showed her into Madame's office, and there was Miss Fanworth—plump, motherly Miss Fanworth—coming towards her with hand outstretched and a kindly yet concerned smile…

Grace burst into tears. Clara wailed. Miss Fanworth fluffed around, like a mother hen.

'Ask Cook to send up tea,' she said to the art master. 'And close the door behind you, please.'

She bade Grace sit on a fireside chair and she sat in the other, picking Clara up and settling her on her lap. She waited until the maid had brought up the tea tray and poured each of them a cup of tea, and then said, 'Tell me all, my dear.'

Between sobs and hiccups, Grace poured out her heart, finally ending with, 'Please don't tell Madame. She'll send us away. Please let us stay for a few days until…until…oh, Miss Fanworth, what am I to do?'

Miss Fanworth shook her head, wisps of light brown hair escaping from her cap. 'I do not know, Grace, my dear. You ever were an impetuous girl, but I really thought *the business* had taught you more caution. Still, we do not have to decide now. Little Clara looks exhausted. You both do. Let us discuss it further in the morning. I am sure it will all seem brighter then. Would you like to sleep in your old room with Clara? It is empty for the holidays.'

'Thank you, yes. And you won't tell Madame?'

'I won't say anything other than to tell her you are here, but you must examine your conscience as to how much you decide to tell her. She is not an ogre, you know. She cares very much for all her pupils, past and present.'

Suitably chastised, Grace hung her head. Miss Fanworth

tood, lifting a now-sleepy Clara, who whinged at being
noved. 'Come. I shall send a light supper for you both
up to your room. You will feel much better after a good
night's sleep and I am certain you will soon see the right
oad to follow.'

Nathaniel sat on Zephyr on the high fell by Shiver Crag,
staring unseeingly over the land that stretched below him.
He was dry-eyed, but there was a hollow inside him as big
as the dale. Not just his heart had shrivelled and died, but
every last cell had withered until all that remained was an
empty, ugly husk.

Why had he sent her away? To punish her? To punish
himself? He had told himself he did it for her own good—
o set her free, as he had set the eagle free—but the truth
was that her vision of their future had completely unnerved
him. He had convinced himself he could never make her
happy and that she would, sooner or later, reject him.

Their final exchange still haunted him.

'Neither of you will ever want for anything.'

*'Except love! What about my heart? How can I be happy
without you?'*

*'Love? You already know my view on that, Miss Ber-
ram.'*

She had said nothing about love until then. Did she mean
t? *Could* she love a man such as him?

The answer was as clear as the view before him. Yes.
She could and she did. She looked at him and she did not
see his scars. She saw *him*. She loved *him*. Her unflinch-
ng courage humbled him.

He had been a fool.

An utter fool.

Stubborn. Heartless. Cruel.

A coward. And, shamefully, he knew that last to be the
truest of all. He had been panicked by her expectations

and too afraid to expose the truth in his heart in case she rejected his love.

He had been scared of losing her, so he had sent her away.

Could any man have got it all so very wrong?

He turned Zephyr's head for home.

The following morning dawned grey and cold. Clara—heavy-eyed and snuffling and asking for Uncle Naffaniel—could not be placated and by early afternoon, when Madame sent for Grace, she was almost relieved to hand the care of her beautiful little girl to Miss Fanworth.

What kind of mother am I?

Heartache, guilt and inadequacy plagued her as she climbed the stairs to Madame's bedchamber, her steps slowing as she neared the door. How could she face the all-seeing, all-knowing Madame when her thoughts and emotions were so utterly confused and raw? She tapped on the door.

'Come.'

That familiar voice was as imperious as ever. Heart in mouth, Grace entered, shutting the door behind her.

Chapter Twenty-Five

Grace had never before seen the inside of Madame's bed-chamber. It was as graceful and tasteful as expected, furnished in elegant rosewood, the walls papered in rose and ivory stripes.

Madame reclined on a rose-coloured *chaise longue* set before a window, her dark, silver-streaked hair draping, loosely plaited, over one shoulder. Madame herself was pale, but her grey eyes were as sharp as ever under her dark brows and as Grace approached her the familiar apprehension fluttered deep in the pit of her stomach.

There was something different about Madame, though—something Grace could not quite pinpoint: a gentler cast to her features that was not solely due to the absence of her customary tightly scraped bun. There was a softening in the lines around her eyes and mouth that made her appear less harsh.

Madame beckoned, indicating a chair near the *chaise longue*. 'Come, Miss Bertram. Sit here and tell me why you have returned, for I cannot think it is because you pine so very much for your old school.'

Grace sat down and haltingly confessed to Madame all that had happened, omitting only the fact that Clara was her natural child.

'This man. This Marquess. He sounds an unhappy man. He is, I think, scared. He rejects you before you reject him.'

'But...I would not reject him. I love him.'

'And you tell him this?'

'He does not believe in love.'

Madame shrugged. 'He says he does not believe in love but he is a man. He wants to feel loved. He wants to be the centre of your world. He is more complex than many men but at heart that is what he needs, even if he does not see it.'

Grace cast her mind back to Christmas morning. 'But.. I told him we could be a family. I tried to make him see how happy we could be: how Clara would benefit, how we could have friends come to visit, how he could take his rightful place in society again.'

'Ah. And did you pause to consider he might not wish to change his life? That your Marquess—who has cut himself off from everyone for so many years—might need time to adjust to a new future?'

'No.' Grace bit her lip as she confessed, cheeks burning as she realised for the first time how thoughtless she had been.

'I thought not. You have not changed, Miss Bertram, you are as impetuous as ever, never stopping to think about consequences. But...still...I find I do not understand the role of this Clara. Have you grown so fond of her in such a very short time?'

'She is easy to love. Everyone at Shiverstone Hall loves her.'

'But her uncle—he sends her away with you. Why did he do so? Does he not love her? Is he not a man of honour? Is *he* not the child's guardian?'

'He adores her! And she adores him.' Grace felt her face flame at the passion in her reply.

'And yet he is prepared to lose her. And you take her from the man you profess to love, even though you know e will miss her.' Her voice grew stern. 'Tell me the whole ruth, Miss Bertram, for how can I help you otherwise?'

Tears prickled. 'She is my daughter.'

'So…' Madame's tone gentled '…*this* is what happened o your baby. I did wonder but, of course, I could not ask.'

Grace's head spun. 'You *knew* about my baby?'

'But of course. I know everything that goes on in my chool. Did you doubt it?'

'But…' Grace stared at Madame, and everything she hought she understood about the Frenchwoman shifted, e-forming into a very different picture.

'But…why did you never—?'

She fell silent as Madame raised an imperious hand. 'My osition was such that, had I acknowledged your foolishness, I should be forced to take an action I did not wish to ake. And so I chose to turn the blind eye.'

Grace hung her head, ashamed her stupidity had forced Madame to compromise her principles.

'You will bring Clara to visit me,' Madame said, 'but I ind I am weary now. We shall talk again.'

Grace descended the stairs, her mind whirling. Madame's words helped her view Nathaniel's actions in a different light; she had much to think about.

Below her, Miss Fanworth had just admitted a distinguished, broad-shouldered gentleman. He removed his at to reveal thick, silvery hair, there was a murmured xchange, and then he headed for the stairs, nodding to Grace in passing.

She reached the entrance hall. Clara ran to her, crying, he minute she saw her.

'She has been very fretful,' Miss Fanworth said. 'I think he fears you will leave her.'

Those words hit Grace with the force of a lightning bolt. What had she done to her daughter?

'And she keeps talking of a sweep, or I think that is vhat she said.'

'Sweep is her kitten.'

'Sweep? Brack?' Clara's sorrowful plea wrenched a Grace's heart.

Grace did not know how to console Clara. She could no promise she would see Sweep and Brack again. She did no know what the future held. She hugged her daughter tight

'Who was that gentleman?' she asked, in an effort to distract herself.

'That is the Duke.'

'The Duke?'

'Of Wakefield. He visits Madame every afternoon a three o'clock.'

Grace gazed up the stairs, but the Duke had already van ished from sight. 'Is it true what Isabel wrote to me abou him? He told her that he and Madame…well, that they had been in love, many years ago.'

'Yes, it is true. And now they have found one anothe again. Oh, it is so romantic.' Miss Fanworth's eyes misted over. 'His visits have done her the power of good; the change in her is astounding. And he has vowed to come every day until she is fully recovered.' Miss Fanworth sighed, one hand pressed to her ample bosom. 'Such de votion. Would that I might so inspire a man.'

Would that I might, also.

Nathaniel. Just thinking his name turned Grace's knee to jelly and set up a wanting, deep down inside, that gave her no respite. Madame's voice repeated through her head and the conviction grew that she must go back.

The very thought terrified her, but how could she not? She must face up to the mess she had made of her life And of Clara's.

On New Year's Eve Grace was reading a story to Clara in the library when Miss Fanworth bustled in, waving two letters.

'They are from dearest Rachel,' she said. 'One for each of us. I dare say she had not received my letter with your address in it by the time she sent these. That is fortunate, is it not?'

She sat opposite Grace and they opened their letters at the same time. Grace read the joyful announcement of Rachel's betrothal to her employer, Sheikh Malik bin Jalal Al-Mahrouky and of their plans to marry in the spring, then stared unseeingly out of the window.

'Well…what splendid news.'

Grace started. 'Yes, indeed. I am thrilled for Rachel.'

Then why was her heart leaden with self-pity? What kind of person envied a friend's happiness? Her three friends were now settled and she was truly happy for them, but…

I am the only one alone and unloved. As I always have been.

Even as a child she had been unlovable. Tears scalded her eyes, and she stood abruptly.

'Would you mind…could you finish Clara's story for her? I will not be long.'

She ran from the room and up the stairs, unsure of where she was going until she found herself outside Madame's door. She did not allow second thoughts. She knocked.

'Well, Miss Bertram? Have you made your decision?'

'No. I do not know what to do.'

'Listen to your heart. It will tell you what to do for the best.'

The best for me? Or for Nathaniel? Or for Clara?

Grace thought of the Duke, with his silver hair and his dignity. Madame had faced heartbreak.

All those years apart.

'Did you listen to your heart, Madame?'

'Ah.' Madame closed her eyes, lost in thought.

'Non, ma chère,' she said, eventually. 'I listened to my

conscience. I gave him up without a fight, because I loved him and because I could offer him nothing. I ignored my heart, believing it was for the best. Perhaps, if he had come after me…if he had tried to persuade me…but he did not. He is honourable, and he put his duty first.

'I have regretted it every day of my life. Now, we have another chance and we both know that love, it does not die. It hides away. It bides its time, until it may shine again.

'You have the chance I did not have: to fight for your love, to reassure your Marquess that what he can offer is enough and that you will be content. He is afraid he will be unable to make you happy. If you are sure he can, go back and tell him what is in your heart. That is my advice. What is the worst that can happen?'

'He might reject me again.'

'He might. You must learn to accept that you cannot mould others' lives to suit your own purposes. And if he does…you are a strong woman; you will survive. Would you be any unhappier than you are now?'

Madame's words haunted Grace as she returned to the library and to Miss Fanworth and Clara, whose woebegone face lit up when she saw Grace.

'I think,' Miss Fanworth said, 'that Clara is scared you will vanish too. She needs a great deal of reassurance.'

My little girl is unhappy and it is my fault.

Could she risk returning to Shiverstone? If Nathaniel did not love her…if he sent her away…she would lose Clara too.

But she is no longer mine. I gave her away and I cannot support her on my own. Whatever the risk, I must return her to Nathaniel. He loves her and he will care for her whatever comes of him and me.

'Miss Fanworth.'

'Yes, my dear?'

'Please, will you look after Clara? I am going to buy a ticket. To go home.'

The teacher's kindly face wreathed in smiles. 'I am so pleased, but I will miss you, and Clara. When will you leave?'

'The day after tomorrow,' Grace called, as she rushed out of the door.

New Year's Day, 1812

Grace was in her bedroom with Clara, packing in preparation for their journey the next day, when she heard a carriage draw up outside the school. It must be three. She peered out of the window for one last look at Madame's Duke.

The carriage outside was mud-spattered. The horses' breath clouded in the chill air and the driver was... *Ned*! Joy erupted through her. She snatched Clara from the bed.

'He's here, Clara. Uncle Nathaniel is here.'

Nathaniel tapped his foot as he waited on the doorstep of Madame Dubois's School for Young Ladies. The door finally opened to reveal a matronly woman with kind eyes and a welcoming smile.

'Good afternoon. May I help you?'

'Miss Grace Bertram,' he said. 'I have come for her and for my niece.'

Her smile faded and she made no move to allow him entry.

'This is a school for young ladies, sir. Might I enquire as to your purpose in seeking Miss Bertram?'

She reminded him of nothing more than a mother hen fluffing up to protect its chicks and, despite his irritation, he warmed to her.

'I have come to take them home.'

She visibly subsided and opened the door wider. 'They are upstairs. Please, come in.'

Nathaniel strode towards the stairs. At the foot, he became aware of several whispering and giggling girls staring at him over the balustrade. He had faced worse on the journey south, but soon discovered that if he ignored people's reactions, they quickly lost interest. A few silly girls would not stop him.

Nothing mattered more than finding Grace and Clara.

He ran up the stairs and there they were. What could he say? What words would heal the hurt and mend the chasm between them? But words were not needed. Her smile shone out and she ran to him, and then his arms were full.

Grace and Clara.

Back in his arms, where they belonged.

They parted, Clara now in Nathaniel's arms, her pudgy arms locked tight around his neck.

'Uncle Naffaniel.' She kissed his cheek.

'Did you miss me, poppet? I missed you. And so does Sweep.'

While he talked to Clara, his eyes were on Grace, devouring every inch of her, oblivious to their audience.

'How did you know where to find us?'

'Ned heard you enquire about a stagecoach to Salisbury when he dropped you off in Lancaster.'

The mother hen arrived at the top of the stairs, puffing. 'Girls! Go to the common room immediately.'

The girls scurried down the stairs and out of sight.

'My lord, this is Miss Fanworth,' Grace said. 'Miss Fanworth, the Marquess of Ravenwell.'

Even Nathaniel, with all his personal misgivings, could hear the pride in Grace's voice and his heart swelled with hope.

'Shall I take Clara whilst you talk?'

Miss Fanworth reached for Clara, who tightened her hold on Nathaniel's neck. Only when she had possession of Nathaniel's hat would she consent to go with Miss Fanworth, satisfied her Uncle Naffaniel would never leave without his hat.

'She has been miserable without you,' Grace said. 'I am so sorry.'

'You have nothing to be sorry for. It was I who sent you away. And I have regretted it every day since. I missed you so much.'

He must say the words out loud. He would not continue to live in fear of rejection. 'I love you, Grace Bertram.'

Grace stepped close, gazing up at him, her green-gold gaze intense. 'I love you too, Nathaniel. And I *am* sorry because you were right. I did presume too much. I never questioned whether the life I *thought* would make you happy was what you truly wanted.'

'With you by my side, sweetheart, I can change. I *will* change.' He brushed her lips with his, stroking a tendril of hair from her face.

She leant into his hand, turning her head to press a kiss to his palm. 'There is no need to change: it is *you* I want, Nathaniel, not the life you can provide. As long as we are together, I will be happy.'

'But I *want* to change. I have had time to think…to adjust…and I no longer wish to hide myself away at Shiverstone. You have helped me to accept myself, scars and all. You have given me the courage I lacked. With you by my side, I can face the world again.'

Her familiar lily-of-the-valley scent weaved through his senses and he crushed her to him, taking her lips in a scorching kiss, losing all sense of time and place as their tongues tangled and he caressed her curves, aching with need.

The bang of a door downstairs roused him.

'Is there somewhere we can go?' he whispered against her lips.

'My bedchamber.' She took his hand and led him to a room containing four beds and a half-packed portmanteau. 'This is my old room: the one I shared with my friends,' she said. 'It no longer feels the same, despite the memories. We have all moved on.'

Nathaniel took her in his arms. 'You have moved on to make new memories. The old ones are still there, to be treasured, but you cannot go back in time.'

'I no longer have any desire to go back in time. All I desire now is a future with you, however you will have me.'

Gentle fingertips stroked his face. He captured her hand and kissed those fingertips, one by one.

'I am sorry I doubted you,' he said. 'I loved you and I wanted you, but I was afraid and I fought my feelings for you with every ounce of my strength.'

'Shh, my love. No more apologies, no explanations.' Her breath whispered across his skin as she pressed her soft curves against him. 'We have no need of words. Come.'

She urged him to a bed. He sank on to the mattress and she settled on his lap, cradling his face as she kissed him. He stroked her lips with his tongue and she opened to him. Silence reigned for several minutes as lips, tongues and hands expressed their love.

Nathaniel wrenched his lips from hers. 'I could never believe a beautiful girl like you would look at an ugly monster like me.' He feathered kisses over her face and neck, the blood pooling hot and heavy in his groin.

She touched his cheek. 'You are so very far from being ugly or a monster. You are a beautiful man, inside and out.'

His vision blurred and he blinked as he forced a laugh. 'Beautiful? Now that is coming it too strong, even for you, my darling.'

She shook her head, loose wisps of blonde hair framing her face. 'Beauty means nothing.' She placed her hand over his heart. 'It is what is in here that counts. Always.'

With a groan, he tilted his head and nuzzled her neck. She squirmed and giggled, fuelling his blood all the more, and he lifted her, laying her back on the narrow bed, crushing her lips with his as he covered her with his body. She was warm and pliant beneath him as she returned his kiss, reaching beneath his jacket to pull his shirt free. Warm hands slid under his shirt, over his bare chest and a quiet sound of satisfaction hummed deep in her throat.

She reached for the fall of his breeches, desire burning in her eyes as her fingers closed around him. The last vestiges of his restraint flew away. He tugged at the hem of her gown. She raised her hips to assist him. He skimmed her satin thighs to play amongst the soft folds between, his touch eliciting a breathy, *'Yes'*. She writhed beneath him, widening her legs, urging him on.

He settled between her legs and pushed into her slick, welcoming heat, then stilled, savouring the sensation as she tightened around him. He took her lips in another searing kiss as he slowly withdrew. Then he thrust, hard. She gasped into his mouth even as her hips rose to meet his and then they were moving together in glorious rhythm.

He knew instinctively when she was ready: he felt the tension build within her, felt her teeter on the edge. He drove into her again, sending them together into a starburst of ecstasy.

Some minutes later, Nathaniel cranked open one eyelid and took in their surroundings. He looked at Grace, still lying beneath him, eyes closed, a satisfied smile curving her lips. She was utterly beautiful. He longed to pull her into his arms and drift into sated sleep, but they could not take that risk. Not here. Not now. He forced himself to his feet, tucking his shirt into his breeches as he crossed the room to peer out of the window.

'Nathaniel?'

The worry in that one word had him whirling to face her. The uncertainty in her eyes near unmanned him. *Hell and damnation!* He reached the bed in two strides, pulled her to her feet, and folded her into his arms.

'I am here,' he murmured. 'I will never let you go again.'

Her tension dissolved and she relaxed into him. She

fitted against him perfectly. He rested his chin on the top of her head, content for the first time in nine long, lonely years.

'I love you, Nathaniel.'

He lifted her chin with one finger. 'And I love you, Grace, very, very much.'

There was something he must do. A question to ask. But…first…he lowered his head and kissed her again, tenderly, worshipfully, the smooth perfection of her lips soothing his soul.

A tap at the door had them springing apart. Miss Fanworth peered in, her cheeks pink.

'Clara started to get upset so I thought I should bring her up to you.'

Nathaniel took Clara from the kindly teacher, thanking her, then ushered her from the room, shutting the door behind her. He turned to Grace and, still holding Clara, heart pounding, he dropped to one knee. Grace's eyes widened.

'It seems fitting Clara should be a part of this,' he said. 'Grace Bertram, I bless the day you came into my life. You have unlocked my heart and my soul and I love you more every day.

'Please, will you do me the honour of becoming my wife?'

'Yes! Oh, yes!' Grace fell to her knees and wrapped her arms around Nathaniel and Clara.

'Me too, Uncle Naffaniel?'

Nathaniel and Grace laughed as one and Nathaniel hugged Clara a little tighter.

'You too, Clara, poppet, you too. We will be a proper family, and you will be our adopted daughter. But we will never forget Hannah and David.'

'No, we will never forget Hannah and David,' Grace said. 'Even though I never met them, they will always hold a very special place in my heart.'

Nathaniel bowed his head, the memories of his sister and her husband still painful, but no longer as raw.

'When they died, I railed against the Fates for taking away my only friends and for forcing my life along a different path. But love and hope and a new future have sprung from that tragedy and I bless the day you both came into my life, my beautiful Clara, and my dearest, darling Grace.'

'Me too, Uncle Naffaniel.'

Epilogue

Ravenwell Manor—23rd December 1812

'Milady!' Alice rushed into the drawing room, her plump cheeks quivering. 'Milady!' She skidded to a halt, hand pressed to heaving bosom. 'There's carriages a-coming. *Three* of them.'

'All three together? How wonderful.'

Grace jumped to her feet, then froze, her hand to her mouth. Alice reached her side in an instant.

'Oh, milady. Again?'

'No.' Grace shook her head. 'No, it is not the sickness. I rose too quickly and felt light-headed, that is all. Now, come. We have visitors to greet.' She cast a swift glance around the room. All was neat and gleaming. 'Will you ask Fish to tell his lordship—?'

'I am here.'

The deep voice came from the doorway and Grace pivoted to face Nathaniel: handsome, inherently masculine, *hers*. Her heart gave its customary somersault and then melted at the sight of Clara, holding his hand. She was growing so tall, her soft brown curls falling down her back in ringlets. Grace could not wait to introduce her new family to her friends.

'Alice, will you alert Cook that we shall require luncheon in an hour, please? Are all the bedchambers prepared? And the servants' quarters?'

'Yes, milady. Shall I take Miss Clara now?'

'No. She will come with us to greet our guests.'

Alice, who had moved back to Ravenwell Manor with Nathaniel and Grace after their marriage, scurried from the room. The Sharps had elected to stay at Shiverstone Hall as caretakers and Ned, Tam and Annie had also stayed behind, to care for the animals and Nathaniel's beloved hawks. Every few weeks, Nathaniel rode over to the Hall to fly his birds and stay the night and, in the spring, they planned to return as a family for a longer visit.

If I am able to. Grace smoothed her hand over her gently rounded stomach, and a warm glow of contentment suffused her.

Nathaniel's gaze tracked the movement of her hand, then lifted to her face and she saw the heat banked in his eyes. Anticipation tugged deep within her, but there was no time to dally.

'How are Ralph and Elizabeth? Have they settled into the vicarage?' she asked, to distract him.

Nathaniel and Clara had been to visit the newly married Rendells in their new home, taking with them a bunch of freshly gathered mistletoe. The elderly incumbent of the local church, St Thomas's, had recently retired and Nathaniel had gifted the living to Ralph Rendell.

'They have and they are as happy a pair of lovebirds as ever I did see—except for us, my darling, irresistible wife.'

He cradled Grace's face and brushed a kiss to her lips. Then his eyes darkened and he lowered his head again, and kissed her until her insides were molten. But, this time, she must resist and, hands on his chest, she pushed him away.

'Nathaniel! Our visitors will be here any minute.'

He chuckled and kissed her again. 'It is precisely because their arrival is imminent that I am taking advantage whilst I may. You must not begrudge me a little sustenance to see me through the next few hours.'

'Papa! Mama!' Clara tugged at Nathaniel's sleeve for attention.

Grace's heart swelled. Clara might never discover that Grace was her natural mother but, once she and Nathaniel had wed, they had agreed Clara would be their adopted daughter and they would be her father and mother from that day forward.

Nathaniel scooped Clara high. He put his lips to her cheek and blew, making a rude noise that had Clara giggling and squirming in his arms as they all made their way to the front door. Their servants were beginning to congregate in the hall, ready to conduct the visitors to their bedchambers.

'The Reverend Rendell was most appreciative of the mistletoe,' Nathaniel said, with a grin, as they reached the double entrance door, standing wide in readiness. 'In fact...' he tipped his head towards Grace, lowering his voice '...nothing would do for our new vicar than to test it out with his bride. I don't know...' he shook his head, his brown eyes brimming with merriment '...if that is the way a man of the cloth sees fit to behave in full view of his benefactor, what hope is there for society?

'They send their pleased acceptance of our invitation to join us for Christmas dinner, by the way.'

'How lovely it will be to have our friends all here,' Grace said. 'Mother is delighted at the prospect of seeing a full dining table at the Manor once again.'

Nathaniel's mother—after a distrustful start with her new daughter-in-law—had soon accepted Grace and they were now firm friends. She now lived in the Dower House on the estate, but she visited almost every day.

The rumble of the carriage wheels and the hoofbeats of eighteen horses—three teams of four, plus six outriders—grew ever louder as they reached the end of the long, straight carriageway that led from the road and negotiated the turning circle that would bring them to the front steps of the Manor.

The sky was uniformly white, with not a hint of grey, and the air was still—almost as though it held its breath in anticipation. Nathaniel had predicted snow and Grace breathed a silent thank you that it had held off until the travellers arrived.

The carriages halted and the silence—punctuated only by the occasional jingle of a bit or stamp of a hoof—was deafening in its own way. A sudden attack of nerves assailed Grace. It had been almost a year and a half since she had seen her beloved friends.

Will they be different? What will they think of me? What will their husbands be like? What if—?

She felt Nathaniel's hand at the small of her back, large and reassuring. She glanced up at him.

'Don't be nervous. You will be fine. You'll see.'

His eyes met hers, steady and confident with no sign of apprehension, and Grace marvelled at the change in him since the day they met. And then there was no more time to worry, for carriage doors were being flung wide and there they were.

Joanna. Rachel. Isabel. Three dear, familiar faces.

Tears blurred Grace's vision and she blinked rapidly, so as not to appear an emotional fool and yet…

They came together in a rush: hugging, kissing and exclaiming.

And tearful—even Joanna, who had never, ever been seen to cry before.

All four of them, in a laughing circle, with tears rolling unashamedly down their cheeks.

Isabel peered out of the window. 'Now that we are safely arrived, I declare it may snow to its heart's content.'

They were gathered in the drawing room after a delicious luncheon.

Grace joined her. 'I believe you will get your wish.' She lowered her voice. 'You will tell me if there is anything you need, will you not, Isabel?'

'Thank you, Grace, darling, but you must not worry about me. I feel exceedingly well. Blossoming, you might say.' Isabel smiled, and placed her hands either side of her swollen belly with a sigh of contentment.

It was chilly by the window and they moved nearer to the warmth of the fire.

'Do you really think it will snow, Lady Ravenwell?'

Grace smiled at the handsome young boy's serious expression. Rachel's stepson, Aahil, had never seen snow in his life. Neither had his younger sister and brother, Ameera and Hakim, who both sprawled on the floor next to Clara, playing with her Noah's Ark.

'I think it will, Aahil. And then…' Grace eyed each of her friends in turn '…we will build a snowman. Do you remember—?'

'The Christmas before last!' Isabel's blue eyes sparkled. 'We all stayed at school and we built the *biggest* snowman…'

Joanna, sitting on the sofa, newly born Edward cradled in her arms, smiled. 'That was such a happy Christmas.'

'This one will be better.' Rachel sat next to Joanna and leaned over to admire the babe. 'He is *soooo* sweet, Joanna.' There was a note of longing in her voice. 'May I hold him?'

'Of course.' Joanna passed her son to Rachel, who crooned softly until he settled again.

'Our snowman will be bigger and better.' Hakim, hopping from foot to foot in his excitement, joined Aahil. 'Will it snow, Lady Ravenwell? Will it snow, do you think?'

Hakim had seemed timid on first arrival, but had soon lost his shyness with all these new people. His father,

Malik—exotically dark and impossibly handsome, with piercing eyes—broke off his discussion with Nathaniel about hawking, a popular means of hunting in his beloved Huria.

'Calm down, Hakim, or I shall send you to the nursery,' he said. 'If the Fates smile upon us, it will snow. Bombarding her ladyship with questions will change nothing.'

'He is excited, Malik. And full of energy after spending so many days cooped up in the carriage,' Rachel said, as she cradled Edward.

'As am I.' Luke, Joanna's husband, stood up and stretched. 'I beg your pardon, ladies, but I need to work off some of this energy. Ravenwell, I believe you mentioned a couple of new hunters? Any chance of putting them through their paces?'

All four men perked up and Grace found herself exchanging knowing looks of amusement with her three friends.

'Indeed. However, before that…' Nathaniel turned to Aahil. 'How would you like to help us bring home the Yule log, young man?' He cocked a brow at Malik. 'I don't know if you're familiar with the tradition, Al-Mahrouky, but the Yule log is specially selected to burn the full twelve days of Christmastide. It is brought indoors on Christmas Eve and lit and then, if possible, a piece is saved on Twelfth Night to light the following year's Yule log.'

'But it is not Christmas Eve until tomorrow,' Joanna said, from her seat on the sofa. 'Will that not bring bad luck?'

'We will not tempt fate by bringing it indoors until tomorrow, but we must drag the log closer to the house before it snows. We can leave it in one of the outbuildings overnight. What do you say, Aahil? Are you feeling strong?'

'May I, Father?'

'Very well, son.'

'Me too!' Hakim bounced up and down.

'May I come too?' Ameera stood up.

'Me, me, me!' Clara shouted, scrambling to her feet, lining up with Ameera and Hakim in front of Nathaniel. 'Papa. Papa. Pleeease.'

'Clara, I do not think—'

'*Pleeeaaase*, Papa.' She turned beseeching eyes to Grace. 'Mama, please.'

Grace raised her brows at Nathaniel. She saw him bite back his smile and she knew he would be helpless to refuse those three pleading faces.

'Al-Mahrouky?' Nathaniel directed his question at the Sheikh, who nodded.

'Very well,' Nathaniel said to the three. 'If you promise faithfully to do exactly as you are told, you may come.'

'Thank you,' they chorused.

Ameera, tugging Clara with her, moved closer to Nathaniel. 'Does that hurt?' She pointed to Nathaniel's scarred cheek.

There was the sound of indrawn breath and Rachel straightened as though to remonstrate with Ameera, but Grace caught her eye and shook her head.

Nathaniel smiled down at Ameera. 'No. Not now,' he said. Then he crouched down before the three youngest children. 'But it hurt a great deal at the time and that is the reason you must always be very careful with fire.'

'I am pleased it doesn't hurt,' Ameera announced. 'May we go outside now, please, Lord Ravenwell?'

Nathaniel laughed as he stood up. 'Yes, Ameera, we will go now.' He winked at Grace. 'We'll take a couple of footmen to help with the children. It will give you ladies a chance to catch up with the gossip.'

William, his light brown eyes creased with amusement, said, 'Judging by the non-stop chatter since our arrival, I cannot credit there is any subject still uncovered. They already appear to have catalogued the happenings of every single day since last they met.'

'You, Mr Balfour, are a tease.' Isabel slapped her husband playfully on the arm. 'Run along and play, you men, and leave your womenfolk in peace. We still have many important matters to discuss.'

'Important matters! Ha!' Luke stooped to kiss Joanna on the cheek. 'Children and babies, I'll be bound.'

'Are you suggesting that children and babies are *not* important, my dear?' Joanna regarded her husband quizzically.

He laughed. 'You have me there, my sweet. Children and babies are, of course, the most important of all things. I stand corrected.' He reached out and tickled Edward's pudgy cheek with a gentle finger. 'I fear you must wait a year or two to join us, my son, but at least you shall stay nice and snug indoors whilst we men brave the elements.'

After the men and children had gone, Edward's nurse-maid whisked him off to the nursery and the four girls were left together.

'Ravenwell Manor is wonderful, Grace. It is so modern, so beautifully appointed, and this room is exquisite,' Isabel said.

Rachel and Joanna nodded their agreement.

'It was completely rebuilt after the fire.' Grace gazed around the drawing room, her favourite room in the house, decorated in shades of green and cream. 'Nathaniel's mother planned the décor.'

'Is that the fire that injured Nathaniel?' Joanna asked in her soft voice.

'Yes. He went back inside to rescue his father, but he was too late.'

Pride swelled at his bravery and at his courage in facing a full life once again, for her sake and for Clara's, and now…she placed her hand against her stomach…for their future family as well.

Grace looked up and found Rachel watching her, an unfathomable expression on her face.

'Are you quite well, Rachel?'

Pink suffused Rachel's cheeks. 'Are you...are you increasing, Grace?'

Isabel's head jerked up, her copper curls bouncing. 'Really? Are you, Grace? Why have you not told us? How exciting. We shall all be mothers together.'

'Isabel! Really. Calm down,' Joanna said, with a laugh. 'Grace has not answered Rachel yet and you are already three jumps ahead of us. You do not change.'

They all laughed.

'I'm sorry, Grace. But...is it true?'

'Yes! We will have a brother or a sister for Clara by the early summer, God willing.'

Then she recalled Rachel's expression. Would her news upset her friend? There had been something...that longing in her voice, earlier, and the look in her eyes when she held baby Edward...

Hoping and praying there was nothing amiss, she said, 'Your time will come, Rachel. You have only been wed nine months and—'

'I think I am with child.' Rachel blurted out her news with a blush.

The gasps were audible, then they all spoke at once.

'Are you sure?'

'How do you know?'

'But you never wanted children.'

'A lady can change her mind,' she said primly, in reply to that last comment from Isabel, and then she burst out laughing. 'I am not certain, but I'm fairly sure. I haven't even told Malik yet... I did not dare, for fear he would stop me journeying here for Christmas.'

A contented glow suffused Rachel's face as she added, 'He is very protective.'

'So we will truly all be mothers. With children by the men we love. How glorious is that?' Isabel stood, flinging her arms wide, and then twirled in a circle. 'Two years ago, we were all dreading our futures as put-upon drudges and now...look at us. Married ladies all and with children we never expected to bear.'

'Except for Grace,' Joanna said. 'Do you know, Grace, for all it was such a terrifying ordeal for you, in a way I envied you. You would be the only one of us to be a mother. Even though you had to give Clara away, still you had experienced the most wonderful thing that can ever happen to a woman.'

Grace clasped Joanna's hands, understanding the pain of her childhood with no family to love her. They had that in common.

'I never knew you felt that way, Joanna. I never believed anyone could envy what happened to me. But I see, in a way, what you mean. I always knew that somewhere in this world there was a part of me. I bless the day Miss Fanworth told me the names of Clara's adopted parents.'

'We have both found true families now, Grace. Although...' Joanna paused, her brow wrinkled with thought '...I eventually came to realise that Madame Dubois did love me, in her own way. She and the rest of the teachers were a kind of family to me, but I was too busy envying the other girls and their conventional families to realise it.'

Rachel laughed. 'No one could ever accuse *my* family of being conventional but, speaking of Madame, it is fortunate she never found out about the baby, Grace, or your life might have turned out very differently.'

'Ah, now that is where you are mistaken,' Grace said. She told them what Madame had told her the previous Christmas. 'She turned a blind eye because she knew my uncle would cast me out.'

'So the sly old thing knew all the time. Well, well.' Isabel subsided into an armchair.

'Talking of Madame,' Joanna said, 'I have some *marvellous* news about her and also about the school and Miss

Fanworth.' She paused for effect, a mischievous glint in her eyes.

'Hurry up and tell us.'

'Stop teasing, Joanna.'

'Tell us quickly before I burst!'

'We-e-e-ll…' Joanna eked out the moment, clearly enjoying being the news bearer.

'Joanna!' Isabel, sitting next to Joanna on the sofa, nudged her. 'Tell us. I am in a delicate condition, don't you know, and I must not be stressed.'

Joanna laughed. 'Oh, very well. Do you remember the Duke of Wakefield?'

'Yes, of course. *I* told *you* about him at that soirée last Christmas Eve and I wrote to Grace and Rachel about him.'

'And he visited Madame last Christmastide, when Clara and I were there,' Grace said, 'and Madame told me her tragic love story. I wrote to all of you about that. And I do know Madame fully recovered from her illness, for Miss Fanworth wrote and told me so.'

'Yes, she has recovered. In fact, she has so far recovered that she wed her Duke last week, and Madame Dubois is henceforth to be addressed as her Grace the Duchess of Wakefield.'

'A *duchess*?'

'How do you know?'

'Why did you not say before?'

'Yes, a duchess. And I know because Luke and I attended the wedding. And I did not say before because we had so much else to share.'

'So Madame has her happy-ever-after as well,' Rachel said. 'I am so pleased for her.'

'And the school?' Grace asked. 'You said you had news about the school.'

'She has gifted it to Miss Fanworth, who is now the principal.'

'So, we four and Madame get our handsome princes, and poor Miss Fanworth gets a pile of bricks and mortar.'

'Isabel!'

'Anyway,' Grace said, with a sly glance around her friends, 'there is always Signor Bertolli.'

She mimicked his Italian accent and twirled an imaginary moustache and the others burst into fits of giggles. They had long speculated over the Italian art master and his apparent liking for the plump, motherly Miss Fanworth.

Without Madame and her iron discipline at the school, who knew what that feisty Italian gentleman might get up to?

Christmas Eve

Grace awoke the following morning and rolled over to face Nathaniel. He still slept, warm and tousled and *delicious*. Stealthily, she leaned over and kissed his lips. He stirred and reached for her, eyes still shut.

'You are insatiable, woman,' he grumbled as he drew her close.

She snuggled against him, reaching between them as his hand delved for the hem of her nightdress and trailed up her bare leg.

When they eventually surfaced, they discovered a world transformed. The expected snow had fallen—so much snow it shrouded the land as far as the eye could see, thickly distorting every familiar feature. The sun shone in a cloudless sky, and the snowcovered landscape glistened and glimmered invitingly.

Somehow—and Grace was not sure quite how it happened—it was arranged that the men would take the excited children outside to build a snowman before bringing in the Yule log, whilst the women stayed indoors to decorate the house with the garlands Grace and the servants had crafted over the past week.

Hmmph! Stay indoors where it's nice and warm, indeed.

She did not voice her frustration to her friends, however. After all, they were not children any more and Isabel, in particular, might not wish to risk going outdoors in her condition.

They had finished decorating the dining room and were about to start on the drawing room when the door flew open to reveal Isabel, clad in her sky-blue velvet fur-lined cloak and twirling a matching bonnet in her hands. Grace had not even realised she had disappeared.

'Why should the men have all the fun?' Isabel said. 'I want to go outside in the snow. We can finish decorating the house later. Grace has done all the hard work already. What do you say, girls? Will any of you join me?'

Grace, Rachel and Joanna, as one, dropped their garlands and chorused, 'Yes!'

Grace rang the bell and sent maids to fetch their cloaks, hats and gloves. Whilst they waited, Isabel continued to twirl her bonnet until, with a sudden exclamation, she stopped, plucked out the short plume tucked into the hatband and discarded it. She then broke a forked branch of mistletoe from a kissing bough and put it in place of the plume.

'There.' She grinned saucily. 'Three berries, as well. I *shall* have fun in the snow.'

They tumbled out into the garden, where Luke and William were rolling a snowball for the body of the snowman and Nathaniel—with Brack by his side—was helping the three smallest children roll another for the head. Malik and Aahil stood aside, watching.

Rachel tutted. 'Aahil needs to play. He tries to emulate Malik, but he is nine years old. If he cannot be a child now, when can he?'

And, with that, she scooped a handful of snow and threw

it straight at Malik, hitting his head and knocking off his hat. He spun around, his dark eyes flashing with an anger that soon melted when he saw Rachel.

Luke, meanwhile, had seen what happened. 'Come on, men,' he yelled. 'War is declared!' And he grabbed a handful of snow and lobbed it at Joanna.

Malik's aloofness lasted all of ten seconds. With a sudden laugh, he joined in, and then they were all throwing snowballs, laughing and shouting, whilst Brack gambolled around, barking and snatching at mouthfuls of snow.

A truce was called only after Joanna slipped flat on her face in a snowdrift. Luke was by her side in an instant.

'Enough,' he panted, grinning widely as he lifted her up. 'You, my beautiful lady wife, are coming indoors right now to get changed out of these wet clothes.' He strode towards the house, carrying Joanna.

'Can we finish the snowman?' Aahil gazed up at Nathaniel, dark eyes wide, hair sprinkled with snow.

Nathaniel patted his shoulder. 'Of course we can. You fetch the head whilst we set up the body.'

Malik helped Nathaniel manoeuvre the larger of the two balls into place outside the drawing-room windows and Ameera scampered through the snow to help Aahil whilst Clara and Hakim chased Brack.

Grace, Rachel and Isabel were content to watch, catching their breath after so much laughter. William joined them, his brows raised suggestively as he looked his wife up and down.

'New bonnet, my dear?'

Isabel preened a little. 'Oh, this old thing? I have merely retrimmed it, Husband.'

He wrapped his arms around her and kissed her soundly, then plucked a berry from the mistletoe. 'Only two more? You disappoint me.' He kissed her twice more, removing a berry after each kiss. 'That is better, for no one else gets to kiss *my* wife.'

The snowman was soon completed and Aahil, as the eldest and tallest of the children, crowned him with an old hat of Nathaniel's. Ameera wound a scarf around his neck and, together, they made his face with coal for eyes, a carrot for a nose and a row of hazelnuts to mark his mouth whilst Hakim and Clara stuck lumps of coal in a crooked line down his body, for buttons. An old clay pipe completed the transformation.

The children stood back, eyes and smiles wide.

'Is he magic?' Hakim whispered. 'Will he come alive and have adventures when it is dark and we can't see him?'

Rachel crouched by his side and hugged him. 'He will if you believe in him, Hakim.'

They were all warm and dry, congregated in the drawing room, when Luke and Joanna eventually reappeared.

'At last,' Isabel cried. 'We are waiting to light the Yule log.'

Two of the footmen had brought the log indoors earlier, setting it in the drawing room grate—only just big enough to accommodate it.

'Sorry.' Luke looked entirely unrepentant.

'We were playing with Edward,' Joanna said, with a blush and a stifled giggle.

'We're all here now,' William said, with a merry glance. 'I have been looking forward to this.'

The fire was lit, using a blackened lump of wood saved by Sharp—bless him—from last year's Yule log, and then all the adults helped drape garlands around the room, adding candles, whilst the children played with Sweep, who was fascinated by all the greenery. Isabel fashioned a dainty headdress for Ameera, using sprigs of juniper, interwoven with red ribbon and tiny fir cones. Clara and Hakim then wanted their own headdresses, so she made two more whilst a delighted Ameera danced around the room.

Finally, all that was left was to hang the kissing bough.

After some dispute amongst the men as to who was the tallest—Malik won, by an inch, over Nathaniel's six foot two—the bough was hung from the chandelier in the centre of the room, just high enough that Malik could stand beneath without it brushing against it.

Then the maids brought in mulled wine and fruit punch and warm mince pies, and cleared away the remaining greenery.

Isabel, her rich copper hair shining in the candlelight, sang a carol, filling the room with her exquisite voice. And then they were all singing, their voices rising and falling in a rich blend, and Grace found herself blinking back tears. Nathaniel, next to her on the sofa, hugged her close and before long, Clara clambered up to join them in a singing, laughing, loving heap.

As the singing came to an end, Malik held up his hand for silence.

'I thank you for inviting myself and my family to join in celebrating Christmas at your home,' he said.

He stood straight and solemn, but Grace was sure she detected a twinkle in his eyes.

'I have found enjoyment in all of your traditions,' he continued, 'but the one I most appreciate—' he grabbed Rachel's hand and tugged her to stand beneath the kissing bough '—is this one.'

He bent his head to kiss Rachel, who wound her arms around his neck and kissed him back enthusiastically.

Malik plucked a berry from the bough and then kissed Rachel once more. There was a moment's stunned silence as the rest of the room watched and then William, with a wink at Isabel, stood up.

'I say, Al-Mahrouky. Leave some for the rest of us to enjoy.'

Malik lifted his dark head. 'You had your fair share of berries in the garden, Balfour. Do not think it went unnoticed,' he said, to a round of laughter.

Nathaniel then stood, raising his glass, and a sudden hush fell over the room. One by one, those still seated rose to their feet.

'I should like to propose a toast.'

Nathaniel's deep voice sent a *frisson* of desire chasing up Grace's spine. As if sensing her reaction, he captured her gaze with his, the faintest of smiles tugging at the corner of his mouth. The angle he stood, next to the fire, highlighted his damaged cheek, but Grace barely noticed it now. It was a part of him and loved and adored by her as much as, or even more than, every other inch of him.

'To Christmastide—a time for friends and for family and a time of joy—to beloved friends from our past and to firm friends in our future, and to happy families, those who are present and—' his fiery gaze lowered to Grace's belly, leaving a scorching trail of desire in its wake '—those we have yet to meet.'

From the corner of her eye Grace saw Malik place his hand, fleetingly, on Rachel's belly. Rachel's gaze jerked to his. He nodded, then slipped his arm around her waist and hugged her close into his side.

So he does *know.* Grace caught Rachel's eye and they shared a contented smile.

Luke and Joanna stood close together, with eyes only for one another as they drank their toast.

'And, last but not least,' Nathaniel continued, 'to the newly wed Duchess of Wakefield, whose discretion and whose sage advice is greatly appreciated by *this* husband at least.'

'And by this one,' Luke said, raising his glass again as he smiled into Joanna's eyes.

'To Madame, for all she has done for me and for sending me away. She was wise, indeed, for if she had granted my wish of staying at the school to teach, I should never have met you, darling Luke.'

'And to Miss Fanworth,' Grace added, 'for if it was

not for her, I should never have found Clara, nor you, my dearest love.'

'Yes. To Miss Fanworth, without whom I would never have travelled to Huria and met Malik and my beautiful stepchildren,' Rachel said.

'To Madame, Miss Fanworth, and their School for Young Ladies,' Isabel cried, raising her glass high as William snaked his arm around her waist.

A quiet bubble of contentment swelled inside Grace. 'To us, to friendship everlasting, to happy memories, and to the brightest of futures,' she said as she raised her glass for the final time.

'We all have so very much to be thankful for.'

* * * * *